VAN R. MAYHALL JR.

Coquille Publishing, L.L.C., a Coquille Publishing, L.L.C. imprint.

Coquille Publishing, L.L.C.
1122 Thoreau Drive
Baton Rouge, Louisiana, 70808
vrm@bswllp.com
1-225-381-8009

ISBN: 978-0-9990513-8-2 (e)
ISBN: 978-0-9990513-4-4 (sc)
ISBN: 978-0-9990513-5-1 (hc)

Library of Congress Control Number: 2017909334

Coquille Publishing, L.L.C. Date: June 1, 2017

Acclamation for Cloe Lejeune Series by Van R. Mayhall Jr.

Judas the Apostle

A thriller with theological underpinnings, set both in steamy south Louisiana and in the Old City of Jerusalem ... a fascinating fictional exploration of the least understood and most maligned figure in the salvation story ... this is the most original work of fiction I have edited.
> —Catherine L. Kadair, freelance editor

Most Christians and many religious scholars accept the story that Judas betrayed Jesus for money. But did he? The author offers the reader a religious mystery every bit as gripping as *The Da Vinci Code*. Set in south Louisiana and covering three continents, this crisply written debut novel is a page-turner full of suspense, with a fascinating look at the motives of one of history's most loathed villains. *Judas the Apostle* presents the possibility of alternative groundbreaking biblical history that is also a compelling read.
> —Jim Brown, author and syndicated talk show host (produced by Clear Channel Communications and syndicated by Genesis Communications, Minneapolis, Minnesota)

An edge-of-the-chair thriller, a stunning history and geography lesson, and an unparalleled glimpse into the past of one of history's most maligned figures ... *Judas the Apostle* tells a great and truly plausible story, against the rich and often diverse tapestry of Louisiana, America's most colorful and mysterious region.
> —Bill Profita, radio talk show host, 107.3 FM, Baton Rouge, Louisiana

This is a page-turner with both mind and muscle. Its thrills and intrigue are offered up with an equal dose of historic heft. It carries you along as it makes you reconsider the well-worn stories you thought you understood.
> —Anne Dubuisson Anderson, writing and publishing consultant

Mayhall, a Baton Rouge attorney, has done the one thing in this book that is essential to keep a thriller thrilling: he has created a bad guy who is truly evil. The Kolektor lives in a bunker under a fake antiquity store in Jerusalem and he is without conscience. He cares only for what he wants. Mayhall has a clear and uncluttered writing style well-suited to the thriller genre. His plot is good. He does his homework on the history of his subject.

—Greg Langley, "Judas Has Compelling Plot, Attractive Local Setting," *Advocate*, October 9, 2012

"Louisiana Author Spins Thriller about Judas Iscariot"
—*Hammond Daily Star*, November 9, 2012

The reader is transported to exotic locales throughout time, including ancient Masada, North Africa during World War II and modern-day Jerusalem and Lyon, France. South Louisiana readers will enjoy iconic venues in the book that include numerous scenes at LSU in Baton Rouge, Madisonville, Lake Pontchartrain and the Tchefuncte River.

—*Point Coupee Banner*, "Louisiana Author Examines the Role of Judas in New Thriller," November 22, 2012

Van R. Mayhall, Jr. has penned a fascinating thriller packed with twists and turns. Ancient language expert, Dr. Clotile LeJeune's quiet life is shaken when she learns her estranged father has been murdered. She travels to her home town to unlock the mysteries of a 2000-year-old oil jar inscribed with the name "Judas Iscariot" that her father left her. The race for answers takes her on a dangerous quest across three continents in order to discover the identity of Judas Iscariot.

—*Legatus* magazine, February 2013

Mayhall has spun a highly original, suspenseful and atmospheric thriller. It is a savvy story of academia, archeology and theology, but you can also taste the warm Louisiana thread that runs through it like a good flavor—the Tchefuncte River, the LSU Campus, the elements of close family ties and the influence of religion.

The story weaves a mystical spell in the timeless story of good against evil that is hard to resist; Judas the Apostle joins my personal rank of books that I call one-sitting reads.

—Jeanne Frois, "Worth Watching: Judas the Apostle," *Louisiana Life*, March–April 2013

A linguistics professor's inherited relic sets an arms dealer on her trail in Mayhall's debut religious thriller. The conversations are weighty but never burdensome thanks to thriller genre conventions: a formidable villain with a penchant for taking artifacts that aren't his; a murder, a kidnapping and a face-to-face showdown; and lots of suspense—indeed, simply opening the jar takes quite some time. The brilliantly open ending steers clear of definitive answers but provides adequate closure. A solid thriller with an invigorating religious theme.

—*Kirkus Reviews*, June 2013

Page after page, Mayhall's dialogue and crafting of suspense draw readers into the mystery of a two-thousand-year-old jar and the murders it has incited.

A fast-paced, changes-at-every-turn intellectual thriller, *Judas the Apostle* is a quality novel that grabs and won't let go until the final page is turned. From the first chapter, where protagonist Cloe Lejeune's elderly father is murdered, through the discovery of what lies in the two-thousand-year-old jar that has sat on her father's mantel her whole life, the novel takes the reader on a ride of discovery as each chapter unfolds.

—ForeWord Review, *Clarion Review*. Five Stars (out of five).

The Last Sicarius

For fans of the award-winning *Judas the Apostle* and newcomers to the Cloe Lejeune series, Mayhall once again delivers a smart, fast-paced thriller with exotic landscapes, a fascinating dose of biblical history, an intrepid heroine, conniving evildoers, twists and turns, and just the right touch of humor that will keep you turning the pages.

 —Anne Dubuisson Anderson, writing and publishing consultant

A rare opportunity to engross yourself in an historical thriller that takes you from New Orleans to the Vatican to the Holy Land ... The action is often intense, and the characters leave you waiting to read about their next adventure. *The Last Sicarius* truly grabs you and doesn't let you go until the final page.

 —Bill Profita, radio talk show host, 107.3 FM, Baton Rouge, Louisiana

An exhilarating companion piece to the first in the series.
 —*Kirkus Reviews*, September 15, 2014

To Mama Lo, now and forever

ACKNOWLEDGMENTS

This is to acknowledge, with love, the efforts of my father, Van R. Mayhall, who passed away at the age of ninety-five in January 2015. From my very first novel, *Judas the Apostle*, Dad read every page of every version. Judas went through twenty rewrites. He did the same with *The Last Sicarius* and now with *7*. In fact, I delivered the last three chapters of *7* to Dad four days before he died. I know he finished the manuscript by the way he always marked paragraphs as he read them. Dad, I hope you enjoyed it and rest in peace.

This is the revelation given by God to Jesus Christ so that he could tell his servants about the things which are now to take place very soon ... Happy the man who reads this prophecy, and happy those who listen to him, if they treasure all it says, because the Time is close.

—Revelations, chapter 1, the Jerusalem Bible, 1966

CONTENTS

PART I

PART II

PART III

PART

I

Gathering

Surely every man walketh in a vain show;
Surely they are disquieted in vain;
He heapeth up riches, and knoweth not
Who shall gather them.
—Psalm 39:6

CHAPTER

1

2017
Madisonville, Louisiana

Clotile Lejeune leaned over her computer and studied digital images of very old writings. The ancient languages expert reached around to massage her overworked neck muscles; as she did so, a lock of her prematurely silver hair swept across her face. Cloe's blue eyes blazed briefly as she thought of the night her deep chestnut hair began to turn. That was the night she spent in the Tunisian mountains with her sisters, the Sicarii. She had learned things that night that changed her forever.

She sat on her front porch in the warm Louisiana evening, the sun having long since set without her notice. A cooling breeze drove away the pockets of heat, and lightning bugs fired in the distance. Although she had been educated in Seattle and lived there for many years, she was a south Louisiana girl and had grown up in the house on the Tchefuncte River. She was home.

She had been at work on the translation since early morning, constantly interrupted by various bulletins about happenings across the world. The news was uniformly bad, consistent with what she had seen and read over the last few months. Now, however, it somehow seemed worse. There was more violence, and the viciousness of such was elevated. There were reports of natural disasters such as storms, floods—and even a volcano eruption in the Far East. Disease in Africa was epidemic again. Food was in

3

short supply in some areas, with famine multiplying the health problems. Populations in several countries were stressed and panicky.

Cloe had been at a particular passage in the journal all day and felt she was on the verge of something. The journal was not a bound volume but a digitalized shoe box of scraps culled from the second jar the Sicarii had left with her. It dated from the first century, and the translation was difficult. Hell, even trying to decipher the handwriting in a variety of ancient languages was a challenge. It was not only a translation problem but a jigsaw puzzle. Once she had some idea of what was said, where did it fit in? She had been working on it for months—no, she had been at it for *years*. Where had the time gone? Still, during that time, she had made monumental discoveries that added to the knowledge of the ancient period in question, namely the three years before the death of Jesus Christ.

More and more, she believed this to be the long-hypothesized but missing detailed account of Christ's public ministry. She had arrived at a point where there seemed to be a conversation chronicled between Christ and someone she could not identify—but whom she thought might be St. John. Yet somehow this was different, possibly even prophetic. From what she had been able to decipher, something terrible was …

As she stared at the symbols, it suddenly hit her.

"I must call Albert. I have to get to Rome!" she said.

CHAPTER

2

Des Moines, Iowa

Zachary Landry glanced down for the hundredth time, nervously fingering the business card he held in his hand. Six hours ago, he had left his downtown office in his home of Des Moines to go to lunch at a nearby café. Now he was on I-55 headed for Memphis, Tennessee, in his old Saab. He was ultimately bound for New Orleans, but he had no idea why. He had no luggage and had eaten only candy bars purchased at gas stations along the way.

There was another person in the car—the girl he had picked up somewhere outside of Saint Louis. He had never picked up a hitchhiker before, but when he saw her standing in the rain, something told him to stop. Other than saying she was going to New Orleans, she hadn't said much. Now she slept, head on the door panel, covered with Zack's jacket.

Looking down again at the card, he recalled the spooky walk from his office toward the café: he never arrived at the eatery. His stomach reminded him of that every few minutes. The candy bars had not helped.

Earlier that day, he had left the office tower where he was second in command in the IT department of a manufacturing business. At twenty-nine, he had a degree in computer science from Northwestern and had earned just enough seniority to avoid the layoffs. He was proud to be the number two at his age, but then again, when he thought about it, there were no old guys in the IT world.

He had turned right onto Church Street, headed for Faye's, a diner that served a variety of sandwiches and a couple of daily plate lunch options. He liked the place because he could sit by himself and read his *Wall Street Journal* without feeling geeky. Zack absorbed the technical information from the *Journal*. What little extra money he had went into a self-advised investment fund that was doing pretty well, all things considered.

It was an unseasonable scorcher of a day, with the temperature somewhere near one hundred. He found himself wishing he had worn a golf shirt to work rather than khaki slacks, a long-sleeve dress shirt, and a black blazer. There had been a series of such days in the last week. *Something about El Niño or whatever*, Zack thought. But there was more than just the heat. The light was weird—like right before a dry thunderstorm. The streetscape had a yellowish tint, and heat waves rippled off the pavement. He half-expected to see a rabid dog come snarling up the street, biting and snapping at the oppressive air.

He looked around but could see no one else out. Perhaps the heat had kept them in, or maybe it was the rampant unemployment. He was rethinking his decision to go out into the heat. Maybe he should have grabbed something out of one of the vending machines in the basement. Well, "in for a penny, in for a pound," as his mother had been fond of saying, and he continued toward the restaurant.

Suddenly, he saw movement ahead of him about a block away. A figure headed in his direction. The thing appeared to lumber along in a slow shuffle as it neared. Zack thought he was going to be panhandled by another one of the growing number of vagrants inhabiting the downtown area. He had already given once that day.

While the undulations of heat waves obscured any detail, Zack could tell there was something wrong with the man—from the size and posturing of the creature, he was sure it was a man. He was a big guy—*very* big. As the distance closed between them, he began to see the figure more clearly. The man was dressed in denim overalls, with a long-sleeved flannel shirt. Zack himself had removed his jacket and rolled up his shirtsleeves a couple of blocks back. *He must be on fire under those clothes.*

As the man neared to within a half block, Zack could see he walked with a stiff-legged gait that reminded him of those flesh-eating zombies in horror movies. In spite of the heat, a chill ran down his spine as the behemoth steadily came closer. He clucked at himself for getting spooked but nevertheless glanced around nervously to see if anyone else was about. *Nobody.* The man and he might have been on the moon—or rather the surface of the sun—for all the company they had.

Now the man was only about thirty yards away. He was enormous, pushing seven feet if he was an inch. Zack was six one, but this guy was head and shoulders above him. He was certainly north of three hundred pounds, and, from what Zack could tell, none of it was fat. The man's hair was long, thin, and a dingy ivory color that with a good washing would probably be white. *This must be what a World Federation wrestler looks like walking around in public.* A sense of foreboding rolled over Zack, and he began to panic. He told himself to get a grip. *For Christ's sake, it's the middle of the day in the middle of town. There's nothing to fear.*

Pow! There was a quick flash of dry lightning and the slam of thunder. Zack jumped and, in spite of himself, was genuinely afraid.

The man was only two car lengths away, and Zack could now see his ruined face. If someone had told him the man had gone through the windshield in a head-on car accident and then had had acid poured on his face, Zack would not have disputed it. His internal danger alarms were firing for reasons he could not fully explain. The man was dangerous, and Zack had no help in sight. He could never take this guy; his only hope was to bolt.

Just as Zack turned to run, the monster man rounded on him where the sidewalk intersected the entranceway to one of the many church breakfast kitchens in the area. He was trapped. He dropped his jacket and backed away from the man, slamming against the locked door. His heart pounded, and a cold sweat rolled down his back, chilling him to the bone.

The huge man studied him as if he recognized him. He didn't say a word but with his big, meaty hand reached into the pocket of his overalls and withdrew a card. The man gazed down at it for a second, as if it were something precious to him. He extended an arm the size of Zack's leg and handed him the card. Zack's mouth fell open as he watched the giant turn and continue up the street.

Zack exhaled, not realizing he had been holding his breath. He glanced down at the card and then looked back up the street for the man. He didn't know if he was safe or if the man was toying with him in some kind of frightening game.

He scooped up his coat and ran to the blind corner, looking up and down the street. There was nothing but yellow haze and the heat radiating off the concrete. The giant had simply vanished. Zack wondered if he had suffered some sort of heatstroke and imagined all of it.

But he could not shake the eerie feeling that this had been real as dirt. He looked at his hand. There was the card. Proof. He held it up and looked at it closely. It shimmered slightly in the odd light. He studied the lone character on it as a single lightning bolt cracked and for a second turned Church Street strobe white.

Now, looking at the card in his hand as he rolled down the highway, he reviewed again the solidary symbol inscribed on the card: "1."

CHAPTER

3

London, England

It was two in the morning in the grungy, dead-end pub, and she had given last call an hour earlier. The woman, having cleaned the tables and stacked the chairs, totaled the night's receipts. It was the last thing to do before heading home to her flat and her two little girls. By now they would have been asleep for hours. Thank God her mum lived in the same building and could watch over them.

The large neon sign in the bar's only window hummed, went out, and suddenly crackled back to life, giving the woman a start. She looked around but sensed nothing except the smell of stale beer and sweat. Her boss had left long ago, leaving her alone to close up. She hadn't minded when he began doing this sometime back, but in the last couple of years, the neighborhood had become rougher and more hostile. She dreaded the six-block walk home at this hour.

Still, she had to have this job. She had two hungry children to feed, and Rachel, her oldest, started church school in the fall. The woman took double shifts every chance she could to save up money for the private school. In England, only three things mattered: family, money, and education. She had neither of the first two, but she had saved for the third. Her girls would have their chance as long as there was a breath in her body. Her girls would be different.

She paused in her task and thought about the girls' father, who had abandoned them after losing his job and being unable to find work. *The sorry son of a bitch.* Failure had broken him. She had no such option. Once again, she told herself how much he had missed and how glad she was that he was gone. The girls were warm, fed, and well loved.

The tavern was located below street level, and patrons had to walk down a flight of steps to enter. It had been an air raid shelter during the war. She felt claustrophobic all of a sudden and hurried to finish up and leave. As she slipped out of her apron, she heard a thump from the stairwell. She spun around. Someone was coming down the stairs. *But that's impossible!* She had locked the door and set the dead bolt herself. She began to shudder.

"Who's there?" she called, her voice cracking.

Silence … but the shape continued down the steps. She could see blue jeans and figured it was a kid. Then there were more figures on the steps.

"What do you want? The bar is closed!" she cried out.

Silence. Now there were at least a half dozen figures, in some kind of loose formation, coming down the staircase. She could see their legs and some of their midsections. All were in jeans or what the kids called cargo pants. As they came farther down the stairs, she could see tattoos. She froze in place, sweating with fear.

The leader, in a leather jacket, reached the bottom step and hopped childlike to the floor. He looked at her with dead, soulless eyes. His cohorts followed behind and spread out right and left. Her heart pounded, and she looked around for some avenue of escape.

"There is none," said the young man, reading her mind.

She studied the group. This was a pack of wolves. *Predators.* She thought about her girls, and her heart broke. She straightened, lifted her head, and said, "I'm not afraid of you. You boys take yourselves back up those steps and get out of here."

The intruders stood rooted where they were.

"Do you want money?" she asked, thinking of the receipts in the cash register.

"No," said the lead boy, giggling. The pack snickered, and the leader produced a thin knife in his right hand. The rest of the group followed suit and brought out knives or box cutters of their own. They began to circle around her. As they moved, they started a low chant. The drone and intonation made her think of some cultish ritual. It was demonic and rang with pure evil. She could not quite make out the words, but they were calling upon the dark powers, she was sure.

The circle around her moved right and then left. She was trapped. The chanting intensified. The woman was terrified but stood straight—her faith like a rock. She saw the white faces and the hollow eyes. She had been a God-fearing woman all her life, and this was the night she would be called home to him. The chill in the room vanished, and the temperature began to rise. She thought she smelled cinders and incense.

"I will fear no evil though I walk through the valley of the shadow of death," she paraphrased.

"Where is your God and Savior, woman?" the leader teased, moving toward her.

"He is here and will overcome all evil—including you!" she responded.

The leader's eyes turned blood-red, and he and his pack fell upon her, tearing and cutting.

CHAPTER

4

Cloe shook herself awake as the phone rang. She was in her bedroom, but the morning light was faint, so it could not be late. She reached for the phone and glanced at the clock; it was a little after six.

"Dr. Lejeune? Cloe? It's Tony ... Father Anton," the priest's voice bellowed through the phone line. "I'm sorry to call so early."

"Yes, Tony, I can hear you now," replied Cloe. "It's okay. Where are you?"

"I am in Rome, but that's unimportant right now," replied Father Antonio Sigliori, vicar general of Vatican Military Field Operations. He worked directly for the pope. "Cloe, I got your message that you had called for Albert. It was routed to me because the monsignor's not here. Something terrible has happened. We need to talk."

"Tony, yes, we do need to talk. I need to see the pope as soon as possible. It's the journal. I may have discovered something ... something important, maybe something critical," she replied, standing and wiggling into her robe. "We must meet immediately."

Cloe walked toward the french doors opening onto the side porch of her home and looked out over the river. The sun was rising over the far shore. It illuminated wispy clouds, turning them a bright red. *Red sky in the morning, sailor take warning,* her mother would have said. Early February on the river was one of her favorite times, especially when the weather was as mild as it had been for the last few days. In the evenings, she loved to watch the sun set on one side of her home and the moon rise on the other.

What could Tony want? Something "terrible" has happened? She marveled at the coincidence of their mutual desire to communicate.

"Tony, how long before you can get here from Rome?" she asked, turning back to the receiver. "Can you come get me?"

"I'll be in New Orleans by lunchtime tomorrow," replied the cleric.

She was now fully alert after Tony's call, so she decided to work. She made coffee and booted up her laptop at the kitchen table. This time, she researched world events. When she finally saved her work and closed the computer, she was more convinced than ever that she needed to see the new pope.

* * *

It was only about forty-five minutes to the famed French Quarter restaurant. She bathed and dressed and then studied herself in the full-length mirror. *Not bad for midforties*, she thought. The jogging and yoga classes were paying off. Then she was off across the Lake Pontchartrain Causeway, taking her over the twenty-four-mile span of the lake between the North Shore and New Orleans. There was not as much traffic as she had anticipated even though people should have been streaming into the city for various functions ahead of the carnival season, which would start soon. If this were any sign, Mardi Gras would be very light—a big disappointment to the city.

As she drove through the New Orleans central business district, it looked strangely vacant without the usual hustle of people on the streets. Cloe thought of the last time Monsignor Albert Roques had come here to meet her. She had been working on a particularly difficult passage in the journal that detailed a conversation between Jesus and the apostle "Jesus loved," widely believed to be St. John, author of the last of the gospels. She had summoned the monsignor, and together they had gone to the library at the Ursuline Convent and found the jars, the treasure trove of the Sicarii. She had been working on the journal and the jars ever since.

To facilitate her work on the first two jars, she left her position as second chair in the Ancient Languages Department of the University of Washington and assumed the top position in the new Ancient Languages Department at LSU, only sixty-five miles from her home in Madisonville.

Now, as a result of the latest gift from the Sicarii, there were scores of jars and endless challenges.

Even though she now headed the department, her staff at LSU was actually doing the work to keep it running. Cloe was required to spend only a day or two a week in Baton Rouge. Her main duties, in the eyes of the university, were to work on the journal and to catalog the jars. While this sounded ordinary, it was anything but, given the historic nature of the find. She had added staff in New Orleans at the library in the Ursuline Convent to assist her. There had already been enormous discoveries from their work, and there were surely more to come. The authentication of the journal as being from the time of Christ had thrown religious scholars into a frenzy.

She turned into the parking garage at the Royal Orleans Hotel and waved to Earl the parking attendant. She wasn't even sure of his last name, but she considered him a friend. Earl might park cars, but he did so much more. He was a travel guide and goodwill ambassador for the city.

"Hi, Earl," Cloe called as she handed him the keys. "How's the family?"

"Hey, Dr. Lejeune," replied Earl. "Everybody's fine, including our brand-new granddaughter. It's great to see you back. Will you be here awhile, or should I keep her close?"

"Just lunch," replied Cloe. "Congratulations on the new arrival. That makes six, doesn't it?"

"Right you are, Dr. Lejeune! It's all good," said Earl as he pulled her sedan up to the nearest spot. "We'll leave her right here for when you're ready. Have a nice meal."

Cloe strode across the beautiful lobby of the old hotel, which was clad in marble and furnished with antiques. A few guests milled about, some checking in or out. She headed down the steps, past the Rib Room and out into the nearly deserted Quarter. A half block later, she stood in front of Antoine's and pushed her way through the narrow french doors.

The mirrored walls glinted back at her as the maître d' led her to the large rear dining room where her waiter, Vinny, joined them. Cloe had been there enough times to know the front room was for the tourists and the back room was where the action was. Today it was nearly empty.

As she approached the table, Father Anton jumped up and came around to seat her. Unlike the monsignor, Father Anton dressed in a dark suit, eschewing the traditional cassock. His dark hair was cut close, but that was the only feature that hinted at the soldier behind his Mediterranean good looks. Vinny chatted with them for a few seconds and then rushed off to start the train of delicacies steaming to the table. Cloe never ordered anymore, putting her complete trust in the staff's choices.

"Hello, Tony," she said.

"Cloe, it is so good to see you," replied the warrior cleric, sitting down ramrod straight as always. "It's been a while."

Indeed, it had been a little over four years, since she, her son, J.E., and the monsignor had nearly lost their lives but had defeated the Karik's forces at Masada. Even now, the sounds of gunfire and men screaming troubled her sleep.

There was also Sergio.

It had all started with the Kolektor, the arms merchant turned ancient relic collector who had wanted her father's jar and had killed him for it. Even though the Kolektor was killed by the Sicarii at Hakeldama, elements of his criminal organization had survived. The Karik, the Kolektor's successor, had been hell-bent on finding and possessing the cave of sacred jars that contained writings from the time of Christ. If that were not enough, the long-thought dead son of the Kolektor, Michael, turned up seeking the jars as well. While she, J.E., and the monsignor were instrumental in defeating the Karik and the heir as well as bringing down the entirety of the Kolektor's criminal organization, she knew that without Father Anton and his Swiss guards they would all be dead. He had intervened at precisely the right time and had "saved their bacon," as her mother used to say.

"Great to see you as well," she said, sipping a nice light Chardonnay. "Is Sky still your pilot?"

"Absolutely! He can fly anything faster and farther than anybody else," replied the cleric, smiling as he recited Sky's personal motto. "We couldn't do what we do, traveling where we have to go, without him."

Sky had originally been Michael's personal pilot. She hadn't thought about Michael in a while. She didn't want to think about him at all.

They were seated against one of the walls filled with autographed pictures and caricatures of famous people who had at various times graced the restaurant. A-list entertainers such as Bob Hope, several presidents, and at least one pope were all represented. Cloe scanned the room.

People-watching in New Orleans was the best in the world. *But not today,* she thought. The surrounding tables were mostly vacant. Vinny laid the three cheese and garlic salad before her as Cloe looked at the priest, wondering how she would explain what she had to say.

"Okay, Tony. Here we are," she said. "What terrible thing has happened? Why have you come all this way?"

"In a moment," he said, "but first the holy father directed me to ask about the progress on the translation of the journal and the cataloging of all the jars the Sicarii shipped to Ursuline."

"Well, the cataloging is proceeding as rapidly as possible. As you know, each jar must be transported to LSU to be carefully opened and the contents indexed. It just takes time," said Cloe. "As I have said from the very beginning, it is undoubtedly one of the greatest finds of ancient literature, if not the greatest."

"And the journal?" whispered the priest.

"Slowly," said Cloe. "There's the hand-writing problem and the piecing together of the scraps. Much of it is mundane; the daily recitation of events. However, it certainly reinforces the four gospels and provides additional details. There is more information about the various miracles and a little more explanation of some of the parables. Each is absolutely fascinating."

"Nothing really new?" asked Father Anton.

"No, I can't agree with that. It adds so much color," she said. "One really amazing thing is the governance structure. The Apostles acted as a sort of board of directors of the ministry. But, we learn from the journal that there was an inner core, an executive committee, if you will."

"Yes?" queried the priest leaning forward.

"There were five of them and Jesus," she replied. "Peter, John, James, Mary Magdalene, and Mary, the mother of Jesus. According to the journal, they talked nearly every day about doctrine, policy, issues, all matters of importance. Elements requiring broader discussion were brought to all the Apostles. Of course, Jesus had the final say but he listened carefully."

"Astounding," said the cleric.

"And then there is the very sad part," she said. "The death of Joseph, Jesus's earthly father, devastated him. He was such a role model for Jesus."

"Jesus was as much man as God, so I'm not surprised," replied Father Anton.

"The most important new pieces that I'm working on are still the passages detailing what seems to be a lengthy conversation or series of dialogues between Jesus and St. John. It's very difficult because it's so new and because…"

"Because?" asked the cleric in his direct manner.

Here it is, Cloe thought. He had skillfully led her to the core of it all.

"Well, if I could be sure, I would say it's because it reads a little like the book of Revelation, which was also reputedly written by St. John," replied Cloe. "You know how difficult Revelation is with all its vagaries and symbolism. To us, it seems to have been written in some sort of code. The section of the journal I'm studying talks about events that might signal the end of the world—floods, famine, disease, etcetera."

"Could you be looking at something that might be the genesis of the book of Revelation?" asked the military priest.

"Tony, you are indeed amazing—you sound like Albert," she replied, thinking of the monsignor's incisive way. "In short, maybe. This section of the journal has the same end-of-times symbolism as Revelation. While there's nothing on the 'four horsemen' per se, the journal talks about, I believe, the rise of evil. Could it have been a precursor to Revelation? I'll have to think some more about that."

"Well, if true, that would certainly 'add some hot sauce to the gumbo,' as I believe you people are fond of saying," said the cleric with a smile.

Cloe chuckled and then, straightening up, said, "Still, you put your finger on why I called. I need to see the pope. I've come to some material in the journal he needs to be personally apprised of."

"Cloe, surely you know what's going on in the world today," replied the priest. "The pope is so busy I'm not sure I could get an audience. Can you tell me what you've found?"

"Tony, I'm not certain yet—but I feel strongly he needs to know what I think I know."

"But, Cloe, you have to help me. The monsignor can't help. He's gone. Tell me something that will assist me in convincing the pope to see you now," said Father Tony.

"Fair enough, Tony. Call the pope and tell him I have reason to believe the end of times is beginning now," she said.

Father Anton studied her, took a last swallow of his coffee with chicory, and asked, "Did you bring an overnight bag?"

CHAPTER
5

A few miles north of Memphis, the girl finally woke up and looked around the car.

"Where are we?" she asked, beginning to twirl her thick brown hair nervously around her finger.

"Not too far from Memphis—headed south," replied Zack. "What's your name?"

"My name is Melanie Washer, and I've been on an army airplane, in the air or on the ground, for about thirty hours since I left Guam headed for Saint Louis. My father, until last year, was in the military and was stationed there," she blurted. "My friends call me Mel."

She had a sweet smile.

"I'm Zachary—Zach Landry from Des Moines, Iowa. I was on my lunch break, and then I was here."

Eyes on the road, he sensed her staring at him and then heard her suddenly gasp. In his peripheral vision, he saw her look at the card in his hand and then hold up an identical card. It shimmered faintly in the evening light.

Oh my God, he thought. *How is that possible?*

He swerved off the road onto the shoulder, stopped the car, faced her, and said, "I think we need to talk."

"Yes. How did you get that card?" she asked. He liked how she got right to the point.

Zack filled her in on his walk to the restaurant and the giant. When she heard the description of the man, she looked shocked.

"It's got to be the same guy," she asserted. "I'm studying nursing at the army school, and I do part-time work as an EMT intern with our emergency medical services unit. The pay is pretty good, and I get a break on tuition. These days the army is about the only place to find any kind of job. The day before yesterday, I was on duty, and we got a call of a possible heart attack at the local mall."

"Okay, but what does any of this have to do with the card?" asked Zack.

"You'll see," she continued. "We loaded the bus and rushed to the mall. We found a large man with a group of people around him. He was lying on his back with his eyes rolled up and hardly breathing. Right away we began CPR and a saline drip."

Zack watched Mel as she talked, liking her pretty face and blue eyes. He thought she was probably in her mid-twenties.

"He began to respond pretty quickly," she added. "As he did, I sat back a little and studied him more closely. Just as you described, the man was huge, with a really scarred face. He had on overalls and a flannel shirt and had longish white hair."

"Sounds like my guy," observed Zack. "But how could the same dude in the same clothes who gave me my card have been having a heart attack in Guam eight thousand miles away a little more than a day earlier?"

"Well, that's the thing. I'm not sure he was even sick, much less having a heart attack," she said. "As I looked at him, he rolled over, stood up, and reached into his pocket. Pretty much everybody backed away, as this guy was a monster. He pulled out this card, looked at it, and handed it to me. He acted like he was serving me Communion or something. Then he ripped the drip from his wrist and walked away, leaving all of us freaked out."

"What did you do?"

"I didn't have any choice," she replied. "My partner and I ran after him and radioed the army squadron that now polices the mall. Calling in a false emergency is against martial law. We ran out the door he had left from, but he was gone. The soldiers couldn't find any trace of him. He just vanished."

"Let me guess," said Zack. "The next thing you knew, you had this irresistible urge to get on an airplane and go to New Orleans."

"It sounds dumb sitting here, but that's it," she replied.

Zack sat back, letting a tenth of his brain drive the car back onto the highway while the rest of it tried to absorb the story and figure out what it all could mean.

CHAPTER

6

Rome—St. Peter's Basilica

It was after nine, but only now were the last of the winter tourists leaving. The old priest wearily thought about the tasks still to be done before the night was over. The church had to be tidied up for the new batch of worshipers coming the next day. Even though there were fewer tourists every day now, he still had to prepare. Then there would be late prayers and the nightly devotional. Finally, there would be a snack and a blessed glass of good Italian wine. By midnight he would tumble onto his cot to sleep for a few hours before the routine started again tomorrow.

A few of the young acolytes had entered the massive building to help him. *These are the good youth,* he thought. There had been so much unrest lately among the young people of the country that everyone was on edge. The newspapers still permitted to operate had trumpeted the violence, scaring the dickens out of the remaining people who bothered to read. For some unknown reason, the young people of the country were angry—and not just in Italy. Ever since the advent of Icar on the world's stage, things had gone from bad to worse. Reports were coming in from all over the world, detailing random acts of extreme violence committed by seemingly normal adolescents. Well, he would have to think about all this later; there was work to be done.

The elderly cleric turned right and then left, wondering where he had misplaced his dusting cloth, when he saw people streaming into the church. *No*, he thought. It was now well past the hours for tourists to enter the church. *How did they get in? Where did they come from?* A few hours ago, there had been a few hundred people in St. Peter's Square on one of the many pre-Lenten pilgrimages. It was a paltry crowd compared to only a year ago. These crashers must have hidden from the security guards. He observed the newcomers more closely. They were all young—late teens to early twenties. Uncertainty and a little fear began to roil in his gut.

He called out to them, "The church is closed. Please come back tomorrow."

The priest heard the young people snicker en masse as if they had some unseen connection. Fear spiked in him for reasons he could not explain, even to himself. He was, however, as safe as anyone could be, here in God's house.

The horde began to flow down the center aisle and both side aisles. So fluid was the movement it reminded the priest of water flowing downhill through numerous linked channels. On they came, as certain as death itself.

Finally, the throng arrived just in front of the main altar, pushing the priest and the young acolytes ahead of them. There, everyone paused as if awaiting further orders. In the hiatus, the old priest stood with shoulders back and confronted them.

"The church is closed," he said firmly. "What do you want?"

"We have come for you, priest," screeched the young man he took for the leader. Leather-garbed and tattooed, he leered at the old man. Carved images of angels and saints adorning the walls looked down on them with birdlike intensity.

"Be gone!" he screamed, knowing his words carried no weight.

"Be gone," murmured the mob, softly taunting the old cleric.

The priest and the novices huddled together. They were completely surrounded.

Slowly, the group began to move to the right, clockwise. Their chanting, barely audible, was in a strange language. The hair was standing on the back of the old cleric's neck. Then there was silence, and the mob stopped dead in its tracks. More rapidly this time, the young men began to circle counterclockwise and once again to chant, this time louder.

"Father, what are they doing?" cried one of the acolytes.

22

The old priest listened carefully and said, "God in heaven … they are calling upon the dark powers."

The horde reversed again and continued their deafening chant, except this time when they stopped between directions, several of the young men from the rear of the circle ran forward and threw buckets of liquid onto the old priest and his charges.

"Father!" screamed several of the young priests-to-be. "It's petrol!"

The old cleric took his rosary from his sash and knelt on the hard floor, "Our Father, who art in heaven …"

Now the mob was in a frenzy, screaming and whirling like dervishes around the priests. The old priest could smell something burning but kept his head to the ground. The chanting and the motion stopped.

"… forgive us our trespasses as we forgive those who trespass against us," he continued.

The circle shrank away from the huddle of priests. The old priest was heartened by this response and once again said, "Be gone!"

"Be gone," echoed the haunting reply, and with these words, each in the horde struck a match or lighter.

The priest stood up straight and faced the leader, "Be gone, Satan!"

The young man only snickered and said, "I am not Satan or fit to tie his bootlaces, but there is one coming who is."

The priest watched in terror as the tossed matches and lighters arched across the transept near the altar where he and the acolytes had clustered together. Many landed in the petrol now covering the floor of the church, giving off a low *whumpf* as it ignited. The young acolytes screamed in horror and pain as the burning fuel consumed them. As the old priest's clothing, hair, and flesh began to burn, he saw the knots of young men clustered around the load-bearing supports of the church's dome.

With his final gasp of burning air, he joined his fellow martyrs in their terminal screams.

CHAPTER

7

As they drove south through Mississippi, the weirdness of the whole situation began to descend on Zack. Now that he and Mel had switched places and she was driving, he had more brainpower to think about things. He was having trouble figuring out what the hell he was doing.

"Why are we going to New Orleans?" he suddenly asked. "Who are you and why are we together?"

"I don't know," said Mel. "But we're bonded together in some way. We're stuck. We've been chosen for something. By whom? For what? I have no idea."

"Chosen? Chosen for what? I'm a computer guy from the Midwest. I don't have any business in New Orleans."

"And you have no connection with the place? None?"

"No, I didn't say that," he responded. "My father was actually born there, but his family moved away when he was just two years old. I have no folks there at all. In fact, my parents are both gone, and I have no relatives whatsoever."

Zack sat glumly as this reality once again hit him. He was alone—completely alone.

"My God," said Mel. "I had only my father, but he was killed in a training accident last year. My mother died not too long after I was adopted by them."

"Adopted? So you're alone as well."

The two grew quiet as Mel drove on into the descending dusk. Headlights began to appear in the oncoming traffic. Zack wondered about the similarity in their backgrounds. Mel had no known connection with New Orleans, and neither of them had any family. Could these be coincidences? They neared the exit for McComb, Mississippi, and his stomach began to rumble.

"Mel, let's look for a place to pull off the interstate and stop for supper," he said.

"Sure," she replied. "We missed the McComb exits, but something will pop up soon."

After a few miles, they came upon a sign that simply said "Smyth" with a symbol for a café beneath the name.

Mel pointed the car down the exit ramp and said, "If we can find gas, we should probably fill up while we're off the highway."

They followed the ramp in the gathering darkness to a stop sign on a two-lane blacktop road, perpendicular to the interstate. It was a little hard to see the signage, but there was a marker indicating Smyth was off to the right.

"Okay, here we go," Mel said, taking the right-hand turn.

* * *

Zack looked out at the two-lane rural road. They had passed through a couple of small burgs, but neither had been Smyth, nor had they seen a café. "Do you have any idea where we are?" asked Mel.

"We're in Mississippi" Zack smiled.

"Oh, you butt! I mean where in Mississippi?"

"Not too far from Smyth, I hope," he said, sneaking a quick look at her. "Are you tired? I can drive."

"I'm fine but let's hope the café is close. I'm hungry," she responded.

On they drove as it began to rain, lightly at first and then harder. Mel was having trouble driving and had slowed her speed.

Finally, they entered Smyth, a small village devoid of traffic lights but boasting a building in a decaying main street area with a flickering neon "Café" sign. The diner was a one-story, flat-roofed structure probably built in the fifties. A few pickups were parked outside in the gravel parking lot, and Zack could see dark figures moving inside through the grimy plate-glass windows. He shivered in spite of himself.

"Finally!" said Mel. "Unless you think the place is full of ax murderers, let's stop and eat."

Zack considered telling her to turn around and get back on the interstate. After all that had happened earlier in the day, his threat assessment alarm was at least vibrating if not clanging. But they both were famished.

"Okay, pull in, and we'll give it a try," he sighed.

CHAPTER

8

"Cloe, I am very interested in what you can tell me about the translation. God knows, it is very important," said Father Anton as they headed from the restaurant to Cloe's car. The sun was in and out among the early afternoon clouds. "Maybe Albert will be able to discuss it with you later in detail, but right now I need to share with you my own news."

"Well, what is it, Tony?" she asked.

"Something terrible has happened, which is probably on the news as we speak—or soon will be."

"What is it?" she pressed him. "I have seen such a blizzard of bad news recently. What specifically are you referring to? In any event, where is Albert? This is a first for you to come here to meet with me."

"Albert is in prison," said the priest.

"What? What in the world are you saying? Albert in prison?" Cloe stopped in her tracks to face him.

"Albert has been imprisoned for his religious beliefs; in effect, he is a political prisoner," said the cleric.

"St. Peter's Basilica has been destroyed," he added.

"My God! *How?*" she exclaimed, the seismic shocks piling on.

"The investigation is ongoing, but it appears that someone broke in last night afterhours, murdered the priests who were tidying up, and blew up the massive loadbearing columns in the church," replied the priest. "The roof, the beautiful dome, imploded of its own weight."

"What of the pope? Is he safe?"

"Yes, the pope is fine. He was removed to a safe location by his security detail as soon as the alarm was sounded. He is under heavy guard at Castel Gandolfo near Rome."

Castel Gandolfo was the pope's personal retreat—his Camp David. It was hard to believe he had been driven from the Vatican by some sort of violence. And St. Peter's destroyed ... *impossible!*

"Tony, how could this happen?" asked Cloe. "Are there any more particulars?"

"No one knows for sure, but somehow it seems that after the pre-Lenten crowd cleared the square, a group of young people hid and then entered the basilica. They set explosive charges against the columns that bore the weight of the church. A number of priests and young men studying to be priests were savagely killed."

"But *why?*" The thought of the priests and the loss of an icon of Christendom weighed heavily on Cloe.

"The pope believes this is part of the worldwide reign of violence we have witnessed over the last few months. It seems to be getting worse and more daring," replied the priest. "Religious of all sorts, both laity and ministry, are being targeted. Nor is it limited to Christians. Some of the worst violence has been visited on Muslim and other non-Christian clerics."

"This looks like it might have political implications as well as religious overtones," observed Cloe. They had reached the garage, and she handed her receipt to Earl.

"Quite right," replied Father Anton. "Many Christians, Jews, and Muslims are blaming each other for the attacks. Each group seems to think the other is responsible. Fighting has broken out among right wing religious factions in several countries."

"Well, many of these religions have been fighting each other for hundreds if not thousands of years," said Cloe. "Why is this different?"

"First, it's not limited to the Middle East where these fights—wars, really—have taken place. England, Russia, the US, and numerous other nations have seen large outbreaks of fighting and violence," stated the priest. "Intolerance, threats, and just plain meanness are all off the charts, pretty much everywhere.

"Second, in more normal times, responsible politicians and leaders try to defuse the violence. In this case, at least one individual has emerged from the shadows by subtly exploiting the situation. This man's creed is a populist spiel that on the surface seeks to uplift those in poor or difficult circumstances, but it does so by pulling others down and by setting people against each other. It's rich against poor, black against white, Muslim against Jew, and so forth. He preaches that all assets, all world assets, belong to everyone equally, regardless of who created the assets. He seeks worldwide redistribution of wealth and of the means of production."

"Even in these modern times, there are those who would believe this." Cloe was beginning to think her interpretation of the journal and world events was correct. "But this has always been just a small minority—not enough to do any real harm."

"It's grown to quite a few people, particularly among the young and disaffected," replied the cleric. "Countless young people have no work and have become used to others providing for them. Already angry, the message is resonating with them, principally, at least to date, in the large population centers such as Paris, London, New York, and elsewhere."

"Who is this guy? Where does he come from, and where is he now?"

"His point of origin is not precisely known," Father Anton responded. "Some say he is from Eastern Europe. Others swear he was born in Israel or in North Africa. There has been speculation that he holds citizenship in more than one country, including the United States, where he apparently was educated."

Earl pulled up in Cloe's car. "Tony, what's his name? Who is this person?"

The priest gazed out across the entrance to the parking garage before he turned to her and said, "He is called Icar."

CHAPTER

9

When they entered the café, a bell over the door jangled; the conversation in the dining room died as everyone turned to look at them. *Was that fear in their eyes?* Zack wondered. There were about a dozen tables, a couple of booths, and a few chrome bar stools around the counter. Aged red vinyl peeked from between the metal bands of chrome on the stools. The decor was a cross between art deco and country. The counter surface was green tile punctuated with stork-necked soda fountains. Several huge, glass-covered cake platters promised German chocolate and strawberry cakes. Behind the counter was a window into the kitchen populated with ancient gas grills and stoves belching fire and smoke.

"Sit anywhere you want," said a woman behind the counter, polishing a glass.

Zack and Mel edged their way to a booth by the front window. The seats were also covered in a red vinyl that might have been new around the end of World War II. The table was Formica, likewise ringed by chrome strips. A jukebox remote was at one end of the table, guarded by oversized salt and pepper shakers and condiment jars.

As they sat down, Zack surveyed the room. The other inhabitants were mainly older: men in jeans and cowboy hats and women in dresses, some of which looked handmade. Zack remembered his grandmother had sewn her own clothes and had a partial mannequin made to her size in her bedroom.

Soon a young waitress came over. She was dressed in a beige uniform with a tiara-style paper cap on her head and a pencil behind one ear. She handed them menus and pointed the obligatory order pad at them.

"Hi, y'all. Help ya?" she asked perfunctorily. "My name's Doris." It sounded like "Door-is."

Zack smiled and noticed Mel watching the waitress out of the corner of her eye.

"What's good?" he asked.

"Well, our burgers are second to none, at least around here," said Doris. "You can't beat our shakes. We use real ice cream."

Zack looked at Mel, and she nodded slightly. "We'll take two burgers all the way and two large shakes."

"Add cheese to mine," said Mel.

As the waitress scribbled on the pad, she glanced over her shoulder a couple of times. When she finished, she squeezed her lips together in a tight smile and left.

"Wow, did I say something wrong?"

"Something's wrong, but it doesn't have anything to do with what you said," responded Mel. "She seemed worried—maybe a little scared."

"Maybe we're overworking this. Let's just enjoy the best burgers and shakes around," Zack replied.

The bell over the entry door rang as the door swung open. A young man appeared in the doorway, and the chatter in the restaurant, which had resumed, came to an abrupt halt again. People quickly looked away. The man was dressed in jeans, boots, and a leather jacket. The boots were more Goth than country, and grillwork shone in the young man's mouth. The café patrons appeared scared.

"What ..." said Mel, softly.

The youth scanned the room, going from table to table, face to face. When he looked in their direction, he focused on them in a way that indicated he was recording their faces. After a bit, eyes shining, he nodded warmly as if it were a Sunday afternoon greeting.

"Whoa." Mel shivered. "What was that?"

"I don't know, but I think we just saw what the waitress is afraid of," responded Zack.

The young man sashayed in a slow, undulating manner into the dining room and up to the counter. Every eye followed him. He threw a leg over an ancient bar stool and sat.

The spell was broken by a yell from the kitchen: "Order up!"

Zack saw Doris grab a to-go order in a tall paper bag and sweep some napkins and condiments into it. He wondered if that was for the stranger.

Doris gripped the bag, spun on her heel, and headed toward their table. She deposited the bag on the table and said, "Your bill comes to twenty dollars even."

"Doris, we didn't order our food to go," said Mel. "We were going to eat here."

"That'll be twenty dollars," repeated Doris, glancing over her shoulder.

"We'll eat here," said Zack.

The waitress was becoming agitated. The young man in leather eyed them intently.

"It's not safe for you here," she whispered, her voice sounding desperate.

Zack looked at Mel and reached for his wallet. He laid a twenty and three ones on the table and said, "Thanks, Doris. We hate to run, but we have to be on the road to meet our schedule."

Doris exhaled sharply and said, "Well, I enjoyed helping you. Y'all come back now."

Zack stood and grabbed the bag as the waitress ran into the kitchen. Mel was too smart not to follow, and they walked toward the door.

The leather punk swung off the bar stool and intercepted them. The crowd in the small diner was riveted on the scene. "What? You too good to eat with us?" he challenged, moving between them and the door. He smiled lasciviously at Mel.

"We certainly don't want to see *you* go, honey," he added.

Zack handed Mel the bag of burgers, stepped up, and faced the young man. They stood about the same height and were about the same build. He sensed Mel move closer to him.

"No, we are needed in New Orleans," said Zack, looking directly into the boy-man's eyes. There was a painful intensity in the kid's stare, but Zack forced his concentration and struggled to back the punk down. Seconds ticked by, building into a minute or two.

"New Orleans?" The young man broke the silence, stepping away from the door. "Then I'll see you again," he said as Zack and Mel passed through the door into the night.

"That's a promise!" he called after them.

CHAPTER

10

"Well, what was that all about?" asked Mel, looking back as they pulled out of the parking lot headed toward the interstate. Zack was driving and not holding back on the Saab.

"I'm not real sure. But I'm glad we got out of there. That guy was walking trouble."

"But what could he have done?" Mel continued. "We were in a restaurant full of adults. He wouldn't have started something with all them around."

"Did you see the fear on their faces?" responded Zack. "I'm not sure we would have had any help—except for maybe our waitress friend."

Mel opened the bag of food and began to organize it. She put a shake with a straw in the cup holder next to Zack and unwrapped his burger so he could eat and drive.

"Damn, that's good," said Zack, now slowing the car a bit as he took a bite of the overstuffed burger.

"This shake is terrific too," added Mel, finally smiling again.

"Well, I told y'all so," said a voice from the backseat of the roomy Saab.

Zack and Mel both jerked around to the back of the car and saw the waitress lying down on the backseat. She was in her uniform, still clutching Zack's check and cash in her hand. Zack looked back, causing the car to swerve, but he easily regained control.

"Oh my God!" said Mel.

"Please don't take me back!" cried Doris. "I can't stand it. It's sick."

"Okay, okay," said Mel. "But tell us what's going on. What's sick?"

"Doris, you're safe now. Tell us what's going on in Smyth," he said, accelerating toward the interstate.

There was silence for a while.

"I'm not from Smyth," she began after she ceased crying. "I'm a student at State, and I needed a job. I saw an ad a few months ago, and I applied and got the waitress job. At first, it was great. The people accepted me, and I could eat all I wanted and made a few bucks plus tips."

Zack munched on his burger and looked at Doris in the rearview mirror. Mel had put her sandwich aside and was sitting sideways in her seat, completely focused on their new passenger.

"What happened then?" asked Mel.

"Well, I think it had something to do with all the trouble going around," she replied. "Smyth is a small community, mainly farming. The people all know each other. Most of the kids become farmers, or they leave. The one you saw at the restaurant is not from Smyth. He came here about two months ago."

"Where did he come from? What's he do?" asked Zack.

"He doesn't seem to do anything except make trouble, and nobody knows where he came from," she answered. "One day he was just here. We don't have local cops anymore to take care of people like him, what with the martial law and all."

"So what does he do that has everybody so afraid and you wanting to run away?" asked Zack.

"Well, Skylark—that's supposedly his name—recruited the youngest, most impressionable kids around here."

"Recruited to what?" asked Mel.

"As far as I can tell, to nothing," she replied.

"That makes no sense," said Zack. "What do you mean to 'nothing'?"

"The kids have quit working on their family farms, stopped going to school, and just don't do anything, including listen to authority," said Doris. The car grew quiet for a minute or two.

"Once he had about a dozen recruits—some say disciples—he began to slowly take over and terrorize everybody," Doris went on. "It was like those old gangster movies. Skylark and his boys shook down people for protection money. Some people laughed, but soon strange things happened to them or to their stuff. Nothing could be pinned on Skylark, and besides, the nearest

34

military outpost is over in Starkville. Now his gang pretty much controls everything, and he punishes, unmercifully, anyone who steps out of line."

"Why didn't you just leave?" asked Mel.

"He won't let anyone leave," Doris replied. "For one thing, he's taken everyone's car keys. We can't get them back except for a specific purpose, and then an escort is assigned to go with us."

"Horrible," said Mel.

"A sign of the times," added Zack. "Everything seems upside down." He looked in the rearview mirror and said, "Oh, oh."

"What is it?" Mel responded, a little worry in her voice.

"Headlights coming up behind us ... fast," he replied.

"That could be just some country boy on his way home," said Doris, hopefully. "They're fast around here. But like I said, the bad boys have taken everyone's keys. That's either a stranger or it's one of Skylark's thugs."

"Maybe," said Zack over his shoulder. "People at the café would have figured out by now that you're gone. Would Skylark come after you?"

"Yes. Nobody has gotten away from him yet," she said.

"Well, we'll know soon," said Zack, watching the vehicle drawing closer and wondering whom to thank for this new threat.

As he monitored the mirror, he could see it was a large truck, the kind with big tires and a large grill. He couldn't yet see the driver.

"He's pulling into the left lane to pass," said Mel, relief in her voice.

"Yes ..." Zack began.

Bam! The huge truck's bumper slammed into the back left quarter of the Saab. Mel and Doris both screamed as Zack struggled for control of the car while the rear end made to skid off the road to the right. The food, now forgotten, flew from their hands and laps.

Zack steered into the skid and managed to stay on the road. He knew the Saab, while old, was in great shape. He cared for it meticulously himself and had recently changed out the shocks and struts. It clung spiderlike to the narrow blacktop road as they sped along with the big truck closely behind.

"I'm so sorry for getting y'all in this," cried Doris. "Here he comes again. What do we do?"

"Strap yourselves into your seats, really tight," yelled Zack over the rush of the road noise. He carefully watched the killer vehicle approach. Soon, it filled the entire mirror, and all he could see was the grill.

"Hold on! I've got a little surprise for our friend," Zack said as he downshifted the Saab 99 and hit the gas. The turbocharger on his old ride engaged, and it leapt forward like a scalded antelope. The big truck receded in the rearview mirror until its lights looked like a white two on a black die. The Saab sped through the night as a tight, thin smile spread over Zack's lips.

"What the hell was that?" cried Mel.

"That was something Skylark would never know anything about. This Saab carries a stock turbocharger to boost the horsepower when needed," said Zack.

"Well, we sure needed it then," said a relieved Doris.

They cruised through the first of the two small towns they had passed on the way to Smyth but this time in excess of eighty-five miles an hour. Everything but the sidewalks had been rolled up and shut down tight. Two years ago, there likely would have been a local cop on duty to snag them in his radar. At this speed, they would have made his day. No longer.

"Thank God, you were able to beat him," said Mel.

"Hmmm, I don't think I did beat him," observed Zack, focused on his mirror. "Here he comes again."

The two girls looked back and saw the monster truck in the distance. It seemed to breathe fire as it roared toward them.

"Oh my God!" cried Mel. "It must be doing more than a hundred!"

"Yes," said Zack. "He's gonna try to end it in one great bull rush. I don't think the turbo trick is going to work again."

The truck had closed to about two car lengths behind them.

"He's crossing into the left lane!" screamed Doris. "He's gonna try to knock us off the road!"

Time slowed down as danger and possible death approached over Zack's left shoulder. It was size, weight, and raw horsepower versus the swift and nimble. He had a plan, and he liked the odds.

The huge truck pulled even with him, with both vehicles going flat out, and Zack looked up into Skylark's leering face, the personification of evil.

"We can't shake him!" screamed Doris.

Zack saw the truck careen laterally toward him, clearly maneuvering to knock him off the highway into the deep, dry ditch at the side. At this speed, the Saab might roll or even tumble.

The distance between the two vehicles closed to within a few inches as Skylark sought to apply the coup-de-grace. Zack hit the brakes hard on the Saab, and the car immediately slowed, causing the truck to rush past. The truck's momentum propelled it into the ditch on the right side of the road, but it did not roll or tumble: it sped along the bottom of the ditch. The driver tried to ascend the steep bank and get back onto the highway, but he overcorrected and shot up the embankment at a terrifying rate of speed.

The Saab coasted to a stop as the truck became airborne, flying across the highway and hitting a stand of pine trees about fifteen feet off the ground on the other side of the road. It burst into flames as the rear end fell crashing into the trunk of the lead tree. The front bumper was twisted around the tree trunk, and the truck hung there while it burned like a Roman candle.

Then it exploded.

CHAPTER

11

"Icar ... yes, I do remember hearing or reading something about him," said Cloe as they drove away from the posh restaurant. "But he's not head of any state or recognized organization."

"No, but he seems to have filled the void created by the US's threat about withdrawing from the worldwide leadership role that it has played for decades," said Father Anton. "Pax Americana may be ending. The world is on the verge of anarchy."

"My God!" Cloe said, thinking about J.E. and his cohorts. "What will happen to our bases? Our embassies and our citizens abroad?"

"The Vatican Opts Center, which provides our intelligence, tells us that the US bases will be legally ceded to the host countries, but in reality, particularly in the third world, they will be overrun and looted. No US citizen will be safe."

"Why?" she asked.

"The president says he needs the troops for martial law purposes at home."

"I can't understand this. How did we get here?"

"Cloe, life has changed very much, very rapidly, and the world stage has dramatically transformed," replied Father Anton. "From an external perspective, experts disagree on whether it all started fifty years ago or five years ago. It certainly accelerated with the Arab Spring. This began the US international disengagement and its leading from behind. Government after government in the Middle East has fallen—in many cases replaced by street mobs."

"I know about all that, but there are other countries … Germany, France, and others," asserted Cloe.

"True, but there are also Iran, North Korea, Russia, and China to name but a few with, let us say, extreme self-interest," responded the warrior-priest. "The US was the great counterweight to all that. Now, Libya, Tunisia, and other North African or Middle Eastern countries have become little more than fundamentalist theocracies. Assad is an Iranian puppet in Syria, and Iraq is now under the nuclear umbrella of Iran. Afghanistan is so lawless even the Russians don't want it. Pakistan and India are again threatening each other with nuclear annihilation. Need I go on?"

"No, I get the picture," Cloe responded wearily. "Things are as bad worldwide as they are in the United States."

They sat silently absorbing the enormity of the world's events as Cloe steered the car onto the highway toward the airport.

"Tell me about Albert. Have you seen him?"

"Yes, he's as well as can be expected. He was on one of his missions from the pope investigating certain ancient artifacts on Malta when the unrest began and the government swung to the fundamentalist side. What had been a rational democracy became a despotic one-man show. The monsignor was arrested and imprisoned," replied Father Anton. "I was able to see him a few days ago by special arrangements made by the pope."

"How do we get him out? Are there diplomatic avenues?"

The cleric paused and stared at one of the above-ground cemeteries in New Orleans. Many of the monuments to the dead were astounding pieces of art. Cloe worried that he might not have heard her question.

"Relations with the new government are strained, so negotiations have been difficult," replied the cleric. "Unfortunately, the government of Malta has, like many current governments, reverted to base concerns."

"What do you mean? Base concerns? Can we get Albert out or not?"

"Yes, but the price may not be acceptable," replied the priest.

"Unacceptable? No amount of money would be unacceptable to free Albert. The pope has the resources."

"Yes," said the cleric. "But …"

"No buts! Pay the money and get Albert back!" she exclaimed.

The priest paused for a moment.

"Cloe, it's not money they want," he finally said.

CHAPTER

12

"Shit!" said the thin, needle-nosed man to himself as he watched the giant approach him on the subway platform. It was like a hundred or maybe even a thousand other dirty subway stations in New York. It was just his damn bad luck that this one had a giant in it. Okay, he had lifted the lady's purse and had stolen her cash—but why would the gargantuan stranger have cared about that?

The man was now within spitting distance.

"Hey, I'll give it back!" shouted Louie. "What's it to you anyway?"

The big man kept coming. He was dressed like some kind of hayseed freak in overalls and a long-sleeved flannel shirt—and he was just plain damned ugly.

Louie fancied himself a pickpocket, but in truth he had no such skills and was merely a petty thief. *At least I'm not a drug dealer or user*, he thought to himself—none of that bottom-of-the-barrel crap. There were others lots worse. Being not as bad as the worst was something to be said. He was not sure his mom would be proud.

Louie considered running. He was very good at that. But the giant rube had him bottled up in a corner of the platform. If he ran in any direction, he would still be within reach of the man's long arms. Any way he looked at it, he was shit outta luck.

Louie took out the cash he had stolen from the old woman and pushed it in the man's general direction. With his other hand, he fingered the switchblade he had in his pants pocket. Louie favored guns, but the freakin' cops in New York were on a tear about guns. He had a gun, a sweet nine mil automatic. It was stashed at his place. With his sheet, if he were caught with it, he would be doing federal hard time. No excuses, no mea culpas.

Louie wasn't afraid, figuring it would be one thing or the other. But he wasn't gonna let anybody, giant or not, beat the crap out of him over some old bitch's stupid purse. If this dung heap farmer wanted a piece of him, he would get it—pointy end first.

The giant eyed the cash, and Louie could have sworn the man was going to break his arm off at the elbow. Instead, he reached into his denim overalls and searched for something. *Who the hell wears overalls in New York?* His meaty hand, the size of a catcher's mitt, produced a card.

The man studied the card for a moment as if to make sure he had the correct addressee and then reached out, dropping the card on top of the bills in Louie's outstretched palm. Louie withdrew his hand quickly, seizing the contents.

The giant did a one-eighty and headed back up the platform at a brisk pace. Louie stood stunned, watching him go. As the eight o'clock roared into the station, he glanced down at the card.

All it said was "3."

CHAPTER

13

"Jesus, Mary, and Joseph!" cried Doris, as she watched the truck and the entire pine stand burn, lighting up the night sky.

Zack nudged the Saab to the point of the road nearest the conflagration. Smoke drifted toward them, and he could feel the heat from the fire. He could see no movement in the engulfed cab of the truck.

"What do we do?" shrieked Mel. "He's dead! No one could have survived that."

"We do precisely nothing," Zack replied. "He's dead. Nothing can be done for him. No one but us knows about this."

"But we have to go to the cops and report this," said Mel. "It's our duty."

"What cops? There's only the military and martial law," said Zack.

The military were big-picture people. If there were battles to be fought, they were the ones to call. Crime, even serious crimes like murder, by their standards, was small ball. Soldiers were not designed or trained to be cops. Nobody would care about Skylark.

"What do we do now?" asked Mel.

"We're going to New Orleans," said Zack, putting the Saab in gear. "Do you still feel pulled in that direction?"

"Yes, I still feel it strongly," she said.

"Pull? What are you talking about?" asked Doris.

"Doris, you may not be part of all this," said Mel. "Have you recently been approached by a giant stranger who gave you an odd business card?"

42

In spite of the gruesome situation, Doris laughed as they resumed their trek to the interstate.

"Giant stranger? What?" she sputtered, giggling. "I saw a big clown in a polka-dot suit at the fair but no giants. What in the world are y'all talking about?"

Zack looked at Mel. What they had to say would sound crazy. Still, there was nothing to do but to fill her in on what had happened. Afterward, Doris sat back and stared at them.

"It's hard to say," she said after a while. "Nobody gave me a card, but I still feel a pull from New Orleans."

"That's new and interesting," said Zack.

"Doris, tell us something about yourself. Where are you from?" asked Mel.

"New Orleans, born and raised. Everyone I know lives there," she responded, smiling.

CHAPTER

14

"Tony, if it's not money they want to release Albert from prison, what *do* they want?" Cloe asked, flabbergasted at the direction the conversation had taken. Surely something could be done to get the monsignor back.

"It's something belonging to the Church, to the pope," said Father Anton. "It's symbolic and precious. It's an unforgivable demand."

"But what is it?" Cloe was losing patience as they drove onward. Because she had come prepared, they were able to head directly from the restaurant to the airport.

"I will tell you, but first, while you were getting the car, I relayed your message to the pope, and he has asked me to bring you immediately to Rome for a personal meeting so you can brief him on your findings."

"Well, that's progress," said Cloe.

"Yes, the pope trusts you and knows you would not have called without good reason," replied the cleric.

"I'm sure the pope will want to hear what I have," said Cloe. "But it's just me this time. J.E. isn't here. He's in the Middle East somewhere on a mission."

"Cloe," Father Anton paused, concern showing on his face, "J.E. isn't in the Middle East. As we speak, he has been attached to the pope's personal intelligence division by special request through the State Department. He's in Rome, at the Vatican."

"My God! J.E.'s in the middle of all that's happening," said Cloe, absorbing the priest's revelation.

"Yes, he is. Cloe, the pope believes he needs you in this fight, and your call has caused him to think he needs to hear from you now."

"Yes," she said, realizing that once again she and J.E. would be in harm's way. "Yes, I need to see the pope."

"Cloe, you are a trained ancient languages expert, fluent in ancient Greek, Phoenician, and Aramaic. You have firsthand knowledge of the contents of at least some of the ancient jars recovered from Tunisia. The pope believes some of what you have learned may be relevant in this new fight."

"A *new* fight? Is it new, or is it just the continuing battle?" Cloe was becoming agitated. She was only a few years away from nearly losing her life in battles with the Kolektor and then with his successor, the Karik. "It seems evil does not rest."

"You and the pope can discuss this. He is fully aware of world events. He believes there is more to all this than mere coincidence," Father Anton assured her.

"More than mere coincidence?" she queried. "Do you mean the pope already suspects there's some link between my research of the journal, the contents of the other jars, and current events?"

"This I cannot say, Cloe. What I do know is the pope is extremely interested in your journal research and, particularly, what the monsignor has reported as to the possible Jesus conversation with St. John that appears to be in the journal."

"Yes," she said. "I am more certain than ever of the connection."

"Do you realize that this dialogue is reported nowhere else in any literature?" asked the priest. "In all of time, no document, no oral tradition has contained this conversation. It is unique."

"Yes," repeated Cloe.

"Do you have any idea what this means?" asked Father Anton.

"Yes, I do," said Cloe. "It means I'm going to Rome."

CHAPTER
15

"Mom!" cried Robby as he crashed through the screen door of his Harrison Street home and ran toward the kitchen in the back of the house.

"Whoa! Slow down," his mother said as he entered the kitchen. "What's all this?" She smiled down at the gangly, curly-headed seven-year-old, now going on eight as he always reminded her.

"Mom, I was over in the park, and this big guy came over to me," said Robby.

Immediately, his mother's ears zeroed in. She really didn't like him wandering around City Park, but it was only a few blocks from the little elementary school where he attended second grade, and lots of children went there after school. She had constantly warned Robby about strangers.

"Did he approach you? What happened?" she asked, kneeling and wrapping his small hands in hers.

"Yes," said the boy. "He was huge. He must have been ten feet tall."

"Ten feet?" asked his mother, recognizing Robby's penchant to exaggerate.

"Yeah, at least ten feet," he confirmed. "Maybe more. He was dressed in overalls and looked like a farmer. He had big black boots on. His hair was as white as Santa's. *Mom!*" he exclaimed in sudden realization. "Could he have been Santa?"

"It seems a little early for Santa, don'cha think?" she responded, amused and concerned at once.

"Yeah," said Robby, clearly disappointed. "Still, it might have been an elf, 'cause he did bring me something. But he would've been a really big elf, like the guy in the movie."

Robby's mother laughed.

"Robby, you're something else," she said. "Well, what did Santa or his really large elf bring you?"

"Well, he brought me a dog," said Robby cautiously. "Mom, can I keep him?"

"A dog? Oh my God! What in the world?"

"I want a pet. *Please*, Mom," pleaded Robby.

"Right, and you will have one," said Robby's mother. "But you aren't quite old enough to take care of a pet."

"What am I going to do then?" asked Robby. "I don't know how to find the man and give it back."

"*Give it back?*" asked his mom, walking toward the door. "Show me, young man."

Robby knew he was in trouble when his mother used that kind of language. He hung his head and shuffled toward the front door after her.

"Come on, Mom. Bully's outside tied to my bike in the driveway," said Robby reluctantly.

"Bully?"

"Yes, ma'am," replied Robby. "That's his name."

When he and his mother walked down the front steps, Robby's bike wasn't in the driveway, and there was no dog.

"Where's your bike?" his mother asked.

"I left it right here in the driveway," he responded, looking left and right.

They turned and followed the driveway up to the carport, and there was the bike, at the end of a strong leather tether tied to a very large English bulldog. The dog, which looked to weigh upwards of ninety to one hundred pounds, was patiently sitting in the shade, having dragged the bike behind him onto the cool concrete.

"Oh my God!" his mother cried. "I've never seen one this big. Where did you get this dog?"

"I told you! From the giant," Robby said, kneeling and scratching the dog's chin. "He really likes it when I do this."

"But ... but," said his mother. "Robby, this dog is huge. He weighs more than you do. And it looks like he's a purebred. He must have cost someone a pretty penny."

"He's smart too," said Robby. "He knows stuff. Can I keep him?"

"No, Robby. The dog is valuable, and you are too young to manage him. We have to go and find the man who gave you the dog. It must be some mistake," said his mother.

Robby got down and scratched the dog's neck and massive shoulders, and the dog grunted in satisfaction, an angelic look of love passing over his otherwise pugnacious expression. Slowly, the massive body rolled over, and the dog lay flat on the hard carport surface. A long, canine fang protruded from each end of a line of short teeth. Just then, the dog yawned, and the mouth widened into a huge chasm that looked like it could gobble a basketball.

"Robby, what else did the man do? Did he say anything? We need to track him down so we can give him back his dog."

Robby looked stricken, but he stood and began to search his pockets. He eventually held out a small fist with something balled up inside it.

His mother accepted the sweaty, wadded-up piece of cardboard and smoothed it out. It appeared to be some sort of business card.

"Robby, the man at the park gave you this?" she asked.

"Yes, ma'am," he said contritely.

"Did he say anything?" she continued.

"No, ma'am. He just walked off."

Robby's mom looked at her son, the dog, and then back at the card and focused again on the simple inscription: "4."

CHAPTER
16

The papal jet headed east into the gathering dusk. Cloe was seated in the executive lounge in the plane's midsection, reflecting on her day thus far. Father Anton had delivered the message he was sent to deliver. Now she was on her way to Rome—but to what?

Cloe had packed a suitcase and brought her laptop, along with her research findings backed up on a flash drive. As she opened the laptop and inserted the flash drive, she watched as the priest consulted with their escort, the Swiss Guard. Cloe smiled at the Swiss. They had been with her in her fight against the Kolektor and then against the Karik. They were great soldiers, and she was glad to have them with her again.

She looked down at the dull glow of the computer screen. Even as she began to review her notes, she had the strangest premonition that she somehow had the answers to the current troubles in front of her. Discernment, as the priests liked to say, was what she needed.

"Cloe," said Father Anton, leaning over in his seat. "I have been on the phone with our Opts Center. The Vatican is being sacked and burned as we speak."

At that, his voice broke, and he could not continue. Cloe watched as unfathomable emotions rolled over the cleric. *The Vatican sacked. How is that possible? What could it mean?*

"Tony, what do you know?" asked Cloe.

The cleric sat up in his seat and struggled with his composure.

"The center of Catholic life and the Catholic Church is being overrun by a mob of thousands of crazed youths," said the priest. "They are destroying everything. The monks and other religious are saving what they can, but it is a disaster of terrible proportions."

"Oh, *no!*" said Cloe, leaning back.

"Tony, that can't be correct," she continued, thinking. "The Swiss Guard would never permit this, and the Italian government would defend the Vatican. It must be wrong."

"It's wrong all right but not for the reasons you are suggesting," the cleric said bitterly. "Most of the Swiss are with the pope at Gandolfo, and the Italian government is in such disarray that it cannot protect Rome, much less come to the rescue of the Vatican. It seems a number of its institutions are also under attack."

"Surely the Germans, the French, or even the American government will come and save the Vatican," Cloe reasoned.

"No one," said the priest. "This is the logical extension of secularism. From their perspective, the Vatican, as a country, must solve its own problems, and as to being a religious center, the nations are indifferent. Indeed, there are elements in every country that actually support the destruction of Christianity. I'm afraid we are largely on our own."

"Is there no one?" asked Cloe.

"Strangely, the only people or institutions who have raised their voices against the persecution of Christians in the past are some of the other religions: Buddhists, Hindus, and other Christians, Protestants. Also, some elements of Islam have protested," replied the priest. "What their reactions will be now I don't know, but none have the actual resources to make a difference."

Cloe considered this and said, "Still, it's important that there are people who will stand against evil. Everything cannot be lost as long as there is hope."

"You are courageous," responded the priest, scrutinizing her. "And what we will need before all this is over will be moral leadership and people of courage."

"Without a doubt," said Cloe, smiling. "My research leads me to believe that we have been given the answer to these persecutions and the other troubles. The problem is we don't yet quite understand what the answer is. This will take more time and more work."

"I'm not sure how much more time we have," replied Father Anton.

"I just feel if we can get these last few paragraphs properly translated, then we will know," she said.

"Then we must solve this mystery." The cleric turned toward her. "*You must solve the mystery.*"

CHAPTER

17

As the plane neared Italian airspace, Father Anton went forward to confer with the pilot. He returned and now sat across from Cloe at the small conference table. Cloe could see the flare of fire against the clouds and the plumes of smoke from below.

"We are about thirty minutes from the airport," said the priest.

"Where are we going to land with all this violence and confusion?" she asked.

"We are going to Ciampino Airport, which I'm sure you will remember from our last trip together to Rome," said Father Anton.

Father Anton, J.E., and the monsignor had stopped there for supplies on the way to try to rescue her from the Karik's hideout in the mountains on the Turkish-Armenian border. Tears came to her eyes as she thought of the young camerlengo, Father Sergio, who had been part of that mission. The pope had assigned "Serge" to them when he had given Cloe and friends the task of finding her father's, Thib's, cave of jars and keeping them out of the hands of the Karik. Serge was brutally executed by the Kolektor's only son, Michael. Michael, the man she might have loved.

Cloe shrank back into her seat as she processed thoughts from that terrible time. She thought about Michael, now dead these years, killed by a mine planted by J.E. in the battle at Masada. *Michael, how could you?* As from a far distance, she saw Tony's mouth moving.

"Cloe, Cloe? Are you all right?" pressed the priest, leaning forward over the table, reaching out to her.

"Tony, I'm fine. I was just thinking of Sergio and the last time I came to Rome."

"That was a difficult time," said the cleric after a short pause.

"I'm not sure 'difficult' covers it," she replied, sitting up. "J.E., Albert, and I were all almost killed by the Karik and Michael at Masada. All the remaining members of the Sicarii, a two-thousand-year-old alliance dedicated to the preservation of ancient Christian writings, were annihilated. Serge was a hero but ended up dead. God, I miss his face, his intelligence, and his wit. I wish he were with us."

"We all wish he were here," the cleric quietly responded.

"Oh dear! I'm sorry, Tony. I didn't mean anything by what I said," uttered Cloe. "It's just that—"

"I know, Cloe. I understand," said the priest.

There was silence between them for a few moments, and then Cloe heard the engines begin to wind down and felt the jet start its descent into the darkness surrounding Rome. As they swept through the low clouds, she looked out a window and was awestruck by what she saw. All she could think of was the image of hell portrayed in Dante's *Inferno*. The holy city was ablaze, and Rome itself was burning.

"No!" she cried.

At the low altitude, in the light of the fires, she could make out the hordes of scavengers burning, looting, destroying man's greatest treasures. The streets surrounding the Vatican were clogged with people. Either fires had spread beyond the walls of Vatican City or more had been set outside. Plumes of smoke and ash rose from the formerly pristine papal campus. Rome itself might be destroyed in the conflagration. The people in the streets seemed to be celebrating. As the jet flew lower, she could see mostly young people apparently singing and clearly drinking. But for the other circumstances, it could have been Mardi Gras in New Orleans.

"Where are the fire crews?" she asked. "There is no one trying to put out the fires. We can't lose the Vatican!"

"Look! There are some fire trucks down there, but it looks like the crews have been savagely attacked," said the priest. "I can make out the bodies of men in firefighting gear. Nobody else is coming."

"If these fires are not contained, it will be the end of Rome and certainly the end of the holy city."

"It would take the army to stop this, and the way these lunatics are behaving, they might very well fight the soldiers. Thousands would be killed, and the people behind this would have a huge PR event," replied the priest.

"People behind this? PR event? What are you talking about?" sputtered Cloe, her thoughts flashing to their discussion on Icar. "Are you saying this has all been organized, that there is someone who expects to profit from all this destruction?"

Tony's face closed—he had said too much.

"Tony, tell me what you know," demanded Cloe.

As the wheels touched down, he looked at her apologetically and said, "The pope will tell you what we know."

CHAPTER
18

"I think the question is whether there are others like us," said Zack as he piloted the Saab across the Louisiana state line and continued toward New Orleans. He stretched his back and looked at his watch; it was after midnight.

"Oh, I can think of a lot of other questions besides just that one," said Mel in response. "Why the hell are we going to New Orleans? Who was the big guy with the card? How did you know to pick me up hitching outside of Saint Louis? And these are just a few that roll quickly off the tip of my tongue."

"Well, I'm just here to get the hell out of that diner," Doris chimed in from the backseat.

Zack smiled at Mel and said, "Doris, I think with all that's happened, there might be a deeper reason you're with us. You're somehow here to help us. Mel and I don't know anything about New Orleans, but you grew up there and know everything. We're driven by something we can't identify, to go somewhere we know nothing about, to do something that has not yet been revealed to us. If anybody needed a guide, we do."

"Whoa!" cried Doris. "I'm the guide? In the movies, you know what that makes me when the going gets tough?"

"What?" asked Mel.

"Expendable! That's what!" spouted Doris. "I'm no guide, no sidekick, and I'm not going out in the dark looking for the fuse box."

Zack tried to keep his eyes on the interstate as he and Mel doubled over laughing.

"Yeah, I've already seen the movie. I know how that role always ends. I'm not dumb, you know. I go to college," said Doris. "I'm getting educated … I'm going to be somebody, someday."

"Well, this isn't a movie," laughed Mel, responding to the intensity in Doris's voice. She turned in her seat to face the girl. "You'll be fine. Zack's right. We need help. We need someone who knows New Orleans. That would be you."

"But what about all the other questions?" asked Doris. "What are y'all doing? Why are you going to New Orleans in the first place?"

"We've racked our brains to try to figure that out," said Zack.

"Do you think the big man might be waiting in New Orleans for you?" asked Doris.

"Maybe," said Mel, "but what could he say to us in New Orleans that he couldn't say in Guam or in Des Moines where he gave us our cards?"

"Good question," responded Doris.

"I think the big guy's mission may be over," said Zack. "His job was to give us the cards. Somehow, their purpose was to urge us to go to New Orleans. *Someone* wants us in New Orleans, so something will happen there."

"But what?" asked Doris.

"Maybe it gets back to what Zack asked about first. Are there others like us?" observed Mel. "If the giant gave out cards to others, New Orleans is as good as any place to gather."

"You mean New Orleans is random, just the place to meet?" asked Doris.

"It does seem like it would be more," said Zack. "But what?"

"How about this?" Doris piped up, trying to contain her excitement. "Ya'll are going to New Orleans to meet the giant, and when you're all together, you'll get some kind of secret mission."

"Doris, you may be closer than you know," replied Zack. "I think it's clear that if there are others, we will get with them in New Orleans."

"Yes, and we'll find out whatever it is we're supposed to do in the city," added Mel.

Zack glanced at the big green reflective sign as they sped past, noting its announcement of "Hammond, Louisiana" in about ten miles. All they could see from the road now were the fast-food restaurants clustered at the various interchanges.

"Anybody hungry?" asked Zack, his stomach grumbling from having lost the last meal at Smyth. "Maybe we can find a twenty-four-hour place along here somewhere."

* * *

As Zack piloted the Saab back onto the interstate headed south, Mel handed a Diet Coke and a BLT to Doris and then unwrapped Zack's burger so he could eat and drive. Soon he had all the essential foods groups arrayed before him: fries, a chocolate malt, and, of course, a bacon double cheeseburger.

As they ate, the car was quiet except for the wind rushing by. There were fewer and fewer cars on the road in the early morning hours. After the incident at Smyth, they had decided to drive straight through to New Orleans.

They had taken the interstate east to Mandeville and were now approaching the Lake Pontchartrain Causeway. It was a twenty-four-mile ribbon of concrete over open water, leading into the soft underbelly of New Orleans.

"Well, we're almost there," said Mel.

"And, we still don't know why," replied Zack.

"No, but I do know one thing," said Mel.

"What?" asked Doris.

"What we're doing is important ... maybe the most important thing in our lives."

CHAPTER
19

Several members of the Swiss Guard were waiting as the plane coasted to a stop at the general aviation terminal at Ciampino. They were dressed in battle fatigues rather than their ceremonial costumes. On high alert, they repeatedly scanned the perimeter. It was near midnight, but the light of the conflagration from Rome lit up the sky. Cloe stood and moved forward as the copilot opened the door of the plane.

"Not yet, Cloe," cautioned Father Anton.

Cloe watched as Father Anton exited and spoke with the soldier in charge of the detail, all the while scanning the area for signs of trouble. Apparently satisfied, he nodded, and the soldier gave a sign. Immediately, three Range Rovers rushed around the edge of the terminal and pulled up sharply next to the jet. There were four soldiers with machine pistols in the first and third vehicles. In the middle SUV, there was a driver and a soldier riding shotgun. However, this time the rider was armed to the teeth.

"Tony, is all this really necessary?" asked Cloe, assessing the tight security as Father Anton ran back to the plane and climbed the boarding steps two at a time.

"Cloe, I assure you it is. Once off the airport's fenced and secured grounds, we will be on our own," replied the priest.

The bags were transferred, and the soldiers formed a sort of human cordon from the jet to the middle vehicle.

"Let's go," said Father Anton, leading Cloe down the steps. They ran quickly to the waiting backseat of the middle SUV. The soldiers boarded their vehicles, and they were off.

"Should I hunker down on the floor?" Cloe smiled.

"No need," said the cleric, studying the surroundings. "The Range Rovers are armored and will stop any ordnance short of an antitank shell."

"Tony, I was only kidding."

The priest turned toward her with real worry on his face.

"Regrettably, I was not," he said.

* * *

Forty minutes later, seated in a small conference room in the pope's quarters, she and Father Anton awaited Pope Francis. It was very late, but they were told the pope had left orders that he be awakened when they arrived. His reign had begun well with a number of highly publicized trips, including one to Brazil where upwards of three million people attended a Mass over which he presided. Some Mardi Gras crowds in New Orleans topped a million souls, but three million all at one Mass boggled the mind.

In spite of the security and precautions—or maybe because of them—they had rushed through the streets from the airport to Castel Gandolfo and arrived without incident. During the trip, Father Anton had pointed out some of the visible features of the area. She learned Castel Gandolfo was a village of about eight thousand people located in the Alban Hills on the shore of Lake Albano, a few miles southeast of Rome. The area was ancient with archeological findings as early as 1600 BC. For many years, it had served as a retreat for the wealthy. The Apostolic Palace had been used as a summer home for various popes, with at least two popes dying there.

Tony said the palace itself was not designed as a fortress, so it could not be easily defended. The Swiss had blocked off its few access ways, the strategy being to prevent anyone from getting near the residence. Cloe and her group had been waved through by the night guard.

She walked to the window overlooking what she thought might be Lake Albano. Being pope now had to be very difficult, considering the worldwide attacks on the Church and on Christianity in general. Everywhere, the Church seemed to be under attack and in retreat.

Cloe could see only darkness as she gazed down the hillside.

Crack! The window before her shattered. The concussion against the window slammed her back onto the floor. The lights went out as she landed hard. Father Anton grabbed her and dragged her out of the line of fire.

"Tony, what happened?" she asked, dazed.

"A sniper, I think, but the glass is bulletproof, and while it partially fragmented, the bullet did not penetrate it," replied the priest. "You were silhouetted against the light inside. Were you cut by the glass splinters?"

"No, but the lights went out," said Cloe, brushing at the tiny glass fragments.

"No, you hit the floor hard," said Father Anton. "*You* went out briefly."

"Oh," she said, getting to her feet and shaking off the cobwebs. "I guess thank goodness for armored glass."

"That and the good Lord must have other plans for you." The cleric smiled.

Before she had time to absorb what had just happened, the door to the pope's inner chamber opened.

Cloe turned toward the sound and stood shocked a second time.

CHAPTER

20

Cloe's jaw dropped. Father Anton turned and rushed to Pope Francis. The pope smiled slightly and extended his ring hand. He was unaware that someone had taken a shot at her. Was it a shot at her? Or just a random shot? The priest bowed and kissed the Ring of the Fisherman. The ring, worn by popes for hundreds of years, was a symbol of their authority ordained by Christ himself, through his anointing of St. Peter as the "rock" on which the church would be built.

The pope glanced around the room and spied the damaged window. Understanding crept over his face.

"Is everyone all right?" he asked.

Straightening, Father Anton said, "Yes, Holiness. No one was hurt, and I have brought Dr. Lejeune."

The pope waved an apologetic hand and said, "This has become too frequent. We try to stay away from the windows, especially at night."

"I'm fine, Holiness. I've had much closer scrapes than that," said Cloe, a smile edging toward her lips.

As the pope turned to her, she was shocked at his appearance. She had thought he looked tired the last time they met a few years ago, at the meeting that had launched the quest for the cave of jars. Now he had aged terribly. There were great dark circles under his eyes, and he had lost weight. He walked stiffly toward her, smiling a bright smile that illuminated his features, the signs of stress instantly disappearing. Cloe was amazed. *There is much to this man*, she thought.

"Hello, Dr. Lejeune … Cloe if I may," said the pontiff.

"Certainly, Holiness," replied Cloe.

As the pope moved away from the doorway, another figure appeared. The young man had close-cropped hair, high and tight, as the military would say. He was taller, and Cloe was unsure how she had failed to see him initially. She looked upon her son, whose six-foot-one frame seemed to have filled out a bit.

"J.E.!" she cried and ran to hug him.

J.E. wrapped his mother in his arms and said, "Hi, Mom. Hey, you've got glass all over you."

"J.E., I'm so happy to see you," she said, brushing tears from her eyes. "Don't worry, I was standing near the window when it was hit by a stray shot. I'm fine. Father Anton told me you had been detailed to work with the pope's security forces."

"Cloe, we must talk," said Father Anton, interrupting.

"Yes, of course," replied Cloe, still smiling at her son.

"My child," said the pope. "Please sit."

They all maneuvered to a table away from the windows and sat; a nun entered and served coffee and cookies.

"Delicious," said Cloe after a bite of cookie.

"It's an eight-hundred-year-old recipe," said the pontiff, a smile crinkling his eyes. "You are unlikely to find a better cookie."

Cloe laughed and wondered at the civilization that could produce that statement, much less the cookie.

"How are you getting along after our last contact?" asked the pope.

"Well enough," responded Cloe. "I have moments where the loss of Father Sergio still overwhelms me. Even so, we kept the jars from the Karik and his evil forces. Indeed, he and his boss, Michael, the Kolektor's son, and their inner circle are all dead. The rest of the organization is scattered and without any apparent leader. They're done. And I have all the jars from the cave, thanks to the sisters of the Sicarii. It's a treasure trove of ancient documents and information that will far exceed the Dead Sea Scrolls."

"Thank God for his many favors in this final good result, and may he have mercy on the soul of our brother Sergio—Serge, as I believe he was known to you," said the pope.

"We could not have won without Serge," said J.E. "He provided key intel in Lyon at the hidden hall of the martyrs and later in Tunisia.

We were badly outnumbered at Masada after the Karik ambushed and murdered the Sicarii. Even gravely wounded, Sergio fought on until he was murdered."

"What courage!" exclaimed Cloe. "We all loved him."

A reverent silence enveloped the group. Cloe saw the pope appeared to be praying. She bowed her head and prayed too for her friend Serge.

"Cloe," said the pontiff after a few moments. "You must be aware of what is happening worldwide concerning the governmental disruptions and violence."

"Holy Father, this is exactly why I asked for Father Anton to fetch me to come here to see you," responded Cloe. "As I sat working on the journal translation and watching the news alerts pop up, it hit me. I believe there is a direct connection between the current trouble and the two-thousand-year-old journal."

"What have you learned?" asked the pope with surprising urgency. "You told Monsignor Roques you thought you had discovered new material about a dialogue between Christ and possibly St. John that might touch on the apocalypse."

"Yes, it seems this part of the journal may have anticipated the book of the Bible we know as Revelation or the Apocalypse of John," said Cloe. "The part I have deciphered describes numerous cataclysmic occurrences that seem to be signs of some kind. These include attacks on religious figures and on religion itself, along with large-scale illness, fighting, and lawlessness. As I read these things from the translation, I was hearing the same things from the news."

"This is critical information," proclaimed the pope. "There is no other contemporary writing from those times that even touches on this subject."

"It may be completely unique," said the low voice of a tall figure who had entered the room unobtrusively.

"Cloe, permit me," said the pope. "This is the Most Reverend Father Dimitri Anatolia. Father Dimitri is the chief historian—we call him the curator—of the Vatican library. He has spent his life studying rare books and scrolls collected by the Vatican over the last two millennia."

Cloe scrutinized the new entrant carefully. He was tall and gaunt, maybe six two or six three. He was clean-shaven but still showed the shadow of a heavy beard. At first, she thought he could have been a young version of Christopher Lee, the actor, but upon further scrutiny, she saw he was considerably older.

"Good day, Dr. Lejeune," said the man with the deep voice. "I look forward to sitting down with you. I'm very anxious to hear firsthand of the journal. It may confirm everything."

"What do you mean that it may confirm everything, Father?" she asked.

"Dr. Lejeune, I have been in charge of the ancient books and writings section of the Vatican library for nearly fifty years, since I was a young priest," responded the cleric. "I'm literate in ancient Greek, Aramaic, and Phoenician. I'm here because of events that occurred a thousand years ago and which have been a source of lifetime study for me."

"A thousand years ago?" mused Cloe. "That would be smack in the center of the Middle Ages or what some refer to as the Dark Ages."

"Yes, Cloe," said the pope. "Father Dimitri is our expert on such things."

"What things?" she asked. "How are events that occurred a thousand years ago relevant when we're talking about a journal written two thousand years ago?"

"We think they have much to do with what's happening today," replied Father Dimitri.

"Why?" asked Cloe, shivering even though the room temperature was warm.

After a moment of silence, the pope turned directly to her and said, "Because we think it's happening again."

"What does that mean? What's happening again? How can anything that may have happened a thousand years ago be relevant to what's going on now?"

"My child," the pope smiled, "we have much to say. How much do you know about the Dark Ages?"

"Not so much," responded Cloe. "Most of my work actually predates that era, so I haven't had much opportunity to study materials from that time. My basic impression is one of chaos."

"Mom, chaos is exactly right," said J.E. "I read a bit about this in my studies and have been in on some of these discussions, and you're right on."

Father Dimitri moved toward the table in long strides.

"Dr. Lejeune, there is much more to the Dark Ages than mere chaos," said the cleric, seating himself. "Evil itself awakened and arose."

"Oh come now, Father Dimitri," said Cloe, smiling. "I have learned to believe in evil, but it seems so dramatic to hear you say that, as if the devil suddenly woke up after a thousand-year nap."

The religious in the room looked stricken. Had she said something that had offended them? After a bit, the pope looked at Father Dimitri and then turned to her.

"Cloe, what you have just said is so shocking because it may be exactly what is happening. We think evil in a very real way is on the rise. As far as we can tell, this is the same thing that occurred in about the year 1000 and resulted in the Dark Ages. What we know about that period may help us defeat the forces of evil here."

"Are you seriously telling me that you believe that some evil force has arisen after centuries of repose to now threaten us?"

"Cloe, do you believe in the devil?" asked Father Dimitri.

She thought about the question. Did she? She certainly believed in good and evil. She had seen evil in the Kolektor and the Karik. Perhaps the worst evil of all had been in Michael, the Kolektor's son. Her face colored slightly, remembering the way he had fooled her.

"Do you mean Satan?" she asked, trying to focus on what she really believed.

"Yes, Satan, Lucifer, or, by any other name, the personification of evil," replied the priest.

"I'm not sure I've ever thought of the subject as such," she responded. "I remember that Lucifer was a prince of the angels who led a revolt against God. Eventually, as the story goes, he was defeated by Michael and the good angels. It seems pride was his downfall. He was cast out of heaven, apparently to the earth."

"Do you know that the story you have just related is not found, as such, in the Bible?" queried Father Dimitri. "Some say there are allusions to it in the book of Revelation or in other obscure references, such as in Isaiah."

"That's really interesting," said J.E. "The creation of the devil, Satan, evil—as important as that seems to be—is not told in the Bible. How can that be?"

"I did not quite say that, young man," said the curator. "I said the story of the supposed battle in heaven and the fall of the angels led by Lucifer is not related in the Bible. There are many references to Satan and to evil. For example, consider the temptation of our Lord in the desert. Satan is prominently featured."

"Yes," said the pope. "The problem is that since the Bible does not tell us of the origin of the devil, whether through the story of the fall or otherwise, we know little about him."

"With respect, Holy Father, don't we know all we need to know? He's the bad guy, the enemy of good," said J.E.

"J.E., think about it like this. On the battlefield or planning for a fight, how much does knowledge of the enemy mean?" asked Father Dimitri.

"When you put it like that, it could mean everything. If you know the foe's history and tendencies, it can mean the difference between winning and losing," replied the young military officer.

"According to the Bible, Satan was a presence from the very beginning," said the curator. "If you read the first book of the Bible, Genesis, the 'adversary' or the devil takes the form of a serpent to tempt Adam and Eve. The adversary is with us throughout the Old Testament into the New Testament; witness St. John's Gospel writings about Satan entering into Judas to betray Christ."

The nuns entered the room and refilled their coffee cups. Cloe added sugar and a good dose of cream.

"Just as Satan was with us from the beginning, he is with us today," said the pope. "We believe he is behind the worldwide rash of violence and destruction."

"But, Holiness, there are secular explanations for what's happening," said Cloe, wondering if she was going too far. "The world's youth are disaffected by unemployment and other grievances. They have simply lashed out in their immaturity. The rise of Satan seems very farfetched as a cause of all this."

"It has eternally been so; the denial of evil has always been its best refuge." Father Dimitri sighed.

Cloe felt as if she had been slapped. The rebuke was soft but very effective. Now she doubted herself. Here she was sitting with the pope, for goodness sake, and he was saying that evil was asserting itself. Who was she to argue?

Centering herself, she asked, "Holiness, why do you believe this is so and what do the Dark Ages have to do with all this?"

"Have you read the book of Revelation?" asked the pontiff.

"Certainly," she replied. "It has been helpful in my current work."

"Then you know what happened to the devil after the initial conflict with God and his son, Jesus?" asked the pope.

"Yes. He was chained up and cast into the abyss for a thousand years. In effect, mankind was free of his overt evil for those thousand years."

"You are correct," said Father Dimitri. "And how long ago was that?"

"Well, that battle seems to have been tied to the reign of certain Roman emperors in the first century, so it would have been about two thousand years ago," she replied.

"Mom, if Satan had been chained up for a thousand years, that would have put him free in about the year AD 1000, give or take, smack in the middle of the Dark Ages," J.E. added.

"Oh my God! If he had been defeated again at that time, and we do know the world emerged from the Dark Ages, the second thousand-year cycle would free him just about now. You believe the Bible has foretold the emergence of Satan now?" Cloe was incredulous.

After some silence, the pope looked directly at Cloe and said, "Yes, we believe he is among us again."

CHAPTER
21

It was early morning as the Saab sped across the twin causeways spanning the enormous lake. Zack looked out at the ink-black water on the west side of the long bridge and alternately to the east at the majestic moonrise.

"My goodness, have you ever seen anything like this?" he asked wistfully.

"It's gorgeous," said Mel. "But on Guam, we get some pretty good full moons and sunsets, for that matter."

Through the windshield, they could see the rising lights of the Crescent City in the distance. The most obvious was the Superdome, with its huge lighted and multicolored rim. But the skyscrapers with the multiple Mississippi River bridges in the background were also amazing.

"Why do they call it the Crescent City?" asked Mel.

"Because it lies between the lake and the river in such way it looks like a sliver of the moon, a crescent," said Doris. "It's very romantic."

"Okay, we're here now. What do we do?" queried Zack.

"I think we need to go to my parents' house," said Doris. "They'll be glad to see me, and you'll be welcome. What else could we do?"

"I guess we could get a hotel room," Zack said.

"I can't see why we'd do that when we can stay at my house for free," said Doris.

"But what will we tell them?" asked Mel. "Won't they be curious?"

"Yeah, they'll wonder why I'm not in school. I say we flat out tell them the truth," replied Doris.

"You mean we tell them we're here because a giant gave us a shiny business card, and we have been inexplicitly drawn to New Orleans for God only knows what purpose?" asked Zack.

"My parents are good Catholics, and they know these are weird times. Maybe they can help," said Doris.

"Catholics? What does that have to do with anything? Why did you say that, Doris?" asked Mel, a little sharply.

"I don't really know," said Doris. "It just sorta came out. I mean this is all religious, isn't it?"

Zack's family was Catholic, and he guessed he had been baptized Catholic at some point, but he hadn't been in a church in years. If this had something to do with religion, why would anybody pick him? Mel said they had been chosen—but by whom and for what? He was not sure it was religious.

"Mel ... are you religious?" he asked.

"There was a time when I was, but not now," she replied.

By the tone of her voice, there was a story there, but she was not ready to tell it.

"Do you think this has to do with religion?" asked Zack. "You said we were chosen. Did you mean in that sense?"

"No. I'm not sure what I meant. I was thinking we had a job to do. I felt we had been chosen to do something," she replied. "But like chosen by God? How could that be?"

"How could that be?" echoed Doris.

Chosen by God? Zack could not get his mind around that at all. There had to be some other explanation.

"Look, this has nothing to do with God or with religion," he said at last. "Mel and I had a funny experience, and it frightened us both to the extent we've acted a little irrationally. We think we're both drawn to New Orleans, but we're really just running away from something that scared us. We've been feeding off each other. We're going to wake up in a day or so and laugh at all this."

"Whoa! You sure had me fooled," said Doris. "Thanks for clearing that up. I wonder if the guy in the burning pickup in the tree stand back in Mississippi would see the humor in the situation."

Zack laughed in spite of himself. Maybe he would have to think more about the religious thing.

"Doris, where're we going?"

* * *

Thirty minutes later, they parked in front of a hulking two-story wood-frame construction that, in the darkness, looked to have been built up about a half story off the ground. Wrapped in a large and deep front porch, it sat on a tree-lined avenue located in an area on the northern edge of the French Quarter.

Although it was early morning, they had been welcomed, and, after many hugs for Doris and a few overflow hugs for Zack and Mel, Doris's mother insisted on a slice of cake and a glass of milk for each of them. They also learned, although it had not occurred to them before to ask, that Doris's last name was Leneau. The Leneaus were very nice people, and being around them made Zack wish for his own family.

After the cake, Mrs. Leneau and the girls went upstairs to prepare the bedrooms. Mr. Leneau led Zack into the candlelit living room where he handed him a cold beer. They settled down in deep, overstuffed chairs.

"Zack, are you kids in trouble of some kind?" he asked directly.

Zack considered the question for a moment because it had never occurred to him they might be in trouble.

"Mr. Leneau, I don't think we're in any more trouble than anybody else in this day and time," he replied.

"Well said, young man," stated Mr. Leneau. "However, that was more of a philosophical answer than a factual one. Let's start over. Why is a young man from Iowa sitting in my living room in the middle of the night and a young lady from Guam upstairs helping my daughter, who should be in school in Mississippi, make up beds?"

"Doris said you would see right through us and we should give you the straight story," said Zack.

"I think that would be a very good idea," replied the older man.

As he filled Doris's father in on what they knew and thought, Mr. Leneau tightly packed his pipe with an aromatic tobacco. Listening intently, he carefully lit the pipe and puffed gently. He let Zack get all the way through the story without interruption.

"And that's how I've come to be sitting here," finished Zack, his clear blue eyes focused on Mr. Leneau. Would the older man believe him?

The room was quiet as Mr. Leneau puffed on his pipe. His dark eyes bored into Zack as if trying to plumb the truth. The light rose and fell as the candles flickered.

"Zack, have you heard that the president has issued an executive order declaring all elections invalid until the martial law crisis is over?"

"Does that mean he's president until it's all over?"

"Yes, whatever 'it' is, is exactly right. Oh, there will certainly be a court challenge, but that takes time," replied Mr. Leneau. "The question is whether the army will back him up. Already, the vice president has resigned in protest, and the former speaker of the house has been appointed by the president as vice president. This is all completely extra-constitutional."

"I can't say for sure, but maybe this is part of the reason I'm sitting here in your living room," said Zack.

"Well, son, this is a pretty hard story to swallow, but even two years ago, if you would have told me we would be where we are today, I wouldn't have believed that either. What do you need?"

"The most important thing we need is to find out if there are others like us," Zack replied. "How can we do that?"

"The easiest way to reach a lot of people quickly would be to put an ad in the newspaper—probably the online version," replied the older man.

"Right. Doris said you worked for one of the local papers—an editor of some type? Could you help us there?"

"No need to," said Mr. Leneau, picking up his iPad from the table next to his chair.

"But I thought you said the easiest way to find out if there were others like us was to post an ad," said Zack.

Mr. Leneau did not respond. Instead, he typed something into his iPad and handed him the device.

Zack studied the personal ads section of the local paper and looked down at a black rimmed advertisement.

It simply said: "Carded and Compelled N.O.," 504.225.8787.

CHAPTER

22

"The devil among us? Now?" asked Cloe. The conference room was becoming stuffy. "This is the twenty-first century. How can we believe such a thing?"

"Good and evil are not time-driven principles," replied Francis. "We cannot even be sure that evil is personified. We have named evil Satan, Lucifer, the devil, and many other names, but we can't be sure there is really a person who embodies evil. It may simply be within us."

"Within us?" asked J.E. "What can that mean?"

"Young man," replied the curator. "As you know, God created us with free will. This means we have the ability to choose."

"Sure, we can choose, but why does that mean evil might be within us?" continued J.E.

"Because, if we can choose good or evil, then we are capable of each. If there is no evil, there is really no choice and no free will. The paradox is that while we are created in the image and likeness of God, who is inherently good, we are empowered by free will to choose evil," said the cleric.

"We must nurture the good within us, or evil will surge to the forefront," said the pope. "If not, we can be overwhelmed by our base instincts and be corrupted."

"Holiness, it seems so hopeless when you put it like that," said Cloe.

"Not at all, my child," replied the pontiff. "God gives us everything we need to overcome evil, but we must believe and work at it."

"Holy Father, if evil may not be personified but merely the bad side of our nature, how can we say God is a person? Perhaps he is simply the good side of our nature," said Cloe. "Maybe it's all just us."

"Very perceptive, Cloe," replied the pope. "But God was here from the beginning, long before man or our free will. Our understanding of God is that he is the source, the uncaused cause. All things came from him. He created us and our free will. Thus, he is exterior to us in that sense, although we believe he is within us as well."

"I think I see," responded Cloe.

"What do we do about all this?" asked J.E. "There's gotta be something we can do. You said God gives us all the tools we need to defeat evil."

The pope smiled at the man of action and said, "You are correct, J.E. There are things that can be done. Right now I need for you and your mother to go to Malta, where Monsignor Roques is imprisoned, as my extraordinary emissaries."

"To do what, Holiness?" asked Cloe, adjusting her shoulders.

"You are to meet with the potentate of Malta, as he calls himself," said the pope. "This man is overcome with his power and is very dangerous, but he has something we desperately need. So we must deal with him."

"The monsignor," Cloe asserted.

"Yes," said Father Dimitri. "We need Albert with us. He has a secular understanding of the forces we are confronting. You must free him."

"What has been agreed?" asked Cloe.

"Malta has Albert and has demanded a ransom that we are loath to pay but we must," said the pope, with resignation. "You will, of course, have a detachment of the Swiss to protect you, but this trip will be very hazardous, in part because of the nature of the people we are dealing with. Malta is on the verge of chaos. While there is martial law, the civil authorities are on the cusp of losing control."

"You will fly into Malta on a papal jet with full diplomatic credentials and protection," said Father Dimitri. "Your Swiss bodyguard will be heavily armed, but we are still relying to a substantial extent on the protection of the Maltese authorities. This is customarily for diplomatic missions. We just don't know how far we can depend upon them."

"Okay, we go to Malta, and we are to seek the release of the monsignor," said Cloe. "Has this been agreed by the Maltese potentate?"

"Yes," said the pope. "The only condition is my representative must personally deliver the ransom. You are my representative."

"But Holiness, surely there are diplomats far abler than I to do this," said Cloe.

"There are Vatican diplomats, but I don't think any are more able than you," said the pontiff. "Your mettle has been tested in the battles with the Kolektor and the Karik. Plus, the monsignor knows you and will trust you implicitly."

Cloe looked around at the faces of determined men. There was no trace of doubt, and their jaws were set. She had no reservation that her mission was right. How could she? The monsignor needed her. She was prepared to do what was necessary.

"Holiness, we are at your service," said Cloe finally. "When do we start?"

"Unfortunately, time is not on our side," said the curator. "We must depart very soon."

"What do you mean 'we'?" asked Cloe, turning to the curator.

"Cloe, Father Dimitri will accompany you," said the pope.

Cloe looked at the pontiff and thought about Father Sergio and his involvement in the previous mission. Sergio's assignment had been a test of his worthiness to be counted among the pope's innermost circle, and before his death, he had passed with flying colors. She was not sure she could bear another such loss.

As if he had plucked the thought from her mind, the pontiff said, "Cloe, Father Dimitri has nothing to prove to anyone. He will be a resource to you and your team. He speaks a number of the dialects that are common in Malta. He has studied the ways of the people. We have certain friends there whom Father Dimitri will be able to access should they be needed."

"All good, Holiness," Cloe replied after a moment's consideration. "Where do we go from here?"

"We will provide a place for you to rest for a few hours and to clean up and put on fresh clothes appropriate to Malta," said Father Dimitri. "Then you will take the ransom and be on your way. You will exchange the ransom for Monsignor Roques, and you will return here."

"Fine. What is the ransom?" asked Cloe, wondering what the Maltese would think the monsignor's life was worth. "Father Anton said it was not money. Is it gold or precious jewels?"

"It is neither."

"What is it, then?" pressed Cloe. "What is the ransom?"

"What they have demanded for the safe return of the monsignor is outrageous," replied the pope. "Still, it must be done."

"What *is* it?" cried Cloe.

"It's the ring, the Ring of the Fisherman," replied the pope.

CHAPTER
23

For the second time in the last twenty-four hours, Cloe was aboard a Vatican jet at the bidding of Pope Francis. She had caught a couple hours of sleep and then had showered and freshened up after the conference. She had donned one of the two spare outfits she had packed—her nicest black slacks and jacket along with suitable shoes. If she was going to be the pope's emissary, she would look the part. Though she felt refreshed physically, she put her head back realizing how tired she still was. With her were J.E., the curator, and a detachment of the Swiss Guard. The group included some of the best-trained soldiers in urban warfare in the world. They were the Vatican equivalent of top US forces such as the navy's Seal teams and the army's Delta Force. Indeed, the Swiss had successfully been through some of the most rigorous US training programs. She was glad they were with them.

They had been with her in the fight with the Kolektor and against the Karik. Her battle with the Kolektor had begun when her uncle Sonny called her in Seattle to tell her that her father was dead. She had not spoken to her father, Thibodeaux Lejeune, in twenty-five years—ever since that terrible fight when she had left home, pregnant and alone. She had been dating Evan … Evan. They had looked at a ring and had talked about marriage, but Evan was killed in an accident, and she had to confess her condition to her parents. Thib was furious, and her mother was too sick to help. Words were said that could not be undone.

Cloe left Madisonville that night and fought to raise her son, J. E., and to make something of herself. Over the quarter century, she had become educated and skilled in ancient languages.

On the phone, Uncle Sonny had said only that Thib had died and that she had to come back to bury him. She and J.E., now an intelligence officer and army ranger, had flown back to Madisonville. Uncle Sonny picked them up at the airport and on the way home told her Thib was murdered in an apparent robbery attempt. After Thib's funeral, she learned he had left her the old oil jar and a letter explaining how he came to possess it. It turned out the contents of the oil jar were earthshaking, and the Kolektor, a man evil by any measure, wanted it and would do anything to get it.

It hadn't ended in the Kolektor's favor. He was crucified at Hakeldama by a secret society, the Sicarii, who guarded the jars, and his criminal enterprise was destroyed. The Sicarii had saved her life and given her a second jar containing what she believed was the journal documenting Christ's public ministry.

One of the Kolektor's trusted lieutenants, known as the Karik, had survived and had taken up where the Kolektor left off. It had been a race to the cave of jars, but in the end there were no jars. Once again, the Sicarii intervened and moved them to a secret hiding place. The new piece on the board had been Michael, the Kolektor's son—more ruthless than his father. Cloe felt hot with shame as she thought of Michael's pretense in caring for her.

It had all ended at Masada, the mountain fortress, where the Karik, Michael, and all his people died. Before that, he and Michael had destroyed all the Sicarii, all but one. In the end, Cloe had all the jars and was the only remaining Sicarius—and she had lost Father Sergio. That was over three years ago.

"Mom." J.E. nudged her. "We're approaching Malta."

Cloe shook herself free of the past and looked down at the small island, or at least the main island in the archipelago. She could see smoke rising from some of the cities.

"There's supposed to be a Malta military escort for us at the airport," said J.E. "They'll take us into Valletta, two miles away, if they show up."

The airplane circled, and from the starboard side, the capital city came into close relief. Cloe's first impression was of a large fortress, as Valletta was encircled by several walls.

"Malta has been a place of strategic importance in the Mediterranean for a long time," said the curator. "Valletta has been the center of many battles and has been fortified by a host of factions over the years. These range from the Phoenicians to the British."

"The monks in the Opts Center tell us that the potentate has moved his headquarters to Fort St. Elmo, which is deep within the walls of Valletta. The government offices are actually outside the walls on the way into the old city. Essentially, from the land, Valletta can be defended by a relatively small force due to the fact that all means of ingress narrow to enter the city gates."

"Sort of a defile," said J.E., "an enclosure or structure designed to let only a few people pass at a time. We encountered structures like this at both Masada and at the Church of St. John in France."

The airplane continued to circle, and Cloe heard the wheels clunk down. They were on final approach.

"Yes," replied the old priest. "So you have had experience with defiles. I'm surprised that such an ancient concept is known to modern soldiers."

"Well, we studied the structure in military history, but we saw one firsthand under the old church of St. John at Lyon, France," replied J.E. "It was pretty amazing. Also, the snake path from the floor of the valley to the top up Masada allowed only a single file of climbers to approach."

"Then you know the prevailing idea behind most ancient cities and fortresses," said the priest. "The structure winnows down the path into the city or fortress so that only one or two people can enter abreast. If they are an enemy, archers or swordsmen can make short work of them. Due to the restricted access, the defenders cannot be overwhelmed."

"Okay, I can see why the potentate has moved his office within the walls," said Cloe. "He's safe from his own people and anyone else. All he needs is a relatively few loyal soldiers."

"That's where we have to go, into the lion's den," said J.E. as the plane touched down at the old RAF airfield. "Once we get inside, we'll be bottled up like rats in a maze. Getting out may not be as easy."

CHAPTER

24

On her way to bed, Robby's mom padded down the hallway and paused at her son's bedroom door, opened it a crack, and peeked in on him.

"*Grrrrr,*" came a low, menacing growl from somewhere in the dimly lit room.

She swallowed hard and pushed the door open a bit more. A low light from the wall-mounted nightlight cast a pale glow. The bulldog was standing straight up on the bed, looking eye to eye with her.

"*Grrrrr,*" rumbled the dog again.

"Whoa, boy. It's me," she whispered.

The dog blinked, sniffed, and seemed to recognize her. He calmed down and lay down on the bed between Robby and the door.

She cautiously entered the room and walked to the bed. Robby was fast asleep in the way only children who felt completely safe could sleep. She patted him on the head and kissed his forehead. He only sighed and continued to sleep.

The bulldog stared at her, eyes glistening in the dark. Bully had massive front shoulders and a huge head. The dog reminded her of a medium-sized bear. There was something wild in his eyes.

The bed was designed to look like a tree house and required a small, two-step stool to reach it. The bulldog weighed at least a hundred pounds, and he was hardly agile. Yet, there he was on a bed that a cat would struggle to reach. He weighed more than Robby, so her son could not have lifted him onto the bed without a small winch.

How in the world did you get up here, Bully? There had to be some rational explanation, she speculated. She recalled Robby's story about the giant from the park who had given him the dog and became further puzzled.

As if the dog had read her thoughts, he seemed to smile slightly. The narrow mouth widened somewhat to hint at a chasm of canine teeth. He rolled slightly to one side, and she had the irresistible impulse to scratch Bully's stomach. As she did, the smile on the dog's lips widened. The dog chuffed with pleasure, but his eyes never left her.

After a few minutes, she headed for her bedroom certain of two things: Bully was here to stay, and they were going to be great friends.

CHAPTER
25

It was midafternoon by the time they arrived at the potentate's official chambers at Fort St. Elmo. The fort itself was an ancient, drab structure that had been retrofitted as offices, meeting rooms, and the potentate's personal spaces. As she waited for the so-called potentate to appear for their audience, Cloe reflected on their trip from the airport. The military escort did indeed show up, if a ragtag group of undisciplined fighters could be dignified with the title "escort." None of them had a full uniform, only individual pieces such as military trousers or blouses—some had merely hats or scarves. However, all were armed to the teeth. Cloe, J.E., and the curator, after being stripped of their weapons, rode in military transports along with the two of the Swiss who were permitted to join them. They encountered no resistance coming from the airport, although they drove through widespread chaos. Stores had been looted, cars burned in the streets, and people milled around, angry and crying out.

After a thirty-minute wait, more formally dressed soldiers drew back the massive doors to the inner chambers, and Cloe and her group were led forth to meet the potentate. A senior aid warned them of the expected courtesies. They were told never to show their backs to the potentate and to speak only when spoken to. He instructed them on the proper method of bowing. Cloe bristled, but she knew she was here on a diplomatic mission and certain niceties had to be observed. The curator absorbed these things silently but with a degree of interest.

They entered what might once have been a large storage area but was now converted into some sort of throne room. It was a huge, open area bisected by a wide, red carpet that led to a dais. On the dais sat an oversized and gilded chair. There was an array of various flags and symbols of office on lacquered poles. A thin film of dust hung in the air. If things were not so serious, Cloe would have laughed at the self-important absurdity of it all.

The senior aid announced the entry of the potentate along with his many titles. The potentate, a slight, short man, swept into the room from a side entrance, along with a dozen attendants and advisers. It was hard for Cloe to measure exactly his height as his knee-high military boots had formidable heels. They gleamed brightly against his flat black riding breeches. This magnificence was finished off by a frock-style coat, militarized by the addition of epaulets and a liberal sprinkling of ribbons and medals. The potentate looked like a Dickens character. He was of indeterminate age—somewhere between forty and sixty.

The potentate strode directly to the dais, mounted it, and stood in front of the throne, facing his subjects. After a moment's pause, he climbed onto the chair and settled in, with his feet hanging about ten inches above the floor.

"Highness, I have the honor of presenting to you the Vatican delegation," cried the senior aide, giving their proper names and titles and handing over their diplomatic credentials.

The potentate studied them and glanced at the paperwork before handing it to one of the advisers.

"*Why* ... have you come to me?" asked the ruler.

His words and tone caught Cloe off-guard, and she glanced at J.E. and the curator in confusion. They were just as surprised.

"Highness, we have come on behalf of Pope Francis to secure the release of Monsignor Albert Roques, whom we have reason to believe has been imprisoned here on Malta," said Cloe in a neutral voice. She could see the curator wince slightly and worried she had been undiplomatic.

"*Imprisoned? Here?* On Malta? *Impossible* ... or I would know of it!" replied the potentate in his strange and distracting way.

"Are you saying the monsignor is not here under your control?" queried Cloe.

At that, the man on the throne jumped down to the dais, rose to his full height, and said, "*Do* ... you dare question the potentate? *Next* ... will you accuse me of holding him for ransom or some such other international crime?" Each emphasized first word was accompanied by some hand gesture, often an index finger pointed upward near his nose as if he were summoning the word at the point of a spear. He seemed to pause for effect after the demonstration.

The curator stepped forward and bowed deeply saying, "Highness, we do not question you at all. We certainly imply no illegality. We seek only your assistance and wise counsel in our inquiries about our friend. Perhaps he is here in some other capacity."

The potentate turned to his group of advisers and nodded. One of them approached and whispered in his ear. A brief but inaudible conversation ensued between them.

Finally, the potentate turned back to the Vatican emissaries and said, "*My* ... adviser tells me the man you seek is here on Malta as our guest. *While* ... he is quite busy with his studies of ancient Maltese relics, a visit might be arranged."

"Highness, Monsignor Roques is needed for other duties and is being recalled to the Vatican by Pope Francis," replied the curator. "We trust he is free to leave with us since he is only a guest here."

"*Out* ... of the question," said the potentate. "*The* ... man's research is valuable to Malta. *He* ... must stay and finish his work."

Cloe picked up on the curator's softball strategy and said, "Highness, we understand the situation. Perhaps the monsignor could be permitted a brief visit to the pope so the pope can consult with him on matters of great importance to the Vatican."

"*We* ... are aware of events on the world stage, and, indeed, we know the Vatican itself has been sacked by the mob," said the potentate. "*If* ... this monsignor left here, what guarantee would we have that he would return to finish his work?"

"We have brought with us an object of great value, which we will leave as security for the monsignor's prompt return," replied the curator.

"*An* ... object of great value?" asked the potentate, pointing and smirking. "*What* ... would that be?"

The curator withdrew the object from one of the interior pockets in his cassock. It was contained in a small, highly lacquered wooden box.

"May I approach, Highness?" asked the curator.

Cloe glanced at J.E. and saw the slightest smirk on his face at this farce.

"*Certainly* … not," gushed the potentate and nodded to his adviser. The adviser stepped off the dais and accepted the box from the hand of the curator.

Cloe's heart went cold when he grabbed the box and turned to present it to the potentate. Now there was nothing to do but to trust this strange man.

The potentate took the box and slowly opened it. As he gazed on the Ring of the Fisherman, his eyes grew wide with surprise, pleasure, and finally avarice. He took it out of the box and slipped it on his ring finger. It was much too big for his small hands, so he tried other fingers, settling on the index finger of his right hand.

He gazed at the ring in wonder, captivated. Without looking at them, he actually said, "*Thank* … you."

The curator cleared his throat, and when the potentate finally focused on him he said, "Sire, may we take our friend and go? Will this serve as adequate security?"

"*Security* … security?" said the potentate. "*Oh* … yes! *Security* … yes certainly. *However* … there is just one problem."

"Problem?" responded Cloe.

"*The* … man you seek is not here," said the potentate, still admiring his hand with the symbol of papal authority now firmly on it.

CHAPTER
26

As it turned out, there were five others—including him and Mel, seven in all. It had taken many phone calls and most of the morning to link up, but Zack was persistent. He was unable to speak to one of those involved but had received a text. They arranged to meet just before noon at City Park at the Morning Call coffee shop. Doris fussed at him that calling Morning Call a coffee shop was like calling a Rolls-Royce a car. It was actually a 142-year-old institution serving its specialty café au lait and beignets 24/7. Still, from a safety point of view, it was the perfect place for a meeting—public and pretty crowded.

When Zack and Mel arrived, they entered the busy restaurant and looked around. Zack wasn't sure what he was looking for. The Australian woman he had spoken to, Zoe, said she would have a sign. They wandered through the café and came to a large table in the breezeway where a woman sat alone. The table was in a corner and overlooked a small lake stocked with geese.

The woman appeared to be forty-ish, plus or minus. She had short, cropped brown hair, bright blue eyes, and an open face—one that you might trust right away.

As they stepped closer, the woman pulled her hands slightly apart, and there on the table was the ubiquitous card. After exposing the card, she quickly covered it up again with her hands.

Zack stepped forward. "Zoe?"

The woman stood and came around the table with her right hand outstretched. "Zack?"

"Yes, and this is Mel," he replied, eschewing the handshake and hugging the Aussie like a long-lost friend. "We are so happy to see you."

They moved back to the table, but no sooner had they sat down than an older woman approached.

"Good day," she said. "I'm Anna. I saw die card. I spoke to you on die phone."

"Yes, Anna, you posted the ad," replied Zack, standing. "Please join us."

"I see die angel visited each of you," said Anna.

"Angel?" Mel queried.

"Yes, das is die way I think of him," said the woman who was probably in her sixties with gray, almost white hair. "When he came to me, he must have been close to seven feet tall, with a horribly scarred face. He vas dressed like a peasant with dungarees and a flannel shirt. He vas very fierce looking and scary but ever so gentle in giving me die card."

"Did he speak to you?" asked Mel.

"Niche a word," said Anna. Zack thought her accent might be Russian, German, or Eastern European.

"Nor did he say anything to me," added Zoe. "He looked at me like he was giving me the bloody crown jewels instead of some strange card."

They were interrupted when two men approached from different directions.

"Hello, my name is Rey," said the one with dark hair and olive skin, holding up a card for all to see.

The other man was silent, almost surly; he simply approached and plopped down at the end of the table.

Zack stood again and said, "Welcome, Rey."

He then looked at the silent newcomer, a smallish man with a large nose and rodent-like features.

"I don't know why I'm here, but my name is Louie and I'm from the Big Apple," the man said.

"Apple? Apple? Vas is dis Apple?" asked Anna.

Zack laughed. "The Big Apple is none other than New York City. Welcome, Louie. We're glad you're here."

Zack looked around at the strange group. Each of the six had his or her card on the table or balled up in a hand. They were numbered consecutively one through six. He had only been in touch directly with these four, but he thought there might be one more, the one who had sent the text. If he was correct that would be number seven.

Rey cleared his throat and said, "Why *are* we here? What is this all about?"

"Maybe we ought to start at the beginning and introduce ourselves," said Mel. "There might be a clue we can learn from something in our backgrounds."

There was general agreement on this, and Mel began outlining where she and Zack had met as well as their adventures in getting to New Orleans.

"So Zack is an IT specialist from Des Moines, Iowa, and I'm an EMS tech from Guam," she finished. "We have absolutely nothing in common except a distant relationship with New Orleans and not much, if any, living family."

Zack looked at the other four and said, "Who wants to go next?"

There was an awkward silence, and then Anna said, "I'm from a little town in what used to be East Germany. I sew, making wedding dresses and other custom garments. I have almost no family because of die purges after the war when the Communists took over. My only brother is a priest in Italy at the Vatican. He cares for St. Peter's. Otherwise, I am alone."

She paused, and Zack was unsure whether she could continue. The old woman recovered, however, and said, "Well, das is ancient history. Der giant came to my tiny shop. He cast a mighty shadow over the doorway, and I thought I vould be robbed by one of die thugs in die town. His hair was white, and his face was horribly scarred, but his manner was very gentle. He reached into his pocket and drew die card. Either die card or his mission was precious, holy, to him. He bowed and put die simple card in my hands. I glanced at it, and when I looked up, he vas gone."

"Yes. That's similar to what we experienced," said Mel.

"And then, it vas the strangest thing. Although I knew little of it, I felt I needed, *needed* to come to New Orleans," said Anna.

"We definitely experienced the same need to get to the city," mused Mel. "We believe we are here for some reason."

"But what?" cried the wry, little man who had introduced himself as Louie. "I don't know any of you people and don't want to. Listening to your stories, it's perfectly clear you are all nuts."

"But here you are a cardholder, one of us," replied Zack. "Tell us your story."

It turned out Louie had a mother in New York, but his only other relative was a sister in London and her children.

And so it went around the table. In each case the giant had approached and had deposited the a card with them. Thereafter, each of them was compelled to make their way to New Orleans. *Why?* Zack had no answers.

"*Rooof, rooof,*" came the deep-throated bark of a dog. Zack turned to the entry of the breezeway and saw an enormous English bulldog on a leash, towing a boy of about seven or eight. The dog dragged his owner along like a team of Clydesdales might tow a beer wagon.

"Whoa, Bully!" shouted the diminutive master.

Bully finally stopped and sat on his haunches near the edge of the table. His massive head hovered above the tabletop. The young boy walked up, hugged the dog, and then looked fearlessly at the people huddled around the table.

"Hi, my name is Robby," he said.

CHAPTER
27

Zack and his companions looked at the young boy in amazement. They were wondering at the strange situation that could involve a youngster like Robby. The small boy was a surprising addition to the group of adults: an older German woman probably in her late sixties, a petty thief from New York, a man from the Philippines, an Aussie named Zoe, himself, and Mel. As Zack mused on the scene before him, he heard the dog growl; Bully was looking directly at him.

He stared back at the mammoth creature. The dog was sitting with his back to the table, between Robby and the entrance, clearly on guard. Bully reminded Zack of a small, very muscular man—a canine weightlifter. He had no tail at all, and his body was covered with a stubbly, light brown fur. His shoulders were large and strong. His massive head was bigger than a soccer ball. Bully's eyes were a deep brown. Zack had the distinct impression of keen intelligence. Bully had a strange way of looking behind him, not turning his head at all but rather extending his head and what neck he had straight up, so that you were looking at his face upside down.

Zack laughed and said, "Nice to meet you, Robby—and you too, Bully." He could have sworn the dog smiled slightly before he went back to watching the entrance, occasionally raising his head to look back in his odd, contorted manner at the table and its occupants.

Mel stood up and walked to Robby.

"Robby, where are your parents? Are you here by yourself?"

"We live a few blocks from the park, and I come here all the time to play," said Robby. "Besides, I'm not alone. Bully is with me. This is where I met the giant."

"Hey, kid! Beat it," said Louie. "We got important stuff to talk about."

"Wait a minute," said Zack. "You sent us a text message, didn't you?"

"Yeah," said Robby. "I saw the number, but I couldn't call it because you would've wanted to talk to my mom, and she wouldn't have let me come. I used my mom's cell phone."

"Kid ... you got a card?" asked Louie.

Robby reached for the back pocket of his jeans and pulled out his card and held it up for all to see. Where the other cards had been numbered one through six, Robby's card said "7." Bully chuffed with satisfaction and continued watching the access way to the outdoor seating area.

"I'm supposed to be here, just like all of you," Robby said.

The group was quiet for a few moments. *Supposed to be here? Is that part of the answer to the riddle of why we are here?* Zack wondered why he had not thought about that word before.

"We all have these 'numbered' cards," he began. "Does that mean anything to anybody?"

"Well, it's more than one thing," said Zoe. "For now it seems there are seven of us. It's not just the number seven, it's our number. But what would that mean?"

"It's a symbol of some kind. The fact that we all have the same cards but each with a separate number means we are linked but each of us is special. It seems clear that we're somehow supposed to be here doing what we're doing," speculated Rey.

"That feeds into what we all are feeling," said Zack, a little discouraged, "but it doesn't move the ball much."

"Robby, tell us about the giant you met here at the park," said Mel.

Robby told them the story, amid chuckles, about meeting the huge Santa or his really big elf "like in the movies" at the park.

"Go on," Zack said. "Were you afraid?"

"No. That's the thing. I probably shoulda been, but I wasn't," continued Robby. "He gave me the card, and then he turned to leave. But he turned back to me and threw me the leash for Bully. He told me to take good care of his dog."

"Vat do we do now?" asked Anna. "Vatever we are doing, it cannot include a child."

"I'm not so sure," said Rey. "My faith tells me there's something bigger here than just us. Somehow Robby's part of it."

"I agree," said Zoe. "There's a lot here we don't understand. Robby's got a card. He's part of it. He's even more special; he's got Bully."

Zack looked at the group and thought about Robby. It was true that he was young and under his parents' authority; nonetheless, he had been given a card, so he was also under someone else's authority, as they all were. To what purpose was this improbable group called, and were they capable of seeing it through?

"Robby," said Zack kindly, "come sit with us while we try to figure out what's going on, and then we'll make sure you get home to your parents."

CHAPTER
28

"Sire, we are confused," said the curator with far more courtesy than Cloe could have mustered. "Our context for this discussion and the pledge of the ring was that the monsignor was here under your authority, although perhaps not a prisoner. The ring was to serve as security that he would return to finish his work here."

"*Quite ... so,*" replied the potentate. "*While ...* he is under my authority, he is not here at Fort St. Elmo."

"Highness, is he on Malta? Where is he exactly?" inquired Cloe sharply.

The potentate looked at her with increasing hostility.

"*Madam ...* I do not think I much like you," he said. "*Here ...* you have asked my help to free your friend, and I'm doing all that anyone could do. *But ...* you insist on questioning me like a common servant. *No! This ...* will never do."

"Sire, please accept my humble apology. I was overwrought and misspoke," said Cloe, anger burning in her eyes.

"*Well ...* I can't be all day about this piece of business," responded the potentate flippantly as he shot a look from the corner of his eye toward his adviser. "*The ...* man you seek is my guest at the Ghallis Tower. *My ...* advisers will write you a pass so you may go there and be reunited with your friend. *You ...* may go."

With that, the audience was over. Cloe, J.E., and the curator were hustled out of the chamber into the same anteroom where they had originally waited. The adviser who escorted them out handed Cloe a handwritten paper inscribed in Maltese.

"Your destination is on the eastern side of the island near Ghallis Point," said the functionary. "The potentate's troops who escorted you here will see you safely to the Ghallis Tower."

"What about our escort, the two Swiss who came with us?" asked J.E.

"They will be safe here until you return," came the curt reply.

Cloe worried the Swiss would be held as hostages against their return; there was little she could do but seek the monsignor without their protection. A few minutes later, they were once again in the vehicles rushing away from Fort St. Elmo and the potentate's inner sanctum.

J.E. spoke up. "I'm sorry I couldn't help back there, but it's not what I'm trained for, and I thought the best thing was for me to keep my mouth shut."

"You're probably right, J.E.," responded Cloe. "I should have kept my big mouth closed. I seemed to only antagonize him. Father Curator, I'm so glad you were with us, or it might have been a disaster."

"*Tsk, tsk*, child; the good Lord guided us though," replied the old cleric. "We can only pray that we have what we came for. I will say, though, that the man had a very strange speech pattern."

"Yes. That thing where he would emphasize the first word of a sentence, gesturing emphatically and then pausing was very unusual," replied Cloe.

"Unusual! It was very distracting," added J.E. "I wonder if he does it intentionally for that purpose. I had the sense he was toying with us."

"Perhaps, but in any event, we are well away from there," observed the curator.

"What does the pass say?" asked J.E.

The curator read it closely. "It confirms our free pass to the Ghallis Tower under the authority of the most high potentate, ruler of all Malta, etcetera, etcetera. It is what he said it was."

"What do you know about this Ghallis Tower?" asked Cloe.

"Well, it is a type of coastal fortification common on Malta. It and several like it were built by the Knights of Malta some four hundred years ago. It had some weaponry, but it functioned primarily as a watchtower," replied the curator. "A series of these towers allowed communications all the way from the northernmost island of Gozo to the knights' home base at Grand Harbour."

"Knights of Malta?" mused J.E. thoughtfully. "I've heard of them. What do you know about them?"

"The knights are an ancient Christian military order that some say began as a group dedicated to hospital care of the poor in Jerusalem a thousand years ago," replied the old priest. "Eventually, they became Malta's defenders from invaders, a role they had for hundreds of years. The series of towers is only one of their works."

"A thousand years ago? In the Middle Ages. That's interesting. Do they still exist today?" asked Cloe.

"That's not entirely clear," replied the priest as they sped north toward their destination. "Over the years, the order has splintered, disappeared, and reformed in other areas such as Rome and as far away as England. Whether there are true descendants of the Knights of Malta is hard to say. Most of the modern groups are more like clubs doing charitable work. The real knights have not been seen in decades, if not centuries."

Cloe surveyed the countryside as they hurried toward the Ghallis Tower. The three-car caravan was traveling on a winding, two-lane highway that hugged the coast. She could see the ocean, or at least one of the many bays that defined Malta, and she could smell the salt air through the open windows. Both sides of the road were covered with flora typical of sandy environs. She should have felt good about their progress, but she didn't. Something was wrong.

"I'm anxious to see Albert and make sure he's all right," she said, putting the thought away.

"Mom, he's okay," said J.E. "He may be a priest, but he's a tough bird—no offense intended, Father."

"None taken," said the priest. "We were all something else before we were priests, son. We might surprise you sometime." He suddenly nodded. "There it is."

Cloe and J.E. looked in the direction he indicated and saw a structure a mile or so off in the distance that looked like the tower of a child's sandcastle. As they drew closer, it was evident the tower rose three or four stories off the ground. It was made of smooth stone and was almost windowless. A stout wall encircled its roof, which featured a small, pillbox-like structure. *This must have been where the knights watched the seas for potential invaders*, Cloe thought. When attacked, it also must have been where the defenders made their stand.

The vehicles pulled up to the entrance, and a detail of six armed guards advanced on the center car occupied by Cloe, J.E., and the curator. One of the guards opened the door as they carefully surveyed them over the muzzles of their weapons.

"We have a pass from the potentate," said the curator, bowing slightly to the leader of the group of guards. "We are here to see Monsignor Albert Roques."

The guard looked down at the pass in the curator's hand and sneered, "Welcome to Ghallis Tower."

The guards formed up around them, and the whole group began to move toward the doorway. The rear door of the car they had just exited slammed shut, and all three vehicles roared off in a cloud of sand and dust.

A chill shook Cloe, and J.E. turned and said to no one in particular, "Wait a minute. How will we get back to the airport?"

CHAPTER

29

"It was the pass," whispered Cloe, as they were marched into the tower. "I knew something was wrong."

"The pass?" asked the curator.

"Yes," Cloe replied. "It was just a one-way trip. It allowed us to go only from Fort St. Elmo to the Ghallis Tower. There was no return."

"Perhaps we will get another pass from here to the airport after we collect the monsignor," the curator speculated.

"Maybe," said J.E. "But I think Mom's right on and the double-cross is on the way. I've got a bad feeling about this."

"Quiet!" screeched one of the guards, in English.

On they went, winding their way through the ancient tower, finally climbing an old stairway toward the roof. The stairway creaked and groaned with age as they passed, and at times the musty smell was almost overwhelming. About halfway up, they entered a narrow corridor framed with ancient wooden beams. J.E. had to bend over slightly to avoid scraping his head on the top of the passageway.

Cloe looked at the man who was the leader of the guards and said, "What are you doing? We have a pass from your ruler."

He snickered and replied, "We are taking you to the monsignor. Is that not your goal? It is most certainly what the pass says."

Before Cloe could reply, the detail stopped, turned, and faced a timeworn iron door mounted squarely in the stone wall. The head guard produced an oversized, old key and opened the ancient door.

"Your friend is just inside," said the officer with a greasy smile.

"Whoa!" said J.E. "It's a trap. I'm not going in there."

J.E. rounded on the escort preparing to fight. The leader, quick as a snake, drew a pistol and put it to Cloe's head.

"Die here or enter the cell," he said. "It makes no difference to me."

Seconds ticked by, but J.E. was beaten. Cloe knew he would not risk her life. As the old door swung wide open, they peered into the gloom of the cell. One by one, they entered, and when they were all inside, the cell door slammed shut behind them.

"I can't see my hand in front of my face," said Cloe into the gloom.

"Well, does anyone have an old Zippo?" came a voice from the darkness.

"As a matter of fact," cried J.E., opening the steel cap with its trademark "*zilk*" and spinning the flint wheel of Serge's old lighter.

There in the flickering light sat the monsignor.

"Oh my God!" exclaimed Cloe. "Albert!"

"Hello, Cloe," he said, rising from his bunk.

As he stood, Cloe studied her friend. His usually immaculate cassock was stained and frayed. Even in the faint light of the cigarette lighter she could see the lines in his face were deeper. Still, the smile in the steel-gray eyes and the sardonic turn of the lip were there.

He hugged Cloe as if he had not seen a friend in a long time.

As he looked at the others, his smile broadened, and he said, "J.E. I see you once again have become entangled in the adventures of your mother and friends. I would have thought Michael and the Karik might have cured you of that."

J.E. laughed and said, "It probably should have, but there you go again getting yourself in need of rescue." J.E. clasped the monsignor's hand in a hearty welcome, but Albert pulled J.E. to him in a manly hug.

The curator coughed and said, "There is some merriment here that escapes me. May I remind you we are all prisoners in a stone cell in a four-hundred-year-old watchtower on Malta—in the middle of the Mediterranean Sea?"

"I'm so glad to see all of you," Albert said. "Even you, Curator. What news do you have?"

"It's not good, Albert," said Cloe. "The pope sent us to ransom you. He needs you. The potentate has taken the ransom, and we are now obviously his prisoners as well. The man has no honor."

"No, he has no honor, but he is a small fish on the world's stage," replied the monsignor. "What is happening outside?"

"Chaos!" cried the curator. "St. Peter's has been blown up, and the Vatican has been sacked and burned. The pope is at Castel Gandolfo."

"The United States has withdrawn from its international role, recalling all its forces and giving its foreign bases back to the host countries. As we speak, its warships, planes, and personnel are evacuating to the US. The world is in disarray; evil is on the rise," said Cloe.

J.E. had been studying the barred door when he turned and looked at his mother, stunned. "Evil?" he asked. "This is a change."

"Yes, I'm convinced this is not merely civil disobedience. This is the rise of evil."

"But, Mom, we have seen evil up close and personal. We saw it in the Kolektor and in the Karik. God knows the worst of the lot was Michael. They are all dead. It's what you said. This may just be the disaffected youth. Admittedly, they are a mob, but evil? I don't know."

"J.E.," said Cloe. "I have had my doubts as well, but priests are being burned alive. Youth are on the rampage with no moral compass. The Vatican has been destroyed, and Rome itself is burning. The pope is in hiding. Martial law has been declared in the US. In past battles, you have always recognized our enemies, and whether it has been the Kolektor, the Karik, Michael, or one of the rogue states, you have seen the influence of evil. Now, the pope has convinced me that it's not just influence. It's the real, direct deal. We are faced with a terrible, all-consuming pure tide of evil."

"But in the past, evil has had a face. Here, what we have seems to be more of a movement," replied J.E. thoughtfully. "Misguided, yes. Evil … I don't know."

"What do you think, Curator?" asked the monsignor.

The old priest scratched his chin thoughtfully. "What we have is unprecedented in our time. We must develop sufficient perspective to understand what is happening. This is why the pope wants you back."

The cell was silent as the younger cohorts absorbed the wisdom of the old man.

Finally, the monsignor said, "The curator is correct. I suggest we table this discussion and put our minds to work figuring how we will get out of here."

"Well, as far as I can see, there's just one way in and one way out," said J.E. "There's no window, just the door—and it's completely solid with a bolt only on the outside."

"They bring me food once in the morning and once in the evening, usually fruit, rice, or some kind of porridge with a little meat in it," said the priest. "I'm allowed on the roof for an hour a day, during which the cell is cleaned. I see no one but the guards."

"Doesn't sound like much chance for escape," said J.E.

"I have been here for several weeks. Believe me, if I could have hit upon a way out, you would not have found me here," said the monsignor.

"Well, this is certainly a dilemma," observed the curator. "It looks like we may be here for a while."

CHAPTER
30

The Burnt Man watched the figure framed in the three-story glass window on the 160th floor of the Burj Khalifa in Dubai. Towering more than a half mile into the desert sky, it was, without doubt, the tallest building in the world. It was the Tower of Babel in a modern world.

The man in the window was tall—over six feet—and gaunt. His hands were clasped behind his back as he gazed at the scene below. He was dressed, as always, in a black suit with a black shirt and tie. His black hair was combed straight back from his forehead.

These three floors had been reserved originally for mechanical systems in this modern wonder. The man standing in the window had acquired these floors at great expense and relocated the equipment. The man told the puzzled property managers that he simply liked the view.

What a view it was. Even a person as ugly and ruined as the Burnt Man could appreciate the vast and beautiful sea. The view to the north and east was of the Persian Gulf, extending to the south around the point of the peninsula on which Dubai sat, to the Sea of Oman. The sunrises were astounding, the sun being visible below the horizon because of the height of the building. The rest of the suite had a view of the desert. and given the sunsets, that, too, was beautiful. *Yes*, thought the Burnt Man, *it is a splendid view.*

He looked around the suite: the figure framed in the window used it as his workspace as well as his residence. It was one of the most peculiar places he had ever been. The interior was painted solid white, but there was absolutely no furniture or any personal articles in it. The man in the window always stood. He never sat, and, indeed, there was no place to sit. As far as the Burnt Man could tell, he never slept or ate either, or if he did, it was when the man went to his room on a lower floor. In any event, there was no food, no furnishings, nothing in the suite.

Almost nothing, the Burnt Man corrected. In a small room off the great living room was the radio equipment. The broadcast station, powered with five hundred thousand watts of FM power, could reach an astounding number of countries, depending on weather conditions. It was strictly illegal, but the figure paid Dubai handsomely to let him be. He spent twelve to fifteen hours a day, when he was in residence, broadcasting to his flock. His believers now numbered in the millions.

The Burnt Man smiled with ruined lips as he remembered the first time he had heard the man's message—from his hacienda in the remote mountains of Brazil. He knew at that instant he wanted in. The changes that had occurred since then amazed him.

Shaking himself from his reverie, the Burnt Man saw the man look over his shoulder. While not afraid, the Burnt Man, nevertheless, was on guard.

"What of the woman?" asked the man.

"Our sniper missed her," said the Burnt Man. "It was dark, and he may have hit part of the window frame. Bad luck."

"I see," was the reply.

At that, the man in black turned and strode toward him. He stopped, smiled, and reached out to touch his mutilated face with the tips of his fingers. He closed his eyes and traced the scar tissue in an almost sensual way. This was the only relief the Burnt Man received from the constant pain.

Then, still smiling, Icar looked steadily at the Burnt Man and said, "Come. We have much to do."

CHAPTER

31

Cloe sat straight up in the narrow bunk on which she lay.

"Oh my God!" she screamed. "What was that?"

J.E. rushed to her. "Mom, what is it?"

Cloe looked around, sweat-drenched from the heavy sleep and the apparent nightmare.

"I don't know," she replied. "I just lay down for a second to rest my eyes, and then, the next thing, I saw Masada and the Karik."

"Mom, you were dreaming, more likely a nightmare," said J.E., putting his arm around his mother. "Masada's long finished, and they're all dead."

Cloe shook her head to clear the cobwebs. "We thought that after the Kolektor had been killed at Hakeldama by the Sicarii, and then came the Karik and Michael. How can I be sure?"

"Mom, for the thousandth time, they're all dead. The Karik was shot and tumbled off the thousand-foot cliff face of Masada. Michael was blown to smithereens by a phosphorous-base claymore mine. They're gone."

"I know, J.E. You've told me that before," whispered Cloe, turning toward the sound at the front of the cell.

"Come," interrupted the monsignor. "It's time for the routine exercise period on the roof. The guards are here."

They were escorted up another flight of steps at the end of the corridor. As they climbed the stairs, the air became measurably cooler. At the top of the stairwell, the sky opened on all sides, throwing off the cramped feeling of the crowded dark cell. It was late afternoon, and the sun was rushing toward its evening destination.

"Well, this is more pleasant," said the curator, stretching and gazing over the bay at the foot of the tower. "I wonder how many legions of knights have stood in this same spot and been witness to what I see now."

"Too many to count, Father Curator," said the monsignor. "We could use a knight or two now."

At that, one of the nearby guards struck the monsignor with the back of his hand, knocking him to the floor of the roof.

The man laughed and yelled, "The knights are long dead, priest. There is no one to save you."

The guard leaned down to the monsignor and spat in his face, causing him to cough and rub his eyes. The rest of the guards laughed at this.

Cloe blinked for a moment. *Did the guard whisper something to the monsignor when he bent over him to spit?*

The monsignor, seemingly humiliated and angry, got slowly to his feet but made no move to challenge the guards and their guns. Eventually, they were led back to the cell.

The cell door slammed shut, and Cloe turned to the monsignor. "What was that?"

The monsignor came very close to her so no one else could hear and whispered directly in her ear, "I think he was a friend. He said only one word—*tonight.*"

The others crowded around and, one by one, were quietly informed in case the cell was bugged.

"Who could he be?" whispered Cloe. "How can we possibly get out of here?"

"I don't know, but there is little we can do but wait and see," replied the monsignor in a very low voice.

"There is one other thing we can do," said J.E. softly.

"What?" asked the curator.

"We can darn well be ready if he comes," replied J.E. "We can look for anything that we might use as a weapon and get to sleep early."

"Yes, the young sir is correct," whispered the monsignor. "Let's find what we can and then get to sleep."

They scoured the cell, and the monsignor found a fist-sized piece of stone he was able to break away from its place near the edge of the door well. J.E. partially dismantled the bunk where Cloe had been resting earlier and secured a length of wire and a flat metal tab that he began to scrape very quietly against the stone wall to sharpen its edge.

After a while, Cloe thought they were probably as ready as they could be, and she lay down to sleep.

J.E. had the first watch and was standing by the cell door; after a while, Cloe awoke to the sound of J.E. snapping his fingers, alerting his dozing comrades. Someone was coming. The bolt on the other side of the wall was disengaged, and the door began to swing open.

"Stand back, faces against the wall," said a rough voice.

As she pressed her face against the cold stone, Cloe glanced over her shoulder and saw it was only the cook and one of the guards, bringing the evening meal. The monsignor had said this usually occurred sometime after eight o'clock. Even so, her heart rate spiked at the thought that they might get out. The cook moved to the center of the cell and sat the tray on the floor. In the murky light from the doorway, Cloe saw the guard move rapidly toward the cook and smash the back of his head with his rifle butt. The cook's dying eyes stared at Cloe, and some muscle reflex caused him to half-rise before he lurched forward and keeled over. The monsignor caught him and lowered him gently to the floor. He crossed himself and leaned over the dying man, whispering in his ear.

Their rescuer slipped back the hood of the cape he wore over the guard's uniform. Light brown, shoulder-length hair tumbled out and surrounded a square-jawed, handsome face.

"Quickly!" he said. "Bind the cook in case he yet lives."

J.E. knelt and wrapped the cook's hands and feet with the wire he had salvaged from the bunk.

"Is there something for a gag?" asked the newcomer.

A moment later, J.E. had torn a strip from his shirt and used it to muzzle the cook. Satisfied, J.E. stood and said, "Who are you?"

"Later. The others will return shortly. Right now there are only two guards here, one on the roof and one at the front door," said the stranger.

"Where are the others?" asked Cloe.

"Swimming at the beach near here. They do it every night while the prisoner, now prisoners, eat," he replied. "They think meal time is the least likely time for a prisoner to think about escape."

The monsignor chuckled and said, "Well, they must eat something other than what they feed us, because when I'm eating this slop is when I most think of escape. How do we get out of here?"

"The Knights of Malta built this tower four hundred years ago, and they devised a hidden means of ingress and egress should the need arise. I will show you," said the man.

They ran from the cell, barring it behind them, and headed toward the stairwell at the end of the narrow corridor. The steps led them down past a second level. The young man signed to them to be very quiet as they came to the first floor; one of the guards remained behind there. One by one, they silently tiptoed around the stairwell to what the stranger had said was an exit downward.

To what? Cloe wondered. It reminded her a little of the church of St. John in Lyon where she had spent much time tracing long-forgotten escape routes.

The stranger stopped at an old trapdoor in the floor under the first-level stairwell. It had a huge, ancient lock on it and looked like it had not been opened for scores of years, if not longer.

"Now what?" whispered Cloe. "We need a key." Once again, a feeling of déjà vu hit Cloe.

The young man produced a stout key from somewhere under his tunic and inserted it into the lock mechanism. He bent to turn the key, but nothing happened. He bore down on the task, producing a shrill squeal of metal on metal. Cloe could hear movement from the front of the building as the guard reacted to the noise. She envisioned the guard turning in his chair and listening intently to try to determine if he had heard anything.

"What do we do?" whispered the curator.

The monsignor bent over the lock and examined it closely.

"Hmmm, rusty," he said and reached into an inner pocket.

"Hurry, the guard is coming," pressed Cloe. She heard the sounds of chair legs scraping the floor, as if being pushed back from a table. Then it was quiet again.

From an inner recess of his cassock, the monsignor withdrew a small vial of oil for anointing the sick and dying, opened it, and poured some of the amber contents into the lock.

"Now!" he said.

The stranger again twisted the key in the lock, and this time there was some movement. He moved it slightly back and forth and then gave it a hard turn. The ancient lock popped open.

"Yes!" said Cloe.

They heard footsteps from the front of the tower coming their way.

"Quickly," said J.E., and he and the stranger grabbed the trapdoor at the same time, ripping it up and open.

Cloe gazed into the ink-black cavity and exclaimed under her breath, "There's nothing there!"

CHAPTER

32

"Who goes there?" demanded the guard from the head of the hallway. Cloe peeked around the stairs and could see the guard silhouetted against the light from his quarters.

Their would-be rescuer, the young man, had a small flashlight and shined it into the dark hole. There was no stairwell, but he pointed to iron rungs imbedded in the wall closest to the stairs.

"Quickly!" he said.

The curator went first, followed by Cloe, J.E., and the monsignor. It only took a few seconds, but the guard was halfway down the corridor before the stranger jumped on the iron rungs and pulled the trapdoor closed behind him. Cloe clung to the rungs in the darkness, listening to the young man bar the door from the inside.

The only light they had was the stranger's flashlight. She could hear pounding on the door above as the guard realized what had happened.

"Everyone, move to the left side of the rungs so I can get down!" yelled the stranger, no longer worried about the noise. With the small light in his mouth, he then shimmied down the right side of the metal rungs. Cloe could barely make him out as he swiftly breezed by her in the darkness.

He went down and down until he and the light seemed like they might soon pass out of sight. With a final jump, the stranger thumped to the ground below.

"Okay ... I'm down," he said. "Come on, carefully." He shined the light on the path that he had followed. Soon, they all stood on a sandy floor at the foot of the old iron ladder.

"Where do we go from here?" asked Cloe.

"Toward the sea," said the young man. "We have friends waiting for us."

"Wait a minute. Who the hell are you?" asked J.E.

"Valent is my name, but we have no time for introductions," replied the stranger. "When the others return, they will be through that trapdoor in no time and after us."

They ran along the sandy floor of the tunnel, the roof of which at times towered ten to twelve feet above them and at other times shrank to five or six feet. When the passage narrowed, they had to use care so that no one was injured by running into the stone outcroppings from the roof. Soon, they could hear the crashing waves of the ocean.

The luminescence of the ocean contrasted against the night as they approached the mouth of the cave. They slowed as they neared their exit to the water.

"Careful," said Valent. "It is likely the other guards have gone back to the tower, but we must be sure. I will go ahead."

The others huddled as Valent moved out to scout the mouth of the cave.

"Do we trust this man, this Valent?" asked the monsignor.

"Do we have a choice?" replied Cloe. "He did get us out of our cell."

"Yes, but to what end?" asked the monsignor.

"If I am correct, he is just what he seems to be—a white knight sent to save us," the curator added cryptically.

"All right, the path seems to be clear," said Valent, ducking back into the mouth of the cave. "We will go out to the left, and about fifty meters down the beach there is a dry reef of large rocks. In its midst is an inflatable that we can use to escape. J.E., you will lead the way and secure the boat."

"Wait a minute. How do you know me?" J.E. asked.

"I know all of you," Valent responded. "Dr. Lejeune, Monsignor Roques, and Father Curator. But there is no time for this. We will talk later."

Valent led them out of the mouth of the cave to where the sea washed ashore and then whispered to J.E., "Go!"

J.E. ran to the left, and the others followed. Just as the stranger had said, they soon reached a group of rocks; in a few seconds, J.E. and the main group had deployed the boat and had it floating in the surf, ready to go.

"Okay, position yourselves on either side to distribute the weight," yelled Valent. "J.E., you are the helmsman."

When everyone else was on board, Valent pushed the nose of the inflatable toward the open sea. Just then, Cloe heard a rifle shot, and a bullet pelted the water a few feet ahead of them.

"Hurry," cried Valent, pushing the inflatable beyond the breakers. "They have found us. J.E., get to the back and start the engine."

J.E. jumped in, and, though it was dark, rifle and machine-gun fire began to rain on them from farther down the beach. Cloe heard the shouts of the guards as they ran toward the boat, firing as they came.

J.E. grabbed the starter rope on the outboard and gave it a mighty heave. Nothing happened. The guards were closer now, and their fire was beginning to bracket the boat. Now the luminescence of the water was working against them.

"Again, J.E.," yelled Valent. "Pull the choke."

Valent, still in the water holding the bow of the boat into the waves, turned on the small flashlight and shined it on the choke lever on the outboard. J.E grabbed it and pulled it out just as another fusillade of gunfire raked the boat. Everyone ducked, and then J.E. ripped the starter rope back, and the engine fired. He threw the boat motor into forward and gunned the engine.

"Get in!" J.E. yelled to Valent, but the young man could no longer be seen.

The monsignor leaped to the bow of the rubber boat and reached down.

"I have him," he screamed. "Go!"

J.E. twisted the throttle, and the inflatable leaped ahead and danced over the low, incoming waves. He juked the boat to the left and then to the right to avoid the gunfire.

"J.E., we are safe beyond the range of the guards' weapons," said Cloe after a while. "Slow the boat so we can get Valent on board."

The monsignor had been holding onto Valent's arm like the Jaws of Life. As the boat slowed, the curator and Cloe grabbed hold of Valent, and the monsignor collapsed in exhaustion.

J.E. joined them, and soon the three of them pulled the young man on board and propped him against the bow of the boat. J.E. went back to the tiller on the outboard and headed them farther out to sea. There was no moon, and now they were beyond the luminance that had guided them on the beach.

"Oh my God!" cried Cloe, leaning over the young man. "He's been shot. He's out cold."

"Look for a first-aid kit—maybe under one of the seats," instructed the monsignor.

"Got it," said Cloe, and she went to work on Valent's shoulder.

"The wound is through and clean," she said after she finished. "I've got the bleeding stopped and the wound cleaned and bandaged, but he's going to be out for a while."

"Well, that puts us in a bind since only Valent knows where we are going," said J.E. "Now what? The Maltese will soon have boats of their own after us."

The curator turned to J.E. in the darkness and, with a smile in his voice, said, "J.E., pick a direction. The good Lord will guide your hand."

CHAPTER

33

The unlikely group of misfits had been talking in the coffee shop for some time, trying to reach an understanding of what was happening to them. Other than a little more detail on their personal backgrounds, not much light was shed on the subject. Robby had gotten bored and dozed off in one of the heavy patio-styled wrought-iron chairs.

"I can't imagine what kind of a team we could possibly make," said Zoe. "We are all so different: young, old, men, women, from different countries, and even a small child. What skills could we have in common that we could apply to one task?"

"I don't know," replied Zack. "Yet we have come from all over the world to this place to do something."

"Maybe we are not to do it here but somewhere else," said Mel.

"Then why were we all driven to come to New Orleans?" asked Rey. "I've come from Manila, halfway around the world. There must be something here."

"We're all here," replied Mel. "This may be where we stage, organize, and prepare for whatever it is. Besides, there's Robby. He couldn't travel far by himself."

"Perhaps it's that simple. If the seven of us are chosen for something, we had to come to the place where Robby was because he's a child," said Zack.

Zack glanced over at Louie and saw he was leaning back in his chair. His eyes were closed, but Zack could not tell if he was asleep. He had not said anything since the first introductions. Anna had also been quiet.

He stood to go get another pot of coffee and heard Bully emit a low growl through clenched teeth. Bully got to his feet and walked to the opening of the breezeway where they sat. He sniffed the air, and the rumble in his throat rose, becoming a clear warning.

Zack walked to where Bully stood and studied the now almost empty dining area. A number of leather-clad boys had entered from the parking lot, and, at first impression, Zack did not think they had come for coffee.

They were all cut from the same mold, with long hair, tats, piercings, and leather jackets or pants. Zack had the impression of dirt and decay. The leader, a little taller and more self-assured than the rank and file of the pack, looked directly at Zack from across the coffee shop and smiled a wicked, greasy smile of recognition.

He and his leather troop advanced on the group like a phalanx of Roman soldiers of ancient times. Halfway across the open space, the chant began, a chant in a tongue so foreign it did not sound human. Zack could not say what it was, only that he hated it. Bully had gone dead quiet.

"What's that sound?" cried Mel, hands on her ears.

The women at the table were now standing. Zoe grabbed Robby and held him tight.

The newcomers were advancing toward the breezeway sanctuary. The chant rose in volume. Bully moved toward the menace, quiet as a midnight cat.

The leather boys and Bully stopped about ten feet from each other near the entrance. The unholy mantra lowered in volume but did not fully stop. Bully sat and stared at the group of young men, continuing to sniff the air.

Zack swallowed and stepped alongside Bully.

"Zack!" whispered Mel.

"What do you want?" yelled Zack, betraying his nervousness.

"We have come for you," said the leader in a high, strange voice. "This is not your place or your time."

"What the hell are you talking about?" Zack asked.

"It is *our* day," said the leader. "One thousand years we have waited."

"Are you out of your mind?" stammered Zack, clearly unnerved by the strangeness of the group and sensing the growing discomfort of his cohorts. "We don't know you!"

"Ah, but we know you and your friends, and you will never accomplish your mission," said the leader of the gang of youths. "The master will not be defeated. Today you die."

With that, the toughs pulled knives, box cutters, and pipes. Zack prepared himself for the fight with his bare hands.

"Zack!" screamed Mel. "Run!"

But there was nowhere to run. Zack stepped up to brace against the charge of the leather kids. He glanced at Bully. The dog appeared bigger than he remembered.

"*Grrrrr,*" came the howl from Bully, louder than Zack could believe was possible. The cavernous mouth had expanded to basketball size, and the teeth were innumerable. Two huge incisors protruded from the corners of Bully's mouth, curving upward. Zack thought that this was what the mouth of a Saber-tooth tiger must have looked like. Bully rose on hind legs and fixed upon the leader at eye level. The leader took an involuntary step backward.

Zack glanced to his left. Louie had joined the line. On the other side of Bully, Rey now stood. Rey had a chair in his hands, ready to swing it into action. Louie stood with a wicked-looking switchblade in his left hand and a crooked smile on his face. No one uttered a word except Bully, whose howl had become a fierce, guttural growl.

The chant from the dirty boys arose again as they voiced their anger and lust. Bully's cry rose to a frenzied level. The dog was going berserk; he would clearly tear apart anyone in his path.

Zack felt a soft, small hand grab his own. He looked down at Robby.

"Zack, what do they want?" asked the child.

"I don't know, but you run back by the table with Mel," Zack said.

"No," he said and reached out for Rey's hand.

Zack could not say why he did it, but he grabbed Louie's hand, the one without the knife. Immediately, he felt ... what? Strength? Courage?

"Well, ain't that sweet!" laughed the leader, and he took a step forward.

Zack knew the charge was imminent. He held Louie's and Robby's hands tighter and braced for the attack.

Just then, he felt a hand on his shoulder. He glanced back and saw Mel. Next to her were Zoe and Anna, holding hands. Anna's other hand was on Rey's shoulder. Power surged through Zack. *What the hell is this?* He felt he could fight a legion of Romans.

As the circle closed, the chant ceased, and Bully became quiet. There was not a sound. The two forces eyed each other. A fight to the death was inevitable. Zack had time to wonder if he would die never knowing why he was here.

As the tension strained to the breaking point, Robby knelt and began, "Our Father …"

CHAPTER

34

Cloe told J.E. to steer the small boat to the north, thinking that if the Maltese authorities came for them, they might be able to escape into one of the coves that formed the eastern edge of the island. Going toward the south would be moving in the general direction of the potentate and his headquarters. She continued to work on Valent, trying to comfort and revive him. Shortly he began to moan.

"J.E., it's pitch black out here. How do you know where you're going?" the curator called out over the noise of the engine.

"The main island of Malta is on my left, and there are a few lights there that I can see. Plus, good old Polaris, the North Star, is up there to help guide us. So, I don't know where I'm going—but I'm not lost," J.E. replied.

Cloe chuckled at her son's humor despite the dire circumstances. Somehow, she had to get Valent awake and alert. They needed him now. She looked in the bottom of the medical kit and found a pack of smelling salts. Quickly, she broke into the package and held it under Valent's nose.

"What ..." Valent coughed, the pain of his wound exacerbated by the raw edge of the stimulant.

"What happened?" he asked as he tried to pull himself up into a sitting position.

"Whoa!" said Cloe. "You've been shot. I've stopped the bleeding and bandaged the wound, but you need to stay as still as possible."

"Valent, we need you to tell us where to go," said the monsignor gently. "We are headed north, but we don't know if that's right."

"North?" asked Valent, confused. He shook his head to clear it and said, "Yes, yes. North. That's right. Look for a light off the starboard bow that blinks thrice on the quarter hour."

Everyone looked at their watches and then began to scan the right side of the boat.

Soon, the monsignor said, "Look! Almost ninety degrees off the bow—there it is."

"Now what?" asked Cloe.

"Take my flashlight and answer with five flashes," said Valent, with fatigue in his voice.

Cloe grabbed the light and made the answering signal. The distant light flashed four times in answer.

"Head toward the location where you last saw the light," said Valent. "They will come to us."

* * *

Ten minutes later, they were aboard a large fishing vessel. Their small boat had been secured on deck. The ship's mate had given Valent an antibiotic and pain medication and served hot coffee to the others. They were now in the captain's tiny quarters.

"Who are you? To whom do we owe our thanks?" asked Cloe.

"We are a small group of patriots who do not like the direction of things," said the captain simply. The captain looked, in the low light, to be about sixty, with a weathered face and sprigs of white hair peeking from under his fisherman's cap. "We will see you back to the pope."

"How do you know where we came from, and how can you possibly get us back there?" asked J.E. "We appreciate being freed, but we are a long way from Castel Gandolfo, and with all respect, this is a slow boat. The Maltese Coast Guard is sure to find us in the morning."

"Ah, the young sir has taken stock of our tactical situation," replied the captain. "As to how we know you are from His Holiness, we have our sources. You must be J.E., the young military officer."

"Yes, sir, I'm a ranger with the US Army, Captain J.E. Lejeune," said J.E., extending his hand.

Cloe smiled at her son's immediate connection with the man as the boat captain took J.E.'s hand and gave it a firm shake.

"Well, that means you must be Dr. Lejeune," he said, looking at Cloe. "And you must be Monsignor Roques, and you, the father curator. Do I have everyone?"

"Quite so," said the curator. "And who might you be?"

He paused before he replied. "The less we know about each other the better. You may call me 'Captain,' but I'm also Val's father. No one else here has a name."

"All right, what do we do?" asked Cloe, realizing the captain and his cohorts were some sort of underground resistance.

"Well, the fastest way back to the pope is by air, is it not?" said the captain.

"Absolutely," said J.E.

"Then, we take you to your airplane," said the captain.

"But our airplane is at the Malta airport and is sure to be guarded. The pilot and copilot are likely prisoners of the potentate," said J.E.

"Yes." The captain grinned. That was all he said.

CHAPTER

35

Two hours later, they had circumnavigated the north and northeastern edges of Malta and arrived at a secluded cove not far from the airport. What appeared at first look to be a slow, weathered fishing vessel proved to have twin modern diesels, a planning hull, and a very respectable wide-open throttle. The captain and his crew, now dressed all in black, carried automatic weapons and a serious attitude. Cloe and her group were similarly garbed, and J.E. and the monsignor had been given pistols. The captain sent a scout to reconnoiter the airport, and a rendezvous was arranged.

Cloe lay in the predawn dampness of the weeds near the airport. She could just see their jet silhouetted in the distance. It was close to the general aviation office. She studied what she could see of the airport and its buildings by the illumination from the overhead stanchion lights.

A dark form appeared in front of them and gave a birdlike whistle.

"Unless I'm mistaken, that is the speckled-belly Maltese patriot," quipped the monsignor.

Sure enough, it was the scout, and he was welcomed into the midst of the assault team to make his report. The air, heavy with moisture, began to congeal into fog as the temperature dropped slightly. The distant outline of the airport grew indistinct. The lights, which had only a few minutes before provided some clarity, became diffuse.

As the men talked, Cloe whispered, "Who are these people?"

"They say they are Maltese partisans," responded the monsignor.

"They are well armed and well disciplined," observed J.E. "They are certainly not tough guys off the streets. They are some kind of paramilitary."

"What about those short swords they carry?" questioned Cloe, thinking of the Sicarii. "Have you seen that before?"

"No," said J.E.

"No," agreed the monsignor.

The curator was silent.

"Father Curator, do you know something?" asked Cloe, now focused on the old man.

"I'm not sure," he responded.

"But what do you think?" asked J.E.

"I think the Knights of Malta are not as extinct as many people believe."

* * *

The captain came to their group and reported what the scout had found. The pilots were being held in a room in the general aviation terminal. Their Swiss guards were there as well, including the two soldiers who had accompanied them to Fort St. Elmo. It was deserted at that hour except for a guard near the jet. There were also guards outside the building. The plan was to liberate the pilots, the Swiss, and to incapacitate the guards as swiftly as possible. If anyone sounded the alarm, it could turn deadly. J.E. and the captain, along with his six crewmen, would dispatch the guards and free the captives. The monsignor would stand guard in case they were somehow flanked.

They all synchronized their watches. Cloe watched from her nest in the reeds for the all-clear signal of three flashes. At that they were to run as fast as possible to the jet. Cloe lay watching the men crawl off in various directions to get some advantage on the guards. The fog had thickened, and she wondered if any signal could be seen from where they were.

All was quiet and dark as a graveyard at midnight. The fog absorbed all sound. The lights had a sunset effect in the growing mist. It was more show than illumination. As the seconds and minutes ticked by, Cloe began to sweat. Her heart beat faster, and her skin prickled. The sweat chilled, and she was cold.

"My God, how long?" she whispered to the curator.

The old man rolled toward her in the weeds and said, "It's only been a few minutes. Have faith."

"Can you see J.E.?" she asked.

Just then, she saw the flashing lights.

"Come on! Let's go!" cried the monsignor. "Run!"

They ran for the jet as planned, stumbling here and there in the reeds and on the uneven ground. By the time they arrived, the now liberated pilots had opened the airplane and were going through their checklist. Cloe glimpsed the slumped bodies of the guards on the tarmac near the office.

As she jumped on the steps to board the plane, J.E. appeared behind her.

"J.E.!" she yelled as the engines roared to life.

"I'm fine, Mom." He smiled. "Get aboard. I have to speak to the captain."

The monsignor and the curator came aboard and strapped themselves into their seats. Nobody knew how rough this takeoff would be. Cloe could barely see J.E. and the captain outside her window because of the fog.

The copilot went to the door and called to J.E., "We've got to go! If the fog gets any worse, we won't be able to find the runway."

J.E. and the captain exchanged a few more words, and then J.E. grabbed his hand, shook it, and bolted for the jet. The doorway was wrapped up and secured, even as the pilot began taxiing the aircraft.

"Everyone, strap in as tight as possible," came the voice of Sky over the intercom. "One of the guards has come to and is about to sound the alarm."

Sure enough, as Cloe looked out her port, she saw the guard running toward the tower building. *Thank God J.E. and the captain took all the weapons*, she thought, *or the man would be shooting at us right now.*

Sky dropped all decorum as the jet roared over the tarmac. The advantage of surprise had been lost with the guard's early recovery. There was no need for stealth or secrecy. Now, it was all about escape.

Lights came on, and sirens screamed to life. Cloe could see people moving at the terminal building. Shots rang out, and at least one hit the plane with a deadly thud. *This is going to be close.*

Sky applied more thrust, and the plane leapt forward on the taxiway. Through the swirls of fog, men climbed aboard trucks and Jeeps and headed toward them. A light drizzle started and cleared some of the heavier fog. Soon they would be sitting ducks. More shots were fired, including from a machine gun mounted on top of one of the Jeeps.

Tracer rounds from the machine gun flew above the jet as the gunner apparently failed to correct for the lift of the muzzle blast. It would be only a matter of seconds before the shooter corrected and the plane was hit. Two seconds later, the commuter jet reached the south end of the runway and pirouetted to the north. The rain quickened. Sky firewalled the throttles on the Rolls-Royce engines, and the plane jumped like a scalded dog down the runway. The engines screamed, and the jet shook. Machine-gun and rifle fire trailed behind it.

Cloe looked out the porthole next to her and saw the trucks and Jeeps rushing after them. They would never catch up. Even now they were slipping back into the distance and the rain. Still, bullets sprayed the area around the jet, and some hit the fuselage. *How much damage has been done?*

The plane continued rushing down the runway as the fog further dissipated. The rain was now heavier and slammed into the plane as it rolled. She had no idea how Sky could see anything without the usual runway lights, much less pilot the winged missile to lift off. Just as she began to think they were locked into some middle-earth universe with nothing else but dark, rain, and regrets, the plane rotated and departed Malta into the safety of the atmosphere. *Thank God*, she prayed.

As the plane gathered altitude over the bay, Cloe looked for the captain and his crew, but she could see nothing. She hoped they had escaped. Surely, God would be with them.

CHAPTER
36

Sky put the plane into the hands of his copilot. He slid from the controls and headed back to Cloe and the others to brief them on the flight. He was whip-thin, with long hair and a handlebar mustache.

"It's a short flight to Castel Gandolfo—no more than thirty minutes," he said. "We will land at a strip south of Rome so we don't have to run the gauntlet of the mob."

"Is the plane okay?" asked J.E. "We did take some fire."

"I think so," said Sky. "Nothing is leaking, and the instruments are good. Thing is everything's always good until it isn't."

Cloe chuckled at the man's fatalism.

"We will see the pope shortly," said the monsignor. "There's a great deal ahead of us. Cloe, I know you are very tired, but we need to talk about the translation."

"Yes, Albert," she said over the jet engines.

"What can you tell me?" asked the monsignor.

He listened intently as she filled him in, waiting until she had finished for his questions.

"Have you determined who wrote it?" asked the monsignor.

"I thought at first the author had to be Judas because of how we found it," she replied. "The references that led us to it were in the Greek version of the Gospel of Judas."

"So it was Judas?" asked J.E.

"I'm not so sure now. It might be, but it could be others. Some of it has that third-person thing we see in the Gospel of St. John," said Cloe.

"You know, where he refers to himself as the disciple who loved Jesus or as the 'other.' Remember, it's in scraps that must be assembled in some order to make sense. Some of it is very clear and straightforward. That's the interesting voice. It's very authoritative. So there may be several authors."

"Okay, so we are not sure who wrote it, but does it give us any help for our current circumstances?" asked the monsignor. "You have mentioned a possible conversation between Jesus and St. John about the end of times. Maybe this is a clue for us."

"Perhaps," said Cloe. "The problem is I'm at a dead end in trying to translate the conversation. I've gotten to the point where I believe Jesus and St. John are talking in a private conversation, and I'm sure Jesus mentions the rise of evil. He talks about the signs that will appear, but the written language departs from Aramaic into what appear to be symbols."

"Signs, symbols?" mulled the monsignor. "Jesus and St. John were very close, often together, and St. John is known as the disciple who Christ loved. Why would there be signs or symbols?"

"What signs?" asked the curator.

"There is talk of famine and plagues," responded Cloe. "Civil unrest and wars emerge, but the persecution and killing of the religious is given as a foremost sign that evil is ascendant. There are many others discussed. Jesus says the evil one will awake, take a familiar form, and there will be a final battle with all the kingdoms of the world."

"Wow!" said J.E. "It does seem that a lot of that is going on now."

"St. John was the only disciple who stayed with Jesus throughout, even unto the cross itself," said the curator. "He and his brother Andrew were two of the first disciples chosen, and he was the one to whom Jesus entrusted his mother as he was dying on the cross."

"Perhaps they had a secret language only between them—that's what the symbols are," suggested J.E.

"All possible," said Cloe. "But it doesn't feel like that. It's not a secret language two people might invent. It's like it's written in little pictures such as Chinese. But it's nothing like Chinese."

"Cloe, are we talking hieroglyphs?" asked the monsignor. "Are these Egyptian-type hieroglyphs?"

"I'm not sure," she replied. "Jesus seems to be giving John instructions on how to deal with the rise of evil, which he says will happen periodically.

He says God will provide the forces to battle evil no matter how bad things seem. We should have faith. Then he says in such times we should look to … something. That's when the strange language starts. Whatever we are to look to is coded."

"If John and Jesus had a secret language between them, why don't we see it in the Gospel of St. John or in his other writings?" asked J.E.

"Well, it might be that the other writings of St. John were for public consumption. They couldn't be in code," said the monsignor.

"John is reputed to have written Revelation seventy years after Christ's death, and it's in a sort of code," responded Cloe. "But it's not the same. The meaning of Revelation is disguised, but it's not written in an indecipherable language. Revelation can be understood by references to then current events. This is different."

"Why would Jesus give John coded instructions on defeating evil?" asked J.E. "Shouldn't we all know about this?"

"We may not be able to answer that question until we can understand what it says," said Cloe. "John may have included it all in the book of Revelation. That may be all there is. But we have to decode it to know what it says in order to see if Revelation gives us clues as to what it means."

"Where is the language?" asked the curator. "I would like to view it."

"It is on my laptop, which I left at Castel Gandolfo with the pope."

Just then the jet engines began to ramp down.

"I've got to go land this thing," said Sky. "We will be with the pope shortly."

"There will be an answer," said the monsignor.

CHAPTER

37

Robby knelt and prayed the "Our Father," and there was little to do but to join him. Zack and his group were hopelessly outnumbered and had little in the way of weapons. The leather boys could easily sweep them away.

So Zack knelt, and Louie, Rey, Mel, and the others did likewise, still holding hands or touching the person in front. Zack could feel the power surge through them. It was not of them but through them.

The young men in front of them stopped as if they had hit a brick wall. The leader looked bewildered and turned to urge his men forward. The leather boys relaxed their grip on their weapons and soon began to drop them to the floor. In short order, the hoods were defenseless.

Zack, Robby, and the rest stood, still praying, and stepped forward toward the entrance to the breezeway. Zack could see the large, inner dining room lined with mirrors in the New Orleans style. The kitchen staff and wait staff had come from the back and were poking their heads out the door to see what the commotion was.

"What's going on?" shouted a man who looked like he might be in charge.

The leader of the dirty boys looked around and took a step back.

"Call the army post," said the manager to one of his workers. "Tell them we need help."

Zack and the others moved slowly forward, one step at a time, still praying as their adversaries retreated. They had nearly crossed the large front entrance area to the restaurant when the thugs withdrew and trotted toward the parking lot.

The leader looked around and said, "Come on, boys. I already had breakfast anyway." They turned and ran—all but the leader. He spun toward them and smiled with down-turned lips and said, "This has only begun. We will meet again."

*　*　*

"Oh my God!" said Mel. "What was that?"

Zack rushed to the end of the breezeway and looked out. He could see the leather boys had mounted motorcycles and were now roaring off to the south.

"Come on, we've got to get out of here," said Zack. "They could come back. Wherever this goes, for so long as it takes, we are together."

"I think it may go farther than we think," said Louie, finally speaking. "Wherever we go, no matter how long it takes, we are *one*."

One, Zack thought. The more he considered it, the more it fit. They were here for a reason, and they were together for the same reason. They were *one,* for better or worse.

After the scene at the coffeehouse, none of them could go back to their hotels. Indeed, they could not separate; they had to stay together. There was only one reasonably safe place, but first they had to deal with Robby's situation. He had to come with them to gather them together, but what would his parents say? If they did not talk to the parents, it would not be long before the military cops were looking for Robby.

Zack faced the others and said, "We have to talk to Robby's parents." They all nodded in understanding.

Robby led them to a small house with a tiny, well-trimmed lawn and single-car carport. After they introduced themselves, all six of them sat in the living-dining room combination, facing Robby's mother. Robby's dad had not come home from a deployment to Iraq. Zack could see the flag and the medals on the mantel, which told the story. The young widow was dressed in medical scrubs and had dark brown hair and a pretty face. Zack thought she could not be too much older than he. As usual, Bully sat between Robby and the door, watching the door but with his ears pricked up, listening to the proceedings.

There was nothing any of them could say that might cause a mother to part with her seven-year-old child. They had discussed several cover stories, but no one had faith in any of them. In the end, they told Robby's mother the truth as they knew it.

"You're not seriously asking that I let a seven-year-old boy go with people I have only just met to be part of some unknown mission?" she asked incredulously. "I think you people need to get out of my house."

"Ma'am," said Zack. "Robby has told you about the strange giant. He told you about the card?"

"Yes," she replied. "That changes nothing."

"It changes everything," said Mel, holding her card up.

They all reached into pockets and purses and held up identical cards, each gleaming in the low light.

"Rey got his in Manila, Zoe in Australia, Anna in Germany, Mel in Guam, and the rest of us in various parts of the US," said Zack. "We have come from all over the world to New Orleans. Robby is one of us and must come with us. He has been chosen."

"Chosen!" she cried, pulling Robby to her side. "I've lost my husband. In a sense, he too was chosen. I can't lose Robby. He's all I have."

The group in the long front room was quiet. The wood floors creaked under their immaculate gleam. There was a neat little dining area adjacent with a table and four chairs that transitioned into the cozy kitchen.

"We understand, and we have all lost people we loved," said Mel. "I buried my dad on Guam. What we are about is important."

"And what is that?" asked Robby's mother, blotting her eyes on her sleeve. "What are you about?"

"We are not sure," said Rey. "We just know it is important; somehow it's critical."

"Critical to what? To whom?" she demanded.

"We just don't know," said Zack, sighing.

"You want me to let my son go with you, God knows where, for who knows what," she remarked. "Please leave my house. This conversation is over."

A small arm tugged at her slacks, and she looked down at her son.

"Mom, I have to go with them," said Robby. "It's part of the plan."

"Plan? What plan?" she asked. "Robby, what are you saying?"

"Well, I'm not all that sure, but I can tell you what I think it feels like," said Robby. "You know when you and I read my Bible studies? We read the deal about Noah and the ark. It's like that."

"Noah?" questioned his mother.

"Yes. He was told to build this big thing and get all these animals and get inside," said Robby. "It seemed crazy. But Noah didn't really need to worry about that 'cause he had faith."

Zack smiled at the innocent wisdom of children. He already loved this little boy.

"I think I see," said his mother. "You're saying I should have faith."

"Yes, ma'am," the little boy said.

"But, Robby, Noah was touched by God," she replied. "He did what he did because he was an instrument of God."

"Yes, ma'am," said Robby.

CHAPTER
38

The pope welcomed them back and after the formalities gave the monsignor a great bear hug. Cloe could have sworn that there was a tear in the corner of the pope's eye. They were seated once again in the conference room at Castel Gandolfo, enjoying coffee and the wonderful cookies prepared by the German order of nuns that served the pope's household.

"That's quite an adventure for what was supposed to be a simple diplomatic mission," said the pope after hearing what had transpired on Malta. "The important thing is Albert is here with us again. Cloe, we owe you and your colleagues a great debt of gratitude."

"Thank you, Holiness, but without this group, whom we think may have been the descendants of the Knights of Malta, we would all still be imprisoned at the Ghallis Tower. Valent, the son of the leader, was very courageous in coming into the tower to get us out," said Cloe. "His life was constantly at risk, and he was wounded in our escape."

"If things ever settle down and Malta once again becomes hospitable, I shall send emissaries to seek out these brave men," said the pope. "I should like to recognize them—that is, if they will allow such a thing."

"Holiness, you may be quite correct in your suggestion," replied the monsignor. "They are underground for their own good reasons, most likely so they can emerge to help Malta in times like these. They may prefer their anonymity."

"Quite so, Albert, but there are many ways to recognize them that do not involve exposing our friends," said the pope. "We shall see."

"Holy Father," said Cloe, "we were not able to complete our mission without the loss of the ring. We had hoped that we could somehow bargain with the potentate in such a way that we could rescue the monsignor *and* bring the ring back to you."

"My child, the ring was committed as the ransom," the pope replied. "The important thing is Albert is back. While the ring is symbolic, it is still only a thing to be gladly sacrificed for the safe return of our people."

Cloe was amazed at the pope's implicit expression of the priceless value of one person's life yet unsure if dealing with terrorists in such a manner was the best policy in the long run. She glanced at J.E., who by his expression was reading her thoughts.

Seeing her look of concern, the pontiff said, "You don't approve of our bargaining strategy? It is well known that it is the policy of the US not to negotiate with terrorists about the freeing of hostages or prisoners."

"That's true, Holiness," said J.E. "The concern is that even a successful bargain only encourages the terrorists to take more prisoners in hopes of more treasure."

The room grew still, and Cloe was fearful she and J.E. had said too much.

"Not all countries have the resources of the United States. While the Vatican is not a poor country, it is the smallest one, and our resources are committed in many ways," the pope kindly observed. "Thus, in situations like this, which thankfully are very rare, we have to use all the tools we have. We bargain, and we look for opportunity. Still, it's not over; the ring may yet be recovered."

Cloe heard the shepherd in his voice, but she also heard something else: steel. She smiled at Pope Francis with a new respect.

* * *

After the pope had retired, the others remained in the conference room as Cloe booted up her trusty laptop. She thought back to when she had deciphered key phrases from the Judas gospel while en route to Lyon, France, to meet the Kolektor. The ruthless monster had kidnapped her elderly uncle Sonny. She and her laptop had been through a lot. She looked down at the screen as the familiar notes sounded. The portion of the journal she had last worked on came up.

"Here's where I left off with the translation," she said as the others gathered around and looked over her shoulder. "You can see my notes of what I had tentatively translated."

"That certainly suggests the other party was St. John," said the monsignor. "That third-person style is classic Johannine verbiage found throughout the Gospel of St. John."

"Quite so," said the curator. "Only John used that special language so one could conclude he wrote it. Do you think this is his journal?"

"It's hard to say," replied Cloe. "I began thinking this was a diary or journal, chronicling Christ's public ministry, probably written by Judas Iscariot. That was somewhat implied by references to it in the Judas gospel. Now, I'm not so sure."

"It may end up that it was written by more than one person," suggested J.E.

"We may find more styles and more authors as we go on. Or it could have been someone imitating John's well-known style."

"Could Jesus Christ himself have written some, or all, of this journal?" asked J.E. "Is this Christ's diary?"

Cloe's mouth fell open. It was as if all the air had been sucked out of the room by J.E.'s question. Why had that not occurred to her? Was it possible? Her head reeled at the thought. *"Christ's diary?"* she asked herself.

"There has never been *any* writing directly attributed to Jesus ever discovered," said the curator. "It has long been assumed that there is none."

"But, Father Curator," said the monsignor, "that answer only begs the question. Is it not equally plausible to believe that no such writing has yet been discovered as it is to believe that none exists?"

"Yes, Albert. Your point is well taken," said the curator. "But how could such a thing ever be proven? We have no other writings of Christ with which to compare it and no contemporary references to verify it."

"Well, it might be possible to speculate as to the author based solely upon the internal content of the journal. We could eliminate other possible authors based upon comparison to their contemporary writings," mused Cloe. "This would take years of work and might never be definitive, but it would be an astounding task. Any number of scholars would gladly devote their life's work to such a project."

"Amazing," said the monsignor. "Just as we peel back one layer of the mystery of the journal, ten more layers present themselves."

"Quite right, Albert," said Cloe. "That's all for another day. Right now we need to know about this conversation."

"Okay, but what does the part you have translated say?" asked J.E.

"It's a relatively long conversation, but the gist is that there will be numerous signs that will announce evil's rise. It vaguely talks about when this will occur, how to recognize the signs, and what to do about it."

"Well, that's good," said J.E. "So, what do we do about it?"

"That's the thing," said Cloe. "The next sections are in this strange code."

They all squinted down at the small screen, studying the strange characters.

"Wait a minute," said the curator, moving away from the table and pushing a button on the wall. As a large screen began to scroll down from a recessed panel in the ceiling, he opened a drawer in a cabinet along the wall and withdrew a USB cable.

"Cloe, plug this into the USB port in the table hub," he said.

Cloe quickly connected the cable to her computer and then to a built-in AV hub. The page appeared in large characters on the wall screen. They looked up at the strange markings.

"This is absolutely incredible," the monsignor finally said.

"What the heck?" added J.E. "It looks like a bunch of tiny insects organized in some strange colony—a little like small platoons of ants forming up on a parade ground."

"Why did you say 'organized,' J.E.?" asked the monsignor.

"I don't know. It just hit me that it didn't seem random," he replied. "Organized, structured."

"Very observant, young man," said the curator.

The monsignor turned quickly to the priest. "Father Curator, I think you have something to tell us."

"Perhaps," said the curator. "I have seen this before."

"Where?" asked J.E. "What's the code?"

The curator stepped back, scrutinized the screen, and said, "It's not insects, not ants, and it's definitely not a code."

CHAPTER
39

They gathered in the living room of Doris's family's home. The room was old school with traditional, overstuffed furniture all grouped around a now cold fireplace. Zack knew the Leneaus did not fully understand what was happening. Still, they were willing to put up with all of them, along with Robby's mother and of course Doris, who was somehow involved.

"In the coffee shop, the hoodlums said they knew us and our mission," said Zoe. "What can that mean?"

"I can't say," replied Zack. "We don't even know our mission. I do know we are here for a purpose, but I haven't thought of it as a mission."

"How could they know anything about us?" asked Mel.

Doris's mother and father had joined the group, and Mr. Leneau puffed on his pipe as he listened carefully to the conversation.

"Have you seen any of these boys before?" asked Mr. Leneau.

"No, sir," said Zack. "We don't know them."

"But how could they know our mission?" queried Rey.

"They were there to stop us from doing something that we don't even know we are doing," said Louie, now more vocal. "This is BS!"

"And how did we repel them?" questioned Zoe. "What was that all about?"

"They were dead set on hurting us or worse," said Zack. "They were crazy."

"Yes, but somehow we ran them off," said Rey.

"One thing I would say is this group has courage," said Mr. Leneau. "From what you have said, Zack, Louie, and Rey stepped forward to meet the threat."

"Don't forget Bully," said Zack. "We all rallied around Bully." The huge bulldog chuffed with pleasure at the mention of his name.

"True, but nothing happened until Robby came forward and grabbed Zack's hand," said Rey. "Then we began to feel the power."

"Yes, but the girls were the clincher," observed Louie. "When they closed the circle, it seemed we could do anything."

"It's plain that you together possess some sort of power or you can somehow call upon a power," said Mrs. Leneau. "I've never heard anything like this. Is ... is this for good?"

There it was. Zack considered Doris's mother's question. Was it good? How could they know for sure? He himself thought it was for good. He looked around at the group and believed them to be good.

"Yes!" he said finally. "Somehow, we are a force for good arrayed against someone or something bad."

"But why me? Where did I sign up for this?" said Louie. "I'm just a petty thief from New York."

"No one knows any of that," said Mel. "But can you deny the power you felt in the circle?"

"No," replied Louie.

"Then you are in it whether you like it or not," said Mel. "You are in it to the finish."

"But what does that mean?" asked Louie. "We all know things are going to hell in a handbasket out there. The cities are a mess with violence that is exploding. It makes the way I make my living look like Sunday school. What do we do? What can we do?"

"It is under such circumstances that evil arises," said Mr. Leneau.

"Evil?" asked Zack. "What do you mean by evil?"

"In my line of work, I read a lot. I have explored the Bible and other religious works. The book of Revelation says the devil was cast into the abyss for a thousand years. That was two thousand years ago. Is this the cycle of evil? Is there a thousand-year cycle and are we on the precipice of the second cycle?"

"Wow, the thugs at the coffee shop mentioned the thousand-year thing and that it was their time," Zack said in surprise.

"My God, you can't believe that," blurted Robby's mom, who had been listening to everything.

Everyone turned to her and then back to Mr. Leneau. The old house groaned and creaked.

Zoe shivered and said, "This is so far above me I don't really know what to believe."

"Well, sooner or later, the same force that brought us here will make known what we are to do," said Mel. "We must have faith."

"Faith?" said Louie. "I'm not even religious."

"Still, can you deny that you have been chosen?" asked Zack.

"No ..." said Louie. "But I don't feel all that chosen."

"No one else does either," said Zack. "But until we know what this is all about, we hide and we wait."

CHAPTER

40

"Father Curator, it's got to be some sort of code," said Cloe. "I'm familiar with many of the old languages—even ones no longer spoken—and this is not one of them."

"Ah, but it is just that—an ancient language," said the old priest. "However, it was never a spoken language. If I'm correct, it may be far older than anything you might have worked with. In fact, it may be one of the earliest known forms of writing."

"Well, that could only be one thing," mused Cloe.

"Yes, cuneiform," said the curator. "It's cuneiform."

"What the heck is cuneiform?" asked J.E. "I've heard the word somewhere before, but what does it mean?"

"Cuneiform itself means having the shape of a wedge or wedge-like," replied the curator. "If you look closely, the tiny shapes you characterized as insects or ants are actually small wedges."

"I have seen examples of cuneiform before in my studies, but this is unlike anything I've ever seen," remarked Cloe.

"You mean someone can read this stuff?" asked J.E., staring at the odd shapes on the screen.

"Yes, the wedges are arranged into various patterns, and those patterns make words, phrases, or sometimes small pictures. It's really quite amazing," said the curator. "We have samples of cuneiform that were used by ancient civilizations in our Vatican library."

"I wonder if there's much left to the library after the destruction of the Vatican by the mob," said Cloe.

The old curator paused. Cloe thought she saw a hint of moisture in his eyes.

"I'm sorry, Father," said Cloe, realizing she had been insensitive.

"A great deal of our library had been digitalized and put on computer. A good deal of it is actually underground and hidden. Even if the ancient manuscripts are gone, the knowledge may still survive," said the priest, with great sadness.

"Do you have any idea what it says or which people may have used this language?" asked the monsignor.

"I have no idea what it says," said the curator. "But I believe it's from the ancient Middle East, somewhere in Mesopotamia."

They sat pondering the strange symbols on the screen, seemingly at an end.

"Cloe, do you think Mike, the supercomputer at Louisiana State University, might be able to analyze these markings and provide some answers?" asked the monsignor.

Cloe thought about her time at LSU and the opening of the first jar, the Judas jar, the computer figuring out the chemical composition in the jar and then some of the verbiage. The supercomputer had also played a critical role in deciphering the biblical clues in the second jar.

"Yes, it's worth a try if we can't get access to the Vatican's information," said Cloe.

"Can't get access to what Vatican information?" came a booming voice from the doorway.

They all turned to face the vicar general Antonio Sigliori, head of Vatican special operations.

"Tony!" cried the monsignor. "How can you be here? I heard you were in Africa."

The priest stepped through the doorway, and the others crowded around him, greeting him with hugs and a tear or two.

"Father Anton, the last time I saw you was at Masada," said J.E. "Where have you been?"

"Well, I went to America to get your mother, and then the pope sent me for a quick trip to Africa to assess the situation. I have only just returned, and I was told you were here," said Father Anton. "So here I am."

"What's happening in Africa?" asked J.E., taking a serious tone with his military colleague.

"It's bad, J.E.," said the priest. "It's no longer just tribal violence in pockets. It's young versus old, rich versus poor, and more, all seemingly inflamed by this mysterious Icar. Whole cities have been looted and are on fire. The people are desperate. The world seems to be coming apart at the seams. We've had to evacuate the religious from all but the most stable areas. In all our years in overseas missions, this has never happened."

Cloe watched Father Anton as he spoke. He looked more fatigued than when she had last seen him in New Orleans and in Rome. His was a terrible responsibility. While the Vatican was the head of the Catholic Church worldwide, it was also a small country and needed to protect its own from time to time. Father Anton, as head of special operations, was that protector along with the Swiss Guard.

"Hello, Tony," said Cloe. "We need to bring you up to speed on all that has happened since you came to New Orleans."

"Good, but what do you need from Vatican sources? Maybe I can help," he said.

"We have a mystery language we believe to be cuneiform. Father Curator believes the Vatican library may have had examples of such writing to which we want to compare our sample," she said. "We need to learn what it says or at least which civilization produced the writing. However, we know the library was largely destroyed in the looting of the Vatican."

"True, but some materials have been saved, and most of the knowledge was put on our computer servers, and we have those. If we can get the sample to the monks in the special operations center, they may be able to help," replied Father Anton.

"Are you saying Father Emilio and the special opts monks are here?" asked J.E. "They saved our skins in the fight with the Karik and Michael, giving us critical intel that gave us an edge."

"They are not physically at Castel Gandolfo, but they are safe in a special bunker near here with all the Vatican computer servers," replied Father Anton. "I can send them an image of the cuneiform, and we'll see what they find."

The priest sat at Cloe's laptop, copied the strange icons, and forwarded them to the monks. Cloe had been amazed that the Vatican had an order of monks manning its special opts intelligence center, but they had proved their worth and their mettle in previous battles. If anyone could find the meaning or source of the cuneiform, they would.

"Okay, that's it," said Father Anton, turning from the computer to face Cloe and the others. "The pope has assigned me to protect you for as long as you are here. Of course, my duties with respect to His Holiness and his household will also continue."

"Thank God, Tony," declared the monsignor. "I have no idea where we are going or what we will be doing, but I feel much better with you helping us."

"Indeed, what do we do?" asked the curator. "Where do we start?"

"A fair question, Father Curator," responded Cloe. "Right now we know only three things: the world is in chaos with evil plainly ascending; a man named Icar is either causing it or exploiting it; and an indecipherable passage in the long-lost journal may tell us what to do about this. That's what we have, so that's where we start."

CHAPTER

41

Later, in her room, Cloe tossed and turned: sleep eluded her. Her mind was going in a hundred directions still trying to answer the old curator's question. *Where do we start?* It was a three-legged stool. One leg consisted of the terrible signs and events in the world and the pope's assertion of evil itself being among them. *Could this be true? What is evil?* Some said it was the absence of good. Recently, she had heard a learned priest say it was the opposite of good. She had pondered the distinction but had reached no conclusions. Still ...

The phone rang with a terrible jangling sound, slapping her awake. Cloe glanced at the window as she reached for the phone on the bedside table. The soft, low glow of early morning came through the curtained glass. At least she hadn't overslept.

"Hello," she said.

"Hi, Mom," said J.E. "I'm sorry to wake you so early, but the overnight intelligence is not good. The pope has asked us to meet in his conference room in forty minutes."

* * *

The heady aroma of rich coffee enveloped her like a pleasant veil. The nuns had also laid out handmade pastries on a serving piece adjacent to the table.

"Please," said the pope. "Have some breakfast and hot coffee."

Cloe helped herself. J.E., the monsignor, and Father Curator were already there and seated around the table. She was just sitting down as

Father Anton entered, bustling with a number of papers and reports in his hands. He laid his burden down and quickly grabbed a cup of coffee.

The pope blessed the meal and paused for a moment of silent prayer. He then looked at Father Anton and said, "Father, what do you have for us?"

"The Opts Center has been processing reports from all over the world. As you know, we still have contacts in numerous places, and we remain connected to the intelligence resources of many countries."

"Yes?" responded the pope.

"The news is very bad, Holiness," Tony began. "You are aware of the riots in most major cities. Many governments have fallen. Mob rule has replaced most of them. Industries have shut down. There are no jobs and no money. There are terrible food shortages, and where civilian authority has broken down there is a scarcity of clean water, heat, and other essentials. Countless hundreds of thousands have died or have been killed. Bodies litter many cities."

"My God!" cried the pope.

"Tony, is there more?" asked the monsignor.

"Unfortunately, there is more," he replied. "Plague has broken out on several continents and is being fanned by the unsanitary conditions and the widespread famine."

"Plague?" asked Cloe. "What kind of plague? I thought most of the really aggressive bugs had been eliminated."

"True, but there are facilities in several countries where even the worst bacteria and viruses have been stored for study or for military purposes," said Father Anton. "A number of these facilities have been overrun and sacked in India, Russia, and in several other countries."

"Oh no!" said J.E. "The people looting those places will make perfect hosts to carry the diseases into the general population."

"Exactly," said Father Anton. "That's just what is happening. In India, thousands have a bacterial plague that is defying exact identification and is resistant to available antibiotics. The same is true in Russia, except it seems to be a type of flu similar to that Spanish flu strain that killed millions in the last century."

"Experts believe fifty to one hundred million people may have died in the flu pandemic near the time of World War I; in fact, war conditions may have contributed to the death toll," said Cloe. "If we are talking about independent plagues on several continents, fueled by terrible hygienic conditions and shortages of food and medicines, the deaths could be in the millions—maybe much higher."

"The very existence of the human race may be at risk," said the pope. "We must act. Father Anton, what else do you have?"

"The United States sits on the sidelines," said Father Anton. "Its ships and planes guard its shores, but, in spite of many pleas, it has not reached out to help. The US must add its wealth and great industrial might to the international resources available to address the plagues. We believe that if medicines could be designed, the US and others could manufacture enough to eventually stop the diseases."

"Cloe, do you have any insight on what is happening in your country?" asked the monsignor. "We have never known the United States not to help in times of disaster."

"Albert, it's a product of decisions we have made over the last few years," replied Cloe. "Some say we have kicked the can down the road instead of making hard decisions. We have moved away from the can-do attitude of the last century and have turned inward in a narcissistic, selfish way trying to equal outcomes for all, squandering entrepreneurism and energy. The leadership at the highest levels has championed a lawlessness that has corrupted the rule of law. Now, I'm not sure the US has the will to mount the effort that will be necessary."

No one spoke as Cloe's words sank in.

After a while, the pope cleared his throat and said, "Our Father will provide what we need to win this battle."

Father Anton's phone rang. He picked it up and listened. When he hung up, his face had a puzzled look.

"Tony, what is it? Who was that?" Cloe asked.

"It was Father Emilio," he said. "They have an answer."

"What is it?" blurted J.E.

"It's just one word—that's all," responded Father Anton. "Uruk."

CHAPTER
42

Several days had passed since the dust up at the Morning Call, but everyone had followed Zack's advice and stayed put. The old house on Esplanade was large enough that everyone was comfortable, but now cabin fever was setting in. The status quo could be maintained for only so long. Zack entered the large living room and found Mr. Leneau puffing on his pipe, reading the paper.

"Hi, Zack," said the older man. "How's the team?"

"Very restless," he replied. "No offense, Mr. Leneau, but we gotta get out of here. Everybody means well, but we've all been cooped up way too long. We have done all we can to figure out what's going on, but we don't have the answer. All we can do is wait, but the waiting for something to happen is getting to us."

"No offense taken," said Mr. Leneau. "Why don't you go down to the Port of Call for lunch? It's just down the street. It should be safe in the daytime."

"Hmmm, that's interesting. We could break up into twos and threes and not attract any attention," said Zack.

"Yes—and a burger and a beer might do you all some good," added Mr. Leneau.

By that time, the others were drifting in, and Zack proposed the outing to the nearby restaurant.

"All right," Mel said. "But I don't have anything to wear."

Mrs. Leneau had gone shopping for all of them because, after the near disaster with the dirty boys, none of them could go back to their hotels for their stuff. She had bought toiletries and jeans, sweatshirts, polos, and blouses of various types and sizes.

"Mel, the Port of Call may have the best burger in New Orleans, but it's not fancy," observed Mr. Leneau. "You'll be fine."

Thirty minutes later, the group assembled in the parlor, this time freshly showered and dressed as nicely as possible. Zack thought Mel looked extremely cute in her jeans and pink polo shirt.

"Okay, here's the plan," said Zack, refocusing his attention. "We need to break up the group for the walk over to the POC in case anyone is watching for a group of seven."

"Well, technically, we are nine including Robby's mother and Bully," said Zoe.

"Hey!" said Doris, looking up from her laptop. "What am I? Chopped liver?"

"Point taken," said Mel. "We need a table for ten."

"I got that," said Zack, "but a group of ten looks like a tour group and attracts attention. We want some couples and a single or two."

"Zoe and I will go together, if she's willing," said Rey with a smile. "After all, we live in the same general neighborhood."

"I go by myself," said Louie.

"Well, Mel, Anna, and I can go together, but that leaves Robby and his mother," observed Zack.

"And Bully," said Robby.

"All right," said Zack. "Louie, you follow behind them and keep your eyes open."

"Hey, college boy! Who made you king?" snarled Louie. "I ain't used to taking orders from nobody."

"Louie," said Mel. "You used to any of this? Zack's done a good job, and I'm for listening to his plan."

"Louie, it's not an order," said Zack. "It just makes sense. Somebody's got to keep an eye on them. You come walk with Mel and Anna, and I'll do it."

"Nah, I'm good," said Louie, looking directly at him. "And I'm hungry. We can talk later, college boy. Let's go."

"I'll go with Louie," said Doris. "We'll watch for Robby."

They decided to leave at ten-minute intervals, with Rey and Zoe going first to reconnoiter the restaurant and get a table out of the way. Thirty-five minutes later, they were all seated in a dark corner of the Port of Call. Nobody seemed to mind a hundred-pound bulldog.

Mr. Leneau had told Zack that the Port of Call had been around for fifty years or so. As Zack looked up, he saw nets on the ceiling and other memorabilia that confirmed its age.

"Gosh, this is fantastic," said Mel. "I want a burger and a beer."

That was pretty much the sentiment across the board, except Robby had a foot long, plain. Bully wolfed down a burger patty.

As the noon hour came and went, the crowd grew. At its height, the bar was jammed and the wait staff challenged, yet everything had somehow come to them in a timely manner and was wonderful.

"Zack, this is great," said Rey. "We've got to get out more."

"Well, there's a great library just a couple of blocks from here," said Zack. "Mr. Leneau told me all about it."

"Maybe, das would be a baby step we could make and still be safe," said Anna.

"Sounds good," said Zack. "It's not open to the public, but Mr. Leneau said he thought he could get us in."

"I like the idea," said Zoe. "Could we go tomorrow?"

"Maybe. I'll check with Mr. Leneau when we get back," said Zack.

"What's the name of this joint?" asked Louie.

"It's the library at the old Ursuline Convent," said Zack. "It has an amazing history, and the order of nuns that founded it were incredible women. There's also an interesting biblical research project going on there."

CHAPTER

43

"Uruk? What does that mean?" said Cloe. "I know of the ancient site, but what does it mean here?"

"It seems to be the place where the monks in the Opts Center think the cuneiform originated, "replied Father Anton.

"Well, that would fit," said the curator.

"Why? What are you saying?" asked Cloe.

"Uruk was a city in Mesopotamia four thousand years before the birth of Christ," said the curator. "It was one of the first large urban centers. Records suggest there may have been as many as eighty thousand people living in Uruk at its zenith. The legendary leader, Gilgamesh, supposedly ruled Uruk twenty-seven centuries before the birth of our Lord."

"My, my. That's a mighty old place," said J.E.

"Yes, but along with the other innovations that Uruk was known for, it had one of the earliest discovered forms of cuneiform as its basic written language. Tablets have been excavated containing this form of writing, including one listing all its kings and others thought to be legal documents," added the curator. "I thought this might be the source of our cuneiform but I was not sure."

"Does Uruk still exist?" asked J.E. "Where is it located?"

"It's in the southern part of modern Iraq, about one hundred plus miles south of Baghdad, but it no longer exists as Uruk," said the old priest.

"You know, I remember reading something on this a while back," said the monsignor. "A museum in London had an exhibit on Uruk. The city went into decline because the bed of the Euphrates River changed course, and it was abandoned over a thousand years ago. Didn't the Germans do a lot of exploration there?"

"Quite right, Albert," said the curator. "Many archeologists have worked there, but the Germans have distinguished themselves with their efforts. Indeed, German scholars have been at the center of the translation of the early writings of Uruk."

"Okay, I think I've got this," said J.E. "We need to get a translation of the cuneiform passage in a two-thousand-year-old journal conversation to figure out how to save the world. To do that, we will need to go to an ancient city in Iraq, one of the most hostile places on earth, and find a German archeologist who understands a six-thousand-year-old language. Is that about it?"

In spite of the circumstances, Cloe laughed. Soon, everyone was howling with laughter.

"J.E.," cried Cloe, coughing and trying to catch her breath, "I think you have it."

After they wiped tears from their eyes, the curator, who had been silent, spoke. "Well, that's not quite correct. We'll be looking for a German epigraphist."

"Oh my God!" Cloe exclaimed, and she and the others collapsed once again into rejuvenating laughter.

"If anyone can translate the passage in the journal, it's possible we can find him or her there," said J.E. as the laughter died out. "Right, Mom?"

"Right. We are going to Uruk," said Cloe.

P A R T
II

Evil

If the devil doesn't exist, but man has created him,
He has created him in his own image and likeness.
—*The Brothers Karamazov*, V, 4

CHAPTER
44

The Burnt Man watched Icar mount the stage that had been hastily assembled in Cairo. There were no musicians, although the atmosphere was one that would have surrounded the most celebrated rock star. The crowd stretched as far as the eye could see. *Certainly, there are over a million people out there and maybe more,* he thought. The crowd was young. Many had camped in front of the stage complex for days. The filth and dirt disgusted him, but Icar seemed to relish it. There seemed to be no level of depravity that would insult his boss.

Today was a big day for Icar.

The crowd was a living thing, rippling back and forth like a beating heart, as Icar strode to the center of the plain black stage. The night was warm, but a breeze cooled the air. While the stage itself was completely unremarkable except for its immense size, the lighting and pyrotechnic effects were world-class Hollywood. Yet there was no crew running the show. There were just the groupies who assembled the stage and then disassembled it once the event was over. In between, it was only Icar and the Burnt Man.

There was no script, and Icar used no notes. When he ascended the stage, the spotlights followed him. Usually, as tonight, he initially said nothing. The Burnt Man watched as his master walked across the nearly half-block-long stage. It was a measured walk, and it always made him look bigger somehow. He paused center stage, and the crowd undulated expectantly in a reptilian manner. He looked out, and the sea of people arose in anticipation, their murmurs lifting to the level of a buzz.

Icar absorbed the crowd's energy. Now the roar of the assembly climbed toward the sound level of a jet engine.

The Burnt Man shook his head. The boss had not even opened his mouth, yet it was always the same. The adoration was cosmic.

Icar let the exaltation wash over him while its volume increased to the intensity of a physical force. Then he bent slightly forward and hunched his shoulders in a supplicant-like position. It was almost a bow. At this, the audience went crazy, and the Burnt Man thought they might rush the stage before the man even said a word.

Just as the scene seemed it could not contain any more emotion, Icar threw his head back and straightened ramrod-tall as pyrotechnics erupted from all areas of the stage as well as from the metal superstructure overhead. Eyes were blinded by the brightness, and ears rang with the concussion of the explosions.

Then all became dark, and the crowd stopped as if it had been smacked. A thick quiet descended like a heavy veil tinged with razor-edged expectation. A single pencil-thin but impossibly bright spotlight blinked on, centering Icar in its beam. His voice rang out like thunder, and everyone could hear him as if he were standing a foot away even though there were no amps, mics, or other such devices. The Burnt Man had no idea how Icar did this.

He spoke of the world and the terrible conditions, including the plagues that had broken out. He told the youth that this was their time and they were being cheated out of it. They should have jobs, families, and above all, they should have the things they had always wanted. The only thing that kept them from all this was money. The wealthy people had stolen what was theirs. On and on the man went, leveling this charge of greed and theft by the powerful. The people there were the victims of this greed. They had been robbed of what was rightfully theirs. They were not powerless, however; they were strong in their numbers and could recover what had been lost.

At each inflection and point of emphasis in the man's oratory, the living pulse, the voice, of the crowd surged forward, but when he lamented the lost, stolen opportunity of the young people, an eerie undercurrent of white-hot anger manifested.

"Are you not in and of this world?" thundered Icar. "Have you and your families not suffered? Yet still you have been denied! Denied your rightful portion! Others have what is yours!"

The crowd was being branded with the fiery iron of insatiable anger toward the older, richer power structure. Such anger could only be satisfied by total destruction of the current order. It must all be pulled down, burned, destroyed. It would be.

His homily complete, Icar walked toward the Burnt Man as screams, howls, and applause rolled over him. When the adulation reached its zenith, Icar turned back to the assembly. He walked to the front edge of the stage. The crowd surged toward him. Screams erupted from those in front now being crushed by the tide of humanity pressing toward the stage.

As he had at so many such gatherings, he threw both arms upward and straight over his head, soaking in the energy of the people. Then he drew one hand across his throat in a cutting gesture and pointed toward the Cairo business district.

The mob roared off in the direction Icar pointed, to begin executing its newly learned lessons. Icar turned back, headed offstage, and motioned to the Burnt Man.

"I have a job for you that will suit your special needs," he said.

CHAPTER

45

They had spent several hours in the library-conference room studying the tactical problems of the mission. Uruk, at least what was left of it, was not located in the most accessible area of the world. In fact, it was extremely difficult to get to, even in the best of times. They would have Vatican diplomatic credentials, but those were no longer worth much in a world of chaos. If they were to be successful, they would need help.

"The best way is to sneak in with a relatively small group and to try to avoid anyone's attention," said J.E. "We can't hope to do that with more than six to eight people. Anything larger than that will be immediately noticed. I have spoken to our friends in Israel, and they will help us."

"I think J.E. is correct in this," said Father Anton. "That area of Iraq is very hostile and does not answer to any government. It's a mixture of Sunnis, Shia, and Al-Qaeda along with local tribal chieftains. To top that off, the Islamic State, or ISIS, continues to make inroads there, having taken Baghdad and now moving south."

"According to the monks in the Opts Center, the Germans are still working the dig, largely because they provide cash and supplies to the locals," said the monsignor. "They are tolerated, but the situation is fluid."

"Interestingly, the person we seek is actually a German cleric, a Reverend Josef Klein," said the curator. "According to the monks, he is the principal epigraphist among the scientists. While he is the world's foremost expert on pictographs and cuneiform, he is a Calvinist—probably not too much disposed to help the Vatican."

154

Cloe looked at the old priest, took a deep breath, and said, "This might be a good time for all of us to put aside our doctrinal issues, long held though they may be, and join in the task of figuring out how to defeat the evil that has brought us to where we are. What do you think, Father?"

"Of course, you are correct," said the curator, after a moment's reflection. "All religions must join together if we are to prevail against our godless adversaries. I pray the Reverend Klein will subscribe to that notion."

* * *

A few hours later, Cloe dozed in her seat on a papal jet flying to the southeast.

The plane rocked in a patch of rough air, and she came fully awake. The pilot came on and advised everyone to buckle up due to turbulence. Cloe briefly panicked, thinking about the flight to Tunisia in search of the cave of jars a few years earlier, which ended in a crash that left them fighting for their lives.

"J.E.?" she called, looking around.

"Here, Mom," said J.E., sliding into the seat next to her. "You okay?"

"I'm all right," she replied.

J.E. gave his mother a hug and said, "We're not too far out from our destination. Another hour maybe."

"J.E., I've been thinking about what we're doing," she said. "We, a bunch of Catholics, are headed for Israel to get help from the Jews to clandestinely enter a mostly Muslim country. Is there some irony here, or is it just me?"

"The Jews are the only people in this part of the world who are able and motivated to try to help us," said J.E. "Survival is part of their national culture. We are all in survival mode right now."

The monsignor unbuckled his belt and approached, hearing part of the conversation. He fell into the aisle seat just opposite J.E. and Cloe.

"The young sir is correct. Some say the enemy of my enemy is my friend. Others say my friend's enemy is my enemy. There are other variations, but, whatever, we share a lot with the Jews, and I'm glad for their help."

As they spoke, Cloe felt the jet's telltale roll and descent. Nothing she had accomplished before could compare with what she had been tasked to do now. The pope needed answers. Events had worsened, and to help the pope on that end, the decision was made to keep Father Anton with the pope. Somehow, Cloe and the rest of her team had to find the answers.

Forty minutes later, the executive jet sat outside the general aviation depot at Ben Gurion airport in Tel Aviv. As the door to the plane opened, Cloe could hear the big Rolls engines shutting down. She looked out, and a complete squad of fully armed soldiers greeted them.

"Good evening, Dr. Lejeune," said a handsome young officer. "My name is Jacob, Captain Ariel Jacob. I'm your liaison and guide."

"Hello, Captain Jacob," said Cloe. "This is my son, Captain J.E. Lejeune, US Army, Monsignor Roques, and the father curator. We also have with us four members of the pope's personal Swiss Guard contingent."

She saw respect flash across his face. He turned to J.E. and shook his hand. "Captain, your reputation goes before you."

"Thank you, Captain Jacob," replied J.E. "What do you have for us?"

The young Israeli spun on his heels and faced the noncommissioned officer standing next to him. "Sergeant, gather their bags and possessions and bring them to the terminal."

"Sir!" said the man and relayed the orders to the waiting soldiers.

"Dr. Lejeune, if you and your party would please accompany me," said the captain.

They entered the small terminal building and proceeded to a medium-sized conference room. The wood-paneled room included a large central table and comfortable bucket chairs. There, they were offered hot coffee and food.

"Please refresh yourselves," said the gallant young captain. "We have much to do, and you will need your strength."

Cloe had slept for most of the flight; she was famished. Everyone was hungry, and they all filled plates and sat at the table.

Cloe looked out the window as she ate spicy lamb, fresh vegetables, and flatbread. A number of sentries placed at strategic intervals protected the outside perimeter.

Captain Jacob walked to the head of the table and secured a map on the large display board so all could see. It was a map of the area from Iraq to Israel.

"Here's the situation. We are here," said Captain Jacob, pointing to the tiny area of the map that formed the Jewish homeland. "You want to go to southern Iraq about here." He indicated an open area south and west of the Euphrates River.

"You will note that Syria and Jordan lie between us and your destination. The fighting in Syria continues to be an extremely bloody civil war with the Islamic State now controlling large parts of the country. Assad is only marginally in charge, but his aircraft and air defense systems are first-class Russian products. To stray into Syrian airspace would be to invite disaster."

"But why fly at all?" asked J.E. "Surely we'd be better going overland?"

"Possibly, we could do that, but it's between six and seven hundred miles from here to there, and it's some of the roughest territory in the Middle East," said the young officer. "There's a much greater chance of discovery as well."

"Okay, so it looks like we don't drive," said J.E. "Unless you have something I don't know about, there isn't a helicopter with the range to get us there and back. I don't expect we'll find fuel on our trip. We have civilians with us, so parachuting in is not an option even if there were a viable way to get us back. Is there a landing strip nearby?"

"There's only a dirt strip for small aircraft," said Captain Jacob. "You are correct on the tactical side as to the equipment, but we have on occasion been able to borrow an Osprey from your navy."

"Of course! An Osprey, it's just what we need!" exclaimed J.E.

"What's an Osprey?" asked Cloe.

"It's a troop/cargo carrier with vertical takeoff and landing capabilities," responded J.E. "It can fly at twice the speed of most helicopters and has extended range that should get us there and back."

"Right. It can land and take off like a helicopter, but it flies like a conventional airplane," added the young Israeli.

Cloe smiled as she watched the two young officers discuss the operational capabilities of the aircraft.

"All right, that's it then," she said. "We have a ride. When do we go?"

CHAPTER

46

Huddled in the foyer of the Ursuline Convent, Zack, his colleagues, plus Doris and Bully stood in front of the staircase to the library. It was roped off, and there was a sign that said No Admittance.

"According to the history in the guide book, it's the oldest building in the Mississippi Valley, having been constructed in about 1750," said Mel. "Listen to this … when the French Quarter of New Orleans burned in 1788, the old convent was one of the few buildings spared."

"Wow, that's amazing," said Zack. "We hear a lot about the Great Chicago Fire but not much about the one in New Orleans."

"Here's something more astounding," said Mel. "'When the Ursuline sisters came to New Orleans from France, they brought a large, life-sized statue of Mary. When they left the convent as the fire advanced through the city, they took with them what they could. One thing they left at the convent was a small tabletop version of the statue of Mary they called Sweetie. They left her facing the south where the approaching fire was burning out of control.'"

"Well, what happened?" asked Louie impatiently.

"Funny thing …" said Mel, continuing to read from the book. "When the conflagration was down the street from the convent, a storm of unprecedented fury came raining down torrents of water. The fire was finally put out just across the last street separating it from the convent. Eight hundred and fifty out of eleven hundred structures in New Orleans were destroyed in the fire."

"Now that's a story," said Rey. "I've got to see this place."

"Hmmm," said Mel. "Here's something."

"What is it?" asked Doris.

"Well, it seems a good portion of the library is taken up by a special research project," replied Mel.

"What's the research project?" asked Zoe.

"It's not real clear," said Mel, remembering her computer search. "Something about a trove of ancient jars being discovered in the Middle East and ending up at the Ursuline library."

"Well, that is special," said Rey. "But there's nothing in the guidebook about that."

"There wouldn't be. When I checked last night, it had just gone up on the website, and that section of the library is not open to the public," said Mel. "Supposedly the jars date from the first century."

Zack looked around the little group. He smiled at his odd collection of new friends. He was certainly a long way from Iowa.

"Hey, it's a library," said Louie. "Get over it. It's bound to have some strange stuff. Anyway, who cares if it's open to the public? We're on a mission from God—right?"

"I got that, Louie," said Mel. "But here's something from an underground blog that says one of the research areas involves fragments from a diary or journal thing that may contain a message from Christ about the end of times."

"Who posted that?" asked Zack.

"Don't know," said Mel. "Someone with the name 'end of times.'"

"How can we believe anything like that?" asked Zack.

"Maybe we can't, but whoever he is seems to have pretty good inside information," replied Mel. "The detail is impressive."

"The end of times? You mean like when up is down and down is up and everyone is going crazy?" quipped Rey.

"Right," said Zoe. "I'm involved in a Bible study group, and we have read a good deal on this. It's when plague, violence, and evil seem ready to overrun the world, when the Vatican has been sacked and the religious worldwide are being hunted and persecuted."

"My God!" said Zack. "Are you saying this is the end?"

"I'm not saying anything," said Zoe. "It's funny, though; we are in unprecedented times that bear some resemblance to the end-of-times forecast in the book of Revelation. Lo and behold, we happen to be on a field trip to a place where they are studying a text in which Christ might have provided guidance on the very subject."

"If you roll that up with how we all got here, I say you have a four-alarmer going on," said Louie sardonically.

"What do we know?" asked Zack.

"Niche much," said Anna.

"We know we are all here in New Orleans for a purpose, but we don't yet know the purpose," said Zack. "We know someone wants to stop us, so what we have to do must be important to somebody."

Anna doubled down and said, "I believe I received my card from an angel—from God. I believe each of you did as well."

"Maybe you got it from the devil," said Louie. "The big meathead who gave me my card looked more like a demon than an angel."

"Oh, Louie, you can't mean that," said Zoe with a look of gentle admonishment.

Louie looked at her, softened, and said, "Maybe not, but who knows for sure?"

"I think if you look at Robby, you'll see the face of God for sure," said Mel. "No, we are sent for good."

"But what about that hound?" asked Louie. "The devil is known to work through animals—what do they call them? Familiars?"

"I think you're mixing up your mythology," observed Zack. "Familiars, usually cats, were mainly thought to be the sidekicks of witches. Bully fought with the rest of us at Morning Call."

"You're right—he did," responded Louie reluctantly. "I felt the energy. It felt good."

"Mel, when you did your computer research last night, did you come up with the name of the lead scientist on the project? Maybe we can go up and talk to her or him," said Zack.

"Uh, it's a woman, an ancient languages expert from the University of Washington at Seattle," said Mel. "She's attached to LSU now, which is underwriting her research."

"What's her name?" asked Zack.

"Dr. Clotile Lejeune," said Mel as she jumped the velvet rope and headed up the ancient staircase.

CHAPTER
47

The Osprey was as advertised—quick and spacious. It easily accommodated all of Cloe's group plus the young Israeli captain, five of his men, and all their gear. They first flew south-southeast across Jordan and then along the border of Saudi Arabia and Iraq. The pilot had said this would be the safest route. Even so, they flew at about two to three hundred feet above the ground once out of the mountains. It was nerve-racking at first to watch the blacks and browns of the desert rush by at such a low altitude.

"I don't see how the pilots can fly this low and this fast," said Cloe to J.E., who sat next to her. "One small mistake would be fatal for all of us."

"I talked to the pilot about that before we took off," responded J.E. "The plane is equipped with a special guidance system that does this automatically."

"You mean no real person is flying the plane?" questioned Cloe. "Some robot has my life in its metallic hands?"

"Yep, and good hands they are," responded J.E., laughing. "Far more accurate than humans. Plus, they don't get tired."

"All right. I guess it is what it is," said Cloe. "What time do we get in?"

"I just checked with the pilots," said the monsignor, flopping down on the seat across the aisle from them. "He says we are on time and will be at Uruk in about an hour, maybe less."

"What's our plan once we get to Uruk?" asked the curator. "By all accounts, it's a pretty big place."

"Right, but from aerial photos, we know about where the dig is located. We'll then need to seek out Reverend Klein," said Cloe.

Cloe felt the vibrations as the big Rolls engines increased the air speed of the plane.

"What's going on?" she asked.

"I don't know," said J.E.

Just then, the Israeli captain yelled to them from the flight deck. "Buckle in ... tight! We have a problem."

"What is it?" asked J.E.

"We are about to get some attention from the Syrians," said the young officer. "Specifically, we have inbound Syrian jets."

"How could they find us at this altitude?" asked Cloe.

"Possibly there is a traitor somewhere along the line." Captain Jacob grimaced. "But more likely we have been detected on Russian look-down radar."

"I've heard of look-down radar, but I thought the US was the only country with this technology," said J.E.

"No, Russia and the Chinese each have this capability," said the Israeli.

"What is it, and what does it do?" asked the monsignor.

"It's positioned in an airplane that flies high, and the radar looks down, much like sonar does on the water," said Jacob. "It can spot moving objects even though they would be blind to conventional radar because of the arc of the earth.

"It has a sophisticated computer that can be very effective in locating objects that regular radar can't see. Turns out the Russians are operating one for the Syrians."

"Okay, things are going to get hot. How long do we have?" asked J.E.

"At most, twenty minutes," said Captain Jacob. "Tel Aviv reports the long-range jets are launched from south of Damascus, and given our speed and their much greater speed, they can be on us about then."

"What's our armament? Can we win a fight?" asked the monsignor.

"We have a fifty-caliber machine gun mounted on the lift gate," the officer responded. "It can be operated only when the gate is down. We have a pod of missiles and an electronic belly Gatling gun."

"Yes!" said J.E. "This baby is really well equipped."

"Most don't have that kind of ordnance," responded Jacob. "But this plane is special. Still we have no hope against four Russian state-of-the-art fighters, even with Syrian pilots. They will chop us up and spit us out."

"Well, that's very interesting, boys," said Cloe. "We're trapped in a machine that can neither outfight nor outrun the enemy. We are a bright, moving target—a bull's-eye on their look-down radar. Is that about it?"

"Simply put, that's about it," said Jacob.

"Can we expect help from Israeli or US fighters?" asked the curator.

"We are too far for the Israeli jets with planning, logistics, and refueling tankers in place," said the Israeli officer. "The US has removed its assets and has nothing in theater that could help us."

"If this plane can't outrun and can't outfight the Syrians, maybe it can hide."

"What? What do you mean?" asked Jacob.

"I mean ... land the damn plane!" asserted Cloe.

CHAPTER
48

Ten minutes later, they were on the ground. They had landed in the flat, sandy bottom of a valley between two ridges of hills, about five to seven hundred feet in height.

"Shut down the engines. Get everything as dark and cold as possible," said J.E. "We need to be invisible."

"J.E., you and the captain said the look-down radar relies on movement to spot its prey," said Cloe. "If we are still and quiet, they may not see us."

"I think that may be right—at least until daylight," responded J.E.

"If we survive the night, we can worry about the light," said the monsignor. "Right now, all lights out … everyone quiet."

The tailgate was lowered, and Cloe and the others ran for the sand mountain nearest them in case the plane was bombed. They took refuge in the lee of one of the huge sand berms forming one wall of the little valley.

"We shouldn't have long to wait," whispered the Israeli.

Just then, four shadows, ink against the black night, flashed overhead from the north, headed south. The jets screamed like eagles in search of their morning meal. They were briefly visible against the faint starlight and then gone.

"Well, they missed us," said the father curator.

"Maybe, or maybe they just overran us," responded the monsignor. "Let's stay quiet and hunkered down for a while."

Sure enough, as Cloe scanned the obsidian southern sky, a few minutes later the sound of multiple jet engines once again hit them. This time, they had the low guttural noise of a prowling reptilian predator on the scent of its quarry. Cloe shivered and thought this sound was even more frightening than the previous flat-out roar.

"They'll use everything they have to find us," said J.E. "Everyone, stay down, still, and quiet—no matter what."

As Cloe stared transfixed, the jets, mere points of dark on the night sky, silhouetted against the stars, began to crisscross the area. At intervals, they would randomly drop flares and fire machine-gun rounds, attempting to spur some response.

"They can't stay on station long," said the monsignor. "At some point, they will need fuel and will have to leave."

"That's unless the Russians have a tanker up there to refuel the fighters," said J.E. "If that's the case, they can stay with us indefinitely."

"Pray they do not," said the monsignor.

After a few minutes, the fighters formed up and headed north at flank speed. Cloe heard the eagle screech as the afterburners of the jets kicked in and then listened as they faded away. Was it her imagination, or was there disappointment in that sound?

"Okay ... they're gone," said J.E. "We have no time to lose. They will be back, and at daylight ground forces will be searching for us."

"J.E.'s right," said the monsignor. "The fighters will return, and this time they will have the logistical support to stay here until we are found."

"What's our timeline?" asked Cloe.

"I'd say two hours," said the Israeli. "That includes landing, rearmament, and changing of pilots. Two and a half hours max."

"Agreed," said J.E. "We need ground transport. Let's go see what's on the Osprey."

They spent thirty minutes inventorying the aircraft in the soft glow of its red, low-light system.

"We have a camo net," said J.E. "Captain Jacobs, can you detail your men to lay out the camouflage and cover the Osprey?"

"Certainly, Captain," said the Israeli, directing his men to use the huge net to hide the plane.

Cloe watched as the soldiers drew the net over the aircraft. It was a dark shadow against the desert. The camo was designed to work in the daylight—but that was not too far off.

"Well, I gotta think it's going to be tough to spot this plane from the air," said Cloe.

"Quite right," said the monsignor. "We also have a solution to the transportation problem."

"What? You found a personnel carrier in the belly of the Osprey?" asked Cloe, smiling.

"No, but we did find a couple of crates of light motorcycles and plenty of gas," responded the monsignor.

A few minutes later, the group had moved back onto the cargo deck of the airplane to pull together the supplies they needed and to assemble the motorbikes. They had agreed most of the Israelis would stay to see to the plane, but Captain Jacob would accompany them because of the need for as much local knowledge as possible. Cloe wanted the father curator to stay with the airplane because of his age. He would not hear of it, and she had to admit they might need his skills in talking with the Germans about the translation, if they could be found. The Israeli captain pulled a map of the area from his map case and carefully studied it.

"Here's about where we are," he said, pointing to a valley formed by sand covering two ridge backs. "Here's where we believe the Uruk excavation can be found. We are about sixty-five kilometers away."

"About fifty miles," J.E. clarified. "We are close. With the motorbikes and no trouble, we can easily be there later today."

"What kind of opposition can we expect in this area?" asked J.E.

"There will be random ground patrols," said Captain Jacobs. "We would have to be unlucky to be discovered by one of them. However, as the Syrian jets report back, this will launch a more organized land search for us. I expect the jets will be back, but so will helicopters from nearby bases. We must be very quick."

Cloe looked to the east and saw the first faint streaks of what would soon be daybreak. She had not slept much, but she felt strangely invigorated.

"Well, gentlemen, what say you?" She smiled.

J.E. looked at his mother, shook his head slowly, and in a perfect deadpan imitation of the famous cowboy actor, John Wayne, he said, "Well, pilgrims, saddle up; we're burning daylight."

CHAPTER

49

At the top of the stairs in the old library, Zack and his friends looked up and down and saw only shelves of books and papers as far as the eye could see. The musty smell of aged documents was strong. *It must go the length of the whole block,* thought Zack.

"Which way?" asked Mel.

Zack listened and heard faint noises from the far end of the library.

"That way," he said.

They walked toward the sounds and soon encountered a small woman with a group of young people who could only have been interns or students.

As they entered the work area, the woman in charge said, "Hello, what are you doing here? This area is closed."

Zack looked around and said, "We're looking for Dr. Lejeune. Are you Dr. Lejeune?"

"Certainly not!" said the woman, a compact brunette with an all-business attitude. "I'm Dr. Jeanne Richard, Dr. Lejeune's assistant."

"We need to talk to Dr. Lejeune," said Mel. "It's extremely important."

"I'm afraid that's impossible," said Dr. Richard. "Dr. Lejeune is unavailable."

"Well, I think she will want to talk to us," said Zack. "We understand she's working on the translation of the journal. We may have information that would bear on that."

"Hmmm, you have information that might involve the journal?" asked Dr. Richard.

"Well, maybe," fudged Zack. "She'll want to talk to us."

"What information is this?" asked the woman. "I'm Dr. Lejeune's confidential assistant. Generally, what she knows, I know. I'll be happy to listen and relay what you say to the doctor."

"We can reveal what we know only to Dr. Lejeune," said Mel.

"Are you sure?" asked the assistant. "We can find a place here in the library that will be completely private."

"Right now we need to see Dr. Lejeune," said Zack.

"Well then, it's quite out of the question," said Dr. Richard. "Dr. Lejeune is not here. The last we heard, she was in Italy with the pope."

"With the pope?" echoed Zack, now sure they were on the right track. "It's urgent we speak to her."

Mel had wandered over to a little television that was playing in the background. She leaned over and looked closely at the picture. Her mouth fell open in shock.

"Oh my God!" she cried, turning to Zack and the rest.

"What is it?" pressed Zack.

"They are fighting in Washington, DC," she replied.

"Who?" asked Zoe.

"I don't know the details, but it seems the president and his inner circle are under siege by forces loyal to Congress," said Mel.

"But the president is head of all US military forces," observed Zack. "Who could be fighting against them?"

"It's hard to say, but from what I can get, it's a number of state militias and their congressional leaders," said Mel. "They say the president has gone too far, has become too despotic, and has not only put the United States at risk but the whole world."

"But that will mean civil war," said Zack. "What will the army do? Will they fight?"

"I'm not sure," said Mel. "But we must talk to Dr. Lejeune and soon."

CHAPTER
50

The map coordinates were programmed into a portable GPS unit, and they were on their way to Uruk. J.E. led the way, he and the Israeli captain each on his own bike. The rest followed, most with two riders. Cloe and the father curator rode together. Everyone who could use a weapon was heavily armed—everyone but the father curator. Cloe was scared but strangely excited. Finally, they were headed toward some answers.

"Close up," J.E. yelled to a couple of stragglers.

The decision had been made to head straight for Uruk. Stealth would only slow them down, and it was certain that the Iraqis knew they were here by this time. Because the bikes were designed for desert travel, they did not have to stick to roads, and they went swiftly as the crow flies. They needed to get to Uruk before the Iraqis, ISIS, or the local tribesmen could find them.

Two hours after sunrise, they pulled up on a knoll overlooking a dried-up riverbed. The GPS said they had reached their destination.

"I don't see much," said the curator, studying the broad expanse below them.

"That's not unusual," replied Cloe, observing the beauty of the red, brown, and sand colors that formed the ancient, barren bed of the Euphrates River. "A lot of what's left of Uruk would be covered by sand and sediment after all these thousands of years."

J.E. scrutinized the riverbed with his binoculars. "There, I see some tents and equipment on the southern edge."

Cloe and the Israeli captain had a look and handed the glasses to the monsignor.

"That's got to be our target," said the monsignor. "How do we want to approach this?"

"I didn't see any armed guards," said J.E. "Best we ease on into the camp and try to make contact with the scientists. I suggest we leave the motorcycles and most of our weapons here. We'll be less threatening that way."

"Agreed," said Captain Jacob, "but we'll leave the Swiss here to cover our retreat if we need to get out fast. They'll also watch our backs in case we have visitors."

Cloe, J.E., the monsignor, the Israeli, and the curator walked down the long sweeping face of what might, at one time thousands of years ago, have been the natural western bank of the Euphrates River. Cloe was astounded at being in the cradle of civilization.

Crossing over the dry, hard-packed riverbed, Cloe could now see more details of the dig. There were the usual stone-and-mud brick walls of houses and storages facilities but without their roofs of wood. The latter had surely long since deteriorated, much as they had at Masada. However, the most amazing artifact confronting them was a piece of what was obviously a wall. As they approached, Cloe looked up and saw it towered forty to fifty feet over them. Portions of it looked like it had been overlaid with tiles or something similar, all forming a pattern. She could see the rough outline of what might have been the earliest version of wall art.

"Imposing, isn't it," said a man standing in the black shadow of the huge wall. He had an accent but spoke excellent English.

Cloe and the others turned quickly in the direction of the voice.

"Hello?" said Cloe.

"Hello," said the voice from the shadow of the wall.

The figure stepped into the sunlight. He was dressed in khaki shorts, a military-style jacket, and a white T-shirt. A pistol was strapped to his hip. His hat had a broad brim with a headband of sweat.

The man strode to the center of the group and stopped. He looked at each of them and then extended his hand to Cloe.

"Madam, you must be the group about which we have heard so much this morning on the radio," said the stranger. "Something about flying into the country under the radar and being sought by every patriotic Iraqi. The gentlemen of the Islamic State are also looking for you."

Cloe smiled, and everyone relaxed a bit. She thought he was probably Scottish but certainly a Brit of some sort.

"*Woof, woof,*" cried a dog that came running up behind the stranger.

"Let me introduce myself," he said. "I'm Miles Welch, a member of the dig team. And this humble canine is my faithful friend Boogie."

Cloe knelt down and scratched Boogie's ears. As soon as Cloe began the doggie massage, Boogie did a one-eighty and rolled over on his back so he could receive a proper belly scratch.

When she stopped, Boogie rolled to his feet and looked at Cloe with an expression of unadorned love.

"Well, it looks like you have a friend," said Miles. "Two friends. How can I help you?"

"We are looking for Reverend Klein," said Cloe. "We have business with him."

"Oh, you mean Tommy," said Miles. "He's in the main dig tent."

"Tommy?" asked the monsignor. "I thought his name was Josef Klein."

"Oh, sure, sure," replied Miles as they turned toward the tents. "The Very Reverend Josef Thomas Klein. We've been out here so long we just call him Tommy."

Just then the group stood at alert as they heard helicopters in the distance. The sound increased until it became a roar. Cloe saw that the helicopters would pass over the camp.

"Come with me, quickly," said Miles. "If they fly over us, wave and smile."

They struck off toward the largest of the tents, and sure enough, the helicopters flew right toward them.

"Wave and smile," said their host. "It's the Iraqi military probably looking for you."

They did so, and Cloe could feel the Iraqi birds eyeing them like flying predators from an ancient time.

The helicopters began to settle as if to land. Dust and sand began to blow in all directions.

"Don't lose your nerve!" cried Miles. "Hold, hold."

Strangely, in the midst of landing, Cloe heard the jet turbine engines on the helicopters wind up, and they flared off to the west.

"Whew! Thank God!" yelled the old curator as the enemy flew off.

"It's an old trick the Iraqis use," said Miles. "They fly in and study you closely. Then they make to land to see if you run. Looks like we passed the test."

Cloe looked off to the west as the threat retreated at flank speed. "Thank God indeed," she said to herself.

As they approached the main tent, a stream of shouts and what Cloe took to be German curses erupted from inside.

"Hmmm, that's Tommy," said Miles, with a sardonic smile. "He can be temperamental."

As Miles swept the flap of the large tent back to allow them to walk in, Cloe saw a barrel-chested man of medium build berating two associates in German. His hair was completely gray, and he sported a neatly trimmed goatee. In fact, everything about him gave the appearance of neatness. He was dressed in perfectly pressed khakis and clean desert boots. He had a large cross around his neck.

As they entered, he turned. "Vas ist das?" he asked.

"Good morning, Tommy," said Miles in a good-natured way. "We have guests."

Cloe strode to the center of the tent and extended her hand, "*Guten morgen*, Herr Reverend," she said, as the others followed. "We have come a very long way to find you."

"Guten morgen," came the guarded reply from the German.

"My name is Clotile Lejeune," said Cloe. "My colleagues are my son, J.E., Monsignor Roques, Captain Jacob, and the father curator. We need your help."

Reverend Klein took in each of them in order. Cloe felt as if his stare would peel off her skin. The man's intensity was almost tactile.

After a moment, he turned away from them and over his shoulder said in very good English, "Go away, I'm busy."

CHAPTER
51

The Burnt Man felt especially hideous as he awaited instructions from his boss. He studied his reflection in the windows of the high-rise tower in Dubai. Once again he cried out silently to all the gods that might be to curse the doctor and her bastard offspring. They did this to him. They would be repaid in spades.

Icar had said he had a task that would fit the Burnt Man's special skills. He longed to hear what his leader had in mind. He needed action. He needed to inflict pain both on himself and on others. This was one reason why he served Icar.

Movement caught the corner of his eye, and Icar appeared. Once again he was not sure whether the man had entered the high-rise suite or had simply appeared there. One thing the Burnt Man had learned was to trust his instincts. He had long suspected that his boss was special, and he believed this now more than ever.

The man was dressed, as always, completely in black, from his glistening loafers to his black tie on his black shirt. His jet-black hair was swept back into a small clutch at the back of his head. Icar walked to him and looked into his hideous face, seemingly absorbing his ugliness. The man was not repulsed but looked at him with love. For a moment, the Burnt Man felt normal, attractive. He would trade his soul for these moments.

"You must go to Rome," said the man. "There is one who defies me yet."

"Yes," he acquiesced. He knew Icar had spies in many places.

"I want you to bring all the resources you need," the dark figure added. "The strength of this one is great. He upholds the many, so they also defy me."

"What would you have me do?" he asked, although he already knew the answer.

As always, Icar laid hands on him, on his ruined face. His delicate fingers traced the scars and took the pain away for a moment.

"Take what you need; you know what I want," he said.

CHAPTER

52

"Busy?" said Cloe, her voice rising. "You're too busy to talk to us?"

Reverend Klein turned back to her and crossed his arms over his chest.

"We've come thousands of miles over brutal terrain and through even more hostile countries, looking for you," she said. "We have been sent by Pope Francis on a mission of extraordinary importance. And you ... you're too busy to even talk to us?"

"Papists. I might have known," said Reverend Klein through clenched teeth. "I don't think there is anything you could possibly say that would interest me."

"Oh really," responded Cloe as the others looked on. "What I have in this bag is more important than all your years working on this dig and anything you might find here."

"Impossible!" shouted the reverend, now both angry and interested in spite of himself. "We have made enormous discoveries and have opened the way for many more if the local fools around here don't all kill each other and us with them."

"How do you know it's impossible?" asked the monsignor calmly.

Cloe watched the reverend struggle. He might be proud and arrogant, but he was, in the final measure, a scientist.

After a moment, the reverend's posture eased a bit, and he said, "Perhaps I was a bit hasty. Let's start over."

He began by introducing his inner circle, and Cloe went around her group, giving names and a word or two on background.

"Ah, Father Curator," he said. "Word of your work with the Vatican archives goes before you. One day I would have you show me around the library."

The curator hung his head for a second and then, looking up, said, "Alas, I fear the library is gone, destroyed by the mob in this trouble."

"Oh no!" cried the reverend with genuine anguish. "Papist or not, that was one of the world's great treasures. I had always hoped to look at some of your old scrolls and maps."

"Maybe we can help, Rev," said J.E., smiling. "We've got a two-thousand-year-old mystery that you might be able to solve."

"J.E.'s right, Reverend Klein," said Cloe, quickly filling everyone in on the origins of the journal and the conversation between Jesus and St. John.

"*Mein Gott!*" whispered the German, lapsing back into his native tongue. "A journal of Jesus's public ministry? By one of the apostles? Can it be so? I must see it."

"Where can we go to show you what we have?" asked Cloe.

He led them to a huge plywood table situated on two sawhorses in the back of the tent.

"Here," he said, sweeping everything off the rough table.

Cloe opened the bag and withdrew the laptop. She booted it up and went to the section of the journal that had confounded them. The cuneiform text came up on the monitor.

For once the loquacious German was speechless. He approached the monitor and traced the strange shapes with his fingers.

"Yes," was all he said.

"Do you know it?" asked the monsignor.

"I know of it," said Reverend Klein. "It's very close to some of the ancient texts we have uncovered here. Close but not quite the same. It may actually be even older than anything we have discovered."

"Can you translate it?" asked Cloe.

"Perhaps," said the German. "I will have to study it."

"Reverend, I hate to tell you, but we have no time for study," exclaimed J.E. "Unless I'm mistaken, that sound is the sound of helicopters in the distance. We need your best guess, and we need it now."

Reverend Tommy Klein looked around and then made to listen. The sound of the rotors was unmistakable. The Iraqis were back.

"You must go," said the reverend. "This time they will land, and they will search everything. If you are here, they will imprison you, and they will kill us. Please, go!"

"Reverend, we may all die, but we cannot go without some idea as to what this says," yelled Cloe. "The fate of the world may depend on it."

As the noise of the distant helicopters came ever closer, the reverend peered at the computer screen. He doodled a bit on the wooden table.

Finally, he looked up and said, "Seven! It's repeated several times in the passage. Seven!"

"Seven?" said Cloe in the gathering stridency of the oncoming helicopters. "What can it mean?"

"I can't say, but if you want 'quick and dirty' as you Americans say, the word is *seven*," said the Reverend. "Seven—and the word seal or seals. I don't know which without spending more time. Sounds like something from Revelation. There is more, but that is all I can get from the translation now."

The war birds sounded like they were circling the dig now, looking for the best place to land. Cloe shut down the computer and threw it in her bag.

"Reverend, we hope to see you again soon," she said as they gathered near the rear of the tent. "Thanks so much. Be safe."

"Not so much as I hope to see you and your journal again," rejoined the German, smiling. "I'm sorry we got off on the wrong foot."

"Thanks, Rev," shouted J.E., as he and the others ducked under the back flap of the tent and ran for the shade of the great wall.

They huddled in the late morning shadow as the two helicopters came in for a landing. The rotor blades stirred sand and dust as they settled in. As the turbines slowed, a group of soldiers from each bird jumped out. One formed up around an officer while another deployed to protect their position.

The officer and his detachment headed toward the main tent. The other group began a casual search of the surrounding area.

"We have to go," whispered J.E. "Mom, you, Father Curator, and the monsignor run for the place where we left the Swiss and the motorbikes. Captain Jacob and I will cover you, if necessary."

Cloe looked at her son and said, "J.E., I love you."

She jumped up and ran for the hillside across the open riverbed. Cloe could feel her calves burning as she dug into the loose sand. The monsignor was beside her, and the curator was only a step or two behind.

A shot rang out, and the curator went down. Soldiers began to yell, and more gunfire erupted. Bullets were hitting all around them as Cloe and the monsignor turned and backtracked to the curator. As they grabbed him under his arms, one on each side, Cloe heard J.E. and the Israeli open up with their sidearms. A couple of the Iraqis went down, and the rest scattered, looking for cover.

"Run, Mom!" cried J.E. "Run!"

Cloe and the monsignor sprinted across the open area as if the old priest they half-carried weighed nothing. The officer and his detachment had now focused on J.E. and Captain Jacob. They were caught in a crossfire with only their handguns against rifles and machine guns.

"J.E.!" Cloe screamed.

She heard and felt the telltale *whoosh* as a rocket-propelled grenade roared over their heads. She flashed back to Masada where she, J.E., and the monsignor had been bludgeoned by RPGs fired by the Karik's forces. It hit the nearest helicopter, and it erupted like a Roman candle, destroying the men who were in it and those who had taken cover behind it when the shooting started.

In the confusion, J.E. and the Israeli ran for their lives. More RPGs arched down from the Swiss, who had stayed behind to guard the motorbikes and their heavy weapons, destroying the second helicopter. Targeted sniper fire soon took out the remaining Iraqis and their leaders.

Cloe and the others collapsed into the camp the Swiss had set up. The Swiss, J.E., and the Israeli ran back to the German camp to make sure all the Iraqis had been incapacitated and to see if the Germans wanted to be evacuated. Cloe rolled over, grabbed a pair of binoculars, and watched the events in the camp.

Later, J.E. reported that the reverend had looked down and simply said, "J.E., you go. We'll be fine. We can't leave our dig. Whatever comes, this is our life's work. The locals survive on our cash. But they will be after you."

"But there's ISIS as well. Your money may make no difference," J.E. warned.

"We'll be okay," said Miles Welch, with a great smile on his face. "But would you please take Boogie with you? I think he's had his fill of the desert."

J.E. hesitated and thought about arguing with them. He wondered at the man who would stay in harm's way but wanted his dog evacuated. He took their resolute expressions into account, then walked over and shook hands with the reverend and his colleagues. He picked up Boogie, tucked him under his arm, and then, as he and the Israeli ran for the riverbank, J.E. looked back over his shoulder and hollered, "Good luck and God bless, Rev!"

CHAPTER

53

By the time they got back to the airplane, it was early afternoon. They had rushed back and had stopped for nothing. The fast-run, lightning strategy had worked since they did not encounter any further trouble. The curator was wounded only slightly, with a bullet slicing the bottom of his right calf. A pressure bandage and some antibiotic salve had taken care of that. The worst of it was he had taken a hard fall when he hit the dirt as the gunfire zeroed in on them. Cloe thought he was suffering from the effects of a mild concussion.

Of course, Boogie was a big hit and had readily adapted to the circumstances. Cloe wasn't generally a dog person, but the pug quickly grew on her and everyone else.

At the Osprey, they dismantled and stored the bikes that had served them so well. Everyone was anxious to return to Tel Aviv, but J.E., the captain, and the flight crew said it would be safer to leave after sunset. As they rested in the shadows of the sand dunes, they heard helicopters in the distance. Once, three of the birds flew almost directly over them, but the camo netting hid their position.

Cloe heard J.E. yelling from a distance and struggled to understand what was happening. She opened her eyes and realized she had fallen into a deep, dreamless sleep. She must have been exhausted. Boogie was curled up with the curator across from her. The sun had nearly set, and the noises she had heard were the soldiers dismantling the campsite as J.E. supervised the gathering up of the camouflage nets.

"Hey, Mom," said J.E., laughing. "We are about ready to go if you and the pug have had your beauty sleep."

As everyone boarded and strapped in, the big rotors flared out into the vertical position. The engines ramped up, and dust and sand erupted from all around the plane. The noise and tumult grew to a deafening level as the big-as-a-house piece of flying metal tried to leave the ground. Boogie howled in fear, but the old priest hugged him tightly. The Osprey shook, and just when Cloe thought it might come apart, it lifted free of terra firma. It was not a leap into space as with a jet taking off; rather, it was a slow but steady ascendency. Soon, the plane had enough altitude to begin tilting the rotors horizontally.

Once again they flew close to the earth, trying to avoid being discovered and tracked.

"J.E., why do you think we can now avoid that Russian look-down radar that located us going in?" asked Cloe.

"We are flying further south and then west to avoid as much Iraqi and Syrian territory as possible," responded J.E. "We believe the radar that found us is generally confined to Syria and parts of Iraq. As we get closer to Israel, we'll get a fighter escort home."

A short time later, Cloe noticed the monsignor and the curator, along with a number of the Swiss, were huddled up in a discussion. Boogie was paying close attention. They were listening to a portable radio. She moved toward them.

"Cloe," said the Monsignor, a stricken look in his eyes. "This is the BBC, about the only reliable news source still out there. The pope is under attack at Castel Gandolfo."

"Oh my God!" she cried. "What's happening?"

"We're not sure," said the curator, fingering the massive rosary strung around his waist. "Apparently, about two hours ago, a mob attacked the pope's quarters at Gandolfo. There has been terrible fighting. The Swiss will defend the pope to the last breath of the last man."

"Tony!" cried Cloe, with concern.

"We should be there," said the monsignor in anguish.

"Albert, have you tried Tony on the satellite phone?" she asked.

"Yes. There's interference. I can't get through."

"Keep trying!" Cloe shouted over the noise of the engines.

"Dear God," said the monsignor, listening to the broadcast. "The Swiss have been overrun, and the mob is in the building."

Cloe looked at the ashen faces of the religious. In the background of the BBC news alert, a huge explosion could be heard. Then static crackled, and a commercial came on. Something terrible had happened.

"What was it?" asked Cloe.

"I don't know," replied the monsignor, beginning to pray.

A few minutes later, the BBC announcer came back on and said that Castel Gandolfo had been completely destroyed by an enormous explosion of unknown origin. The man choked back tears and said that no one could have survived.

The monsignor rose unsteadily and walked toward the rear of the plane, head down and shoulders slumped.

Cloe had never seen her friend, the monsignor, in such pain and defeat.

"His Holiness ... gone?" asked the monsignor. "It's not possible."

The enormity of the announcement overwhelmed her. How could the pope be gone? What would become of them all?

"We don't know for sure," said J.E. "Perhaps he escaped somehow."

They listened to the broadcast until they arrived in Tel Aviv, but there was no word on survivors. They had been to the ruins of a five-thousand-year-old city and had come away with two words: "seven" and "seal." These were important clues, but the events in Rome had crushed them, and they could no longer focus.

Captain Jacob's people met the plane and made arrangements for the soldiers. Cloe and the others were taken to a conference room at the airport. A solemn group of high-ranking Israeli officials greeted them there.

"Dr. Lejeune," said the leader of the group. "Our intelligence indicates a heavily armed body of men attacked Castel Gandolfo. It was not just a mob as reported by the media."

"What?" asked the monsignor.

"There was a mob," said the officer. "But the destruction of Castel Gandolfo was caused by highly organized terrorists using heavy weapons and explosives. The mob was just the cover. The Swiss could have easily disbursed the crowd, but they were overrun and annihilated by the armed thugs."

"What of His Holiness?" asked the curator.

"Sir, I have the terrible duty to inform you that the pope is dead," said the officer reluctantly.

"Impossible!" cried the monsignor. "I cannot accept this. We need him. God would not take him now in our hour of desperation."

"Albert," said Cloe, taking his hands. "We must get hold of ourselves. Will you surrender to this evil?"

"Cloe, this amazing man has almost singlehandedly held together Christianity in the face of this unprecedented onslaught," said the monsignor, looking away, blinking back tears. "He can't be gone. What will we do?"

"Albert, we will do what Francis would have wanted us to do," said the curator. "We will carry on,"

Shaking him, Cloe said, "Will you let him down?"

The monsignor looked back at her, his tear-filled eyes now hard and cold. "No."

CHAPTER
54

They had the Vatican jet and were tempted to fly to Rome. But if the pope had been assassinated, what would they do there? The Israelis had told them the conference center was theirs as long as they needed it. They also had made arrangements for sleeping quarters until Cloe and her friends figured out what to do.

Now they were back together again, having cleaned up and slept for a few hours. Cloe poured coffee and surveyed her colleagues seated around the table. They had been through a lot together, but for the first time they were really stumped about their next move. *God, I wish Serge were here,* thought Cloe. *His big brain would find something.*

The Lejeune stubbornness in her, however, would not let her admit defeat.

"All right, what do we know?" she challenged.

The monsignor looked up from his thoughts and said, "Well, we know the world's on fire due to the rise of evil. The pope said as much. He said it is the one-thousand-year anniversary of the casting of the devil into the abyss. The evil one will be free unless we can put him back in his prison."

"We know that famine, disease, and war are galloping across the globe," said the curator. "The four horsemen have been loosed."

"My God, is that Revelation?" asked J.E. "Is that what you're saying, that this is all happening now?"

"Revelation tells one version of the end of times, although many scholars believe it was specific to the Roman Empire," said the monsignor. "Still, others argue the words of the book of Revelation have a broader, more universal meaning."

"This all ties in with the passage in the journal," said Cloe. "I believe that St. John and Jesus are telling us specifically about *how* to deal with the rise of evil."

"Right, and what we know from Uruk is that it has something to do with *seven* and *seal*," said J.E. "This is what we have to solve."

"In the early parts of Revelation, St. John talks about the seven seals, and in his vision they play a vivid role," said the curator.

"Right. The opening of each of the seals portends some new apocalypse visited on mankind," said the monsignor. "The seals are opened by the Lamb, the only person deemed worthy to view the contents of the sacred scrolls to which the seals are affixed."

"Wow, what can all that mean?" asked J.E., amazed.

"No one knows for sure, but it's an apocalyptic vision where evil arises and somehow the Lamb, Jesus Christ, rallies mankind, and evil is squashed in the end," said the monsignor. "But we know that the beast will always try again. He is not finished, only banished."

"If this is the right track, this means the beast is here. Could he be this Icar?" speculated Cloe. "The beast represented the devil, but he had a henchman ... what was his name?"

"He is sometimes called the second beast or more often the dragon," said the curator. "He was an operative for the beast, Satan, who bore the number of the beast."

"Ah, the mark, which is the name of the beast, or the number of his name," said the monsignor. "Curious phrase. But the followers of Satan are marked with the number 666."

"Well, if the seven seals opened the scrolls in Revelation that visited all kinds of disasters on mankind, what we need now is someone who can seal everything back up and throw Satan into the abyss for another thousand years," said J.E.

"Even though it's not clear that everything in the scrolls was bad, your point is well taken," responded the monsignor. "How to undo what has been done?"

"Christ must be telling us how in the journal and it has to do with seven and seal," said Cloe. "But that only seems to get us back to the beginning."

"Yes, the beginning is the alpha and the end is the omega," said the curator. "But Christ is the Alpha and the Omega. Is that a clue?"

"It gets back to J.E.'s thought—that this may the journal of Jesus Christ himself," responded Cloe.

"Imagine, the very words written by Christ himself telescoping two thousand years into the future, telling us what to do. We have only to understand the message," said the monsignor.

As they pondered the mystery, the monsignor's satellite phone rang. Cloe saw him look at the others. The phone had been silent since they had departed Castel Gandolfo. Cloe saw Albert's hand tremble slightly as he reached for the phone.

"What could it be?" asked the father curator.

"God only knows, but right now almost any news would be good news," said the monsignor.

He punched a button and said, "Hello."

CHAPTER

55

"My faithful servant, I'm well pleased with your actions and more specifically the results," said Icar, standing in the window and staring into the darkness. "You have rid me of a petty annoyance that has been a distraction. The weak rallied around him, but now he is gone. They will be lost."

"It worked out just as you planned," said the Burnt Man. "The mob arose spontaneously, which gave us the opportunity to launch the real attack. The Swiss were there, but none of the pope's inner circle was seen. How did you know he would be vulnerable?"

"I have my intelligence resources," Icar said.

The Burnt Man wondered about this. His boss seemed to have amazing, inside intel.

"You mean your spies," asserted the Burnt Man.

"Were you seen?" Icar asked, turning the question aside.

"The whole thing was likely taped or filmed," he responded. "That could not be helped. Still, there was a great deal of confusion, and we were dressed to blend in with the people."

"And you set the explosives?"

"Yes, we mined the entire place. No one could have survived when they detonated," responded the Burnt Man.

"Did you actually see his body?"

"No," he replied. "The destruction was total. The debris was too much to search. The local citizens and reporters began to converge on the site. I had to get my people out."

"Yes, of course," said Icar.

He then pivoted and walked over to him and reached out. The Burnt Man thought he was to have his scars smoothed as before, but his master seized his face with different hands, and the pain was excruciating. He screamed in agony and fell to his knees.

"Is the pope dead?" cried the man in a bestial scream.

"Yes, yes!" croaked the Burnt Man, shocked and wracked with pain. "He could not have survived."

"Indeed, I do not feel his presence," said Icar, pausing to sniff the air.

His hands changed in an instant. They released the Burnt Man and traced his scars, caressing the pain away.

"He is gone, but surely another will follow quickly," said the Burnt Man when he had recovered.

"No, the Vatican has been destroyed. Only the cardinals can appoint a successor," said the dark man. "And many of them are dead. Their traditional meeting place, the Sistine Chapel, has been destroyed. Even if they could agree on a new meeting place, the survivors will be weeks and more likely months getting there. By then it will be over."

"The Church is resilient," observed the Burnt Man. "Nothing can be taken for granted."

"True, my friend," said Icar, looking directly at him with eyes like arrows. "But for now, pray for yourself that the pope is indeed dead."

CHAPTER

56

In the conference room of the airport at Tel Aviv, the satellite phone crackled with static. The late-afternoon sun streamed through the windows.

"Albert, are you there?" came the tinny voice.

"Yes, I can hear you but just barely," said the monsignor. "Who is this?"

"Albert, it's Tony," said the voice.

The monsignor squeezed the handset, and Cloe thought tears might again bloom in his eyes. He looked at them and said, "It's Father Anton. I don't know how."

"Albert, talk to him," said Cloe. "What has happened?"

"Tony, what can you tell me?" said the monsignor into the phone. He hit the speaker button so all could hear.

"Albert, the pope is not dead," yelled the priest into the phone. "Don't believe what the news media are saying."

"Oh my God!" cried the monsignor. "His Holiness is alive!"

Cloe looked around and saw everyone had tears of joy.

"But how?" asked J.E. "How could he have survived the explosions?"

The monsignor turned back to the phone and said, "Tony, tell me how this all happened."

"The supposed mob was just the cover for a very well-orchestrated, professional attack. As soon as we realized that, we decided to evacuate the pope. When the blasts went off, we were in the underground redoubt of the monks who handle our intel."

"Yes. And then what happened?" asked the monsignor.

"The blasts were devastating, but we were a step removed," said Father Anton. "The pope was slammed against one of the stone walls and is now in a coma. But he lives."

"A coma?" said J.E. "Who leads the Church?"

"Albert, there must be some provision for continuing the governance of the Church in this situation," Cloe said. "I hate to ask a stupid question, but is there a vice pope who carries on if the pope is disabled? I can't remember any discussion about this as I was growing up."

"There is no vice pope or assistant pope. There is only the pope," said Father Anton. "Even if there were, we cannot announce the pope is in a coma because the evil one will try to finish the job. So the world, including what's left of the College of Cardinals, must think the pope is dead. It's the only way."

"I can't believe there's no provision for papal succession when the pope becomes unable to carry on," said Cloe.

"It's true," said the curator. "There is the one and only pope. Otherwise, there would be a line of succession as with kings of various empires. The possibility of succeeding to a throne has been enough to cause many pretenders to plot murder. This cannot be the case with the papacy. Once elected, there are only two ways out of the office: death or, as recently demonstrated, retirement. In either situation, only the College of Cardinals can appoint the new pope."

"Where is he?" queried the monsignor.

"I cannot say," said Tony. "He is getting the best medical care in a secret facility. For the time being, he must remain dead as far as the world is concerned. His safety depends on it."

"But who will carry on for him?" asked Cloe. "If he is supposed to be dead, will not the cardinals convene to elect a new pope?"

"Yes," said Father Anton. "The cardinals will convene. At least those who are left. Word on this will be made public soon."

"But where will they go?" asked J.E. "The Vatican has been destroyed. Their tradition has been ruined."

"I do not know," said Father Anton. "Where would be safe in these times?"

"Suppose the pope does not survive his condition?" said J.E.

"Then whomever the cardinals appoint will wear the ring of St. Peter," responded Father Anton.

"This is bizarre," said Cloe. "Everyone must be deceived as to the pope's death, including the cardinals who have to appoint his successor. Whomever they appoint—if they can get together—will have legitimacy depending on whether the pope lives or dies. This at a time when the world's Christian religions need leadership that only the pope can give."

"Albert, while you and your friends know the truth, I must impose upon you the strict duty to keep silent as this plays out and we see what is God's will as to His Holiness," said Father Anton. "You must keep this confidence no matter what."

Cloe looked at the grim faces of her companions and said, "Tony, we understand what's at stake. Still, we must act to put an end to this evil."

She relayed what they had learned at Uruk.

"Seven and seal," mused Father Anton. "I'll ask the monks to look into it. "By the way, you must have heard, the scientists at the Uruk dig were executed by ISIS agents."

"Noooo!" cried Cloe. "We only left them yesterday."

"Yes. The German press said that they were accused of plotting against the government and that they were shot at the dig site," said Father Anton. "There was no trial and no time for diplomacy. All their notes, writings, and work were burned or destroyed."

"The bastards! Those men were scientists, not spies!" said J.E.

"All those lives and lifetimes of scholarly work have been lost," decried Cloe, throwing her arms up and wringing her hands. "Is there no end to this barbarism?"

"It seems not," said the monsignor. "Tony, we're in good hands here. We haven't worn out our welcome with the Israelis yet, so we may stay for the time being and work on the clues."

"That's a good idea," said the priest on the phone. "With the destruction of both the Vatican and Gandolfo, we can't really secure you here, and I can't tell you where we are even if we could provide a safe place. I'll keep the monks focused on the project … it's the best I can do."

"Until we meet again, Tony, God's blessings on the pope and all of you," the monsignor said.

"And you," came the tinny reply just as the line went dead.

CHAPTER

57

The small group looked at one another around the table in the Israeli conference room. Some were seated, but Cloe stood at the end of the table. It was just Cloe, J.E., the monsignor, and the father curator. They also had Boogie, the sole survivor of the Uruk massacre. Boogie sat in the father curator's lap as he scratched the dog's ears. Captain Jacob had left earlier on other business, and the Israeli sentries were picketed outside. They could not go back to where they had come from, as the Vatican and Castel Gandolfo, along with much of Rome, had been destroyed. The Israelis had also said Europe was in the midst of the worst plague since the Middle Ages. There was nowhere to go.

No one had used the cuneiform from Uruk in six thousand years. The German had given them two clues off the top of his head. They might mean something or nothing. Cloe could not remember feeling so alone and so isolated and ... so useless. She looked at the team around the table and had the impression of a locker room after a losing season.

She stamped her foot and cried, "Enough! This will not do!"

"Enough what?" asked J.E.

"Enough of this down-in-the-mouth attitude," she said. "We've taken some blows, but we've been in tough places before. We'll just have to figure it out."

The monsignor smiled and said, "Amen."

"J.E., get on the computer and start working your magic," Cloe said. "Check with your intel buddies and see what's happening in the US."

"Roger that, ma'am," said her son, rising from his chair.

"Father Curator, try the sat-phone to see if the monks in the Opts Center need anything we can give them," she instructed. "Also, if we can get some of the oldest translated samples of Uruk cuneiform from them, maybe we can add something to what Dr. Klein told us. I'm going to call New Orleans to see if my staff there can help."

Twenty minutes later, Cloe felt very lucky. She reached her second-in-command in New Orleans in spite of the disturbance in global communications. The jars sent by the Sicarii were being methodically opened and carefully catalogued. There would be no real analysis of the individual manuscripts until all had been opened and accounted for. This was good progress.

The plan had been for Cloe to work on the journal, and, at some point, she and her colleagues would all converge and compare what they had learned. Everything was up in the air now, and the journal was the center of importance. Cloe told her assistant, Jeanne Richard, about what she had learned from the cuneiform passage and the trip to Uruk.

"My goodness!" said Jeanne. "Seven and seal. My first instinct is that it is reminiscent of Revelation, but otherwise it's a mystery."

"Yes," replied Cloe. "It's one we must solve and as soon as possible."

"We'll talk about it here, Dr. Lejeune, but I don't think we've seen anything from the jars we have opened that might help."

"I understand," Cloe replied. "Don't limit yourselves to the jars. If there's anything in your experience that might be brought to bear, no matter how remote, please let me know."

"Well, Dr. Lejeune, now that you mention it, a strange thing happened a couple of days ago," the scientist replied.

"Yes?"

"We were working in the far end of the second-floor library, and we looked up to find ourselves almost surrounded by strangers," said her assistant. "At first we were a little afraid, but on second glance, even though they were in a restricted area, they did not seem threatening. Their apparent leader, a young man named Zack, said he needed to talk to you."

"Zack?" asked Cloe. "Did he give a last name?"

"Yes, it was Landry," she replied. "He said he was from Des Moines, Iowa, but he had some connection to Louisiana."

"I don't think I know the name," mused Cloe. "He said he *needed* to talk to me?"

"That's right. It wasn't that he wanted to or anything social like that," she replied. "He needed to. He was very insistent."

"What of the others?" asked Cloe.

"Well, it was a real menagerie," the woman responded. "They were young and old. At least a couple of them were from other countries. Two of them did not seem to be a part of the core group. One was a large dog ... at least a hundred-pound English bulldog."

"A large dog?" laughed Cloe. "My goodness."

"All I can tell you is the dog seemed to be part of the extended group. He was well behaved, listening to everything. He and the little boy."

"A child?" asked Cloe.

"He was seven or eight years old, but his eyes seemed older," replied the woman. "His parents weren't there, but the dog appeared to be looking after him. It was all very odd."

Cloe wondered what this could all be about.

"Did this Zack say why he needed to talk to me?"

"Not specifically, but he said it had to do with your work on the journal, which he had read about on our website," she said. "He said he had information for you."

"Jeanne, this could be important. I need to know what you can remember. Tell me a little more about the relationships between them, anything you can remember. How did they behave toward each other?" asked Cloe.

"Well, there was a young woman, Doris, if I remember correctly. She was from New Orleans, and they were staying somewhere in the area," said the scientist. "The rest seemed to have no relationship to each other whatsoever. Zack said he was from Iowa, and the young woman who accompanied him was from somewhere in the Pacific. One of the islands. There was a man from the Philippines and one from New York. There were a couple of other women from other parts of the world I did not get."

"You've done a very good job remembering these things," said Cloe. "Of the people who did not appear related or local, how many were there?" She held her breath as her colleague mentally counted the visitors.

"With or without the dog?" the woman finally said.

"Without," replied Cloe.

"Seven."

CHAPTER

58

On the 160th floor of the tower overlooking the Persian Sea, Icar stood in the frame of the floor-to-ceiling window, watching, once again. It was as if he were a king observing his many subjects. Of course, the Burnt Man knew that individual people looked like mere insects from this great height. What was he always watching?

Suddenly, Icar turned and caught him staring. He smiled slightly and advanced on him. As Icar strode in his direction, the Burnt Man began to feel somehow ... assaulted. There was a strange aggression in the approach. His mouth fell open in shock, and he began to experience fear—something he had felt only a few times in his life.

"The pope lives," said Icar. His eyes, burning, fixed upon him and held him fast.

"Impossible!" he replied.

"Yet he lives," said Icar.

"How can you know this?"

"Do you seek to question me?" asked Icar. "Your existence is already forfeited because of your failure. I can make your death feel like a thousand deaths."

"Master, there's just no way he could have survived the explosions," replied the Burnt Man. "There must be some mistake."

"And yet you survived an explosion—really, two explosions," his boss reminded him.

"The explosives my team used destroyed the entire building. Somehow your intelligence is wrong."

"There is no mistake," replied Icar. "My sources are impeccable."

"But what can be his condition? He cannot be whole."

"He is in a coma. While I'm not happy that you did not kill him, I find that luck sometimes exceeds skill in result. The pope in a coma may be better than dead for my purposes."

The Burnt Man relaxed slightly, hoping that events had somehow turned in his favor.

"Master, where is he? This time my men and I will see him dead," he said.

"He has been hidden somewhere even my sources haven't been able to find … yet," said Icar. "Even so, we will let this scenario play out for a while. This will create great confusion among my enemies."

"Well, someone will simply fill in for him," suggested the Burnt Man.

Icar laughed. "There is no mechanism for that. The Catholics have certainly boxed themselves in on that. No, if the pope is incapacitated, they are dead in the water. They will be little more than mute witnesses to my final triumph."

"Are you saying this takes the Catholics off the board?" asked the Burnt Man incredulously.

"There will always be isolated resistance, but as an organized force they are finished. I have won," Icar declared.

It hurt the Burnt Man to smile, but he beamed at this news. He would reign in glory with the new order. His revenge for insults to his father and to himself would be complete.

"Master, this is wonderful news," he said.

"Yes, but there is one remaining significant threat, and I want you to go and personally deal with this one as well—terminally."

Another threat? What could possibly threaten his master now that the Catholic church was paralyzed? Still, his master had many enemies.

"What is it?" he asked humbly.

"The woman you failed to shoot in Rome has an ancient writing in her hands," said Icar. "I did not believe it could be useful until now. You will go and eliminate her. You are not to fail me this time. Luck will not again be your ally."

"I understand, Master. Whatever must be done will be done," replied the Burnt Man. "Where am I going this time?"

"New Orleans."

CHAPTER
59

"I must go to New Orleans," said Cloe.

"But why?" asked the monsignor. "The monks have just sent us some templates of ancient cuneiform that might serve as our Rosetta Stone in the further translation of the journal. They're saying the words *seven* and *seal*, translated by the German scientist at Uruk, are keys that have been very helpful."

"I know, Albert," replied Cloe. "You and the curator will have to work on this, but J.E. and I must go to New Orleans to meet with this group."

"Cloe, that group in New Orleans may be nothing," he said. "We have real leads here."

"I feel it is something," she said. "I can't say exactly why, but I have to go. It's the right thing for me to do. I have told you what my assistant told me. This might be the answer."

"Very well then. The papal jet will be ready for you tomorrow," said the monsignor reluctantly. "We'll do our best. At least take Captain Jacob with you. You don't know what you'll find in New Orleans."

* * *

The sleek Vatican jet headed east at maximum speed and ceiling. Cloe stared out at the ethereal clouds below and the streaming sunshine above. *So beautiful. How could anything be amiss in a world so utterly wondrous?* It was an illusion. Beauty masked evil in many cases.

"Did this Zack indicate how to contact him?" asked J.E., breaking into her thoughts.

"No. In fact, he said he would get back in touch with my staff in New Orleans. He said that people were after them and had tried to harm them before. He could not take a risk by disclosing their location," said Cloe.

"How will we find them then?" Captain Jacob asked. "Is New Orleans not a big city?"

Cloe smiled and said, "Yes and no. We'll find them because they want us to find them. New Orleans is a big city from a population standpoint, but the area where we are going is compact and tightly knit. We'll find them."

"Yes, that's what worries me," said J.E. "If we can find them, I would think the people who want to hurt them can do likewise."

"Right you are, J.E.," replied Cloe. "We must hurry."

* * *

The plane dropped like a stone through the midlevel cloud cover and formed up for landing parallel to the causeway spanning the great inland lake just north of New Orleans. They landed at Louis Armstrong International Airport and cleared customs without incident. Serving as appointed emissaries from the Vatican certainly helped. Cloe had to smile as she thought of Captain Jacob, a Jew, presenting his credentials as a Vatican representative. The customs agent was clearly confused, but the paperwork was all in order. They headed for the downstairs departure area to hail a cab.

As they waited for the taxi to arrive, Cloe thought of Uncle Sonny, her father's big brother. Thib and Uncle Sonny had been so different in so many ways but so alike. Now both were gone—Uncle Sonny only a year. At least J.E. and Cloe had been able to spend a few years with Uncle Sonny.

They had decided to stay at the Hotel Provincial, deep in the Quarter not far off Esplanade. The hotel was one of the many small gems in the French Quarter. It also happened to be a couple of blocks away from the Ursuline Convent where her team was working on the jars.

Cloe sat with J.E. and Captain Jacob in the tiny bar of Hotel Provincial, now deserted, tucked away opposite the registration area overlooking the street. They had considered sitting in the small courtyard but had opted for the bar. *A trip to New Orleans just to tour the interior block courtyards was well worth the effort,* she thought. Most of the public were unaware these urban oases existed, but many were amazing and unique. Ancient brick work, iron tables and chairs surrounded by tropical plants and gnarled live oaks was a common theme, but each was different, with its own history.

"I called ahead and made arrangements for my assistant on the journal project, Dr. Jeanne Richard, to meet us here to get updated," said Cloe.

At that moment, a young woman entered the bar area and headed toward them. She was a petite brunette with brown eyes.

"Hi, Dr. Cloe," she said, sitting in the open chair.

"Hey, Jeanne," said Cloe, making the introductions. "I appreciate you coming on short notice."

"Sure, Cloe. I've been anxious to talk to you anyway," replied the assistant. "We have been working on cataloging all the jars, and a couple of us have also been working on the translation. Everything is going well but for the area with the strange code. We've just never seen anything like it."

Cloe was shocked to hear her assistant was working on the journal. She was the only one who was supposed to be doing that. She wondered if her young assistant had set out to eclipse her work, a theme all too common in academia. Now she was angry with herself at having left this woman in charge without her closer supervision. As she cooled off somewhat, she was disappointed in herself for such thoughts.

"It's ancient cuneiform," said Cloe, eyeing Dr. Richard. "The Vatican curator recognized it, and we eventually traced it to the Old Testament city of Uruk."

Cloe filled her assistant in on the trip to Uruk and the German scientist's quick assessment that in the cuneiform were two recognizable words, "seven" and "seal." There was a lot omitted from this short version of the papal mission, but time was of the essence, and now she wasn't sure she could trust her assistant with the full story.

"Okay, you know a lot more than we do about the translation," Jeanne replied.

Cloe did not think there was much conviction in her words. *Could she be hiding something?*

"Tell me about our visitors," said Cloe.

"Well, there's not much more to tell other than what I said on the phone," responded the woman. "It was a strange group, and the leader was insistent you would want to talk to him."

"He was right," said J.E. "There must be something else. Did they say or do anything that might lead us to where they are?"

"No, nothing," she replied. "Wait a minute. I almost forgot. A while after they left, I sent our runner up to the Port of Call restaurant to get some takeout."

"Yes?" Cloe wondered where this was headed.

"He thinks he saw the dog," said the assistant.

"Dog?" Captain Jacob broke in. "What dog?"

"The big bull dog, the one the little boy called Bully," explained Dr. Richard.

"He said he had never seen a bulldog that big around here, and there couldn't have been two of them. The dog was lounging in the small front yard of a house not far from the restaurant," she continued. "Funny thing was he said he felt like the dog was watching him, even from a block away. He said it was like the dog wanted him to take notice."

"Whoa!" said Captain Jacob. "The dog *wanted* to be seen?"

"It does sound strange, I grant you, but that's what he said," she replied. "The dog wanted him to know he was there. Our runner told me exactly where the house is located."

"Okay, I can understand ancient cuneiform, five-thousand-year-old cities, and conversations between Jesus and an apostle on the end of times, but now a dog acting human? I feel like I've fallen through the keyhole. What could possibly be next?" said J.E.

"J.E., you're right; we have seen some strange things," said Cloe.

"Well, this is right up there with the strangest of them," he replied.

Cloe looked around the table at her companions. "Well, what are we waiting for? Let's go find Bully."

CHAPTER
60

They headed north on Chartres Street as the evening's gloom began to gather. The dark crept like tendrils down the streets running from east to west of the French Quarter. At Esplanade, they walked to the west for a bit, onward just past the Port of Call, which was already beginning to rock with after-work and neighborhood patrons.

"Let's see," said Dr. Richard, pausing to get her bearings. "Yes, it must be just up the block a ways."

They crossed another north-south street and walked under dense live oaks that filtered what little remaining light there was to the point where the grays shaded toward dark. The first wisps of a nighttime fog emerged.

As their eyes adjusted, Dr. Richard said, "There it is, a half block up."

Cloe gazed up the tree-lined boulevard at the front of a large wooden home with a deep front porch. The house was dark. Moreover, there was visible damage to the front area of the house. It appeared vandalized and burned. Military police tape lined the property.

"Oh my God!" said Cloe. "The military police have been here. Something terrible must have happened."

"*Shhh!* Mom, there's someone sitting on the front porch," said J.E. quietly. "He's in the shadows, smoking a cigarette—he's all in leather, like some Goth."

"I see him," Cloe replied softly. "He's waiting for someone."

"He may be waiting for us," urged Captain Jacob. "I suggest we continue our stroll."

"I agree," said J.E., now taking Dr. Richard's arm as if they were boyfriend and girlfriend, walking the Quarter.

They continued at a leisurely pace, not looking back at the dark figure crouching on the porch. Soon, they came to the next corner and turned south back into the Quarter.

* * *

Returning to the hotel bar, Cloe, J.E., Dr. Richard, and Captain Jacob regrouped. The atmosphere was somber. Now fully dark outside, the bartender was lighting candles on the tables and at the bar. The room was nearly deserted, and they had their pick of the tables, settling in at one in a corner and ordering a round of drinks. Something had happened at the home on Esplanade. They still had no idea as to the whereabouts of Zack and his mysterious crew.

"Zack told us at the convent that he and his group were being pursued by some people," said the assistant. "He called them the leather boys and said they had tried to hurt them at City Park. They had been in hiding ever since."

"According to the news, there are lots of those types around since the troubles began," said J.E. "They band together and terrorize whatever area they are in. They prey on the weak."

"I'd have to say, based on what I'm hearing, there was just such an individual on the porch of the house," said Captain Jacob. "I think he was waiting for us."

"How could he be waiting for us?" asked Cloe. "No one knows we are here, and no one knows we have any connection with Zack and his group."

"I hope that's true. But I'm not saying he was waiting specifically for us, but for someone like us who came looking for the people who were in that house," said the captain. "He was a sentry posted at the scene of the crime to see who came after."

"Why would anyone do that?" asked Dr. Richard. "I mean, if they got to Zack and his friends, it's all over. That house was virtually destroyed. Zack said they would kill them all."

"You're right. Why would they post a sentry if they had achieved their goals?" questioned J.E.

"The answer is simple," said Cloe. "They didn't. They might have destroyed the house, but they didn't get Zack and his friends. Somehow they got away."

"That's got to be right," agreed J.E. "The leather boys didn't get what they came for and don't know where Zack has gone."

"All right. Tomorrow, we start again looking for Zack," said Cloe.

As the group was getting up, the desk clerk rounded the corner as if on a mission.

"Dr. Lejeune!" he called out.

Cloe said nothing as he approached and stopped in front of her.

"Ma'am, we have a hand delivery for you," the clerk said, beaming.

Cloe accepted the envelope, tipped the clerk and plopped back down in her chair. The envelope contained a single sheet of paper with a very brief message.

"It says, '*Be at the dock by the Coast Guard station, West End, at 11 p.m. tonight*'," she read.

"What can that mean?" asked Captain Jacob. "Do you know this place?"

"Sure, it's out on Lake Pontchartrain near the causeway," said Cloe, musing. "The original Coast Guard station itself was destroyed in a recent hurricane, but it's been rebuilt. There is a channel and dock that run right next to it. There's also a big, popular restaurant next door."

"Who would leave such a message? As you said, no one knows we're here," said Jacob. "If the leather boy at the house on Esplanade somehow identified us, this could be a trap."

"It's signed Leneau," said Cloe.

"That sounds familiar. He may be one of the members of Zack's group," said Cloe's assistant.

"It might be a trap."

"Mom, I think this is a real lead, the only one we have," said J.E. "If this were a trap, I don't see why it would be set right next to an active Coast Guard station and a busy restaurant. That makes no sense."

"I think you're right, J.E.," responded Cloe after some thought. "There're places within a few blocks of here that are way more dangerous." Cloe looked at her mates. They were all on board.

"Here's what we do," she began. "Jeanne, you go home. This may be dangerous, and you didn't sign up for it. You continue the work."

"Cloe," said the assistant. "I'm not sure why or how, but I'm part of this now. If it's all the same to you, I'm in."

"But, Jeanne," said Cloe. "You could be hurt or worse."

The two soldiers carefully studied the assistant, trying to determine what she could possibly bring to the table and how big a liability she would be.

"You know, that's the same thing they told me when I wanted to join the marines after 9/11," said Jeanne.

"Well, it's a good thing they convinced you not to do such a crazy thing," said J.E. "Marines are half-navy, half-army, and all trouble. They get the worst and most difficult gigs of any conventional force."

Jeanne Richard turned directly to J.E. and said, "Who said they convinced me?"

CHAPTER
61

The young thug and his cohorts stood before the Burnt Man, whose scowl was more an attitude than a fact, as his facial muscles were destroyed. The leather boys had a rat's nest of a residence in an old and partially falling down wood-frame house in the residential area north of the Quarter. There was no electricity. A couple of stolen hurricane lamps gave what light there was.

"You say nobody came to the house?" asked the Burnt Man.

"Yeah, that's it, man. Ain't nobody come to the house during my shift," squirmed the punk.

"*Nobody?*" repeated the Burnt Man.

"Nobody come to the house; only some walked by it," he replied.

"Describe them."

"All 'em?" asked the hood. "There was maybe ten to twelve."

"Did anybody stand out?"

"Well, there was the guy walking his dog; I remember 'cause the bitch crapped in the front yard."

"Anyone *else?*" He was beginning to lose patience.

"Well, near dark, there was a group that came by, and I thought they was a coming in, but they strooled on by," replied the leather kid.

"Strooled?"

"Yeah, dude, you know, hold'n hands and what."

"Describe them."

After the Burnt Man had exhausted the limited memory of the youth, he was convinced that two of the group were the lady doctor and her son.

He had no idea who the others were. *How had Icar known they would be here?*

He turned to the assembly of young toughs and said, "You find out where they are staying and let me know if they are there or not. If they're not there, you find out where they have gone. I don't care if you have to burn down every building north of Canal to do it!"

As the soldiers in his dark army joyfully piled out of the old house on their mission, the Burnt Man smiled, thinking about his next meeting with Cloe Lejeune.

CHAPTER

62

Semper Fi. When Jeanne Richard rolled up the sleeve of her drab sweatshirt, the tattoo on her bicep said it all. They had changed into more appropriate garb, some of which they purchased from one of the secondhand stores nearby. The three soldiers discussed their military experiences on the cab ride to West End. J.E. and Jacob were impressed. The cab let them out in the parking lot of the seafood house next door to the dock.

Fifteen minutes before the appointed time, they approached the dock next to the Coast Guard station and in the light from the parking lot saw a midsized cabin cruiser cleated down tightly to the dock. While the station house had been rebuilt, they had to step over or around traces of storm debris even after so many years. Cloe could hear the deep-throated engines idling. The salt air off the lake was beginning to cool, and she was glad they had bought sweatshirts. A wisp of gray fog floated by.

"Ahoy!" came a deep voice from the wheelhouse of the cruiser.

The dock was in shadows and the cruiser unlit, so Cloe could only see the vague outline of a man against the dark recess of the boat. She detected an orange glow and smelled pipe smoke.

They stopped at the dock to assess the situation. J.E. stepped forward. "Mr. Leneau?"

"Right you are," said the man. "Come aboard quickly. We need to move."

"Whoa!" said J.E. "We're not going anywhere until we know who you are and what this is about."

"Son, you do what you want, but in the last twenty-four hours, people have tried to kill me and my family and have destroyed my house. I will take you to Zack. In fifteen seconds, this boat is leaving. Make up your minds."

They all looked at Cloe, who said, "Let's go."

"Anybody know anything about boats?" asked Mr. Leneau. "I need the dock lines tended so we can get out of here."

"Where's our marine?" asked J.E.

"She ducked into the restaurant to use the restroom," said Cloe.

"Restroom?" questioned the Israeli. "We were supposed to stay together."

Just then Dr. Richard appeared. "Here I am! What do you need?"

"Can you handle the dock lines?" asked Leneau.

"Are they controlled on the boat or the dock?" asked Jeanne, stepping up.

"On the boat, of course," said Mr. Leneau, smiling.

With that, the diminutive marine grabbed a handhold on the side of the cabin and swung around to the narrow gunnel, "Fore or aft first, sir?" she asked.

"Fore," cried the older man. "With what little wind we have off the lake, the bow will swing out."

"Roger that, sir," said Jeanne, running up the narrow walkway and crossing the foredeck. She quickly untied the bowline and secured it. Then she ran back and did the same with the stern line.

The sleek cruiser drifted off the dock, and Mr. Leneau gunned both engines. With two solid clunks of the gears, the boat made immediate forward progress, and the trip, to wherever, began. The vessel fast-idled up the short channel and turned to the starboard to dog leg into the lake. To their right, the lights from the lakeshore shone weakly through a growing haze.

Cloe stood next to Mr. Leneau on the pilot deck. At the outer marker to the West End harbor, he expertly swung the vessel almost due north and slowly pushed the throttles toward the stops.

"Well, looks like we're headed to the North Shore. You know, that's my neck of the woods," said Cloe over the rising roar of the engines. "Madisonville is my home."

Mr. Leneau looked at her and said, "What makes you think we're headed for the Tchefuncte?"

He's right, she thought. Eight or ten rivers and bayous fed into the lake where a cabin or camp could be located with Zack and his cohorts. She had just assumed …

The sleek old cruiser was on high plane and skimming the surface of the almost flat lake. With no moon, low clouds, and the gathering fog, it was as dark as a well digger's elbow at midnight. They could have been on God's own blessed scow, cleaving the River Styx on a holy mission.

"How do you know where you're going?" yelled Cloe in Mr. Leneau's ear.

"I have programmed our GPS, and the radar tells me what's out there," he replied.

Cloe observed the reddish glow of the bank of marine night-vision tinted instruments and thought of her father's stealth-lighted flashlight he had used all those decades ago during the assault on El Guettar. She took a deep breath and watched the radar sweep a 360-degree circle, painting hard objects. The main contact on the screen was a glowing line, maybe a mile away, stretching from south to north to the port side of the vessel.

"What's that?" asked Cloe.

"That's the causeway that you probably took to travel from Madisonville to New Orleans," he replied.

They were on the east side of the causeway, so they were probably not going to the Tchefuncte River but maybe Bayou Castine near Mandeville or even somewhere in Slidell on the east end of the Lake.

Before she could ask, she heard Leneau say, "Uh-oh."

"What is it?" she asked.

He pointed, his face grim. "See that dot on the radar?"

She looked at the green screen, and sure enough, she could see a white dot just on the inside of the last ring on the radar. It was on the bottom of the screen, so she took that to mean it was behind them.

"Yes. What is it?" she asked.

"Well, there aren't too many boats out tonight, but there's one, and it's coming on fast," replied Leneau.

"How can you tell that?" asked Cloe.

"He's watching the time it takes for the bogey to advance from one ring to another. The rings are a known distance apart, in this case two miles," said Jeanne, who had joined them.

"Right. He's transiting the rings about twice as fast as we are. We're at thirty knots, so our friend must be flying at something north of sixty knots," said Leneau.

"Wow!" said Jeanne. "That's got to be a go-fast."

"A what?" asked Cloe.

"A go-fast, as yachtsmen on the lake call them. A damn nuisance, I call them," yelled Leneau over the engines, which he now pushed to the full throttle stops. "They're capable of doing sixty to eighty miles an hour, and they sound like a freight train coming. With a flat lake, they'll be on us in a little while—if we're their target. We can't outrun them."

* * *

The pilot of the sleek Fountain speedboat studied the instruments, turned to the Burnt Man, and shouted over the scream of the engines, "They can't have gotten too far ahead of us. Our spy said they turned due north at the outer marker. We'll catch them shortly at this speed."

"Good," was all the Burnt Man replied as he scanned the lake ahead. The Fountain roared on; he took pleasure in its power and speed and the knowledge that every second drew him closer to his quarry, the honorable Dr. Cloe Lejeune.

He turned and looked at his men, who were armed to the teeth.

"Make ready!" he shouted.

* * *

"I make their ETA in about fifteen minutes," said Jeanne, watching the green dot on the radar grow in size and proximity. "Do you have any weapons?"

"Yes!" Leneau replied loudly over the roar of the cruiser's engine. "All I have are out on the forward bunk below."

Jeanne turned to the companionway and called for J.E. and Jacob, then dropped below decks. The other young soldiers followed her.

The cruiser was now making thirty-two knots, according to the GPS. "That's all the old girl has in her," said Leneau. "We're going to be overrun."

Cloe looked at the oncoming image on the radar and studied the area around their boat. She wondered how their adversary could possibly have known where they would be. The air was crystallizing with water droplets as she watched. This might be the beginning of one of those lake fogs like she had seen in her childhood.

"Maybe," she said, thinking she was starting to sound like the monsignor. "But the good Lord does provide."

Just then, J.E., Jeanne, and Jacob emerged from the cabin, carrying the meager arsenal that Leneau had aboard.

"Well, we have a twelve-gauge pistol grip shotgun with a Ziploc bag of shells, a twenty-two long rifle and a forty-five automatic handgun, each with extra shells or clips," said J.E. "Jacob and I each have our sidearms. We're in good shape for close quarters or varmints."

"We got what we got," cried Leneau. "I suggest you figure out their best use because the speedboat is almost on us. It's out there to the starboard off the stern quarter. She's as black as this night and running without any lights."

Cloe turned to the stern and stared off to the starboard. She could see nothing, but she began to hear something. The cruiser's inboards were churning in a deep bass, but she heard a louder, higher, banshee-like cry as well. As the go-fast approached, the sound grew louder and higher in pitch. The beast was upon them.

CHAPTER

63

"Sir, the old cabin cruiser is off our bow on the port side. She's running with her lights still on," declared the pilot.

"Take us in parallel so we can bring our weapons to bear," cried the Burnt Man. "We'll blast that old boat from under them."

"Roger, sir!" responded the pilot, squeezing the throttles further toward the stops.

The Fountain engines shrieked, and the boat leaped ahead and moved to the port toward the now visible, lighted cruiser.

"Now, men, let her have it!" sounded the Burnt Man, his lipless smile broadening.

* * *

Cloe saw isolated muzzle flashes from the speedboat, but nothing seemed to happen. Then, several more guns lit up from the go-fast, and rounds began to whiz overhead, splashing in the water around them. A few smashed into the old wooden cruiser.

"Down!" cried Leneau.

The three soldiers took cover behind the starboard gunnel and made to return fire.

"Hold!" J. E. hollered. "The only thing we have that might reach them is the twenty-two, and it will do little or no damage. Better we let them think we're unarmed. If they think that, they may close in and be within range of our weapons."

This was a dangerous game because the men on the speedboat were very well armed. If she was not mistaken, Cloe had heard AKs and AR-15s. They could not let the speedboat come abreast of them with those weapons. They were in serious trouble. She looked around for some strategy.

"Slow down and let them run by. Then head for the causeway," she cried in Leneau's direction.

Leneau immediately throttled back, and the heavy wooden cruiser stopped as if he had put on the brakes. The speedboat flew by in excess of seventy miles an hour, streaming a two-story rooster tail behind it. It screamed off into the distance but began to slow and turn.

* * *

"Blast it!" cried the Burnt Man as the Fountain flew by the old boat. "Turn this thing around and go after them!"

His men were still firing at the profile of the cabin cruiser, now a good distance behind them.

"Save your ammo!" he shouted, but it did little good.

The Fountain began a long, looping clockwise turn back toward the cruiser. The Burnt Man nodded at the pilot's skill. He was executing a man-overboard-type turn, and if he was accurate, this would put them just abeam of the cruiser at the circle's completion.

"Now, we will have them!" the Burnt Man cried, smashing his left fist into the palm of his right hand.

* * *

Leneau had now throttled up again and was headed dead west toward the causeway. He had turned off the running lights, and the cruiser was dark. As the boat leaped in the direction of the concrete twin spans over the lake, the fog thickened. As they progressed and it enveloped them, Cloe became concerned they might actually hit the causeway.

She looked behind them. The chase boat was invisible in the gloom, but she could hear its engines as it came about. She looked ahead and saw nothing but a dense fog bank.

Leneau backed down on the throttles and eased farther into the heavy mist.

"I need a lookout!" he called to Jeanne. "Here, take this. You may need it."

Jeanne grabbed the headset and portable communication unit, swung up on the handhold, and ran forward. About halfway to the bow, she passed out of sight in the fog.

As the cabin cruiser slipped deeper into the fog bank, its own engines at idle could barely be heard. The speedboat's roar increased as it came nearer. It sounded like a beast cheated of its kill.

"Quiet, everyone!" whispered Cloe. The men aboard the speedboat were firing wildly now. Most of the slugs hit harmlessly in the water around them.

Then Cloe heard Leneau cry out.

He was slowly collapsing to the deck, holding his left upper arm. Cloe could see blood—a good deal of it. She jumped and threw her arm under Leneau's good arm and helped him slowly to the deck.

She turned to J.E. and Jacob. "J.E., we need a medic and a boat driver."

"I'm certified as a military medic," said Jacob, stepping in. "Is there a medical kit?"

Leneau growled, "In the head."

As Jacob went below for the kit, Jeanne came in from the bow. "What's going on? We're all over the place!"

"Leneau's been shot," said Cloe. "Can you pilot this boat?"

"Yes, that's one of my certifications. When I joined the marines, I got trained only in support roles. Driving a boat is one of them," she said. "Of course, that's all changed."

"Well, you're the captain now," said Cloe. "Get us out of here!"

Jeanne stood behind the wheel on the small pilot deck and studied the instruments.

"Okay," she said. "Where to?"

"I think we have an advantage," Leneau whispered. "Many of the go-fast boats don't have radar because they don't have a mast to mount the hardware and don't want the weight. Our pursuers will be blind in this fog."

"Okay, what do we do?" asked Cloe.

"The causeway is just ahead. We should hide between the spans and cut our engines. We'll make no noise and be invisible in the fog," gasped Leneau before he passed out.

The classic cruiser traversed the thick mist and crossed under the eastern elevated highway that headed north. Jeanne cut the engines, and the silence was overwhelming.

"Everyone ... we have to be completely quiet," Jeanne said in a low voice.

* * *

"Sir, they have entered the fog just ahead of us," said the pilot. "I have to slow down or we may hit the causeway pilings."

"I don't care about the pilings!" screamed the Burnt Man. "You stay after them and don't lose them."

His men had fired everything they had just before their quarry entered the fog bank, but he couldn't tell if they had hit anything.

"Shut down the engines and listen for them!" ordered the Burnt Man.

In the minutes that followed, the only thing they could hear was the sound of what little auto traffic remained on the causeway, and that was moving very slowly in the fog.

"Okay, start the engines and perform a grid search," said the Burnt Man to the pilot. "They can't hide forever."

"But, sir, we have no radar, and I can't see past the middeck," protested the pilot.

"Do it!" the Burnt Man commanded.

* * *

Cloe assisted in cleaning up Leneau's wound while Jacob administered a local pain killer and patched him up. Soon the bleeding had been stanched and the wound dressed and bandaged. J.E. and Jacob carried Leneau into the saloon and laid him on the settee. They covered him with blankets, and Jacob stayed with him.

Back on deck, they could once again hear the angry sound of the speedboat. It was diffused in the pea-soup fog, so it was difficult to tell exactly which direction it came from. The sound reminded Cloe of that of an angry bumblebee.

Then … the crunching sound of fiberglass on concrete, followed by screaming and cursing reached them.

A muffled voice said, "Let's go! We just scraped the piling. The boat's okay. I know where they are headed." Soon, the go-fast moved off to the north.

"Wait a minute! I know that voice," said Cloe to herself. "But from where?"

"Okay, I think we can move out," said Jeanne a moment later, interrupting Cloe's thoughts. She cranked the engines and slowly headed north.

CHAPTER
64

As the cruiser headed northward, the satellite phone in J.E.'s holster began to vibrate. J.E. reached for it, listened intently, and then walked toward her.

"Mom, it's Albert. It's for you," he said, offering the phone.

"Hello," said Cloe into the receiver. "Albert? What is it?"

"Cloe, there is news," came the response.

Cloe gripped the receiver. Whatever it was, she did not expect it to be good.

"Cloe, the cardinals are convening in Iceland," said the monsignor. "Father Curator and I have been called to Reykjavik for the convocation."

"Is this about the pope?"

"Yes, the remaining cardinals believe the pope is dead, and they are convening to elect a new pope," responded the monsignor. "After the attacks on the religious, there are only about a third of the cardinals left."

"It's very courageous of them to do so," said Cloe. "They could make themselves convenient targets."

"Yes, but the Church must go on," sighed the monsignor.

"Why Iceland?" asked Cloe.

"With the Vatican destroyed, this decision is about security," responded the monsignor. "Reykjavik can be secured in ways few other venues could be. Whatever remains of the Swiss Guard will be there and, of course, Father Anton as well."

"When will you go?" asked Cloe.

"Immediately," said the monsignor. "We have been tasked to get there as soon as possible."

"Will there be time? Events seem to be accelerating," she observed.

"Yes, the worldwide news is not good," said the monsignor. "The plagues have killed nearly a third of the population in countries where they have struck. The destruction, violence, and now famine have killed millions more."

"It's as if the pale horse of Revelation has been loosed upon the earth," Cloe said.

"His rider is Death, and Hades follows close behind with power over a fourth of the earth to kill by sword, famine, and plague—or words to that effect," said the monsignor. "What the pope said about the rise of evil and the apocalypse cannot be disputed."

"So it seems, but I was taught that God never gives us a challenge that He does not also give us the ability to meet."

"I believe that as well," said the monsignor. "This means that good is also rising to meet the evil, and we have the tools to defeat it. We just have to figure out how."

"Have you and Father Curator and the monks made any progress on the translation?" she asked. "We need answers."

"We have a sentence or maybe two, depending on how you look at it. The words from the scientists at Uruk have helped. In time, we will be able to translate the entire text."

"But what do you have now? We have no time," said Cloe, a little more forcefully than she intended.

"We have this translated from the cuneiform: 'Evil must be sealed at the Mount; Good will serve the Seven,'" he said.

Cloe let the translation wrap around her as she considered it. Without more, it seemed almost as incomprehensible as the cuneiform. She balanced herself in the speeding boat; her neck hurt, and her shoulders were sore from the tension. Nonetheless, they were making progress.

"Albert, I'm sorry. I know you and the curator have been working with the monks night and day on this, but it doesn't ring any bells with me. Even so, I can't come back just yet. I want to be with you, but I sense this trip to New Orleans is critical," responded Cloe.

"What have you learned?"

As Cloe filled him in on what had happened, she realized she really knew nothing more than when she had arrived other than that some bad actors wanted to kill a strange group of people. She didn't know why or what it could have to do with her mission.

"The sentence you have is absolutely fascinating," said Cloe, ruminating on the language. "It has both the words *seven* and *seal* in it that the German said he saw. But the seven what? What is the mount? How will evil be sealed?"

"In Revelation, the personification of evil, the devil in the form of the beast, was cast into the abyss for a thousand years," the monsignor explained. "In other words, Jesus and the forces of good defeated evil and cast it away. That's the thousand-year cycle we have talked about."

"In a sense, evil was sealed away from mankind in the abyss," said Cloe. "But where is the mount, and who or what are the seven?"

"Is the abyss a real place and is it near the mount? I think we have to assume the term 'mount' refers to a mountain or hill of some sort," posited the monsignor. "As you know, the Bible is full of mounts—for example, the Mount of Olives and Mount Calvary."

"Right. Much of significance in the Bible occurred on or around one of these mounts, but what does that get us? Some were not even real mountains. Calvary itself was more of a rock formation than a true mountain."

"If Father Sergio were here with us, he'd tell us we need a working theory," said the monsignor. "I think we need to find seven souls who can lead good against evil, and the end game will occur at some mount. How's that for vague?"

"Well, it's at least a theory that fits the known facts," said Cloe, smiling, thinking of her affection for Serge. Then she thought about Zack and his cohorts. *The seven*, she thought. *Is that it?*

"In my opinion, you should get to the end of whatever you are doing in New Orleans and then come to Reykjavik as soon as possible," replied the cleric. "That's where the action will be. We will need you. The curator and I will continue on the translation, but you are critical to that work."

Stung by the mild rebuke from her friend, Cloe wondered whether she was just chasing phantoms or if what was happening was a key to the solution. Her initial, although indirect, contact with Zack and the rest left her with a clear notion that they were involved. Was it possible? Doubt yanked at her sleeve.

Gathering herself, she said, "Albert, we will join you in Reykjavik as soon as I run this down. I'm on to something here, and the attack on us proves it. Why would anyone try to hurt us unless what we're doing matters?"

"Cloe, right now, there's no accounting for what people do. Sometimes, random just happens. But you do what you must, and we'll look for you in Iceland."

CHAPTER

65

The cabin cruiser entered the narrow channel in the northwest quadrant of the lake. Cloe watched her assistant deftly pilot the vessel through the shallow waters. A string of orange markers became visible as white dots on the radar guided them.

Leneau had regained his senses and had given Jeanne a bearing that led them to their current location. "Port Louis," was what he had said.

Now he stood next to her, swaying a bit but watching carefully as she guided his baby into the bayou at the end of the channel.

"Easy here," he whispered. "The channel silts up and is very shallow. Stay toward the right bank."

They had not seen the go-fast since they had left the fog bank, but J.E. and Jacob were armed and on alert. Leneau had slept solidly for the forty minutes or so it had taken them to arrive at whatever this Port Louis was and awakened somewhat refreshed if groggy from the painkiller. He was very sore but determined.

"Where are we?" asked Cloe. "I know this is west of Madisonville, but what is this place?"

"Port Louis is a development project that was probably started in the early to mid-eighties. It was meant to be a modern, upscale mixed-use project but has fallen on hard times and now has a few camps on the bayou that empties into the lake. I have a little place here," said Leneau. "It's very isolated."

Cloe looked ahead and could see the bare silhouette of a string of what looked like two-story townhouse-styled structures in the low light emanating from the windows of two of them. The rest, maybe ten to twelve structures, struck her in the darkness as long vacant and possibly abandoned.

"Here," said Leneau, pointing to one that was completely blacked out.

Jeanne nudged the craft toward the dock and coasted in. Soon they were tied up and helping Leneau off the boat. J.E. and Jacob stood as sentries. Cloe looked back and saw the lake-effect fog rush up the little channel behind them, blanketing everything. Whoever was after them would not find them this night.

* * *

"Good Lord!" was all Cloe could say as she gazed at the huddled menagerie seated in the glow of a hurricane lamp in the living room of Leneau's camp. They looked like a group of refugees discovered by the border patrol.

A young man stood, walked toward her, and said, "Dr. Lejeune, I presume. I've been anxious to meet you."

"You must be Zack," she replied. "We need to get Mr. Leneau to bed. He's been wounded."

"Oh no!" cried Doris, arising from her camp chair and coming to her father. Her mother, who had been laying out sheets and blankets for the night, joined her to help him toward a nearby bedroom.

"He needs a hospital!" screamed Mrs. Leneau.

"No," said her husband. "I'll be fine. Just put me down on the bed so I can rest."

Introductions were made, and then Zack asked, "What happened?"

As Cloe filled him in, she took in the group before her. Zack's eyes said he had seen many things in his young life. Louie looked rough and talked tough. Mel and Zack meant something to each other. The others just looked lost.

"Well, Mr. Leneau is a pretty tough bird and certainly game," said Zack, after hearing of the attack on the water. "When the dirty boys came for us at his home on Esplanade, he saw what was happening and got all of us out through an old coal chute in the rear of the house. He took us to his boat at West End, and here we are."

Cloe looked at the jumble of human beings and at the giant bulldog. She took note of the boy. The dog always maneuvered to be between him and her, an occasional low growl escaping his throat.

"Hello, ma'am," said the child.

"Hi, Robby," Cloe responded, remembering his name from her assistant's phone call. "Are you okay?"

"Yes, ma'am," he said. "I'm a little tired and hungry, but we have work to do, don't we?"

"Yes, we do," Cloe replied. "We'll have some snacks that Mr. Leneau brought, and then we need to talk."

As J.E. distributed the treats, Cloe sat down in the middle of the odd group. She paused to examine them further while they tore into the food, refreshing themselves. They looked completely ordinary—except when she looked at Louie, she wanted to hold her purse a little tighter, if she had had a purse.

Finally, she asked, "Who are all of you?"

"We've told you who we are individually," said Zack. "The only thing that makes us special and that we have in common is the card. Seven of us have the card. We've told you about the giant or angel or whatever he was who gave it to us."

Cloe watched as each of the seven reached into pockets or purses and produced the cards. She took the one held up by the boy. The front side said "7." She turned it over and saw there were lines of very small markings on the back.

"What in the world?" she said to herself. She peered at the minute marks and then held the card near the lamp. *They look a little like tiny insects in some kind of formation.*

She held it closer to the light, "My God! It's cuneiform!"

J.E., Jeanne, and Jacob looked at each other, and J.E. asked, "How is that possible?"

"What's cuneiform?" asked Mel. "I thought the lines were just some type of decoration on the card."

"Okay. It seems we have a story to tell you," said Cloe.

After she told them about the journal, the cuneiform passages, and the trip to Uruk, the little living room was hushed.

"So what does it say?" asked Mel. "Can you read it?"

"No, it's an ancient form of writing that very few people can decipher, and then it takes study," Cloe responded. "My friends are developing a key to translating it, but it's not finished."

"Mom, look at all the cards," said J.E.

Cloe assembled all seven cards on the nearby kitchen table. She gazed at them for a long moment.

"I don't know what they say, but whatever it is, it's the same on all the cards. The formations of wedges are exactly the same," said Cloe.

J.E. took a picture of one of the cards with his cell phone and then said, "I'll e-mail this to the monsignor. He may be able to get something off this."

Zack leaned forward and said, "We don't know what it says, but what does it mean?"

Cloe looked around the living area. The faces surrounding her were wide-eyed and frightened. This was too much.

"How ...?" one of them asked tentatively.

Cloe considered the question and the astounding fact that the same ancient cuneiform she was studying from the journal also appeared on the back of these seven strange cards. These cards had driven them to New Orleans, for what they still did not know. *Who the hell are these people?*

Finally, she said, "I don't know how and I don't know what it says specifically, but what it means is we are somehow linked together and we have work to do ... together."

"What work?" asked a suspicious Louie.

"I'm not certain yet, but I believe it has to do with the trouble," said Cloe. "I have a feeling we'll know for sure soon."

CHAPTER

66

The Vatican jet rose from the runway at Louis Armstrong International Airport and headed east, clawing for altitude. By any standard, the jet was overloaded, and if it had not been a private, diplomatic airplane, it would not have been permitted to take off. It had a full fuel load and more passengers than it was certified to carry. Somehow, Sky had made the taxi and the liftoff.

The seven were aboard, as was Robby's mom. Cloe had insisted that Leneau stay behind, although he argued forcefully against it. In the end, he needed to attend to his wound. Mrs. Leneau and Doris stayed with him. Jeanne Richard returned to her work at the library. The biggest problem was Bully. When the dog figured out he wasn't making the trip, he raised hell. It was as if a miniature Brahma bull had been set loose in the living room of the Leneau camp. He had to be restrained as a tearful Robby was pulled away. J.E. and Jacob used all their combined strength to hold Bully back. Finally, the dog was somewhat subdued, and the traveling group left.

"Well, this looks like old times, Dr. Lejeune," Sky had said when he greeted them—to which a weary Cloe replied:

"Light 'em up, Sky. We have work to do."

The sleek jet climbed to forty thousand feet, rushing toward the rising sun. Red and orange streams of light colored the cabin. Cloe thought about the events on the lake and the voice giving commands on the speedboat. *Was that a trick of the fog?*

Cloe examined the back of Robby's card and shivered in the cool of the jet's interior. She pulled a sweater from her bag and draped it around her shoulders. She glanced back at the seven, alert and probably wondering what they were doing. Her eyes dropped again to the card.

"How can this be?" she asked, more to herself than to anyone else.

Captain Jacob was sitting across from her at the table at the front of the executive jet.

"God's hand," he said.

"What's that?" asked Cloe.

"Sometimes, the only answer to things is that it's the hand of God at work," said the soldier.

"Do you really believe that?"

"Ma'am, I live in a tiny nation that by all odds should not exist. I have fought many battles for our very survival," he said. "I have seen God's hand too many times not to believe."

Cloe looked around at the strange, courageous group of people in the aircraft. Young, old, male, female—all together to see the end, whatever that end might be. Could this be God's bicep poised to hammer evil? She did not know.

"But how can five-thousand-year-old cuneiform be on the back of what looks like a modern business card?" she asked.

"Perhaps it's there to say something to you," said Jacob.

"You think this is a message to *me*?"

"Why not?" responded the Israeli. "Someone has to be the tip of the spear. Your destiny may be to defeat this evil. Everything you have ever done in your life may have put you in position to be here," said Jacob. "In my culture, a single individual from time to time has been positioned or was thrust into the role of making a huge difference. Look at Moses or Noah. Ordinary people, yet God decided they would make a difference. Perhaps God has decided you will make a difference."

"How can I know?" asked Cloe, shaken. "I'm certainly no Noah or Moses."

"You can't," responded Jacob. "It's the faith thing."

"Good will serve the seven," echoed Cloe.

"That's part of what the monsignor said has been translated," said J.E., who had been listening to the conversation between Cloe and Jacob. "The question is whether our seven is *the* seven."

"I certainly can't tell you for sure," said Zack from across the aisle. "But this group is special and has a certain power about it."

"Power? What do you mean?" asked Cloe.

Zack related the events at the coffeehouse.

"I can't say how or why, but evil was defeated in that small way at that time," said Zack. "We joined together and prayed. Evil backed down."

"Hmmm, evil defeated," mused Cloe, looking out at the layers of clouds and light outside the window.

"The strength we had as a group was like a physical force," said Zack. "I've never experienced anything like it before."

"Well, whatever it was, I'm not sure it would help us today. We seem to be arrayed against an adversary who is powerful enough to drive events worldwide. I don't see how seven random souls could stand against it," said Cloe.

"Perhaps," said J.E. "But you know three hundred Spartans stood against two hundred thousand Persians at Thermopylae and would have won, except a lowlife betrayed them, allowing the Persians to get above and behind them."

"I would have to add that a small boy named David was sent out to meet the Philistine champion Goliath, and he defeated him with a sling and a small, smooth stone," said Jacob.

"Point taken," said Cloe. "Still, this is the twenty-first century, and things like that don't happen."

"Well, you might say they don't happen until they do," replied Zack. "Nine/eleven could not happen until it did. Our history is full of firsts."

Cloe observed the earnest faces of the three young men seated around her.

"Are you saying God has sent you to defeat this evil?" she asked directly.

With a defeated look, Zack said, "I don't honestly know. But I do know this without fail. We have been chosen for something. It has to do with what you're doing. Perhaps your translation will give us more."

Again, the translation. Cloe felt guilty she was not working on it. It might be the answer to everything. She stood and felt disoriented.

"I'm going to check on Robby," she said.

She headed for the rear of the airplane where they had made a bed between two seats for the boy. Robby's mother was in her seat, dead asleep. She envied her innocent slumber. *The poor woman is exhausted. We all are.*

Then she heard it. It was low and almost inaudible at first over the sound of the engines. The hair on the back of her neck stood up, and she froze, her eyes fixed on the rear of the plane. She took another step, and the growl came again, louder this time.

Cloe leaned over and looked around the set of seats where they had made Robby's bed. She came face-to-face with the clear brown eyes of a hundred-pound English bulldog, who filled the entire space between the seats. She jumped backward.

CHAPTER
67

"She's gone," said Icar into the sat-phone link.

"How can you know that?" asked the Burnt Man from the rear of the speedboat. "She and her pals were just here on the north shore. We're very near to catching up to them. We will catch them."

"You're too late," responded the voice on the phone. "They're gone. You have been outsmarted."

The Burnt Man was silent. He had been so close to confronting the lady doctor. The damn fog had prevented him from catching her. How could Icar know what he himself did not know—here, on the scene? He had long recognized that his boss knew things of which he had no knowledge and that no human could know. *Was it spies or does he just somehow know?* He was trapped between the lady doctor's escape and Icar's superior information sources. *Now what?*

As if he could read his thoughts, Icar said, "The action moves to the convocation of cardinals. You must get back to New Orleans and go to Iceland. The cardinals will convene to elect a new pope. Dr. Lejeune and the monsignor, along with all your old friends, will be there. Plus, I sense there are new players on the board. Together, they are strong. But they will all be in Iceland where we can break them apart. There is a child. You must bring me the child. The circle will be broken. With my faster plane, you should be able to get to Reykjavik ahead of them."

A child? Broken circle? What the hell?

"But you said the pope is still alive," responded the Burnt Man, hand signaling his pilot to crank the engines and head south.

"True, but the masses do not know the pope lives," said Icar, laughing. "Whatever is left of Christianity will demand a new leader. The cardinals will appoint a new pope, not knowing the current one has survived. Chaos will reign. It's possible this will even create a schism within the Church, with one group following the new pope and the other clinging to the old pope."

"How does that help us and our plan?" he asked.

"Internal conflict and division within the Catholic Church will be our ally. They will not be able to recover in time. The whole thing will fall. The entire world will burn."

The Burnt Man thought about this and realized that Icar had one objective, and he had another. While he had been initially enchanted with the scope of the man's vision, now, he realized, he could barely stomach this strange being. He was completely devoid of any humanity. The Burnt Man smirked at the thought of his own lost humanity. He was as ruthless as they came and willing to do anything to reach his goals, but Icar would destroy all, including him.

"What do you want me to do?" the Burnt Man yelled into the phone, as the go-fast came onto plane and slashed southward.

CHAPTER

68

Cloe looked over at J.E. and said, "How long before we get to Reykjavik?"

"We're about thirty minutes out," he replied as the plane banked toward the north.

Cloe looked back and saw that nearly everyone was asleep. She had dozed and now felt somewhat refreshed.

"How did that dog get on board? We left him at the camp. There's no way he could have followed."

"Mom, he must have tagged along and stowed away on the cruiser in the fog," said J.E. "Then he simply followed us to the airport and slipped on board when no one was watching. It was dark and unbelievably foggy."

"J.E., do you really believe that?" asked Cloe, under her breath.

"Well, what's your explanation?" asked J.E. "You think he sprouted angel's wings and flew across the lake and somehow materialized on the plane?"

"Maybe. Between him and Robby, I'm not sure which explanation is more farfetched."

At that point, the Vatican jet rolled and began its long descent. In spite of the lengthy flight and the time-zone changes, the sun still shone on the plane's six. This was not the land of the midnight sun, but it was the next closest thing.

"Reykjavik is within a mile or two of our destination, the Basilica of Christ the King, known today as Landakot's Church or Landakotskirkja," said J.E. "It's the Catholic cathedral where the cardinals will meet."

"J.E., I'm very worried about this," she responded. "We need to be focused on the ascent of the evil one, but here we are in this strange country to elect a replacement for a pope who is not dead. We seem to be taking our eye off the ball."

"But no one knows that except us."

"Perhaps that's why we're here, J.E.," said Cloe, after a moment's consideration.

* * *

As they taxied toward the general aviation hangar, Cloe could see there was another airplane ahead of them. It was parked near the entrance, and several men were deplaning.

Sky skirted the parked jet and brought the Vatican plane to a stop about fifty yards away from the entrance to the business side of the hangar. As Cloe closed her computer and prepared to stand and move down the aisle toward the open door, she glanced out the window again at the men departing the other airplane. She did a double take when she saw one of them. Did she know him? Was it the way he walked? The way he held his head? She saw him for only a second before he passed under the wing of the plane.

"J.E.," she said.

But J.E. had already exited the plane.

Cloe shrugged and went back to help Robby's mother with her son. Robby was awake and alert, and Bully was excited. He growled at her again.

Robby's mother gathered their things, and Cloe held Robby's hand as they moved toward the cabin door. Cloe looked out the door in the odd, somehow alien daylight, so unusual for this hour of the evening. She shivered even though it was not cold.

Bully rushed forward, entangling himself in Cloe's legs, nearly knocking her aside. His growl was louder, more insistent. He stood between Robby and the door.

"What is it?" asked Robby's mother, catching up with them.

"I don't know," responded Cloe, now beginning to worry but not wanting to alarm Robby or his mother. "Bully's upset about something. Perhaps it's the weird light."

Cloe emerged from the door of the aircraft and heard the pilot of the other plane begin to start up its jet engines. She descended the short flight of steps to the tarmac. J.E., Jacob, and the others were milling about in a tight circle, talking to some of the men from the other jet. One of the men, near the rear of the pack, dressed in an overcoat with its collar pulled up almost to the brim of his hat, stepped toward them. At that, Bully leaped from the doorway of the plane, flew over Cloe and landed squarely between them. He issued a single loud bark of warning.

Cloe half-turned toward where Robby and his mother were standing at the top of the steps and saw armed men under the fuselage, holding their weapons trained on J.E. and the others.

"I'm sorry, Mom. They got the drop on us," said J.E.

He, Jacob, and a couple of the men from the seven were looking for some opportunity to fight back. One of the men held a wicked-looking stiletto, hidden against the back of his sleeve. Things were about to spiral out of control.

"Hold on, here," Cloe said, advancing on the nearest of the newcomers. "What do you want? We are a diplomatically protected group of papal representatives."

The man looked unsure and backed up a step. He glanced back at the man in the overcoat.

"We want the boy," said the clandestine figure in the background. His words were soft but clear.

The nearest man advanced on the airplane. Bully stood on his back legs and emitted a terrible roar.

Robby's mother cried, "*Noooo!*"

Cloe stepped forward and said, "You can't have him or anybody else! The police are on their way. You'd best crawl back into whatever hole you came from!"

She felt her chest clench in fear. Her people were greatly outgunned, and the element of surprise was with the intruders. Cold sweat dripped down her back.

The man in the background laughed softly and said, "Go get him."

The laugh and the voice were familiar, but she could not say why. It came at once from long ago but also from the recent past. Was it the voice from the speedboat?

The man Cloe had addressed initially advanced on the boy and made to grab his arm.

"Come on, son," he said gently.

Bully launched forward, grabbed the man's arm, shook it in his great mouth, and tore it from the socket at the shoulder. Blood spurted everywhere as the man's arteries began to empty. Bully stood with the stump of the man's arm in his teeth while the man screamed.

The background man nodded, and three men took pistols from their overcoats and simultaneously fired at Bully.

"Bully!" cried Cloe at the same time that Robby screamed, "No, no, no!"

Where there should have been the earsplitting blasts of handguns, however, there was only the spit of compressed air.

"Our friends in New Orleans made us aware of the dog, and we have come prepared," said the disguised man, who was obviously the leader. "We certainly don't want any animals harmed in this endeavor."

Cloe watched as the darts crashed into Bully, all three direct hits. Bully jumped and snapped at them, trying to remove them. He circled, trying to find the enemy. Finally, he began to slow. Still, he was fierce, and no one could get to Robby.

For Cloe it was like watching a movie, frame by frame.

As the drug took effect, Robby huddled next to Bully with his small arms around his great neck and shoulders.

Robby's mother screamed, and Jacob kicked one of the newcomers in the groin, sending him crashing to the tarmac. Jacob grabbed the man's gun, spun, and squeezed off a three-round spread in the leader's direction, but his shots went high.

The leader drew his own weapon, snake-quick, and fired a single shot at Jacob, hitting him square left center in the chest. Jacob went down hard. J.E. bent over him to try to help.

Now all was still except for Jacob's labored breathing and the startup whine of the jet's engines.

"Robby, come here!" said the leader of the band of thugs.

Robby's mother screamed again, and then her knees buckled. She toppled off the top step of the doorway and would have fallen to the tarmac except that Sky, standing at the foot of the steps, caught her.

Robby walked toward the man, straight up and unafraid.

"Robby!" cried his mother, her arms stretched out.

Robby turned and said, "Don't worry, Mom. God will take care of me."

The leader took Robby's hand, and they turned toward the jet, now ready for takeoff.

As he walked toward the jet with Robby in hand, the Burnt Man paused, looked back toward Cloe, and called out, "Dr. Lejeune, won't you join us?"

He and his men then began backing away and boarding the aircraft, with chaos erupting on the tarmac. J.E. jumped up from where he was tending to Jacob and ran toward his mother, who was now with Robby and his captor. One of the thugs raised his AK-47 and pointed squarely at J.E., but before he could shoot him dead, Cloe intervened.

"I don't know who you are, but I'll go with you only if my son is not harmed."

"You will go with me one way or another," said the Burnt Man. "But I do not wish your son's blood on my hands, at least not today. Warn him to stay away."

"J.E.!" screamed Cloe. "We will be all right. Stay away. I'll see you at the mount."

The Burnt Man's servant loosed a volley of gunfire just over J.E.'s head. He hit the ground and rolled over as the Burnt Man and his hostages boarded the plane.

Then it quickly roared down the runway, tearing itself from the earth, and headed southeast.

CHAPTER

69

J.E. rose to his knees, looked after the plane, and swore a terrible oath that he would find his mother and Robby and he would put the people responsible in their graves—but now he had work to do here.

He ran back to Captain Jacob, who was coughing and spitting up blood. Sky was holding Robby's mother and gently laid her on the tarmac. Everyone else was shaken but unhurt.

"J.E.!" called a voice from the terminal.

He turned and saw the monsignor and the curator coming out the door to the depot.

The monsignor took one look, assessed the situation, and then he was on his cell calling for an ambulance.

"Father Curator," said the monsignor. "Please go inside. There must be a medical kit and maybe someone trained in using it."

The curator departed at once. The monsignor came over to him and the Israeli.

A blond-headed man in jeans and a sweatshirt crashed through the terminal door carrying a medical kit the size of a small foot locker and ran toward them.

"My name is Hans Taj. I run the general aviation terminal here," he said. "I'm a certified medic. Let me see what I can do."

He bent down over Jacob and, using a blade, cut his tunic and undershirt away.

"Hmmm," he said.

He rolled Jacob over to his side and cut away the rest of his shirt. He examined the captain's back. J.E. could see there was no exit wound.

"He needs a hospital as quickly as possible," said Taj. "The bullet must come out."

"We've called for an ambulance," said the monsignor. "They said three minutes."

Taj took materials from the kit and cleaned and sanitized the wound. He applied a powder that J.E. took to be an antibiotic. He then quickly and expertly bandaged the wound to stanch the bleeding. He gently laid Jacob's head on a large roll of bandages and said, "That's all I can do."

As he stood, J.E. could hear the siren of the ambulance in the distance.

"Could you look at the woman?" asked J.E. as the siren grew louder.

Taj went to Robby's mother and gave her some smelling salts. Sky still squatted by her, fanning her and trying to make her comfortable. She quickly revived and began to scream for Robby. He talked calmly to her and gave her an injection from the bag. She began to settle down.

Walking back to where J.E. was, he said, "She's fine physically, but she seems to have had a shock. What happened out here?"

"Didn't you hear the gunshots?" asked Zack.

"No," said Taj. "The observation tower is on the other side of the airport. They did not report any problem. The terminal here is very well insulated because of the jet engines and because we have sleeping quarters within. Our pilots must have a quiet place to rest."

"We need information on the plane that just took off. One of the men on the plane shot this man, and they took two hostages. Can you contact the tower and get a flight plan, coordinates, and a destination?" asked J.E.

"I'll see what I can do," said Taj, heading for the terminal. "The police must be alerted."

"J.E., what happened?" asked the monsignor.

"Mom and one of the seven have been taken," said J.E. "They got the drop on us as we deplaned. Jacob fought back and was shot. He seems to be hurt pretty badly."

"Who was it?" asked the monsignor. "Did you recognize any of them?"

"I don't know—I mean, I'm not sure," J.E. stammered. "One of them was familiar, but I did not see any one I knew. I know that's a contradiction, but that's it."

The monsignor said, "Well, in any event, I have alerted the monks in the Opts Center, or what's left of it, and they will be tracking the airplane."

J.E. called to Sky, "Get some rest and have the plane fueled. We are wheels up in thirty minutes."

"Aye, J.E." replied Sky. "We'll find them."

The ambulance arrived, and the med-techs carefully examined Jacob, nodding their approval at the measures taken to save his life. They loaded him and tore off in the direction of the nearby hospital. J.E. and the monsignor went with Jacob to watch over him, and the curator stayed behind to make arrangements for Zack and his crew.

"J.E., you said one of the seven had been taken," the monsignor shouted over the screaming ambulance. "What does that mean? Who are 'the seven'?"

Exhausted by the long day's events, J.E. quickly filled him in on what they knew.

"Mom thinks the seven, including the boy who was taken, are somehow involved with us in our fight against the rise of evil," said J.E., holding on with one hand as the ambulance swerved through a corner. "We don't know how they are involved, and they don't know either. But the fact one of them was taken says something."

"Yes," replied the monsignor as they arrived at the emergency room. "One of the seven has been taken. You might say the circle is broken."

PART
III

The Mount

And he gathered them together into a place called in the
Hebrew tongue Armageddon.
—Revelation 16:16

CHAPTER

70

"Who are you?" screamed Cloe as the jet lifted off the runway. "What do you want?"

"Calm yourself, Dr. Lejeune," said the Burnt Man, just loud enough to be heard over the engines.

"Where are we being taken?" she demanded.

Cloe had been strapped into a seat next to Robby. The kidnapper sat at a table, tapping text into a laptop. *Probably a message to whomever this man works for*, she thought. *Mission accomplished.*

She looked at Robby. He was wide-eyed, not taking his eyes off the man. She put her arm around him and pulled him as close as the seat belts permitted.

"It'll be okay, Robby," she whispered.

"I know, Dr. Cloe," the child responded.

Cloe looked up at the figure across the table, who had now finished what he was doing on the computer and was staring at her. *Do I know you?*

"You think you know me?" asked the man, stealing the thought from her mind.

She glared at him. His coat collar was up, and his hat was still pulled down. She could not see much of his face except his eyes and part of his nose. The nose was a pitted husk, as if disfigured in a fire, but the eyes were clear and bright.

"Yes ... no. How could I? Have we met?"

The man paused for so long that Cloe thought at first that he must not have heard her.

"Yes," was all he said.

He stood with some effort and walked toward the back of the plane, apparently checking on his men. The walk was once again familiar. Cloe turned, and out of the corner of her eye she saw that he was removing his coat and stowing his hat.

He strode back to the table and sat opposite her. Cloe stared into his face and gasped in shock. His skin rippled like midday heat against his bones. Red-and-blue scabs and scars repulsed her as nothing else had in her life. He had no ears, no eyebrows, no hair of any kind. She had never seen a visage so damaged. *Ruined*, was all she could think.

"Good God!" she said, shooting a look of concern at Robby. She was stunned; Robby had not turned away or averted his eyes. He stared at the man. She wondered if he was in some kind of shock.

"I'll pray for you, Mister," said Robby abruptly. "Does it hurt?"

"Yes, the scars hurt," the Burnt Man said after a bit. "But I've gotten used to the pain."

"I don't mean the scars," said Robby.

The Burnt Man stared at the boy.

"I once knew a boy about your age," said the Burnt Man.

Cloe saw the man flinch slightly as if in pain. He hid it very well, and she was not sure at first that she had seen anything. But as she studied his ravaged face and—she had to admit it—beautiful eyes, she knew that Robby had somehow evoked a strong reaction in him.

"My boss takes away the pain when he lays hands on my face," said the Burnt Man. "He's the only one."

"He's not the only one," said Robby, slipping out of his seat and walking directly to the Burnt Man. "Your boss causes the pain so he can take it away. Let me look at your face."

The Burnt Man was taken aback and hesitant at first, but he leaned down closer to Robby. Robby looked upon his disfigured countenance and then spat in his hands and placed them across the Burnt Man's face. Robby bowed his head and prayed. The Burnt Man moaned and fell toward Robby, ending up on his knees in the aisle.

Cloe glanced around for some means of escape or defense, but there was none.

The Burnt Man came swiftly upright and said, "What did you do? My face is burning!"

"I'm not sure what it is, but this will help. I know that," said Robby. "You will be healed."

"Healed?" mocked the Burnt Man. "My face is on fire from whatever you did, and you say it will be healed? Only my boss can heal my face!"

"He's not your boss, and I didn't say anything about healing your face," said Robby in a small child's voice.

The Burnt Man sat back on the seat behind him and stared in apparent confusion at the boy.

"I'm beyond healing."

Boss … boss, thought Cloe as she flashed back to what Tomas and his men called him. An old memory surfaced.

"Oh my God! *Michael!*" she cried.

CHAPTER

71

The monsignor stood in the rear of the Cathedral of Christ the King and watched the cardinals enter. He could smell the incense wafting through the air from an alcove to the right of the main altar. While it was dubbed a cathedral, aside from its age, it was not much more than what would be found in an average parish church in Europe or America. It was the oldest Catholic church in Iceland, dating from about 1864. *Still, it is not the Sistine Chapel,* thought the monsignor. The usual sea of scarlet was today a mere trickle of barely thirty cardinals, who came from all over the world to elect a new pope.

"What will they do when they find out the pope is still alive?" asked the father curator.

"I don't know. We are sworn to secrecy," said the monsignor.

The monsignor glanced over at his colleague and friend and saw a tear in the corner of his eye.

"They are so few," said the monsignor, understanding his pain.

"Yes." The curator sniffed. "And the centuries-old tradition of the conclave at the Sistine Chapel is finished."

"My friend, you are very knowledgeable and wise, but I would beg to have you consider what the Church has versus what it is," said the monsignor. "It has many traditions, some ancient such as the conclave and the sealing of the Sistine Chapel to elect a pope. But that's not what the Church is. You will recall that the first pope, Peter, was simply anointed by Christ as the rock on which the church would be built. There was no vote and certainly no Sistine Chapel."

"Yes, quite right, Albert." The curator shrugged. "It's just that I miss the tradition of it all."

"Yes, we all do, but the Church, as the worldwide body of Catholics, has survived for two millennia and will continue to do so," replied the monsignor. "It's the spirit of the body of Christ … it's the people."

"But how will we carry on?" asked the older priest.

The monsignor turned and looked directly at his old friend and said, "We are now leaner, and we will get meaner if that's what it takes to defeat this evil that has gripped the earth. In the book of Revelation, Jesus himself defeated the beast and threw him into the abyss for a thousand years. We must be ready to do likewise."

"I wish I had your courage, Albert," said the curator. "It just all seems too much."

"Take heart, Father Curator. We have the wherewithal to overcome this latest challenge. We must find the right tools, the correct approach."

The monsignor looked around as a commotion arose at the heavy wooden entry doors to the church.

"Father, look!" he cried. "It's Father Anton! He must have come directly from the pope."

The monsignor and the curator moved toward the porch on the front of the church.

"What's the meaning of this interruption?" cried the camerlengo, who was responsible for the conclave and the gathering of the cardinals. "We are about to send all but the cardinals out and seal the doors for our deliberations."

Father Anton stood tall and said, "By all means, Father Camerlengo, please proceed to do so, but the monsignor and the curator will stay. I have a message they must hear, along with the cardinals."

"Impossible! And you are impertinent, young man!" declared the camerlengo, now beginning to grow angry. "It will not do."

"Father Camerlengo, please clear the church and seal the doors," said Father Anton. "I have an urgent message to deliver that may be heard only by the conclave and my colleagues."

"From whom does this message come?" asked a nearby cardinal.

"The source of the message may only be known by the conclave," said Father Anton firmly but respectfully.

The camerlengo glanced over at the monsignor and crossed his arms over his chest in a gesture that clearly communicated his disdain.

"Camerlengo, I pray hear this man out," said the monsignor. "He comes directly from an unimpeachable source."

Audible chatter issued from the cardinals now gathered around the camerlengo and Father Anton as they speculated on the source of the message and its contents.

"The pope is dead!" cried one of the cardinals. "We are here to elect his successor."

"Has the camerlengo performed his sacred duty and pronounced the pope dead?" challenged the monsignor.

Again, confusion reigned with all eyes turning on the camerlengo.

"He was reported killed when Castel Gandolfo was sacked," was all he could say.

The curator stepped forward and said, "You all know me. I have overseen the Vatican library for a half century. I have served each of you. Hear this man out!"

"Empty the hall and seal the doors!" cried the camerlengo, raising his right arm and pointing to the entrance.

The personal servants of the cardinals and a few trusted administrative personnel were all sworn to secrecy, and then they left the church to await their call.

When only the cardinals and Father Anton, the monsignor, and the curator were left, the camerlengo stepped to the front of the group and said, "Father, please deliver your message."

"Thank you, Father Camerlengo," said the priest.

He then turned to the cardinals and in a loud voice so all could hear, he said, "The pope lives!"

Chaos ruled in the old church as the cardinals came to this truth and began to shout questions.

"How? Where? Praise God!"

"The pope is in hiding, recovering from his injuries suffered in the blast that destroyed the Castel Gandolfo," said the priest.

"My God! I understand you cannot say where he is, but to know he is alive and recovering is a miracle!" exclaimed the camerlengo.

"It is God's will," said the curator.

"It is both," replied the soldier-priest. "Now, Camerlengo, would you examine this writing from the pope and verify its authenticity?"

The camerlengo took the scroll, which had been sealed in heated wax, and examined it.

"There is no stamp of the papal ring," said the camerlengo.

"No, the Ring of the Fisherman was used as ransom for my release from Malta," said the monsignor. "Do you know the pope's hand?"

"Certainly," said the camerlengo, looking over the writing very carefully. "It is the pope's handwriting."

"Read the message!" one of the cardinals called.

CHAPTER
72

Cloe and the boy stood in an enormous suite on top of an impossibly tall building in what she thought must be the Middle Eastern country of Dubai. They had deplaned and come here in a blacked-out Suburban, so she saw little of the surrounding area. The elevator, however, was a dead giveaway as to the size of the building. *So this is the tallest building in the world?* Somehow, it was fitting.

As they rose toward Michael's mysterious overlord, she had felt again the shock of recognizing him. She had thought him dead and long out of her life. *How could he have survived?* Cloe's mind went back to that night with Michael on the terrace of the old hotel in Tunis. *Magic,* she thought, and her heart ached.

The suite was entirely empty. There was not a stick of furniture. There was no art and no window treatments. There was only white and the huge windows. There were no light fixtures, yet light was omnipresent. She and Robby cast no shadows. The light was not stark or oppressive but just a source of illumination. That was the only way she could explain it. She had entered the cave of the creature, but she wondered if the cave might actually be the creature, or at least a part of it. *How else to explain this?*

She and Robby moved toward the huge floor-to-ceiling windows. She could discern nothing on the ground below them but a light here and there. The emptiness outside swept over her, and she stepped back, slightly nauseated.

The Burnt Man waited in silence.

248

Cloe caught movement out of the corner of her left eye. She spun in that direction to see a tall man dressed all in black standing a few feet away from her. He was studying the boy. Cloe watched him carefully. He was perfectly coifed and garbed. His eyes were flat black with no depth at all. Shark eyes. His skin was lily-white, but his lips were rosebud red. Was this the center of the evil now loosed on the earth? He was only a man. Only a man—but much more.

"Good evening, Dr. Lejeune," he said. "My name is Icar. Now that you are here, welcome to my home."

"We had little choice," replied Cloe. "Your man was most insistent. Why are we here?"

"Ah, directly to the point, I see," replied Icar. "The boy is here to remove him from the other six. Without the seventh—the boy—they are harmless to me. But the boy himself—is he harmless? I'm not sure."

"Robby is a seven-year-old child," said Cloe. "What threat could he possibly be to you?"

"One never knows. It pays to be on the safe side," said Icar. "Have you not translated the journal passages of the dialogue between St. John and that man?"

"Yes, I have completed the translation," said Cloe, wondering if he would hear the lie.

"Then you know that one of the seven rises and becomes the leader," said Icar. "It might be this boy."

Cloe laughed. "So you think this seven-year-old child is the leader of the seven? That is assuredly not so. I have met their leader. Who are the seven anyway and what possible threat can they be to you?"

"They have been here from ancient times in different forms, different people at different times, waiting, always waiting for me," said Icar. "We have tangled before."

"Without much success, I gather," said Cloe.

"Well, this has been pleasant, Dr. Lejeune, but why are *you* here?" asked Icar, turning to the Burnt Man. "I sent for *one* of the seven, did I not?"

Cloe gawked at the change in Icar, from the chatty colleague to the terrible taskmaster. *Why am I here?*

"And I brought you one of the seven," said the Burnt Man. "You said nothing about the others. I used my judgment. She is the leader of the Vatican group. Perhaps she can be used as leverage to achieve your plan."

"My plan needs no leverage. It has been set in motion. Nothing can stop me. Plagues and chaos abound, and the US sits on the sidelines. The Vatican is destroyed, and the pope is in hiding. There is nothing that can be done to oppose me," spewed Icar.

"Impressive," said Cloe. "So why kidnap a child?"

Icar turned on her with fire in his eyes. The lights in the suite dimmed slightly and then burst forth with a brightness that was painful.

"You do provoke me!" he hissed.

"The mighty Icar," Cloe mocked, gaining confidence or maybe just shedding her fear. "Afraid of a boy. Your plans may be in motion, but I sense an Achilles' heel. There is a card here that, if pulled, brings the whole house down."

"You have obviously read the prophecy," said Icar. His eyes swept over her.

Until that very moment, Cloe had not thought of the coded passage in the journal as a prophecy. Now it all made perfect sense. These were not Jesus's instructions as to what to do upon the rise of evil. This was his foretelling of how events would unfold in this second cycle of evil. This was why Icar was so afraid of the boy.

Cloe laughed and pressed, "What a waste. All this destruction and death. Only to end with another thousand-year nap for you."

Icar roared, and the whole place went black and then brilliant white again.

"You task me!" he snarled. "Your life hangs in the balance! Do *not* provoke me further."

"Nothing original to say, Icar? I'm not a whale, white or otherwise." Cloe smiled demurely, wondering whether his allusion to Melville was deliberate. "The boy is just a boy, and I demand that we be set free. If your plans truly cannot be stopped, there can be no harm in letting us go."

"Perhaps you are correct, Dr. Lejeune," replied the demon-man with a thin smile on his face, turning to the Burnt Man. "Michael, take them immediately to the observation deck and set them free."

CHAPTER

73

"Brothers," the message began. The enclave of cardinals was completely silent. A pin dropping would have made a racket.

"Brothers, Father Anton bears my message, and I bid you to heed him," said Father Anton, reading the papal missive.

Father Anton put the scroll down and looked at the assembled group.

"Read the rest of the message!" cried one of the cardinals.

"That is all that is written," said the warrior-priest. "The pope would not trust the rest to paper."

"What else is there and how can we know it is true?" questioned another cardinal.

"I will tell you the rest, and you will judge the truth," said Father Anton.

Father Anton looked at the monsignor, and he nodded for him to continue.

"His Holiness says we are at war," started the priest slowly. "We are in a thousand-year struggle with the beast. Evil appears now at every quadrant. But it has all been foretold. This is the second cycle of evil. Originally, in the time of our Lord, it ended with Jesus banishing the beast to the abyss for a thousand years."

"Yes, yes ... that is written in the book of Revelation by St. John," observed one of the cardinals. "But what of today?"

"The first cycle occurred during the Dark Ages, and again, evil was vanquished," said the priest. "The second cycle is now upon us. It is up to us to confront and to pitch evil into the abyss. To do this, we need a warrior-leader of the church. We need someone of proven mettle who can lead us into battle."

The cardinals murmured amongst themselves as they heard this. The monsignor thought he heard agreement in the whispers.

"The Church requires a person who can assume the mantle of battle and take the fight to the beast," said Father Anton, his voice rising.

Now the assent among the cardinals was louder with some saying, "Yes!"

"The pope has designated such a person," shouted the priest. "He will assume the post of vicar of St. Michael, a position vacant for a millennium. To him shall fall the sword and lance of St. Michael the archangel. These are among the most sacred of the Vatican treasures. Upon his shoulders shall rest the fate of the Church and of humanity."

The room was dead silent now. No one shouted or cheered as the weight of the incredible responsibility fell upon the assembled group. Cardinals prayed aloud that this not be their lot.

"Who is it?" whispered the camerlengo.

"The pope has decreed that the vicar of St. Michael the archangel," cried Father Anton, "the one to confront and to defeat the beast, shall be Father Albert Roques, the monsignor!"

CHAPTER

74

"Boss, I can't take them to the observation deck; if there are people up there this evening, they will notice and ask questions," warned the Burnt Man.

Icar turned on Michael and walked closer to him. "Michael, is there something different about you? I sense a change."

"No, boss. It's the same old me, but this is a dumb plan. It goes too far," he replied.

The dark man smiled and said, "No one will care. There's no security in the building, and no one would have the gall to question me. Be done with it."

Cloe could see Michael processing his choices.

"Follow me," he said forcefully.

Neither Cloe nor the child made to move.

Michael spun on his heels and grabbed Cloe's arm with one claw-like hand, laying his other hand at the nape of Robby's neck. Cloe fought back, trying to tear her arm away from his grasp, but it was like being pinned by an iron vice.

Robby held up his small hands and said, "Dr. Cloe, don't worry. We have nothing to fear." He began to walk slowly toward the door.

Icar laughed softly and headed out of the room.

Cloe at last wrenched her arm from Michael's grip, straightened her clothes, and moved toward the door.

As he unlocked the door, Cloe whispered to him, "Michael … not the child."

He simply smiled. "Why not?"

"Michael, is there no shred of decency left in you?" asked Cloe as he opened the door and ushered them into the all-white elevator lobby. He pressed the call button for the elevator.

She could hear the mechanical voice of the building as it began its metallic speech, and in a couple of seconds she heard the rush of the high-speed car. It would be there shortly.

Michael had not answered her question. He seemed lost in thought. What little brow he had left convulsed, and he bent slightly as if he had been punched.

The elevator arrived, and the doors opened. Michael pushed them into the car, and the doors closed. The elevator awaited instructions.

As the seconds ticked by, Cloe noticed the button for the observation deck was at the top of the panel while the button for the lobby was at the very bottom. They could be at the observation deck in a matter of moments.

It was plain that Michael was engaged in some terrible internal struggle. He turned to the panel of buttons.

"Don't worry, Dr. Cloe. He will do the right thing somehow," said Robby.

Michael turned to her with fire in his eyes and screeched a bloodcurdling scream. Cloe and Robby clapped their hands to their ears. Then Michael spun back to the board and pushed his thumb directly onto the top button.

The car rocketed toward the upper deck.

Fear seized Cloe, a cold, greasy feeling roiling up from the pit of her stomach. *Not the child.* Cloe prepared to fight as she had never fought before. She prayed for God to give her the strength to save the boy.

The elevator stopped at the observation-deck level, and the doors began to open. Cloe looked out but could see nothing but blackness beyond the wall surrounding the deck. Time began to slow down as Michael turned toward her. She balled her hands into fists and growled at him.

"Where are we?" asked Robby, breaching Cloe's concentration.

She half-turned to him on the other side of the elevator, but before she could speak, the doors began to close. She rotated back to Michael and the panel of buttons and saw he had mashed the lobby button.

"We're going down!" she cried.

"You're going home," Michael said, "if I can get you there. The man up there will be after us and will kill me and you in a most unpleasant way when he realizes what I have done."

"Why, Michael? *Why?*" asked Cloe.

"I can't kill this child," he said. "He's only a little younger than my youngest was when he died."

"But you have killed so many."

"Yes, including my own children, although that was not intended. It was a terrible accident," he said, slumping with the weight of his awful guilt. "I was terribly burned that night on Masada, and I thought all humanity had been seared from me. I joined Icar to take my revenge."

"So what has changed?" Cloe asked.

"I don't know. I only know I cannot harm this child," he said as the elevator began to slow for the lobby stop.

CHAPTER

75

Michael walked quickly from the elevator through the lobby of the unholy building. Cloe and Robby had to trot to keep up with him. He burst through the double glass doors and headed for the black Suburban parked in front. Icar might even now be after them.

"Get in quickly," he said hoarsely.

Cloe sat Robby in the passenger seat next to her and strapped them both in.

"Do we have a chance?" Cloe asked.

"Yes," said Michael, backing away and heading the Suburban out to the highway. "He's not God. He's not even a god. While there's much mystery about him, I believe him to be an angel, a fallen angel but in human form. Right now he's just a man—although in some ways he's very special. He's in human form so he can reach the masses. This dilutes his demonic powers as best I can understand it. But he's still not your average Joe, and he grows stronger day by day."

"Where are we going?" asked Cloe.

"The airport, and as fast as we can get there. The more distance we put between ourselves and Icar, the less he can sense us and know what we are doing."

"Why isn't he after us now?" she asked, looking back but seeing nothing.

"He may be, but I think he's gone to the place where he goes to withdraw and somehow recharge himself," said Michael. "He does this most nights, although sometimes he lingers to see if I'm doing what he told me to do. The man has no trust."

"I see," said Cloe. "That's why you took the elevator up first instead of straight down to the lobby."

"Yes, that and, in part, because I had not fully decided what to do with you," Michael responded. "The boy touched something in me, something deeper and more profound than just my face. He reminded me of a lot of things."

Cloe considered this and looked down at the young boy sitting beside her. His eyes were drooping, and he was beginning to nod off.

He turned slightly to get more comfortable and said, just before closing his eyes, "The bad man is gone for a while."

They raced over deserted highways and roads and entered the general aviation area of the airport. No guards were in sight as Michael parked the vehicle.

"Everyone's scared to death and in their homes or have gone into the desert," said Michael.

He picked up Robby, and they headed toward the hangar. There Cloe saw what looked like a beautiful new Lear jet. No airplane had ever looked better to her.

"Now, all we need is a pilot and some fuel," she said.

"The jet is kept fueled in case the boss needs it. It's all ready to go."

"We need Sky, your old pilot," Cloe said with a nervous smile.

"I can't claim to have taught Sky, but I did learn from him," he said as he opened the hatch to the jet's interior and then ran around and unchocked the wheels.

Returning, he helped them onto the plane and to get strapped in.

"Unless you are a licensed jet pilot or have a better offer, I'm going up there and get us out of here. While I was recuperating from the bomb blast in Brazil years ago, I did the work and got my license. Sky helped me a lot."

Cloe watched as he trotted up the aisle to the pilot deck. Soon the engines fired and the jet began to roll out of the hangar. She could hear his communications with the tower, which was apparently telling him he was not cleared to take off since no flight plan had been filed.

He looked back and yelled, "Hang on! This might be rough!"

He taxied rapidly over the tarmac and turned onto the main runway. Official vehicles with lights flashing rushed toward them, some of which were heading in front of them to block the runway.

Michael firewalled the throttles and simultaneously released the brakes. The little plane shot forward as if launched from a slingshot. It tore down the runway, both engines screaming, drifting slightly from side to side as he fought for control.

From her aisle seat, Cloe saw the flashing red lights through the cockpit and out the windshield. Emergency vehicles had been set up as a sort of mobile barricade across the runway. There was no way this airplane was going through the wall of trucks ahead.

Faster and faster the little plane rushed at the line of vehicles that now looked impossibly close.

"We're not going to make it!" cried Cloe. She grabbed the sleeping boy and held him close.

She felt the plane rotate, but she knew it was too early. Still the jet fluttered airborne just enough to clear the barricade. This early leap killed the airspeed, and the plane slammed back to earth on the outbound side of the line of trucks. As the plane drifted over the official line, she could see the men below with their mouths open in surprise.

When the Lear hit the runway on the other side of the trucks, the impact was so hard she did not know how the jet stayed upright. She bit her tongue, and blood flowed from her mouth. Robby slept on. Somehow Michael steadied the hurdling plane and pushed the throttles over harder. The jet shook with stress but continued down the runway, again gathering speed. *How much runway is left?* she wondered. Ahead, she could see dark silhouettes that might be buildings. *How far?*

This time the jet shot off the end of the runway like the phoenix reborn. The plane immediately rolled violently to port, and Cloe wondered if it had been damaged. Her stomach leaped into her throat, and she gagged briefly with the beginnings of motion sickness. Then they were over open water that she knew could only be the Persian Gulf. They were safe but still not higher than a few hundred feet.

Cloe unbuckled her seat belt and moved into the companionway leading into the cockpit.

"Michael, where are we going and what's our plan?" she said loudly over the engine noise.

"We have to stay low and fly north toward the Mediterranean," he replied. "If we can stay at this level, we may avoid the fighters from several countries that will be looking for us. Egypt, Syria, and Saudi Arabia come to mind."

"But where will we go? My friends are all in Iceland," Cloe said. "I must join them and finish my work. I have important new insights that will help us."

"We don't have the range for that," Michael replied, looking up and back at her. "I would have to stop for fuel, and we would certainly be picked up, arrested, or worse."

"Where can we go?" she asked.

"There's only one place that might be safe—at least for a while," he replied.

"Where?"

"The sanctuary ... we go to the sanctuary."

CHAPTER

76

"I'm not sure what to call you," said J.E. to the monsignor as they sat at a table in the old church and tried to figure out ways of finding and rescuing Cloe and the boy.

"Albert, or Monsignor if you prefer, J.E.," responded the monsignor. "I'm not changed because of the pope's confidence and designation. If anything, I'm humbled by it."

"But, Albert, you have been tapped by the pope to lead the Catholic Church against the evil that is now here," argued J.E., his eyes open wide. "What more important or greater role is there than that?"

"I don't know, J.E., and I don't know what I will do next," said the monsignor, putting his coffee cup aside and turning directly to his friend. "I'm just as shocked as anyone by these events."

"Well, I guess you'll have to figure it out. It seems all of Christianity is on your shoulders."

"We will need to gather Zack and his cohorts," said the monsignor. "Cloe was right: they are part of this. The father curator has kept them safe, but it is now our time."

Just then J.E.'s satellite phone on his belt buzzed. He picked it up but did not recognize the number. He pushed the button to answer and put his ear to the receiver.

"J.E.," said a voice. "Can you hear me?"

"Mom!" cried the young soldier, his voice full of emotion. "Are you all right? Where are you?"

"I'm fine, J.E. Is Albert there with you?"

"Mom, he's here, but there are things you should know," responded J.E., filling his mother in on the developments at the church in Reykjavik.

"J.E., this is astonishing, and I can't think of anyone more worthy or capable of leading us against this terrible evil we face than the monsignor," she said.

"Where are you?" he asked.

Cloe hesitated and then said, "Robby and I are in the mountains near the Turkish-Armenian border. We've been here before. Michael is with us."

"Mom, what are you talking about? We went over this so many times. Michael is long dead. I saw him blown up at Masada," said the young soldier.

"All true, J.E., but you did not actually see Michael's body. Somehow he was not killed, although he was horribly burned. He's nearly unrecognizable," she replied. "He survived and rebuilt the lodge in the mountains. We are there now."

"But how did you find him?" asked J.E., walking around the ancient wooden table.

"We didn't. He found us," she replied. "He led the group that attacked our plane at Reykjavik. It was he who took the boy."

"But I don't understand," said J.E. "He's our enemy. He proved that at Masada and at Reykjavik."

"J.E., put the phone on speaker so Albert can hear as well," said Cloe. "I'm not sure how to explain what has happened, but I need both of you."

There was a gush of noise as the external speaker was engaged, and then the monsignor said, "Cloe, it's so good you and Robby are well. I've been following the conversation. Are you in physical danger?"

"I don't think so, Albert—at least not immediately," she said. "Our danger is from Icar. He is the evil that is behind all that is going on. He believes he's on the cusp of completely disabling the Church. He is aware the pope lives, but he knows everything is in confusion and the leadership is not there."

"What about Michael? He's not our friend," asserted the priest. "Are you in jeopardy from him right now?"

"I don't think so," said Cloe. "The boy has had some effect on him. He's different. He was with Icar, but when Icar gave orders to have us killed, he could not do it. I can't explain it. It's extraordinary. He knows

Icar will search for us, so he has brought us to the mountains where he feels safe. He believes Icar doesn't know of the place and it's far enough away from him that he cannot easily detect us. But his spies will find us eventually. I'm worried that it is only a matter of time."

"I wonder if Michael has really changed. Can he be trusted?" asked J.E., now back in his chair leaning over the phone on the table.

"I'm not sure," said Cloe. "But Michael is afraid of Icar and believes he will search for him because he cannot let the betrayal go unpunished. I think we are okay at least for the time being."

"Cloe, we have some further news," said the monsignor.

"What is it, Albert?"

"The monks in what's left of the Opts Center have been able to give us a complete translation of the cuneiform sections of the journal," he replied. "They used the clues from the German scientist and their own research to create a template for the translation, a kind of Rosetta Stone. We think we know what it says."

The line was quiet for a moment as the monsignor summoned the words to tell Cloe the answer to what she had been seeking for the last several years.

"What does it say?" she asked, simply.

"Understand, this is just preliminary, but we think it's close to being right," he cautioned.

"Yes?"

"I'm sending it to your phone, but what they have come up with is this:

Evil must be sealed at the Mount;
Good will serve the Seven.
Rely upon the innocent;
For these will suffer to come unto Me.
But who is innocent?
Such a one will arise, and
The evil one will be cast into the Abyss."

The men heard Cloe exhale deeply through the receiver. "This is the most obscure section of the most important document ever unearthed in the history of man. The prophecy of Christ, himself, on the defeat of evil. This is the core of the journal."

"Yes," confirmed the priest.

"Albert," she said as the static crackled over the phone and she studied the text. "What do you think it means?"

"Cloe, all I can tell you is what the monks told me when they called to give me the translation," responded the monsignor.

"What did they say?"

"They said they could tell us what it says, but somebody else will have to tell us what it *means*."

"I think I have an idea or two," said Cloe thoughtfully. "How soon can you be here?"

"Wait!" said J.E. "They also sent us a translation of the writing on the back of the 'seven' cards."

"Yes," said the priest. "According to the monks, it says, 'The time is close.'"

"That seems pretty plain to me. When can you leave, and when will you be here?" she asked.

"Sky is waiting at the airport for us now," replied the monsignor. "Even so, if you are where I think you are, it will be several hours."

"Albert, I will need you, J.E., and the curator along with as many of the Swiss Guard as you can muster," said Cloe. "This will be a fight much worse than Masada. I need you to tell Captain Jacob we will need him and his people as well. Bring Zack and his friends. I will have the boy."

"But, Cloe, where are we going?" asked the monsignor.

"We are going to the mount," she replied. "To Israel."

"Israel ... of course," he replied after a moment.

"And, Albert ..." whispered Cloe.

"Yes?"

"Hurry."

CHAPTER

77

Cloe hung up the phone and wondered how long it would be before the monsignor arrived to take her, Michael, and the boy to what she thought might be the final ... what? Battle? Confrontation? *No*, she thought, *this will be a war, a thousand-year war.*

She looked down at Robby, and she smiled back at his smile. He was a trouper and had stayed close to her. She and Robby were on the long couch in the chalet's great room. They had been there for several hours, and although they had dozed a bit, it seemed it must be approaching midday.

"Robby, are you all right?' she asked.

"Sure, Dr. Cloe. I'm fine," he responded. "I just wish Bully was here."

"Well, Bully should be with us soon. I think my friends will bring him here. Where's Michael?" The chalet felt otherwise deserted.

"He's gone," replied Robby.

"Gone? What do you mean? Where could he have gone?"

"He's gone back to the bad man," said Robby. "He left while you were on the phone."

"How could he do that? What did he say?" asked Cloe, dread making her skin clammy.

"He just said he had to go, but he left you a letter," said Robby, handing her an envelope.

"Oh my God!" whispered Cloe, flashing back to Tunisia, years before, to the last letter Michael had left her, one of error and apology.

She carefully opened the message and read the two lines it contained: "Cloe, I've made a terrible mistake. I must go back to where I belong now that you and the boy are safe. I'm sorry."

She stared at the note from the man she had thought at one time that she might have loved. He had betrayed her at Masada. He had never been what he had pretended to be. Now, another betrayal. She had to face it: Michael was evil to the core. He was incapable of change. Even the boy's effect on him was only temporary.

She shook her head violently and turned away from Robby so he would not see the tears. Even so, she was not sure if these were tears of loss or anger or something in between. One thing was certain; Michael had been lost to her at Masada, and his own acts now, once again, condemned him.

Dabbing her eyes on her sleeve, she faced the boy and said, "Okay, Robby, we need to get ready. Our friends will be here after a while."

"We're going after the bad man, aren't we, Dr. Cloe?" asked the boy.

"Yes, Robby," replied Cloe. "We're going after the bad man."

"You know it's our job, don't you?"

"I know that's somehow true. How do you know that?" she asked.

"Bully told me," he said.

Cloe thought about this and could not say otherwise.

"Do you know who the bad man is?" she asked, testing the boy.

"Yes."

"Do you know his name?" persisted Cloe.

"Yes."

"Well, can you tell me?" she asked.

"No," he said.

"Why not?"

"It's not safe."

"Not safe? It's just you and me here," she replied. "Even Michael is gone."

The boy looked at her, and his eyes widened.

"Dr. Cloe, to say that name out loud would be to open a door that couldn't be closed."

CHAPTER

78

"Cloe, it is so good to see you," declared the monsignor, giving her a huge hug.

"And you too, Albert."

No sooner had she greeted the monsignor than J.E. grabbed her in a bear hug. They had assembled in the chalet's great room with its magnificent view of the mountain range on the border separating Armenia from Turkey. The furnishings were rustic and oversized as befitted a mountain lodge.

"Mom, you're safe. Thank God!" said her son.

"*Waraff!*" cried Bully, standing on his hind legs.

Robby ran to him, and Cloe saw he was at least a foot and a half taller than the boy. Robby hugged the huge dog and would have been rolled over by Bully but for his great strength.

"Good boy, good Bully!" whispered Robby, giving Bully's ears a world-class scratch. "I missed you so much."

Cloe looked around and said, "Where's everyone else? Where are Zack and the others?"

"They're at the airport with the Swiss," said J.E. "Robby's mother is still being tended to in Iceland, but she said to tell Robby she's fine and she loves him."

Cloe looked at the boy. His eyes were moist—he was missing his mom.

"We came to get you, Michael, and the boy," said the monsignor. "The plane is being refueled. We figured you would want to go as quickly as possible."

"Yes," replied Cloe.

"But where's Michael?" asked J.E., looking about. "I still don't see how he survived the Claymore at Masada."

"He's gone, J.E.," she replied.

"Gone? Gone where?"

The monsignor, who stood near the window gazing out across the mountains, turned full around to face them. "I'm guessing he's gone back to Icar."

"That seems to be the case," said Cloe, showing them the letter. "I don't get it. He seemed to be free of Icar—the boy had a positive effect on him. We would be dead but for Michael. Why would he go back? He has to know Icar would suspect him and likely kill him. Why did he leave?"

"Cloe, I don't know for sure, but the child must have appealed to some small part of him that remained good. But away from Icar and with you safe, he could not resist his fate," said the monsignor. "The temptation of power and greed is strong."

J.E. hugged his mother. They listened to the crackling of the fire, laid by Michael, in the huge fireplace.

Then Cloe turned and clenched her right hand into a fist and said, "All right, we know the score. Now, let's go put Icar to sleep for another thousand years."

* * *

The airplane was noisy with the engines and the Swiss clinking and clanking weapons as they cleaned them and prepared for battle. People shouted back and forth, and spirits were high. Cloe sat with J.E., the monsignor, the curator, and the others in the middle of the executive jet. Cloe had checked in with Jeanne in New Orleans to see if they had developed any more information, but there was nothing new. She told her of the prophecy, and they speculated on its meaning.

Zack and Mel were helping them work on a plan. Rey and Zoe talked quietly, and Louie sharpened his blade. Robby dozed a few seats away with Bully curled at his feet. They barely had a platoon of the Swiss, but it was all the monsignor could round up. *Still, it's a game bunch,* thought Cloe.

"Cloe, the translation," said the monsignor. "You said you thought you knew what it meant?"

Cloe looked at her friend, Albert, precious Albert, now a virtual member of her family. She looked at J.E., who she knew had studied the Bible while deployed in Iraq. Then there were Zack and Mel and the curator all watching her expectantly. Robby and Bully both stared at her, exuding a kind of knowing confidence. Well, it had all come down to this. Now they had to be right.

"Here's what I think I know," she started. "The first line of the translated section of the coded part of the journal says, 'Evil must be sealed at the Mount.'"

"Yes," said the curator. "I think we can say whatever and wherever the finale will be, it will occur at the so-called mount."

"No, Father Curator, it's more than that," said Cloe. "'Evil must be sealed' has to mean something, and I believe it means evil will be defeated at the mount. Remember, I now believe this is not a formula for the conquest of the beast but a prophecy."

"You're telling us that you think Christ is saying this is what *will* happen," observed the curator. "If so, we must believe this will happen. We will be victorious. The end is foreordained."

"Yes," said Cloe. "That seems correct, but it doesn't feel right. It seems to say evil has no chance."

"Here's the thing," said the monsignor. "It's the difference between *must* and *will*."

"I think I see," said Zack. "The prophecy says evil must be sealed at the mount, which suggests this is where the battle has to take place. It's a prophecy as to the location of the fight and not as to the outcome."

"Good Lord! Of course, you're right," said Cloe, turning to Zack. "The end is not preordained, only the venue of the deciding battle. So, what we know is that if the beast is to be defeated, it will be at this mount."

"If we are correct in our thinking, we must find this place ... this mount," said the monsignor. "There we will find Icar."

"But what about the next line, the one that says 'Good will serve the Seven'?" asked J.E.

"The number seven is a very common reference in biblical history and may be thought of as a lucky and perhaps holy number," said the curator. "The most obvious reference is to the creation of the world with God resting on the seventh day. With its derivatives, such as seventh and sevenfold, it is used almost nine hundred times in the Bible, fifty-four times in the book of Revelation alone."

"Quite right. In Revelation, there is a reference to the seven seals. It's part of the unfolding of the apocalypse," said the monsignor.

"Seven seals?" Cloe observed. "It cannot be a coincidence that the words sealed and seven are used in the first section of the translation. Also, our German friends at Uruk mentioned these words. Let's carefully go over once again what we know."

"This is connected," said the curator, over the noise of the engines.

"But in the book of Revelation, the seals are opened by the Lamb and presage the final battle, the apocalypse, including the unleashing of the four horsemen," observed the monsignor. "How does that relate to 'evil being sealed' in the translation?"

J.E., who had been listening intently, said, "It's all Revelation. When the Lamb opened the fourth seal, it loosed a pale horse. Its rider was named Death, and Hades was following close behind him. They were given power over a fourth of the earth to kill by sword, famine, and plague and by the wild beasts of the earth."

There was no sound among the core group except the droning of the jet engines.

"There can be little doubt that the pale horse and its rider are now among us," said the curator. "The prophecies foretold in Revelations are playing out now."

"But Christ says in the journal that evil can be sealed at the mount and good will follow the seven," said Cloe. "This must mean that what has been unsealed or opened can be resealed by the seven. This can be stopped."

"Yes, in modern terms, good, led by the seven, can defeat evil at the mount, and this will all be sealed or stopped," said the monsignor. "That's the key."

Cloe turned to Zack and the boy, now wide awake. She looked upon him and the others with new realization.

"Zack, you and your friends *are* the seven," she said finally.

"*Whooof*," cried Bully, as if in confirmation.

Zack looked as if he were crushed by the weight of responsibility. After a moment though, she saw him stand tall and strong. He was ready.

Robby smiled that slight, enigmatic smile of his as if somewhere inside he knew something.

"Let it be," the child said.

CHAPTER
79

The executive jet was nearing Israeli airspace when Sky came on the intercom and said, "Everyone in their seats and buckle up tight. There are targets on our radar headed toward us that are not answering our radio calls. This may be trouble."

Cloe tightened her seat belt, fear creeping into her shoulders and neck. She recalled the flight from Lyon, France, to Tunisia, which was sabotaged by the Kolektor's people. Now, compared to Icar, the Kolektor seemed like a piker and his brand of evil like amateur hour. J.E. went forward to see if he could help Sky.

"Albert," called Cloe, "were you able to contact Captain Jacob and the Israelis for their help?"

"Yes, I spoke with him," replied the monsignor. "He's in a hospital in Jerusalem, recovering. At the airport, we thought it was touch and go there for a while, but on closer examination, the doctors found it not to be as serious. He's already much better. We will have as much support as he and his people can give us."

J.E. had left the cockpit door open so Cloe and the monsignor could see onto the pilot deck and through the windshield. She saw Sky feverously adjusting controls and using the radio. He had put the radio on the speaker so everyone could hear the radio traffic.

J.E. had belted himself into the copilot's seat. Cloe glanced down at Robby and saw his eyes, big with wonder. There was no fear in them. *What a kid*, she thought.

An unidentified voice came on the intercom. "Vatican jet, this is the leader of the flight ahead of you. You are directed to reduce speed to two hundred knots and fall into formation with us."

Sky keyed his mike and said firmly, "Leader, identify yourself and your flight."

Cloe wondered briefly how the intruders knew this was a Vatican airplane. The leader had an accent, but it was slight and hard to identify, especially over the scratchy intercom.

"Vatican jet," said the leader, "I repeat, reduce your speed and follow us. If you do not comply, you will be shot down."

The interceptors had formed up around them: there appeared to be four in total.

"Who are they? What are they?" Cloe asked.

"They're MiG-21s, obviously fully armed," said the monsignor, studying the aircraft bristling with weapons. "As to who they are, I would have to speculate that they are soldiers of Icar or his allies."

"Leader, we are a diplomatic mission under the full protection of the Vatican," returned Sky. "You are to remove yourself from our proximity and cease from impeding our progress."

Cloe smiled at the moxie of her pilot. Sky was a piece of work. What was it Michael had said to describe his former pilot? *He could fly anything farther, faster, and better than anyone on earth.* She knew it was true.

At that point, two of the MiGs dropped off and slipped behind them.

"Hang on!" cried Sky over the intercom. "They're lining up behind us to aim their missiles."

Just then, the jet to their starboard fired a burst of machine-gun bullets. The tracers arched over the front of the Vatican jet and fell behind.

"Vatican jet, this is your last chance," said the leader of the bogies. "Drop your speed and fall in with us."

"Mayday, mayday!" shouted J.E. over the radio. "This is Victor, Romero, Mike, niner, niner, seven; we are under attack by unknown assailants. We need help immediately! We are a Vatican jet on a diplomatic mission. We need help!"

Cloe listened as J.E. continued to broadcast the distress signal and Sky coiled into a striking position. Whatever was going to happen was coming at them like a runaway freight train.

Then Sky, strangely calm, spoke into the intercom in an almost conversational voice, "Tighten those seat belts down as much as you can, scouts. We don't have guns, but we're not defenseless."

Two seconds later, the Vatican plane barrel-rolled and dropped like a stone. Cloe watched as four missiles shot past where they had been and hunted for a target. One of the MiG-21s ahead of them peeled off, and the last she saw, the missiles followed. *Blam! One down*, she thought, hearing a thunderous explosion. Her heart felt like it would lodge in her throat at the zero-to-negative gravity drop.

She turned and stared out the port and saw at least two of the jets following. She had no doubt that the remaining MiG was also hot after them. Three to one was not good, particularly because they had nothing to shoot back with.

"Fifteen thousand feet!" the monsignor shouted as Sky went to full power in an almost vertical drop.

"What?" Cloe called out over the noise of the screaming jet's descent.

"We're headed below fifteen thousand feet. The 21s are superb platforms, but they have their weak spots," cried the monsignor. "They are basically high-altitude interceptors, and below fifteen thousand feet they lose high-speed maneuverability and weapons systems tracking. Piloting becomes a lot of work, and control can be tough to maintain."

Is there nothing this man does not know? Not for the first time, she considered how much of his background was religious and how much was military. Just then, J.E. turned to her and gave her the thumbs-up signal. Obviously, J.E. was aware of the MiG's vulnerabilities as well.

"Mayday, mayday!" J.E. yelled into the mike on his headset. "We are a civilian jet on a mission from the Vatican under attack by military jets, MiG-21s. We need immediate help. We are descending below fifteen thousand feet."

Sky leveled the plane, virtually squashing everyone with the g-force of the maneuver. The jet was quickly at or near its rated high speed at this altitude. Cloe wasn't sure, but she thought it might be north of five hundred miles an hour.

"With this special jet and its modifications, top speed is closer to six hundred miles per hour," said the monsignor, reading her mind. "But we would need to be higher, in thinner air to achieve that. The MiGs are a lot faster, but at this altitude they lose maneuverability and fire-tracking capability."

Whoosh! A missile flew by to starboard.

"Damn, that was close!" cried Cloe.

Sky banked the plane hard starboard in the lee of the missile. Cloe saw the MiGs lumber into the turn but not as precisely as the Vatican jet. A small spark of hope kindled in her breast.

The remaining fighters opened up with thirty-millimeter cannon fire, and Cloe watched as the tracer rounds stitched the air around them.

Sky pushed the plane back to port, but it was too late as the impact of the large rounds hit the jet below the wing and tore something lose. Immediately the jet began to lose speed.

"Mayday, mayday!" J.E. shouted into the radio again, but there was not much hope of help now.

The Vatican jet's speed continued to bleed off, and now the MiGs had caught up. Cloe could see them dropping off to the rear to administer the coup de grâce.

"J.E.!" cried Cloe.

J.E. looked back and smiled a great, loving Lejeune smile at his mother.

Cloe returned his smile. She was so proud. She was sorry they would not complete their mission, but they had done everything they could do. She leaned back, grabbing the armrests in a death grip, and awaited whatever might come. She thought of her long-gone mother and her father.

Four thundering silver shadows, with afterburners raging white-hot, blazed by the cabin window to her right.

"No!" she exclaimed. "There are more of them!"

Blam! Blam! came the deadly explosions from behind.

Cloe thought they would explode or fall from the sky, but neither happened. She looked out the window and saw two F-16s forming up on their wingtips. The Star of David was plainly visible under the cockpits of the jets. She had no doubt that two more jets were on the other side.

"Victor, Romero, Mike, niner, niner, seven, this is Israeli flight Halo One with the compliments from Captain Ariel Jacob and the State of Israel. It seems the remaining MiG has decided to go home."

CHAPTER

80

Once again Michael slammed into the outside of the massive window on the south side of the penthouse on the 160th floor of the tower. His hands were tied behind his back, and he dangled upside down from a rope around his feet. He looked down and saw that it was a long way to the ground, but he was not afraid. If tonight was his time to die, so be it. He had put too many people in their graves to cheat the reaper if it were his turn.

Blood dripped from what was left of the end of his nose; he thought it might be broken from the last hit against the window. Well, his face hadn't been pretty in a while. The other end of the rope was fastened to a fixture on the observation deck of the tower. Icar stood inside watching as the wind blew him out and then back into the side of the building. How long had he been out there?

Icar had not been sympathetic to his story of being somehow overcome in some strange psychic way by the child. Michael had sworn that the boy had seized mental control of him and he had not come to his senses until the boy had gone to sleep at the chateau. That's when he had escaped the influence of the child. While not inclined to believe his story, Icar was nevertheless extremely interested in every detail about the boy and made him repeat it over and over. He could not get enough information on what might be the boy's powers.

"Why didn't you kill them both then and there?" he had asked.

"I thought only about escaping and getting back here," Michael had replied.

He knew Icar was weighing whether to trust him or not. His master was not so much watching him as observing him. This was his trial by fire. If he were Icar, he would just cut the rope above and be done with the problem.

Suddenly, he felt himself ascending. In a few minutes, he was sitting on the wall surrounding the observation platform, looking at his boss.

"Your thoughts are clouded from me," said Icar. "Why?"

Michael knew the beast, in human form, had lost some of its demonic power and perception.

"I don't know, boss," said Michael. "Tell me what you want to know, and I'll tell you."

Icar smiled at his number one and said, "I need you with me. Your experience with the boy may prove valuable."

"I don't know what he did, but somehow he overwhelmed me." He shook his head as the blood returned to his lower body.

"I thought you had betrayed me," said Icar. "I told you to throw them off the observation deck. The next thing I know, they are gone, and so are you."

"It was like I was in a trance or a fog," Michael replied, trying to sound convincing. "What is he anyway?"

"What is he?" mused Icar. "He's nothing, just interference from an old adversary. He taunts me by sending a child to thwart me. It's so like him. But it's too late. Everything is in motion. Even he cannot stop me."

"Good," he responded. "What do you want me to do?"

"The doctor and her friends from the Vatican are on the way to try to stop me," said Icar. "It seems my efforts so far to dispose of them have not succeeded. My fighters had them until the Jews intervened. Send my special troopers to terminate them. They will have the boy, and by now all the seven will have reunited. Kill them all. I want no last-minute interference."

Michael considered these instructions. How did Icar know Cloe was coming? Either his powers were growing or he had someone close ... inside. The special troopers were a short platoon of the absolute dregs of humanity, or what was left of humanity. They were born killers and highly skilled. Most had been mercenaries in one war or another. They were led by a bearded giant of a man with fiery red hair. Once unleashed, he knew they would follow their prey to the very gates of hell.

"As you wish, so shall it be," he said, bowing his head.

"Make preparations to move our forces to Israel. It will end there," said Icar, gazing out to the east.

"It will be done as you say. Where in Israel?"

Icar looked out over the sea far below and did not answer at first. Michael thought he might not have heard.

Just when he considered asking again, Icar said, "We go where all things end, of course."

CHAPTER

81

Cloe, J.E., the monsignor, Zack, and the curator gathered at the center table of the jet after the deadly excitement. The plane was level and stable in spite of some damage to its underbelly beneath the wings. Sky was flying in formation with the Israeli F-16s.

"How the hell did Icar know we were coming?" stormed Cloe.

"Mom, I don't know," said J.E. "But Sky says the MiGs came directly for us. This wasn't a random patrol."

"Cloe, Icar could not have known beforehand," said the curator. "Everyone here is absolutely loyal."

"True, and everyone who knows what we are doing is right here," said the monsignor.

"I wonder," said Cloe, thinking of her phone call to her office in the States. "But that's for later. Now we have to focus on the remaining elements of the translation. The passage gives us two clues as to location. The first is that it refers to evil being sealed at the mount, and the second says the evil one will be cast into the abyss."

"If I'm thinking about this correctly," said the monsignor, "we must locate the mount and then everything else will fall into place—one way or another."

The jet engines droned in the background as everyone considered the import of the monsignor's words. *One way or another.*

"We just go to the mount then," said Zack. "That's where the final battle will take place."

"Young man," said the curator. "Do you know how many mounts there are in Israel and the surrounding countries that have received some mention in the Bible?"

"Judging from your comment, I'm guessing quite a few," said Zack sheepishly.

"Just so," said the old priest. "There's the Mount of Olives, Mount Zion, Mount Ararat, Mount Sinai, and Mount Calvary just to name a few."

"We need something to narrow down the search field," said J.E. "If we have to check out all the mounts, the battle will be over before we even arrive. We need some good intel."

"There are three real possibilities," said the monsignor. "It is true there are many mounts in this area that are mentioned in the Bible. Most do not fit the context. As far as the journal tells us, this is a final battle between the forces of good and evil. Father Curator, most of the sites you mention are prominent for some other reason."

"True, Albert," replied the old priest. "We need the biblical site of God's judgment of good versus evil."

"Right, and scripture tells us a likely place is the Valley of Jehoshaphat," said the monsignor.

"The Valley of Jehoshaphat?" questioned Cloe. "I've never heard of it. Why would that be our target?"

"The prophet Joel says, 'Let the heathen be awakened and come up to the Valley of Jehoshaphat,' which is referred to as the Valley of Decision," said the monsignor.

"Yes, God says he will sit to judge all the heathen round about, 'multitudes and multitudes,' in the Valley of Decision," said the curator.

"Where is Jehoshaphat Valley, this Valley of Decision?" asked J.E.

"Some believe it is the Kidron Valley, which lies near Jerusalem between the Mount of Olives and the Temple Mount," replied the curator.

"Well, that could supply the mount part of the prophecy," said Zack.

"That's true, but the Kidron Valley is physically steep and rocky. How would a large-scale battle be fought there?" asked J.E. "Tactically, it doesn't seem to be the best site."

"There's that, but also another problem is that it was the Roman empress Helena, Constantine's mother, who identified the Kidron Valley as the likely site of the Valley of Jehoshaphat," said the monsignor. "Scholars have questioned this for years."

"Isaiah says the judgment of the Lord shall descend upon Edom and the Lord will visit his wrath on all the nations and their armies," said the curator.

"Perhaps that is the place we seek. It does sound like a place of final judgment. Where is it?" asked Cloe.

"Edom is located in southern Israel, south of the Dead Sea," replied the monsignor. "It is more open and suited to a great battle. But other than the Isaiah reference, it has little history to recommend it as the site of the final battle for our times."

"Is there any other place you can think of that might be our site, the one with the mount where evil will be sealed?" asked Cloe. "We're running out of time."

Just then Sky came on the intercom to tell everyone they were preparing to land.

She looked around and could see everyone was racking their brains for a solution.

"I'm sorry, Dr. Cloe, but I can't help with that biblical history shit," said Louie.

Rey laughed and looked closely at Anna and Zoe, who were talking intensely but had no answers.

The monsignor smiled slightly. Cloe had seen that look before.

"Okay, Albert, out with it," she said. "You have something."

"Well, there is one other possibility," he said. "It's a very ancient place that is at the foot of a very old trade route between Egypt and Assyria. It was strategically very important in those times, and many great battles were fought there."

"Ah! Well said, Albert," said the curator. "Of course, you are speaking of Har-Magedon, or sometimes Har-Megiddo."

"Quite so, Father Curator," replied the monsignor.

"What is this Har-whatever?" puzzled J.E.

"It's a hill, thus the Har, located in northern Israel at the end of the Jezreel Valley," said the monsignor. "One might consider it a mount. It has been the sight of many famous battles, including one noted in Second

Chronicles where Josiah, the king of Judah, was killed in a fight with the Egyptian Pharaoh Necho."

"Right. As late as 1918, the British defeated the old Ottoman Empire at Megiddo," added the curator. "Wars have been fought there by the armies of the world for millennia."

"Interesting," said Cloe as she heard the wheels lock down for landing. "This sounds promising. But the name Har-Megiddo is not familiar to me. Is it mentioned in the Bible?"

"Yes," said the monsignor, "but only once."

Cloe sensed something was coming. Normally, she did not have to draw information out of the monsignor.

"Albert, where is it found?" she asked.

"It's found in the New Testament but is only seen one time, and that is in the book of Revelation."

"Okay, this place is referred to in Revelation but how and where?" asked Cloe.

"In Revelation, St. John speaks of the great day of God Almighty when he gathered all the kings of the earth and their armies into a place of final judgment," said the monsignor.

"Yes?"

The monsignor paused for such long time that Cloe thought he might not answer.

As the wheels hit the runway, he said, "And that place was, in the Jewish tongue, known as Har-Megiddo or, as translated into our language, Armageddon."

CHAPTER
82

The jet taxied toward a massive hangar at one side of the airport. Two of the F-16s had landed in tandem with them and were now escorting them to the hangar. The other two fighters were flying cover watch above them.

"Looks like they're expecting trouble," commented Cloe.

"Unfortunately, they are trained to always expect trouble," replied the monsignor. "Now, it's just more so. We can't know what information Icar has gotten out of Michael. As we speak, he and his forces may be after us."

"True," said Cloe. "Icar certainly identified Robby as some sort of threat. But for Michael, he would have had us thrown off the top of his building."

"We have to assume he will try anything to stop us," said J.E. "He probably sees us as one of the last obstacles to his dominion of the planet."

That thought chilled Cloe's heart, and her stomach fluttered as she considered the possibility that the beast had marked them specifically as the final hurdle to his goals.

"Dr. Cloe, we have the answer to this," said Robby. "We just have to see it."

The massive doors to the hangar began to slide back on motorized tracks. The two fighter jets slowed and stopped on either side of the pathway into the hangar. Cloe could see two military helicopters in the dark chasm of the huge building. Technicians surrounded them, apparently making them ready for the next leg of the trip. The rotors were beginning to twirl. Sky pulled up within twenty yards of the helicopters and braked the executive jet. The engines came to a full stop as he threw open the hatch and lowered the steps.

Whoosh! came a sound from the mouth of the hangar.

"RPG!" cried J.E. "Off the plane!"

Everyone piled out of the jet with their weapons as a massive explosion erupted just outside the hangar. Cloe saw one of the Israeli jets hit by the missile detonate and burn. Her face grew hot with the force of the flames. Shrapnel rained down all around them. Immediately, the other pilot firewalled his throttles and roared across the tarmac, searching for flight.

"What's happening?" cried Cloe.

"We're under attack!" J.E. yelled. "Run for the helicopters!"

Several rockets were fired at the fleeing F-16 from assailants out of sight. The two overhead jets blasted the entrance to the hangar with cannon fire. Powder, dust, and grit filled Cloe's mouth and nose as she watched the Israeli jet try to get airborne.

The jet reached the main runway and twirled to the north. The pilot gave it all it had, and the jet roared down the concrete strip. Faster and faster it went until Cloe was sure he would make it. Even as the fleeing plane began to rotate into its take off, it skewed to one side to evade incoming fire.

Blam! the jet exploded as it lifted just off the runway. The RPGs had found their target. Approaching its takeoff speed of 160 knots, the jet's momentum caused it to continue on briefly into the air even though the missile had destroyed it.

Cloe screamed for the fate of the pilots who had saved them, and she heard her comrades cry out in their anguish. The rotors on the helicopters spun faster, and dust was blowing everywhere.

"To the helicopters!" J.E. repeated.

Sky went first, running for the nearest helicopter, and jumped behind the controls. The young military officer who was warming the helicopter slid into the copilot's seat.

Small-arms fire came from the mouth of the hangar. The Swiss set up a covering formation and returned the fire. Several attackers fell under their accurate, disciplined assault. One of the Swiss fell. Two of his fellow soldiers grabbed him and ran for a helicopter.

Cloe picked up Robby and sprinted for the nearest bird. The downdraft from the helicopter's blades stormed against them, and the dust in the air stung her eyes. Bully galloped along beside them, looking over his shoulder.

"It's the bad man, Dr. Cloe!" yelled Robby.

Cloe, Robby, Bully, and the remainder of the seven piled onto the helicopter with Sky. The old curator, surprisingly spry for his age, dove for the deck of the helicopter. The monsignor was right behind him but turned, knelt, and continued to squeeze off shots from a large bore handgun. Cloe had no idea where he kept that weapon.

The monsignor exhausted his rounds and leaped aboard the helicopter even as he swapped magazines. Sky lifted the helicopter off the concrete but did not immediately try to fly the gauntlet staging at the mouth of the hangar. Instead, he hovered the bird about ten feet off the ground and moved to the side of the giant hangar where the door would provide some shelter from the fusillade of gunfire now inbound.

Sky then turned the helicopter sideways to the door in the lee of the enclosure as the monsignor grabbed the handles of the fifty-caliber machine gun mounted in the doorway. He cocked the weapon and sprayed the doorway with a deadly, withering fire. Light streamed in through the huge bullet holes in the metal walls. God help anyone who might have thought the walls could provide shelter.

Under shield of the onslaught from the monsignor's covering fire, J.E. and the Swiss sprinted to the other helicopter and piled in. In a second, J.E. manned the fifty and begin to rake the entrance and near walls with the large-caliber bullets. *That will slow them down*, Cloe thought.

"Will we be able to get out?" Zack yelled. "The jet couldn't get away from the missiles. How can we?"

Cloe could hear Sky and the other pilots talking calmly on their radios. Whatever their fate was, they would meet it shortly.

As the pilots began to rev up the power on their birds, they curiously began to fly in a large circle in the huge hangar. Faster and faster they went.

A deafening roar came from outside as the remaining F-16s screamed toward them like angry eagles diving for their prey. Missiles and bombs rained down from the jets, obliterating everything outside the hangar. Such was the skill of the pilots, however, that the hangar itself was not touched.

Cloe heard the launch of a slew of RPGs seeking the jets at the same time she heard the jets go to afterburners. As if on a signal, the lead helicopter roared out of the hangar, propelled by the centrifugal force built up inside of it. Cloe's helicopter rocketed out not thirty yards behind the lead bird. As she shot by what remained of the attackers, who were frantically trying to reload their missiles, she saw a huge, redheaded man behind a military personnel carrier who bore the mantle of leadership. The man, who was badly scarred, looked directly at her with hate in his eyes. He raised his right hand in a fist as he realized he and his men had been beaten.

The lead helicopter stayed about ten feet off the ground but quickly peeled to the left while Cloe's ride went right. They passed swiftly out of the line of sight of the attackers as their exit was protected by other hangars and buildings. They were, for the moment, safe.

The image of the redheaded man burned into Cloe's mind. She had no doubt he was the leader of the men Icar had sent for them.

"Until we meet again," she whispered.

CHAPTER

83

"Destination?" yelled Sky inside Cloe's helicopter.

Cloe looked at her team and read their faces.

"Har-Megiddo," she said forcefully.

"Aye, ma'am," responded Sky, smiling. He twisted his dials, punched a couple of buttons, and said, "ETA thirty-five minutes."

The monsignor smiled at her and said, "This is right. Megiddo is the omega, the end."

"Albert, what are the logistics we need to know about Megiddo?" she asked.

"Well, Har-Megiddo is actually a hill, not a mountain, overlooking the Plains of Megiddo," said the priest.

"Yes," said the curator. "It has been made by many civilizations building their dwellings on top of each other for thousands of years. Thus, it rises above the plains around it and may be considered a mount."

"The top of the hill is flat and contains the ruins of many houses, stables, palaces, and churches. It has been excavated by archeologists many times," said the monsignor. "That's where we will find the beast."

At that point, the man in the copilot's seat turned back to them and said, "Good afternoon, Dr. Lejeune."

Cloe studied the young man, now in a military headset and helmet. Did she know him?

"Jacob!" screamed Cloe, "Captain Jacob. How? How are you? We thought you were in the hospital!"

The young Israeli glanced at Sky and then rotated in his seat and slipped back onto the deck facing the passengers.

"I was in the hospital, but I was feeling better, and when I heard about this, I thought I might tag along," he said with a huge smile.

Cloe hugged the young man. Bully nuzzled him with his massive face, almost knocking him backward.

"Whoa, boy!" said the captain, giving Bully a scratch around his ears and back.

Soon the smile faded from the young captain's face. "Dr. Lejeune, what have you learned? We need all the intel we can get."

Cloe and the monsignor, shouting over the noise of the helicopter, quickly filled him in on the events in Iceland and what they had discerned from the translation.

"So you think the mount where evil will be sealed is Har-Megiddo?" he said, more as a question than a statement.

"Yes," said the monsignor, recounting the possibilities and why they thought the final battle would be at Megiddo.

"I tend to agree," said Captain Jacob, turning back toward his headset and radio. "I will notify my people. We will be there in force."

* * *

"Albert, we haven't really had time to talk about this, but what does your designation as the vicar of St. Michael the archangel mean ... exactly?" asked Cloe, as Jacob spoke quietly to his superiors.

"It's an ancient designation, an office in the Church that has been unfilled for a thousand years," the priest started. "Michael the archangel led the fight to oust the fallen angels from heaven. He is Satan's equal and opposite. We can never replace St. Michael, but this is the Church's way of saying we are in the fight to the end."

"Amazing," Cloe said.

"Albert has been imbued with what are reputedly St. Michael's spear and sword," said the curator. "These have been in the care of the Church from its earliest days. Our tradition says these weapons were used to vanquish Satan in the battle mentioned in Revelation."

"What good will a spear and sword do against modern weapons?" asked Cloe. "You saw what happened at the hangar. Megiddo will be far worse."

"True enough," acknowledged the monsignor. "We shall see."

Cloe could see her friend's heart was heavy as he considered his responsibilities. This man was the Church's best hope to lead it into battle against its ancient enemy. Cloe's money was on the monsignor.

"Albert, the prophecy in the journal says that good will follow the seven. We know who the seven are, and we have them. Good will follow us."

"True and useful," he responded. "It also says that we should rely on the innocent."

"Yes, an innocent will arise, and the evil one will be cast into the abyss," added Cloe.

"Quite so," he agreed. "That's the part I'm uncomfortable with. I don't view myself as an innocent."

* * *

The helicopters flew steadily across the rough terrain toward Megiddo and whatever destiny awaited them. Cloe thought she had been here before. She remembered flying to the Church of St. Irenaeus and later flying to Masada where, in each place, she and her colleagues were to confront terrible evil. Each time, they had been successful, not because of their planning but because of the grace of God. Yet they had faced nothing like Icar, the beast. She knew this would be their greatest challenge, and she was mortally afraid. She poured out her heart in prayer for God to give her strength.

"Captain Jacob, do your people have any kind of intel for us on Megiddo? Do they have spies or satellite information that can tell us what's happening there?" asked Cloe.

"Our satellite links are down for some reason," said the young officer. "Our on-the-ground intel tells us large numbers of armed people are gathering near Megiddo. There are hundreds of thousands, maybe many more spoiling for a fight."

"Who are they?" asked Cloe. "How did they know to go there?"

"As best we can tell, most of them are Icar's legions. Some are not," said Jacob. "Our people tell us many opposed to Icar simply followed his soldiers."

Cloe thought of Valent and the Knights of Malta who saved them when they broke the monsignor out of prison. Could they be at Megiddo? It wouldn't surprise her at all.

She turned to the monsignor as he said, "I suspect we will see some of our friends from Malta. There are many groups like that throughout the world. We could do a lot worse than to have them fighting with us."

"Ariel, is there any news as to what's going on beyond Megiddo?" asked J.E.

"Some say the earth's population has been reduced by 25 percent. In places with poor health care or weak governments, anarchy reigns."

"Blast it!" said Cloe. "Has anything changed in the States?"

"Yes, it seems the worm has turned in Washington," said the Israeli. "The fact is the president has resigned in disgrace and the new vice president has been sworn in as president. Congress has aligned behind the new leader. The US is gathering a great fleet of ships for humanitarian purposes. This will bring aid and medicine. But unless we are successful, the US effort will be too late."

"Can we expect military help from them?" asked the curator.

"There may be some isolated help from bases not fully evacuated but not much," said Jacob.

"Okay, we're going to have to do this ourselves," said Cloe.

"The full might of the Israeli forces is behind you," said Jacob. "We also have some Arab countries and what's left of the Europeans. As you have said, there may also be the knights. Some have been deploying for days, and some are on the way. Word has it a group from Malta is there or nearby."

"I can't think of anybody I'd rather have on my side," said Cloe.

"Dr. Lejeune, come look!" cried Sky. "There's something you must see."

Cloe crawled toward the front of the helicopter and looked out the windscreen. She thought it looked like some kind of enormous dark tower in the distance.

"What is it?" she asked.

"I'm not sure. I've never seen anything like it," said Sky as they came closer. "I can't see any movement. It looks like a stationary sandstorm thousands of feet high."

Cloe saw the black wall-like apparition churning in place. It did look like a sandstorm, but it was not dashing across the desert, as it should have been—it was standing still. It constantly mixed and folded in on itself. She could not tell how thick it was or whether it was safe to fly through.

"Sky, can we get through it?" she asked.

"I can't take us into that," he responded. "I don't know if it's a yard thick or a mile. There's a lot of sand in it, and my engines don't breathe sand. We've got to land. Megiddo is only about two thousand meters from here. We can walk in."

"This is the work of Icar," said the monsignor. "For some reason, he wants us on foot."

Captain Jacob turned back to them and said, "My people tell me some of their airborne units have tried to penetrate the wall."

"Yes?" asked Cloe.

"They are gone. We have lost contact with them completely," he replied. "It's like your Bermuda Triangle. They are just gone."

"Okay, Sky. Put us down," said Cloe. "We're gonna need a different approach."

Bully growled.

Robby shivered and said, "The bad man is in there, Dr. Cloe. He's calling us."

CHAPTER

84

Icar surveyed the surrounding area, a young woman at his side. The sandstorm wall encircled the entirety of Megiddo, as he knew it would. In many ways, it reminded him of Roman siege walls back in the day. He smiled slightly as he thought of some of those battles. Masada was one of his favorites. It had taken the Romans three years to break the Sicarii there. Even then, there was no real victory, as the Jews took their own lives rather than submit to the Romans.

Turning, he saw Michael and the leader of his shock troops.

"You were weak," Icar said to the redheaded man. "They were trapped in the hangar, and you let them get away."

"Sir, the Israeli jets above us made it impossible for us to hit our targets," said the man with the long, fiery beard. "I lost half of my men."

"Why not destroy the hangar?" replied Icar.

"We had only small arms, sir."

"All you had to do was wire the place with explosives!" Icar shrieked.

The man was quiet and then said, "We rushed the job. We should have wired the building with explosives."

"That's right," said Icar. "This battle would have been won."

"We can still stop them," said the redheaded man.

"I wonder," said Icar. "When I drop the sandstorm curtain around Megiddo, the final battle will be joined. I want them dead before that."

"It will be as you say."

"Go then, and cement your place in hell!" said Icar, voice rising. "Kill them and bring me their heads. Your modern weapons are no good inside the wall. Prepare yourself for hand-to-hand battle!"

The redheaded giant smiled. He threw his rifle and handgun down and drew a wicked-looking machete from a holster on his backpack.

His remaining eight men did likewise.

As the mercenaries trotted toward the wall near where Cloe's helicopters had landed, Icar laughed with derision as he considered the prospect that the cursed doctor and her force, largely consisting of old men, women, and children, could possibly prevail against these killers. He certainly would not let the Swiss soldiers through the wall. Michael had told him that J.E.'s military genius had beaten the Karik's vastly superior force at Masada. *That, and the devil priest, the monsignor.* Indeed, J.E. had laid the Claymore that had burned Michael so badly. Now, he and the others would get theirs. He had lured them to the trap.

Icar grinned at the human notion that it was better to rule in hell than to serve in heaven. And God himself had wanted him to bow down before these idiots! Soon, they would all bow to *him*.

Icar glanced to his right and smiled at the young woman. She had been invaluable with her information, but there could be only one ruler in hell. She and Michael would have to learn that lesson.

C H A P T E R
85

Both helicopters landed, and Cloe and her crew hunkered down in front of the lead helicopter near the wall of howling sand.

"The helicopters can't go any farther," said Cloe. "We need intel on how to get through the curtain."

"Dr. Cloe, we can walk through," said Robby.

"Robby, I know you mean well, but all manner of soldiers, tanks, and planes have tried to penetrate the barrier and have failed," responded Cloe. "A person couldn't simply walk through."

Robby looked at Cloe, hurt in his eyes, and then turned and ran for the wall.

"Robby!" screamed Cloe.

"Come back!" yelled J.E.

Robby ran, and Bully followed, Robby with his head start and little-boy steps and Bully quickly catching up on his great muscular legs and shoulders, powering across the gap to the wall.

They hit the wall at full speed and simply went in. *Absorbed.* Cloe had half-expected them to bounce off some impenetrable, hard surface, but it was as if they had passed through some living membrane.

Cloe ran and stopped at the wall's edge.

"Robby!" she screamed, but there was no answer. They were gone. Over and over she called out his name.

J.E. came to her and wrapped his arms around her. The monsignor, the seven, the Swiss, and the others gathered around.

Cloe looked at them and said, "If we believe in what we're doing, we're going through this barrier. We will find Robby."

"The lead helicopter pilot just told me that a young man went through the barrier a few minutes ago," said the monsignor. "Just like Robby and Bully did. He was one of the knights from Malta."

"Who?" asked Cloe.

"The pilot did not know, but he watched him remove all his weapons, except his knife, and then he just went in," the monsignor replied.

"That must be the key," shouted Cloe over the noise of the blowing sand.

J.E. turned and told everyone to gather their gear but strip away all modern weapons of any kind.

When everyone had done so and returned, Cloe drew her .45 sidearm and stood in front of the group. She threw it in the sand, took off the holster, and started toward the wall. The monsignor, armed with the sword and spear of St. Michael, followed behind her.

The monsignor, J.E., and Zack joined Cloe at the front of the group. Zack cried out, "For Robby!"

Cloe ran for the wall and hit it at full speed. She expected to be flattened by the crash, but she passed through and fell head over heels on the other side.

Dazed, she looked around and saw the monsignor, J.E., Zack and his friends, and the old curator. None of the Swiss had come through, and Captain Jacob was nowhere in sight. Cloe wondered if they might have passed through at some other place or if they could not quite bring themselves to dispose of all modern ordnance.

Cloe stood. "Where are the others?"

"This seems to be it," said J.E.

"How could some of us get through but not others?" asked the curator.

"It seems the people Icar either wants to confront or from whom he feels no threat have been admitted. Otherwise, our fighting men have mainly been rejected," said the monsignor. "We are on our own."

"Where's Robby?" asked Zack.

Cloe looked around at the smoky, dark landscape but could not see the boy or the dog.

"I don't know, but he couldn't be far ahead of us," she replied.

"We'll head toward Megiddo. We will find them."

The small troop gathered themselves and began to walk toward the mount on which what was left of Megiddo was located. The terrain was very rough with jagged boulders and fractured shale. The smoky atmosphere limited visibility, and Cloe wondered if this was the "fog of war" she had heard so much about. The sun was not visible, just varying degrees of gray.

When they had gone perhaps a thousand meters toward Megiddo, the ground began to rise slightly. Cloe heard a dog bark in the distance—it was Bully.

"Hurry!" she said. "They can't be far now."

She ran forward and suddenly stopped. The others caught up and stood confronting a phalanx of mercenaries. The men were dressed in military fatigues with desert camo colors and high-top leather boots. They were hard men and bore visible scars likely from other battles. They were obviously fighting men who were there to stop them from finding Icar. They also stood between them and Robby.

J.E., the monsignor, and Zack came abreast of her, and they all stared at the opposing force. Louie and Rey joined the front line. Cloe looked around and saw the courage in their eyes—but they were mainly amateurs against obvious professionals.

"We have no business with you," cried Cloe. "Stand aside!"

A man stepped from the ranks of the hostile force.

Cloe gasped. It was the fiery-haired man from the hangar.

"Good evening, Dr. Lejeune," he said with a smirk. He drew a razor-edged machete that reminded Cloe of the fabled Roman short sword she had seen in paintings and drawings. "We know you are virtually unarmed, as mechanical weapons are useless here behind Icar's wall."

"He's right, but we are not unarmed," said J.E., drawing from its scabbard a threatening knife designed for hand-to-hand combat.

The man laughed and took a step forward. "I have come for you and the boy, Dr. Lejeune. Where is he?"

So Icar does not have Robby ...

"He is safe and beyond your reach and that of your master," she responded.

"Nothing is beyond Icar's reach," said the redheaded giant, becoming angry. "Where's the boy?"

"I'm here!" said Robby, stepping from behind a rock fall near the middle of the two groups. "Go back to the bad man and tell him to leave us alone."

At that, the redheaded man and his cohort howled with laughter.

"Hey, kid, that's funny, but you don't know our boss," said the soldier. "He's a hard case and wants you and the doctor. Come here, and we'll take it easy on the others."

Zack and the other five came up to Robby. He and Mel flanked the little boy. The others lined up behind the three of them. Robby reached out and grabbed Mel's and Zack's hands, and the rest of the group also joined hands. Power surged through the line.

The monsignor stepped away from Cloe and moved opposite the leader of Icar's troop. There was no hurry in his steps but a reluctance.

The monsignor squarely faced the mercenary. "You can still save your own souls. Move out of the way. We are only after Icar."

The leader did not smile but only brandished the menacing machete. It made a terrible sound as it slashed through the air.

"Our boss would not understand," he replied. "We only want the doctor and the kid, but we will kill you all to get them if necessary."

The monsignor drew the sword of St. Michael from his belt and said, "So be it."

Cloe watched as the monsignor advanced toward the monster. On her right, the seven arrayed on either side of Robby advanced, and a humming began like high-voltage electric lines. Cloe thought about the prophecy about relying upon an innocent. *Robby?* She glanced back toward the monsignor, who seemed to have grown in size and power to equal the redheaded man.

The leader of Icar's thugs took a step backward. He then lunged at the monsignor with his machete, swinging in a gigantic, powerful arc.

Surely such a blow would cleave the monsignor shoulder to breast!

"Albert!" she cried.

But the monsignor lifted his sword and blocked the hammer-like blow as easily as a child might swat a fly. The giant went flying as the monsignor deflected the swing's momentum. He landed in a heap at Robby's feet.

Rolling and half-kneeling, the redheaded man drew back the machete and thrust it toward Robby's little body. The point rushed toward Robby's heart—the monsignor could not possibly get there in time.

"Robby!" she screamed.

A huge body flew through the air, and a terrible roar overtook them. Bully seized the hand wielding the machete and slammed it away from Robby's small frame. He bit down hard into the hand and wrist with his massive jaw and violently shook them. As big as the man was, he looked like a ragdoll in Bully's jaws.

Cloe heard a sickening snap and, one final shake of Bully's head separated the man from his hand about halfway up the arm. The man screamed as blood squirted everywhere. The devil's mercenary rolled on the ground and cried in pain.

The monsignor turned to face the others who had drawn their machetes. He took a step toward them, the sword of St. Michael raised and flashing even in the dim light. They bolted in all directions.

CHAPTER
86

"Ha!" cried the monsignor as he watched the devil's brigade run for the hills. Without their leader, they were nothing.

Cloe looked down at the red-bearded man, now near death from his blood loss. He was trying to say something. She leaned in close to his face.

"Priest," he whispered faintly.

He knows he's dying and wants a priest. The leader of the devil's troops wants a priest.

"Albert," she said. "Will you minister to him?"

The warrior-priest spun around, his blood still high from the fight. He seemed to deflate a bit.

"Of course," he said, stooping and drawing the vestments and oils for the last rites from his inner pocket.

The monsignor carefully bent over the man. "Albert, watch out in case this is a trick," said J.E.

"Thanks, J.E. A priest I may be, but a fool I'm not," said the monsignor as he observed the fallen man. Apparently satisfied, he began to intone the blessings of the last rites. He anointed the man and took his last confession. Regardless of what the man might have done in life, the monsignor seemed pleased that he had the opportunity to deliver a soul into paradise.

Cloe had never thought about it before, but it was as much a blessing on the priest as on the dying man to reclaim a soul for heaven. A man had been lost but at the last hour was saved.

When the man had gone, the monsignor stood wearily and looked around. Everyone was staring at him.

"Bless you, Father," said Robby at last.

* * *

Smoke and mist swirled around them, and visibility was very limited. They had piled some stones over the redheaded man and now were once again headed for Megiddo. The group included the seven, J.E., the monsignor, the curator, and of course Cloe. Bully jogged along with them.

As they hiked up the incline toward the rise that was Megiddo, Cloe wondered what awaited them at the summit.

"Do you believe this has all been foretold?" she asked the monsignor.

"Yes, Revelation has told us this was coming or, maybe, coming again," said the priest. "Left alone, evil will begin to grow. Good must rise up periodically and tamp it down. Indifference only allows evil to bloom."

They approached the crest of the hill on which the old city had once been located. At first, it appeared to be a nondescript plateau. Gradually, while the mist shrouded the periphery, Cloe could make out seams and formations that might have been ancient walls and buildings.

There, in the center of the hilltop, stood two figures, one tall and straight and the other shorter and bent as if in pain. A third figure was off to the right. Cloe looked at J.E. and at the monsignor.

"Now what?" she asked, softly.

"Oh, come now, Doctor! You've come this far ... approach!" said a voice that she knew must come from Icar. They were still some distance from the two figures in the center, but the voice sounded as if the speaker were right next to her. There was a smile in that voice.

Doubt leaped on her back and sought to weigh her down. Her mind spun, and she could not think clearly. The horror of the evil that they now confronted washed over her. How could they possibly prevail? What had they been thinking?

"J.E.!" she cried, but her son and the others had been similarly affected.

As she wondered what they could do, she heard a small voice.

"You are a bad man," said the child as he gathered the seven to himself. "Stop hurting Dr. Cloe."

They clasped hands, and that thing happened again. The power within them rose up. Cloe felt she had somehow awakened from a deep sleep. She shook the devil's cobwebs from her head and focused on the figures in the center of the plateau.

The seven moved forward with Robby at the point. Bully was completely silent, but he stood on his hind legs and snapped his jaws. He stared at the taller of the two figures. Icar had a huge hound on a tether of some sort—a hellhound.

As they moved a little closer, Icar raised his hands and moved them in a circle. Immediately, the wind arose and began to blow like a cyclone. It was as if a tornado was trying to touch down within Icar's wall. Icar was standing in the eye of the storm, but where they were, the agitated air screamed around, trying to tear them apart. Dirt and small stones filled the air, and still the wind speed grew.

Cloe saw a stone hit the curator, a glancing blow in the head, and he fell in a heap. The monsignor leaped to his side and helped him up. Blood trickled from a cut above one eye. Quarter-sized gravel pelted them like hell-sent hail. If this continued, they would all be stoned to death.

"What do we do?" cried Cloe.

J.E. yelled, "To Robby!"

Robby and the other six were enveloped in a cocoon of some sort against Icar's storm. She and the others fell in line behind them. There, the air was calm, and no dirt or stones penetrated. Above and away from that sanctuary, the air roared and whipped. It had become very dark and hard to see.

They were now no farther than thirty yards from Icar and Michael and they continued to push forward. The third figure appeared, still indiscernible.

The tornado roared, but in the lee of the seven, it was still calm. Soon enough they would be face-to-face with the beast. Then, Cloe thought, she would know for sure who was innocent.

CHAPTER

87

The seven bent into the blast of the wind and debris. The power that pulsed through them warded off most of the storm. Still, their progress was only in inches. It was the brute force of the devil versus the power of good. Robby and his cohorts kept moving forward like a small fleet of battered ships in the face of a hurricane. Cloe wondered how such a young boy had the strength to keep going. She remembered the simple prayer of the congregation of St. Anselm Catholic Church in her hometown so long ago. They had prayed to Our Lady of Prompt Succor to protect them against the storms of the Gulf Coast. She reached out and prayed to the Lady now. She prayed hard, but she looked for opportunity.

They were now within fifteen to twenty yards of Icar, and Cloe could see his menacing leer. Not a hair on his head was out of place. The wind had died down considerably.

"The storm's abating!" she called to the monsignor to her right.

"No, we have only entered the eye wall," said J.E., on her left.

Sure enough, as she gazed outward, she could see the monster storm still raging. Strangely, the eye was very tight, possibly no more than fifty yards. It was more like a tornado than a hurricane.

Now in the center, the air was calm and clear, but the light was low and filtered due to the wall. Cloe felt like she was in a nightmare landscape. The mega-storm roared around them, howling in rage, tearing everything in sight to pieces. Thousand-year-old stone dwellings were flung like toys.

Cloe turned back to the middle of the plateau and saw the beast, Icar, smiling. The redheaded man's troop had reformed with their ruler as its center. They brandished their machetes and hollered obscenities. Once again, the holy warriors were outnumbered by the fighting men.

The monsignor moved close to her and said, "They have no heart. If we can strike a strong blow, they will run again."

Icar, seemingly anticipating this tactic, moved forward and released his giant hellhound. The dog stood immobile for a second, contemplating his freedom, and then Icar screamed, "Kill!"

The hound bounded for Robby, covering the distance between them in a handful of seconds. Bully screeched a horrific canine roar and leaped forward, intercepting the hellhound in mid-leap. The hound must have outweighed Bully by fifty pounds, but the bulldog had the mass of a brick wall.

Bully bowled the hellhound over backward and rolled on top of him. Jaws of glittering teeth from both dogs snapped with the force of bear traps, each seeking the vulnerable tissue. The hellhound's maw found Bully's chest beneath his massive chin. He bit into the soft flesh, and Bully squealed in pain. The hound held tight and shook his head, opening a large, shallow wound that began to bleed.

Robby, distracted from the seven, cried, "Bully! Run!"

Bully shook himself free of the devil's pet and rolled over trying to regain his feet. It was no good, and he collapsed on his side. He struggled to get up, but the hound was fast approaching, seeking to press his advantage. He plowed into Bully and sank his teeth into his shoulder.

Cloe screamed and ran toward Bully. She grabbed him around the shoulders and made to protect him from the next attack. She could hear Icar laugh at her meager efforts.

"J.E., Albert!" she cried. "Help!"

Before either could even move, the hound sprinted at Cloe and Bully and slammed into Cloe with the force of a small locomotive. Cloe went sprawling, and the hellhound stood over Bully, ready to administer the final blow.

As he bent down to seize Bully's vulnerable neck, he briefly exposed himself, and Bully, seemingly near defeat, leaped for the monster dog's jugular. He clamped down with bulldog ferocity, severing the artery, mauling the hellhound's throat.

The devil's dog stepped back, bleeding profusely, with a terrible look of mortality on his face. After a few seconds, his front legs simply crumpled, and he fell face-first onto the rock-strewn plateau. He rolled over, twitched, and then was still. Bully somehow climbed to his hind legs and let out a primal, animal roar of victory.

* * *

Once more the seven advanced. It had only taken a second to regroup. Robby grabbed the hands of the others, and Cloe felt the power surge and dance. It seemed more powerful than ever and was growing stronger.

Icar actually backed up a step when he saw this, but it was only for a second. He screamed at the devil's brigade, exhorting them forward. The mercenaries advanced toward the seven.

Once again, the monsignor stepped forward with the sword and spear of St. Michael. Cloe saw Louie finger his switchblade, ready to help. J.E. drew his combat knife from its scabbard. They were outnumbered two to one.

They were no more than five yards distant from each other when the monsignor stopped and cried, "Lucifer, come forth! These men do not have to die!"

As he said this, the soldiers stopped and seemed confused. Cloe watched as they considered the monsignor's words. Why didn't Icar come forth and make an end to these people? Surely, he could do so. Why didn't he? Was he afraid?

An awful silence hung over the battle scene while the storm, unabated, howled on outside. The two groups faced each other. Robby and his six cohorts advanced with Cloe and the others following behind them. The monsignor was slightly off to one side at the point.

Robby stopped, and so did the others.

"Lucifer, come out!" cried Robby.

CHAPTER

88

Cloe stared at the beast and saw him smile. He was not afraid.

He stepped forward, moving toward the point of his soldiers. His youth, good looks, and arrogance awed Cloe. His victory was dialed in. He had no doubt. He would brush them aside, and his future as Earth's ruler would be secured.

The phalanx of mercenaries parted, and Satan stepped forward in human form.

"Where are you, Michael?" he asked.

Confused, Cloe thought he was asking for her scarred nemesis. Then she remembered the archangel and the monsignor's assumed mantle.

"I am here!" said the monsignor.

"Ha!" said the beast. "You are but a pale imitation of my ancient adversary. I have not forgotten."

"I am enough for the likes of you," responded the monsignor. "Be gone, Satan! Get thee hence, in the name of Jesus Christ our Lord."

Icar laughed and said, "Oh please, not that crying in the wilderness thing. I don't think I got very good press on the temptation in the desert. Your boss was tempted. I almost had him."

"Repent, Lucifer. Even now it's not too late," cried the monsignor. "God loves you and will accept you back."

Icar turned as if to walk away and then spun back to the monsignor. "By all accounts, I'm the only being God does not love. I was thrown out. Think of it! God loves all humans—even, *especially*, the sinners. Christ made that clear. Only Lucifer, once his favorite, is now unloved. I have no path to redemption."

Cloe had never had the opportunity to consider such things. Was the beast saying he had no free will, no path but evil? Yet at some point he had made the decision to revolt against God, and this was the result. Was this his hell? Could he repent as the monsignor was suggesting, and would God accept him? Or was the relationship between God and his angels entirely different from God and mankind, made in his image and likeness? She had nothing but questions.

"Dr. Lejeune, I see you are puzzled," said Icar, stepping toward her.

"Stay away from her!" cried the monsignor, moving to intercept Icar.

"Surely, Dr. Lejeune, you have given this all some thought," replied Icar. "Where do you think my power comes from? You have studied Judas. I'm as much a pawn in the great scheme of things as he was. Without me, without evil, of what use is free will? If there are no choices, free will is but a pale ornament on a barren tree."

"But what you're saying? I don't know," struggled Cloe.

"Cloe, the devil is trying to appeal to you by presenting himself as some sort of victim," said the monsignor. "He is not. He is evil, the very embodiment of evil."

"Albert, where does his power and authority come from if not from God?" asked Cloe.

"No one can say for sure, but I believe when the angels were formed they were given certain powers," said the monsignor. "Lucifer received the gifts all the angels received and indeed, probably more since he and a few others were favored by God and are sometimes referred to as archangels, the leaders of the other angelic hierarchies. But he perverted his gifts and chose evil to lead a revolt in heaven."

Icar laughed. "This is probably closer to the truth than you can know, priest."

"Icar is not a victim. He is right where he wants to be, doing just as he pleases," said the monsignor. "He only wants to tempt you to his side."

As the monsignor said this, Cloe felt as if she had been awakened. The devil's ways of persuasion now became clear to her. She had almost fallen for Icar's line.

"Be gone, Satan!" she screamed.

CHAPTER
89

While the beast was focused on Cloe, the seven had moved closer. They formed a tight circle with Robby at the point with clasped hands. Cloe could hear that humming sound, like a high-voltage power line, coming from them. It rose steadily in volume. Energy radiated from them like an electrical bonfire, aimed toward Icar.

Icar turned back toward Robby.

"Ha! Led by children, are you?" he taunted. Still, as the power from the group became stronger and surged over him, he stepped back.

Behind him, a terrible, tearing sound vented from the earth, and stone and dirt flew upward. A pit appeared, and smoke and fire belched from its recesses. Cloe put her hands over her ears as the screech of stone upon stone grew louder, drowning out even the storm. The force from the seven redoubled and drove Icar back toward the noise. A deep, gaping hole in the earth appeared behind him, beckoning. Cloe reckoned it to be about fifty yards wide. As the crevasse widened, she was pulled toward it.

"It's the abyss!" cried the curator. "The seven have opened the abyss, and they are pushing Icar toward it. He will be imprisoned for another thousand years."

Icar slid toward the chasm, but a few feet away from it, he suddenly stood straight, anchored himself, and faced the seven. He extended his arm toward them and pointed directly at Robby. The boy faltered for only a split second—it was enough for Icar to recover the advantage. Power emanated from the beast, a dirty elemental energy. The devil's strength met the faith force of the seven and began to counter it. The seven stopped and began to slide backward, slowly. They fought back and channeled every bit of the power of good that they possessed. Once again the devil was forced back.

Cloe saw that the contest had come to a virtual draw. The seven had stymied Icar's advance, but they could move no further against his power. Each side struggled and pushed. She could think of nothing else to do, so she picked up a good-sized stone and heaved it toward Icar. The rock exploded about three feet from its target and was blasted into sand.

In spite of his efforts, Icar laughed.

Cloe saw the beast take a half step forward and then be pushed back slightly. Still, he had gained a few inches of ground. He took a larger step, and Cloe saw the seven were beginning to weaken. Their efforts had clearly exhausted them.

The monsignor ran by her and heaved the spear of St. Michael toward the beast. It caught him full in the shoulder and pierced his body.

Icar fell backward and landed a foot or two in front of the abyss. Cloe looked at the seven and saw that they had collapsed in disarray under the fatigue of the effort. All the power and energy that had filled the battlefield a moment earlier fled. Now all that could be heard was the never-ending howling of the wind surrounding them.

Icar rolled over on his side and tried to stand. He fell back but tried again. He sat full upright and stared at the lance. He looked at it almost quizzically, as if he could not believe he had been wounded. Black blood streamed from the wound.

He said, "Well, it's been a while since this has happened to me. There must be something of my old nemesis in this spear."

The monsignor strode toward him with the sword of St. Michael in his hand, surely to apply the coup de grâce to the beast. As he approached, Icar broke the shaft of the lance and reached around and pulled the tip out of the back of his upper shoulder.

The monsignor swung the sword in a mighty arc that would have separated the beast from his head, but Icar rolled and came up with what was left of the lance, pointing it at the priest. Cloe could see the hole in Icar's shoulder closing. In a few seconds, as the combatants circled each other, the wound had completely healed, and Icar's face once again bore his sardonic smile.

306

The monsignor swung the sword again, but Icar ducked and came up, plunging the remnant of the lance into the priest's midsection.

Cloe screamed as Monsignor Albert Roques went down hard and did not move. She ran to him, but there was little she could do. Still, Cloe tore pieces of the monsignor's tunic and tried to stanch the bleeding.

"You bastard!" she screamed at Icar. "He's badly hurt."

"I hope he's dead," said the beast, grinning in triumph. "I'll see him in hell!"

"Not today!" cried Zack.

Cloe turned and saw the seven were back together, and the dire intensity on Robby's face spoke volumes. They clasped hands, and the power surged.

"Go away, you bad man!" screamed Robby. "You hurt my friend!"

The devil was thrown back toward the abyss. If the fight with the monsignor had not carried him away from it, he would have been cast into the pit. Again he rallied, stood, and launched his counterattack.

"I'm not going anywhere, you annoying brat!" Icar shouted. With that, he gathered himself and shot a huge burst of energy toward Robby and the seven.

Cloe cried and clutched her heart.

The burst caught Robby full in the chest, and he went down like a sack of potatoes. The circle was broken, and all power drained away. The beast stood straight and howled a cry of victory.

Icar glanced over his shoulder at the abyss. Without the power of good to keep it open, it had slowly begun to close. He had won.

He smiled at the figure who now appeared on the edge of the clearing and beckoned her to him. Cloe watched as her assistant, Dr. Jeanne Richard, walked to Icar. Dressed in all black, tight-fitting fatigues, she looked different ... seductive. Even in this light, the red lip gloss gleamed.

Cloe stared at her assistant, suddenly realizing how Icar knew their every move in advance, and said, "How could you?"

"My reward will be great," said Jeanne, looking up and smiling at Icar and then back at Cloe. "You were nothing to me, another arrogant academic to be pushed out of my way."

"You were my closest colleague. I trusted you with everything I knew!" said Cloe, her anger swelling at the magnitude of the deception.

"Yes, and I was able to use every bit of it against you," she laughed.

"You bitch! Rot in hell!" shouted Cloe.

"Ha! Rule in hell is more like it. Kill her!" commanded the devil's assistant.

Icar turned, his face dark and fierce. He grabbed Jeanne by the neck and twisted until a gruesome snap was heard. He then tossed her lifeless body away like so much garbage.

"There is only one ruler in hell!" snarled Icar.

CHAPTER
90

"You shouldn't have hurt the boy!" said Michael, whose voice was muffled by the wind.

Cloe looked up and saw Michael's scarred features emerge from the shadow of one of the ancient walls, where he had been watching everything.

"What ...?" asked Icar.

A low growl issued from the other side of the clearing.

Cloe turned and saw that Bully had dragged himself from where he lay bleeding from his wounds and was now standing on his hind legs, teeth gnashing.

"Satan! Today you return to the abyss!" shouted a man with shoulder-length brown hair who had stepped out from behind the rocks.

"Who?" asked Icar, turning to the newcomer.

Cloe surveyed the man and cried, "Valent!"

The beast's attention was riveted on Valent as he slowly, deliberately moved toward him.

"Icar, do you recognize the ring on my finger?" cried Valent.

"The Ring of the Fisherman," said Icar.

"Yes, we retrieved it from the dying hand of your servant on Malta," barked Valent with a triumphant smile on his face. "You have lost the ring. You have lost."

Michael advanced surreptitiously toward the distracted Icar, as did Bully.

The devil glanced belatedly at Michael and then back at the monster bulldog. His vision walked back to Valent. He inched backward toward the nearly closed abyss.

"You're too late!" laughed the beast. "The abyss is closed. I have won."

"Not yet!" shouted Michael as he broke into a sprint toward Icar.

Bully raged and galloped at Icar, shoulder muscles bulging, launching himself into a great leap at the throat of the beast.

At the same time, Michael lunged at Icar. They moved so quickly Cloe barely had time to suck in her breath.

Dog and man hit the beast in mid-chest, and their combined weight carried him backward toward the narrow crevasse that remained. A horrible scream of despair issued from deep within the black gut of the beast. In but a moment, man and beasts were gone.

Everything became calm. The wind lay down, and the wall fell. Rays of sunshine pierced the gloom.

Cloe jumped up and ran toward the place where the opening to the abyss had been. Valent ran after her.

"Michael!" she cried.

But they were gone. The earth had sealed over, and the devil was cast down into the abyss for another thousand years.

"Michael!" she screamed.

"He's gone," said the monsignor, now by her side, arm around her shoulders. "It seems Michael sacrificed himself for all of us."

"Albert, how?" she asked in shock. "You were on the point of death."

"I'm not sure, but the boy had something to do with it," he replied.

Cloe looked back at J.E and the seven. There was Bully by Robby's side, his great tongue licking his wounds.

"How?" she cried.

"Perhaps it is God's will," said the knight.

"But the prophecy—it was supposed to be Robby, the innocent, who vanquished evil," she said.

"Consider the next line in the prophecy," said the monsignor. "Who in God's eyes is innocent? Why not the man who has given his life for his friends?"

"Albert, is Michael …?" asked Cloe.

"Michael is with God," said the priest. "No greater love has any man than the one who gives his life for another. Somehow, Michael was redeemed at the last."

CHAPTER

91

A week later, Cloe sat on the front porch of her Madisonville, Louisiana, home with the monsignor. The ever-present laptop was open. She had been working while awaiting Albert's arrival. The porch overlooked the crystal waters of the Tchefuncte River. Every now and then, the sun would catch a diamond ripple on the water, blown upriver by the southeasterly wind. Children were playing in the late afternoon on the grassy area abutting the river, referred to by local residents as "the wall." The vista was a far cry from the chaos of a mere week ago.

"How are you, and how is the pope?" asked Cloe.

"I'm fine. Not even a scar. His Holiness is recuperating; he's now able to be treated in a proper hospital, so we expect him, eventually, to fully recover. Right now he has a touch of pneumonia in addition to his injuries from the explosion. Of course, he has much on his mind."

"How much of the Vatican was reclaimed?" asked Cloe. "Is there anything useable?"

"Yes, surprisingly," said the monsignor. "Most of the destruction was mob generated. It was random rather than organized. The biggest damage is to St. Peter's and of course the fire and smoke damage. Contrary to the news reports at the time, the father curator says the library with its books and records and the museums holding much of the historic treasure of the Church remain intact, although some have been damaged. As you know, most of this was belowground in secure areas. It will take a while, but even now the pope is beginning to rebuild the Vatican staff. Once that's done, the work of resurrecting the Vatican itself will proceed. Swiss guards have been deployed to protect the grounds and buildings. The Italian government is back in charge in Rome even though martial law continues."

"Amazing. That's real progress in just a week," said Cloe. "And how is the curator?"

"He's fine. His days are very full now, and of course his new pal, Boogie, is his constant companion."

Cloe looked down and thought of Miles and the other scientists at Uruk.

"Where's J.E.?" the monsignor asked.

"He's in Washington, DC, on a new assignment," she said, looking up. "It seems the US government is badly in need of good intel and competent people who can process and assess it. Washington is mobilizing to move supplies, medical, food, water, and various services on a scale not seen in decades. They need to make sure everything gets to the right places and people."

"The seven have gone back to the lives they led before Megiddo," said the monsignor.

"Surely not everyone?" laughed Cloe. "Hopefully Louie will find a better line of work in New York than he had before. Something legal, I hope."

"They all seemed a little dazed by what happened, but all have been profoundly changed. I suspect Louie will find something more constructive to do with his time. Each seemed imbued with a new energy to make a difference."

"Were they God sent for this purpose, Albert?" Cloe asked.

"Yes, I believe so, and I think they or their counterparts have been with us always," he said.

"Are we good for another thousand years?" she asked. "It would be nice to think that."

"With the speed of everything and the worldwide reach of events now, I tend to think the cycle might compress, but who can say?" said the monsignor. "I don't think we can consider ourselves safe by any measure."

"You know, I flew back with the boy," said Cloe. "Robby, his mom, and Bully all came back to New Orleans with me. It's remarkable to think they live just across the lake from me."

"How is Robby?" he asked.

"I rented a car and drove them to their little house," she replied. "They asked me to come in for a while. His mother missed most of the excitement, but what she did get was plenty. She had a million questions I could not answer.

"You know, when I was talking with her, Robby went to his toy box and pulled out a small car set and began playing with it like any other seven-year-old," she continued. "Bully sat watching, between him and the door."

"Perhaps that's just what he is now, a regular seven-year-old," said the monsignor. "Children have remarkable curative and coping mechanisms. In a few weeks, he may not even remember the events."

"Maybe, but I had no answers for questions like whether he was permanently different or was he now someone else or was he from heaven," she said.

"No ... who can say?" said the monsignor. "I just know he was empowered by God to do what he did. They all were."

"After all her questions had been asked, our conversation died away, and it was time for me to leave," Cloe said. "Robby's mom walked me to the door, and I thought for a moment Robby was too engrossed in his game to notice I was leaving. Just as I was slipping out the front door, I heard him call out, and he came running. He gave me a great hug and whispered in my ear, 'Dr. Cloe, it's not over.'"